Jigsaw

Guide to the James Caldwell papers 1903-1906
United States Naval Institute
589 McNair Road
Annapolis, Maryland

Dan Ryan

AuthorHouse™
1663 Liberty Drive
Bloomington, IN 47403
www.authorhouse.com
Phone: 1-800-839-8640

This book is a work of fiction. People, places, events, and situations are the product of the author's imagination. Any resemblance to actual persons, living or dead, or historical events, is purely coincidental.

First published by AuthorHouse 9/10/2010

ISBN: 978-1-4520-6186-3 (e)
ISBN: 978-1-4520-6184-9 (sc)
ISBN: 978-1-4520-6185-6 (hc)

Library of Congress Control Number: 2010912436

Printed in the United States of America

This book is printed on acid-free paper.

ALSO BY DAN RYAN

Novels

Admiral's Son General's Daughter
Admirals and Generals
Lull After the Storm
Death Before Dishonor
Calm Before the Storm

Reference

Lean Modeling for Engineers
Lean Office Practices for Architects

Engineering Education

Robotic Simulation
CAD/CAE Descriptive Geometry
Modern Graphic Communication
Computer-aided Design
Computer-aided Architectural Graphics
Computer Programming for Graphical Displays
Principles of Automated Drafting
Technical Sketching and Computer Illustration
Computer-aided Kinetics for Machine Design
Graphical Displays for Engineering Documentation
Mini/Micro Computer Graphics
Computer-aided Graphics and Design
*Computer-aided Manufacturing (*Russian Language*)*
CAD for AutoCAD Users
Graphic Communication Manual
Computer Graphics Programming Manual
Computer Aided Graphics (Chinese Language)

Acknowledgments

The publication of this ninth book by Authorhouse has been special. In addition to the many hands at the publishers, the author and copy editor wish to thank our Mayan guide, Sian Ka'an, who met us at Playa del Carmen and agreed to take us to the newly discovered ruins at Estructura, 7H-3 map coordinates. It was an all day trip driving up the coast highway, turning onto back roads and then single lanes cut through the jungle. We left our vehicle and hiked the rest of the way. We went last winter to avoid the rainy season and the summer mosquitoes. The many photographs described in this story were taken at this site. Sian's help was invaluable to understanding the Maya Culture of the Yucatan.

Contents

Prelude

LIKE A CHILD'S PUZZLE BOARD, the maps, documents and charts spread out before me were the keys to my success. I am Lieutenant L J Caldwell. I am a lawyer and I work, officially, out of the Judge Advocate's Office. Unofficially, my time is spent 'on loan' to the Office of Naval Counter Intelligence, NCI. I have been with JAG for two years, joining right after law school. My father and brother were overjoyed with my decision to join the US Navy. I came from a long line of Naval Officers, beginning with my grandfather, five star Admiral Jason Caldwell. My father is three star Admiral James Caldwell and my brother was Captain J. Jason Caldwell, commander of the submarine fleet stationed in Norfolk, Virginia. I am the black sheep of the family because I did not go to Annapolis like both of them. I was valedictorian of William and Mary and first in my law school class at Georgetown. My office was wherever I was sent to work on the most difficult cases. My rank went up and down like a yo-yo. I was undisciplined and unaware of most of the requirements for climbing the ladder of advancement within the US Navy. Because I was a lawyer, I was given a commission to join the investigation division of JAG. Rank meant nothing to me, I thought it was a cumbersome system to start with, an ensign and then shift to lieutenant, and what was all this junior grade and lower division crap? Either you could do the job assigned to you or you couldn't.

The whole family was home for Thanksgiving at Seneca Hill. I wanted to see my grandmother who lived with them, she always understood me, we were two of a kind. When she asked me how I was doing with my appointment at JAG, I told her that I was a brand new LTLG or something close to that. I knew I had been given a reduction in rank, but I did not want my brother to know it. My brother overheard our conversation and asked, "What happened, Louis? Why were you busted?"

"No one hit me. They were upset at how I solved the case given to me, but that has become almost routine lately. I get results which turn into convictions and that is why I love my job."

"It is not a job, Louis. You have a career and you come from a long line of US Naval Officers."

"No, I did not graduate from Annapolis, therefore, the Navy is not my career. The law is my profession. I can practice it anywhere. Whenever the Navy wants me to quit and get a real job with a much higher salary, they will tell me." I knew my jab about a real job would get to James.

"Why do you think naval rules and regulations don't apply to you, Louis?"

"What? Of course, naval regs apply to me, I am in the US Navy."

"Then why don't you follow them?"

"I follow them to the letter, otherwise, no convictions!"

"That is not what I am talking about. You use the regs against the criminal actions of others in order to prosecute, but you think they don't apply to you."

"Yes, they do. If I committed a crime then the regs would be used to punish me."

"Do you see a demotion as a form of punishment?"

"No, I see it as a warning to be more careful in pursuit of the bad guys."

"Don't you care what rank you are?"

"I am not impressed by titles. My income does not come from the Navy. I sign my check over to the Naval Widows and Orphans Fund every month. My income comes from my seat on CI, just like yours does, brother."

I would have liked to continue my discussion with my brother, but I was on my way to see my other grandparents who lived in Georgetown. When my Grandpa Schneider heard that I had joined the Navy right out of law school, he said, "Louis, my son, I am so proud of you. The men on both sides of your family have served their time in the Navy. The only exception is your Uncle Tom Schneider, that ungrateful, little shit is going to get himself, or one of his family killed. He lives in

Washington without knowing how to defend himself. Come down to the basement and change clothes and I will teach you that to help you through the eight weeks of basic training."

We spent several hours that day and I returned the next day with a few questions.

"I now know how to stop a man's fist or knife coming near me. How do I take that knife or weapon away from him and kill him with it?"

"Louis, Louis. That is not self defense! You are just beginning to learn how to defend yourself, it will take days more with me before you are ready to start your basic training."

It was then that I told him what I wanted to do with my JAG career.

1

Georgetown Law School

June, 1903

The Navy JAG recruiters had a representative at the Georgetown Law School for interviews and I stopped and filled out an application. I was using an ink pen and trying to make a neat and professional looking job of the process. I was about halfway through the first page when this Navy guy in his dark blue uniform stopped me. He was reading over my shoulder.

"You are Admiral Caldwell's son?"

"Yes, let me finish this, please. Can I schedule an interview with someone?"

"I think you can, Mr. Caldwell! Have you graduated yet?"

"I should be finished in June, why?"

"Do you have any time today?"

"No, I am really jammed up with this crazy contracts course."

"Are you free any time tomorrow?"

"In the morning, sure."

"I will give you this card and I will sign it on the back. This will allow you into the Army Navy Building and the NCI office."

"I am applying for the Judge Advocate General's Office, not the Office of Naval Counter Intelligence. I am going to be a lawyer not a spy." I was smiling.

"The NCI has lawyers working for them, too. In fact, there is one division that is shared by both, the Criminal Investigation Division."

"What time do you want me there?"

"8:30 hours will be your appointment, Mr. Caldwell."

I took his card and turned it over, it was signed Rodney Lowe. I looked up at him and he was smiling.

"I sandbagged you, Louis. I know your father and he said you might be applying this week. I have been here every day. I thought you might have changed your mind."

"How do you know my father?"

"I was his first commanding officer when he graduated from the academy. All I do now is look for talent."

"You are a talent scout?"

"Sort of, if you decide to join us, you can not mention that I talked to you on the Georgetown Campus. Is that alright with you?"

"What? Why?"

"It is a matter of national security. If I tell you why, I will have to kill you." He was not smiling, all the warm fuzzy emotions were gone. He looked like he had just swallowed something bitter. His jaw was pulsating like he was chewing marbles.

I looked him square in the eye and said, "You look just like my Grandpa Schneider, only younger."

"I am younger than retired General Schneider. He is a pussy cat. I am still an old lame tiger with a bad attitude. Piss me off and I will bite you in the ass. We understand each other, Son?"

"Aye, aye. Sir."

"Wait until after you have joined the Navy to use that phrase, Son, only a few are strong enough to understand what it means and the total commitment it implies."

"Yes, Sir. Sorry to offend you."

"Show up tomorrow ready to listen and learn, all will be forgiven if you do that."

When my last class was over, I left the law school with every intention of catching a cab over to the Army Navy Building and asking my father to give me some background on this Commodore Lowe. I changed my mind and headed for Grandpa Schneider's. When I asked about Commodore Lowe, he smiled and said, "Be careful of what you wish for, my Son. Sometimes you get it. This is what you told me you wanted the last time I threw you on your ass in my basement."

"I love you, Grandpa, I was letting you throw me around the mat down there."

"Sure you were! I had to be careful not to break your neck. You probably can not cut the program that Rodney Lowe has laid out for you. When you see him tomorrow, he will ask you to sign away your right to about every freedom we Americans hold dear. Then he will tell you that you need some introduction to the USN, via San Diego, eight weeks worth. Then they will test you for language aptitudes and send you up the coast to Monterey. A year later you will end up in OTC, probably in Virginia at the NCI 'farm'."

"What is that?"

"Commodore Rodney Lowe's school, 'so you want to be a spy.'"

"Who is this, Commodore Lowe? I never heard of him."

"Ever hear of the USS Maine? Rodney Lowe was the Commodore in command of that fleet when the Maine was sunk."

"I thought Admiral Sampson had the fleet."

"After the board of inquiry, Captain Sampson became Admiral Sampson and the rest is history."

"Why is Commodore Lowe a recruiter for JAG?"

"He is not, NCI does not exist, he can not recruit for something that does not exist. They have to put you somewhere and guess what, you are a lawyer, so off to JAG you go like a good little boy. NCI officers are housed all over the Navy depending upon where they went to college and what their 'cover' can be. If you 'wash out of the farm' - then you have a permanent home in JAG."

"Because, I can no longer return to the civilian life because I 'know too much'."

"I always knew you were the smartest of all my grandchildren, Louis. Keep your wits about you. Remember, when facing the bad guys, close the ground between you, never take a step backwards, it screws up the timing for converting self-defense to instant death for your attacker. Want to go down in the basement?"

"No thanks, Grandpa. I want to show up for my interview tomorrow without any marks on my body!"

At eight hundred hours the next day, I was at the Army Navy Building and showed the guard at the entrance Commodore Lowe's card. He turned it over and said, "Report to Room 378, that's on the third floor." He waved me through and I found the steps and took them two at a time. I hit the landing at the third floor and found the room marked 378. Two large men in marine green stood in front of the door. I handed them my card. The guard on the left looked at it and slammed it back into my chest. I took a step backwards and my grandpa's words came back to me, "Never take a step backwards, it screws up the timing for self defense." I took a quick step forward and was face to face with the two shaved gorilla types that barred the door.

"Which one of you ass holes would like to apologize for wrinkling my dress shirt?" I had a giant smile on my face. The words and the facial expression were in conflict. The man on the right began to relax and began to return my smile. The one on the left still had a scowl on his face. I folded my fingers on my right hand at the first joint just like my grandpa had showed me and I drove them as hard as I could, just above the Adam's apple of the guard on the left. As he was going down, I drove my right foot into the side of the right guard's knee. I heard a soft crunch and he bellowed in pain grabbing his knee and hopping around like a little girl.

The office door flew open and a naval officer, I did not know bellowed, "What the hell is going on out here?"

I said nothing. The left guard was red in face and could not speak a word, my grandpa said it would be one or two days before his voice would return. The guard on the right was now sitting on the floor still bellowing something none of us could understand. I thought maybe it was time to say something. "Hello, I am reporting to the Navy Recruiter's office and I ran into these two."

"I can see that. What happened?"

"I handed my card from Commodore Lowe to this man here." I pointed to the one unable to speak. "He dropped the card and we both tried to pick it up and we bumped heads. Don't you just hate it when that happens? Then this other recruit over here tried to help us and we bumped knees, you know knee cap to knee cap, boy that smarts." The officer dropped all pretense and said, "Rodney said you were a smart ass. You two get down to first aid and send the next two up here on the double." He motioned me into his office.

"How did you manage to get the drop on both of those marines?"

"Those were US Marines? Maybe I better rethink my choice of military options for someone like me with a brand new law degree from Georgetown."

"You did not learn how to disable those two in law school."

"I am General Schneider's grandson."

"Your application says, Caldwell not Schneider."

"My mother was a Schneider, you want to see someone tough, recruit her!"

He burst into laughter. "Rodney said you would not agree to join us after you were given the conditions of service, but that I should meet you anyway. We have not been introduced, Mr. Caldwell, I am Captain Yandle. I run this office." He offered his hand and I shook it.

"Tell me the conditions of service for joining the Judge Advocate's Office, Sir."

"You will begin your service at JAG, but you may be transferred to any other unit within the Navy at your commanding officer's discretion."

"That is totally out of the question, Commodore Lowe was correct, I can not accept those conditions. I want a law career not a Navy career. Tell me the conditions for joining another branch of the Navy, like the Office of Naval Counter Intelligence."

His eyes widened and he said, "I can only tell you about JAG since that is what your application indicates."

"Can I fill out an application for NCI?"

"There are no applications for NCI, all members are selected from other branches of the naval forces."

"Can I modify my application to JAG to indicate that I will accept a transfer only to NCI, after a trial period of service? I do not want to waste four years of time when I could be practicing in a law office."

"No one has ever asked me that, Mr. Caldwell. I will find out and contact you. Are you still at Georgetown Law School?"

"No, I am staying with my grandpa until I ship out for San Diego and Monterey."

"His eyes widened even further, do you a speak foreign language?"

"Yes, the Schneiders are German and my great grandmother taught me the lower version of German before she died. I have spent some time in France and seemed to get along alright there. I am not sure about my accent, though."

"Was war thre UrgoBmutter der namin?"

"Sie war aus Bayern. Sie war aus haus der von Hingleburg."

I had not realized that we had slipped into German until Captain Yandle returned to English, "Mr. Caldwell, I am going to go ahead and recommend to JAG that you be accepted with the proviso that you share your assignment only with NCI. If you are transferred anywhere other than NCI, then you will muster out at the time of transfer. How does that sound to you?"

"Sounds like that will work."

"Good, read and sign this. You will leave for San Diego on Monday of next week."

I picked up a pen and signed the next several years of my life away. I left the Army Navy building and caught a streetcar heading for Georgetown. I rode a few minutes and got off at my grandparent's corner and walked the rest of the way to their house. My grandma was baking something and the whole house smelled like a bakery. I found my Grandpa Schneider in his basement. He was punching a body bag fastened to one of the floor joists. The chain that hung the bag rattled with each jab and left hook that my grandpa landed. He looked up and said, "Are you a Navy man now, Louis?"

"Yes, Sir. I talked to a Captain Yandle. He said he knew you."

"Sid Yandle, Captain, nice guy, a little stuck on himself. What did he tell you?"

"He said I was going to San Diego next Monday."

"Have you told your parents and your brothers and sisters?"

"No, I came here first, you have some idea of what I will face. My father and brother did not go to basic training. They went to the Academy and went through Plebe year instead."

"It is not the same, Louis. Trust me, in eight weeks you will be able to toss your father or your brother on their ass."

"My father and brother are not physical, they are more mental in their approach to things."

"Yes, the really physical members of your family are your mother and sisters. I remember your mother taking a paddle to you and your sisters whenever she thought you needed it. Now that you mention it, I do not remember your brother ever getting paddled or your father ever striking any of his children."

"I do not remember him even raising his voice, he was always under control. Do you suppose I am adopted?"

"No, you are more like the Schneider side of the family. Hit first and ask for forgiveness second. That is not a very nice trait and I am sorry for that. I suppose I always got away with that because I was bigger than most of the children that I played with and went to school with. You and your sisters are small boned like your father and it is remarkable what you have learned to do in this basement gym. Now go and kiss your grandmother, eat her cookies and see your parents."

The ride home was very enjoyable, the brown paper bag of cookies was gone, only crumbs were left and I wadded it up and threw it in a trash can as I left the streetcar terminal. I had to ride the streetcar from Georgetown into the Washington Streetcar Terminal and change cars to ride out to the southern suburb of Forest Heights. My parents had found a small acreage there. My father had left the Navy in retirement just before the Spanish American War and he was called back to service and we lived in Beaufort while he was in command of the Marine Training Depot in Port Royal. After the war we moved back to Seneca Hill for a short time and the Vice President, my Uncle Teddy, found us this place in Forest Heights.

The end of the streetcar line was about a half mile from our house and I walked the rest of the way. My father was not home, but my mother was and she asked what my Grandfather had said about my joining the Navy as a lawyer.

"How do you know I talked to Grandpa?"

"Because you are a Schneider first and a Caldwell second, Louis."

"I know, Grandpa Schneider apologized for that not thirty minutes ago."

"You take after the hot headed German side of the family, Louis."

"I often wonder what my father's heritage is. He was raised by his adopted family as an Irish Protestant."

"Louis Caldwell, don't you know that your genes are what got you here, but your parents are responsible for what you think, how you act and even what you will do in a crisis? Do you remember the earth quake in Beaufort when you were a child?"

"Not everything, tell me about it!"

"It began in Charleston. It progressed to Beaufort where buildings swayed back and forth while terrified inhabitants rushed into the streets in their night robes. There were lesser shocks in Memphis, Nashville, Raleigh, Chattanooga, Selma, Lynchburg, Norfolk, Mobile, Louisville, Wilmington, and as far away as Chicago and Cleveland. None of these cities, however, suffered to the extent of Charleston and Beaufort. Telegraphic communication with the rest of the country were cut off and the president declared a national emergency. In Beaufort, the first shock was felt about ten minutes before ten pm and lasted just under a minute. From the rocking and tumbling buildings, the people of Beaufort rushed into the streets, many believing that the end of the world was at hand. By the time your father and I got you four children up and dressed, it was over."

"I do remember you coming into James and my bedroom and telling us to get dressed."

"Your father told us we should not go back inside the house until someone came to check for damages. You asked if anyone was hurt and needed our help. I asked,'Who is up at this hour?'"

"Your father said, everyone in town. We are dressed and we can walk down Bay Street and see if there is any damage there. If the buildings there are alright, maybe we can put the children back to bed. You said, 'I want to help, I am not ready to go back to bed.'

We began walking and we met our neighbors doing the same thing. A second shock began and lasted less than a minute. Everyone was lying on the ground with our heads covered, except you. We sat up and I checked my watch. Is was about twenty minutes after ten."

"I remember that night, I was laying beside an old man who was crying."

"It had been 30 minutes since the first one. You said to the man next to you. Stop crying and you tried to comfort him. We got back on our feet and began the trek down Bay Street. We heard the fire bell ringing and men began to run to the firehouse two blocks up Scott Street as far as Craven Street. A series of fires had broken out in Beaufort. You, your father and brother joined the team of men pulling a pumper to the first fire nearest the fire house, the women of the family just watched our men at work. A third shock was felt, but it did not knock us off our feet. I checked my watch, it was about 30 minutes since the second shock knocked us over. Ten distinct shocks were felt during the night, each about 30 minutes apart with the last just a slight tremor. A total of twenty fires were fought that night. You and your brother were exhausted."

"I do remember that no element of terror was lacking. The people of Beaufort camped in the open streets or fled to the countryside for refuge. At sunrise, we began to get a clearer picture of what damage was caused. The dead were placed in the lobby of the Sea Island Hotel, 105 in total. Nearly two-thirds of the town buildings needed major repairs. Father, James and I found the rest of you sleeping in the park."

"The point I am trying to make here is that it was you and your father that took control."

"I remember when it was over. We needed to see what the damage was to the house. We slowly walked back to our house and stood and looked at what had happened. The beautiful carriage portico was a pile of rubble. The long side porch on the opposite side of the house sat at an odd angle torn away, but somehow trying to cling to the house."

"Yes, your father said to keep you children off the porch. You and he went around the outside of the house to see what damage has been done to the main core."

"I remember the carriage house was flattened. Nothing was inside, the steamers were all in the warehouse on Scott Street. We continued walking and looked at all four corners of the house. They had not shifted. They looked solid. We entered the back stoop and found our housekeeper asleep under the kitchen table. I thought she was dead until I heard her snoring."

"That would have been Mrs. Willowoee, do you remember her?"

"Louise and I loved her. She opened her eyes and said, 'That was quite a night. I tried to get out the back door but as things began falling so I dove under the table here and stayed put. I must have fallen asleep. Oh, my. I do believe I have soiled my underwear!'

We all began laughing and you found us sitting together with our arms around each other. You asked what were we doing? We tried to answer but we were laughing too hard. Mrs. Willowoee said, 'We are celebrating life, Mrs. Caldwell. Where is Louise she is never alone, she is always clinging to Louis?'"

"Louis, I do not worry about you. I worry about your father and your brother, but you are different. You enjoy your basic training and the other training that will be required of you. Write to your father as often as you can, he worries about you."

"I know he does. The one I worry about is Louise. We have never been apart in our entire lives, except for one summer. When she was frightened by a storm or the earth quake you described, she would come and sleep with James and me. Three of us in a double bed."

"I know, it was comical to see the three heads all in row when I would come looking for you in the morning. James would be asleep clinging to one side and you and your sister in each others arms like an old married couple."

"Oh, Mom, the four of us are very different. We all handed our sibling relationship in a different way. Louise and I shared everything when we were little. We became very co-dependent. For that reason, I am glad that the Navy is sending me away for several months. Louise is a school teacher now and a grown woman. She needs to begin her life without her twin brother to kiss away her fears every time there is a bump in the road."

2

San Diego Training Center

July 1, 1903

My trip across the country was uneventful. One train ride is pretty much like another. My sister and I were born in San Francisco and we had traveled to the family resort in Virginia City, Nevada, so I thought I knew the west. San Diego would probably be different. It might be more like Mexico, or what I thought Mexico should be like, I had never been to Mexico. We had lived on the east coast, traveled to Bermuda and spent a summer in Paris attending the Ecole des Hautes Etudes. We had asked my parents to send us there after our second year of study at William and Mary. They did not think it was a good idea, even though it was a sponsored summer course from William and Mary. We talked to our Grandmother Caldwell and she understood, she always did. After a twenty minute conversation with grandma, my father announced that my twin sister and I could go to Paris, on one condition! That condition was that we go in different summers. I went the first summer and Louise went the second.

The train ride would be three days long. I tried to remember why my sister and I became so co-dependent. We had been apart both of those summers, but when our classes began again in the fall at William and Mary we were inseparable again. The co-dependance must have occurred earlier than that.

When we were small we took baths together and swam nude together in the ponds at Seneca Hill. She said I had a bigger thing than she had. As soon as your things began to grow beards our parents tried to separate us as much as possible. Louise became modest beyond belief after she witnessed the many spankings my mother gave me for not respecting other people's privacy. The beatings never had an affect on me, I ran around nude all the time. Whenever she saw me nude, she called me a pervert and I called her a prude. When I lost my virginity in Paris that first summer, and I was stupid enough to tell her, she was beside herself with grief about my "immortal soul". I told her she was jealous that I was growing into an adult and she was still a child. She did not speak to me for a week.

After a week, she said, "Louis we need to talk." That was always a sign that she had made up our minds about something. Even after we went to William and Mary as freshmen she would leave the girls dorm and I would leave the boys dorm and we would spend the night together until curfew. I did not date girls and she did not date boys. Now she had decided to have the conversation that might end our special relationship of being a twin in all respects. I was terrified that we would not have that after the discussion. I remember it started this way.

"Louis, did you ever wonder why I never dated boys the last two years at William and Mary?"

"Yes, It was probably why I never dated girls. I never met any that excited me as much as being with you. You finish some of my sentences and know what I am thinking most of the time. Most girls I know are rather silly and not interested in what I am interested in."

"What was different about Madeleine, Louis?"

"I wondered what sex with a girl might be like. May be it was because it was my first time, but it hurt my thing and I did not enjoy it. Couples that have children must really want to have them to put up with that."

"I thought all boys and especially some men could not get enough sex. You seemed interested in it all the time. I had to be careful not to be nude around you. What is wrong with me?"

"Nothing is wrong with you. You are beautiful. Anyway, I think you are beautiful, it has been a long time since I have seen most of your body but what shows is beautiful. Besides it is what is inside a person not what their thing looks like that attracts you to them. I can not remember a time that I was not attracted to you, Louise."

"Oh, Louis, I love you too. I will try to be less bashful around you."

"It is your body, Louise, save it for someone who appreciates it." She began crying and I did not understand adult women at all.

When our college days were finished and we graduated, Louise checked out of her dorm and I checked out of mine. We found a tiny apartment near her teaching position and a short walk for me to start law school. It had one bedroom with twin beds and one bath room. It was impossible not to see your sibling in some sort of undress. We even saw each other nude and it did not make either one of us blind. We understood that we were special to each other and that in order to preserve that we would continue to be each others safety net for all things that life can throw at you. We said we were comfortable with each other, in truth the co-dependence got worse.

This upcoming year would be the first time that we would be apart since we were born. I would always remember the look on Louise's face when I told her that she needed to keep the apartment for herself or move in with our parents who lived in the Washington area. I would be away from home for at least a year, may be longer, depending where the Navy decided to sent me. She was heart broken and I was not much better. I was already sad that I would not see her bring her papers home from school and correct them. I missed not seeing her get excited over something and hug the stuffings out of me in response. I loved my sister.

It was two more days until the train arrived on the west coast. Each night I would dream about Louise and what we had shared during our life times together. The train finally arrived in San Diego.

The train station in San Diego was only a short ride by city trolley to any part of the city. But I did not see any part of it, we were met at the train platform by a group of drill instructors. These guys were something else in their stiff mounted policeman hats and knee high shined brown boots. They yelled at us and I smiled at them. Most of the kids getting off the train to meet their basic training sergeants were eighteen years old. I was five or six years older and I bet none of them had a Grandpa Schneider with a basement full of training devices.

"Hoist your gear and get moving towards the trucks."

We grabbed our suitcases and followed one of the DIs as the others began to shout insults at us.

"Try to look like you can keep in step, will you? What the hell is wrong with you, Sailor? You look like you miss your mommy, well, I am not your mother!"

I began to chuckle, I remembered stories told to me when I sat on my Grandfather Caldwell's knee. I wondered if I would meet my Chief Gunnerman sometime during the next two months.

"What are you grinning about?" A mean looking DI, a half a head taller than me, was in my face. I continued to walk in step.

"I am talking to you, Sailor!" He reached out and grabbed my arm and spun me out of the line of recruits. The rest of them continued on while this DI was red in the face from yelling at me. I did not say a word. Grandpa Schneider said it was best to let them exhaust themselves from yelling than try to get emotionally involved with any DI. When he finally stopped to take a breath I asked him, "Here are my enlistment papers. How many Ensigns do you get to bully around during basic?"

"If you are an Ensign, I will kiss your ass!" He grabbed the papers from my hand and began reading. "It says here you are an Ensign upon completion of your basic training. You have not even started basic yet, you smart ass!"

"That is true. In two months, a brand new Ensign can make your life miserable, however. Think about that the next time you get in my face." He blinked hard and shoved the papers back into my chest, I took a small step forward. He backed off and started yelling at some little pimply faced kid from Nebraska.

Our barracks was long and narrow, full of cots and foot lockers. We had been processed and given our brand new Navy grey underwear, blue jeans and white tee shirts and hats. We even looked like sailors. We were told to report for physical training in front of the barracks. The same DI that had read my papers was standing with his hands on his hips and glaring at us.

"I am your drill instructor for the next eight weeks. My name is Henderson. You will call me Mister Henderson. Is that clear!" No one said a word.

"Is that clear?" He shouted at the top of his lungs!"

"Yes, Mr. Henderson." We all shouted back at him.

"Good, usually we start with some warmup exercises and then we do a five mile run. Today, I have modified a few things so that some of you will get the idea of what you can do after your eight weeks here is finished. Those two DIs standing right here beside me will demonstrate self-defense for you."

The two DIs squared off and demonstrated how to break a choke hold, throw an attacker over our hips by using the forward motion of the attacker and all the rest of what I learned in the Schneider's basement. When they were finished, Mr. Henderson said, "They are experts, no one expects you to defend yourselves like that."

He looked down his clip board and said, "To demonstrate what I mean, I will pick one of you at random. Mr. Caldwell, please step forward and try to defend yourself against either one of these two DIs here."

"Are you sure, Mr. Henderson?"

"Front and center, Mr. Caldwell."

I stepped forward and assumed the stance for naval basic judo training. The two DIs looked at each other and started laughing,

"Let me take this one, Ed." He walked toward me with a mean look on his face and started to say something. I stepped forward and placed my foot between his legs, crossed under and swept him off his feet. He bounced back up and charged me, he was angry. I used his forward motion and threw him over my hip. He landed with a surprised look on his face and shouted, "Get him, Ed."

The second DI came charging at me, pivoted on one foot to land a body kick. I stepped inside and drove the flat of my hand into his Adam's apple. He went down in a heap gasping for breath. The first one had gotten up and he charged me with another of the basic judo moves and I threw him on his back, placed my foot in his armpit and twisted his hand at the wrist until I heard a snap. I was watching out of the corner of my eye because I expected Mr. Henderson to be next. Instead, he started writing on his clip board and he acted like he had not seen a thing. I stepped back into formation while the two friends of Mr. Henderson limped out of sight. I never saw them again during the next two months.

I did not have to see his friends, Henderson, the DI, was always in my face about something. I never showed any disrespect and always remained calm. First rule of Grandpa Schneider's School of Self Defense: never begin an argument, never throw the first punch, never go on the offensive. I waited for Henderson to lose his cool, he never did. He had been a DI a lot longer than I had been "a ninety day wonder". That is what the DIs called anyone with a college education. I had no idea where that came from. Naval basic training was eight weeks or fifty-six days. Maybe when I arrived in language school, I would be known as a "56 day wonder."

No one was given any leave time in San Diego, it was 56 days from beginning to end. On Sunday morning there was one hour for chapel, temple or mosque. The Moslems thought that this was ridiculous, they never went to mosque on Sunday mornings, they prayed three times a day and went to mosque sometimes twice a day. When this was denied to them, they left basic training and were given discharges. The rest of us, Christians and Jews, learned to cope with what was thrown at us and we survived as a group until the last week. The last week was known as hell week and you had to get through that to get through naval basic training. We were given our survival packs after church on Sunday and told to begin our march south from San Diego into the wilderness known as Lower Otay Indian Reservation. The reservation was abandoned by the tribes placed there in the middle 1800's. They had been assimilated into the Spanish and American populations, some going north and some going south into Mexico. The reservation was still federal property and the Navy used it as a survival training area. When we entered the area, it was like walking into an 1846 Mexican War battlefield.

"What the hell were sailors going to do for week on an army battlefield?" I asked myself. I soon found out. A detachment of soldiers came out of the brush and fired their weapons over our heads, close enough so that we threw ourselves, face first, on the ground. I looked up and saw a mean looking guy in a strange uniform speaking Spanish. I understood what he was trying to say, "You are my prisoner, Yankee Dog. Take off your clothes and open that pack of supplies." We all looked at each other in amazement, "Was this some kind of graduation joke?" I thought. When we did not move, our captors fired into the ground near us and small stones began to draw drops of blood from our hands and faces. I began to peel off my field utilities on the double. In less than two minutes the entire basic training class was sitting in a circle, naked as jay birds.

The leader of our captors spoke to us in broken English.

"I am the supreme leader and you are all prisoners of the 'Peoples Liberation Army of Northern Medico'. When I ask you to stand, you will stand. Those that do not will be shot."

One smart ass sailor among us said," Sure you will!" He was dragged out of the circle and into a gulch just beyond our vision and we heard automatic gun fire and several screams of pain. The troopers who dragged him into the gulch came back with blood on their boots and pant legs. I was shocked, wait a minute, this is play acting, isn't it? We never saw that sailor again, not during the next week, or at graduation. I looked around the circle to find our DI, Henderson, there he sat nude like the rest of us with a smirk on his face.

The supreme leader saw him and he screamed, "Why are you smiling? Do you think this is funny? Drag him off and cut off his nuts, then put a bullet in his head. Henderson began screaming as he, too, was dragged into the gulch with the same results.

"Who else, among you, are the leaders of this bunch of boys from north of the border, I wonder? You!" he screamed. He pointed his finger at me. "Point to the leaders of this rabble." I pointed to myself, then the man sitting next to me and the next, until I had pointed to everyone. Then I said in Spanish, "You have killed our leader, Generalissimo Henderson, may he rest in peace."

The supreme leader of the captors tried to keep a straight face but his face cracked into a slight smile. "Silence in the ranks. You will stand and you will march into the prison camp over that hill."

We all stood and marched barefoot over the hill. On the other side was a barbed wire enclosure with three shacks along the back edge of the compound. It was August 22, 1903, and the temperatures in southern California had set record highs that summer, it was 102 degrees in the shade and we were standing in the sun.

"You may all rest in the shade of your barracks, except for you." The supreme leader pointed at me. "Come with me into my headquarters."

I walked behind him and followed him to the smallest of the three shacks. The temperature inside was as bad as the outside. "Please for you to sit young man." I understood that was meant as permission to sit, so I sat in the only chair before a makeshift desk. The desk was an old house door and two saw horses but the chair behind the desk was a plush, leather covered office chair. I began to see better as my eyes adjusted from the bright sunlight to the dim light of the "head quarters". There was electricity into the camp because I saw a light bulb hanging over the desk and heard the hum of an icebox.

"Would you like a cold drink, young man?" He walked to the icebox in the corner and brought out two bottles of Mexican beer and sat them on the desk. He pulled an opener out of a shoe box that served as his in-out box and popped the cap off one of the bottles. He began drinking it and watching me.

"What is your name, young man?"

"Theodore Roosevelt, Sir."

"You think you are amusing me, no doubt. Why did your military group invade Mexico?"

"The United States has declared war on Mexico and we are the first wave of invaders. I would not get too comfortable, thousands are following, even as I speak." He finished his beer and took the second bottle of beer to return it to the icebox.

"I will offer this drink to the next prisoner who will tell me his name. A simple question, no?"

"I told you my name, my rank is commander-in-chief of the armed forces of the United States. I was visiting the San Diego Depot and decided to join the first wave of the invasion. I have not led troops in battle since Cuba, I was too young to come to Mexico in 1846 to kick the shit out of you Mexicans, so I decided to have a bully good time on this trip south."

"Then you admit that you invaded Mexico, Senor Roosevelt!"

"Of course, a state of war exists between our two countries, don't you listen? I prefer to be called, Senor President." The supreme leader could not keep a straight face. He withdrew his revolver, pointed it at the ceiling and pulled the trigger. The sound was deafening. It must have been a signal for one of his men to come inside and throw a cup of pig's blood in my face. I was hauled out of the chair and thrown out the door of the shack. It happened so fast that I did not have time to react and went sprawling in a heap in front of the headquarters. The rest of the naval basic training group looked on in disbelief. I got myself together and walked over to them. I was a sorry sight. I looked at them and said, "I plan on forming an escape party as soon as it is dark, anyone interested?"

"What the hell are you talking about, Caldwell, this is just an act. Sit down and shut up." The man who said that was jerked up and hauled off to the head quarters shack. I was shoved down into his place. The man next to me said, "This is a little extreme, even for an exercise. What happened in there?"

"I was offered a cold drink for basic information. I cooperated with them but they did not like my answers."

"Did they beat you? Are you hurt?"

"No, they just threw blood in my face. I am fine." About that same time my replacement came sailing out the door of the head quarters on his ass. He was covered with blood and he was crying. The supreme leader came out the door and screamed, "I will kill the next son-of-bitch that does not give me his name, place of birth and rank within the United States invasion force." Several of the seamen rose to their feet and began giving their names, where they were born and where they were stationed.

"These sailors think they are in Mexico." I thought. Within an hour everyone of us gave his name, where he was born and the fact that we had indeed invaded Mexico from San Diego. We were given water to drink for the cooperation. No food was offered. The sun began to set in the west and the temperature began to drop. The sweat on our bodies began to dry and we shivered together like a bunch of little girls.

"We need to exercise to keep warm I whispered to the group closest to me." I stood and began to do jumping jacks and calling cadence, soon the entire group was up and exercising.

Inside the head quarters, the resurrected Henderson said, "That is the Caldwell kid, he will be the toughest to break, he can take care of himself, we need to separate him from the rest, he will give them hope. He is a natural born leader.

"What do you suggest?"

"Let him escape. Where can he go? He is nude and in the middle of nowhere. Keep two trackers on him and if it gets hairy we can get him water and food. He will have a hell of a week out there in the wilderness."

"Agreed. Turn off the lights behind the barracks and get everyone inside for the night."

We were herded into the barracks where we found cots and blankets. Many just grabbed the blankets and covered themselves to keep warm. I stood and considered my options. I needed food and water, boots and my survival gear. I did not need clothing, I liked being nude. Maybe Louise was right, I am a pervert. Three others were standing beside me.

"Where do you think they stored all our packs, Caldwell?"

"That is, Ensign Caldwell. If you three are coming with me you obey my orders, agreed?" They shook their heads, yes.

"See if there is a way out of here that is not through the doorway, I will be back in a few minutes or the escape attempt is off and you three can go to bed."

"Aye, aye. Sir." I grinned and crawled out the doorway on my belly. I returned in twenty minutes.

"Okay, this is what I found. The packs are stacked inside the corner of the head quarters shack. I doubt that we can get four packs without taking out some of the guards."

"There are twelve guards with guns, Ensign Caldwell. We can not do that. These are American trainers, not real Mexicans."

"Did any of you three go to college?" Two of them nodded, yes.

"Okay, did any of you join a fraternity? They nodded, yes, again.

"Do you remember hell week? This, gentlemen, is a case where the actives take us for a ride off campus, bump our asses in the middle of nowhere and expect us to get back to campus on our own. They want us to try to escape so they can rub our noses in our failure. Suppose I can get one of the packs tonight, remove all the contents and pass it out to everyone in this barracks? We can replace the pack and hide it in plain sight back in the head quarters shack. While I make an attempt, the three of you talk to each one of the men in here. Tell them what our plan is." It was now dark behind the barracks, so I stayed away from there. The trainers would be watching us make an escape in the darkness and then round us up in the morning. I waited and crawled back to the head quarters shack. I was outside the building on the corner which contained the packs. The shack was constructed of tree trunks, limbs and branches. The trunks formed the frame work, the limbs formed the cross members and the branches covered the outside walls. I heard voices inside talking about when Caldwell would attempt his escape.

"He will not try anything until later tonight when he thinks everyone is asleep!" I heard one of the trainers say. His voice belonged to Mr. Henderson. I had reached my hand through the branches and carefully slid the first pack that I could reach, toward me. Slowly, slowly I thought. What seemed like hours passed and I finally had the pack outside the shack. Carefully I crawled back to the barracks. My three enlisted men were ready to pass out the goodies. We emptied the pack and replaced everything that was not edible or drinkable. The missing weight was replaced with stones and I crept back and replaced the pack and took another. When I got back everyone was up and eating.

"Police this area. Don't leave anything for the trainers to find in the morning. Bury the trash under the shack. Be careful, stay out of the darkness behind the barracks, that is where the trainers are watching."

THE SUNRISE WAS BETWEEN 5 AND 6 AM. The trainers came charging into the barracks screaming for us to get up and fall out for inspection. Some of the trainers had been up all night watching for the escape and they were down to nine guards instead of the twelve. We needed for another three to get sleepy and we could turn the tables on them, after all, we all had a good night's sleep. Henderson and the plant that they pulled out and into the gulch, had to stay out of sight. We formed into two lines and faced the trainers.

"Today, there will be no food and no water unless you confess to your crimes." The first man in formation said, "I confess." The chorus of, "I confess," followed throughout the ranks. The supreme leader smiled and said, "Pass out the water canteens." We all drank heavily and waited for the food. There was none. Each man was drug into the head quarters shack and was grilled for information. It was noon time and the trainers lit a fire composed of wood and grilled some sort of wild game that they had shot. The smell was mouth watering. The trainers ate in front of us. We sat in the shade as the temperature began to rise.

"It will not be long and one of them will break." The supreme leader smiled and said, "It never takes more than two days for everyone of them to give up their citizenship and become a Mexican, in order to get something to eat, maybe by tonight, time will tell."

At dusk, the temperature began to drop and we were herded into the barracks when one of my helpers took my place and lead the men in jumping jacks. As soon as it was dark, I crawled out of the barracks, keeping away from the darkness and crept over to the head quarters shack. I heard voices.

"I do not understand, why did another seaman take Caldwell's place? Why is he still here with the rest of us?"

"He will try his escape tonight double the guards behind the barracks, we need to track him to keep him safe."

I smiled as I reached into the shack for my third survival pack. I got it safely out and then slid another out the same way. Two trips were risky. I found everyone up, not just my three enlisted seaman. Everyone was beginning to enjoy this exercise. We ate and drank and I replaced the two packs. The trash was buried beneath the barracks.

"Tonight, I make my escape!" I said. "Where can I hide inside the compound?" Confusion filled the faces of the men. "Tommy, you crawl out after I am hidden and make it look like someone slid under the fence. If you have time, make barefoot prints into the brush and back using the same foot falls, can you do that?"

Tommy Carlise was one my three trusted lieutenants he nodded yes. "Do it now, they will expect a late departure after everyone is asleep. I need to find a place that the trainers will never think to look."

"Ensign Caldwell, how strong is your sense of smell?"

"I guess like everyone's, why?"

"You can crawl under the latrine. I will bring you food and water for as many days as it takes. No one will think to look for you there."

"Tommy, you are a genius. Each night another one of us will escape using the same technique. It will drive the trainers crazy when they can not find us out in the desert. They will think they have killed a seaman during basic training."

The sunrise on the third day brought panic. One of the trainers came running into the head quarters and said, "Caldwell is missing."

"What do you mean missing? He never left the camp last night, we were watching."

"Oh, yes, he did. I found the opening in the fence and his foot prints leading off into the brush."

"Son-of-a- bitch, why didn't someone see him leave and keep tabs on him? He won't last eight hours in this heat. Get everyone you can spare, including Henderson and Ellington and pick up his trail."

The two line formation of seamen stood at attention before the barracks as the supreme leader yelled at us. "Where is Caldwell? I know he did not escape. Every one of you will help in the search of the camp."

That was a fatal mistake. The guards were armed, but outnumbered. Three were asleep. Four were out looking for me when Carlise said, "I know where he might be."

I was in deep shit, literally. The smell was not too bad. I got used to it after a couple of hours. I was waiting for Carlise to bring the supreme leader to the latrine. I heard someone coming. I got away from the hole and waited.

"I think he might be in the latrine." As the supreme leader bent over to look down the hole, I reached up and grabbed him by the front of his shirt. I pulled his head into the hole cut in the rough boards. He was trapped and Carlise took his weapon and tried to tie his hands behind his back with his boot laces. He was screaming for help until I kissed him right on the mouth and he started to gag. I shoved some used toilet paper in his mouth and he fainted. I said, "Eat shit, supreme leader."

Carlise had an easier time after he fainted and I called up through the hole, "I am coming out of this shit hole. How are the others doing?"

"It is eight to one, Ensign. The tables should be turned." I came around the corner of the latrine and said, "I am going down to the stream with a bar of soap. Find the seaman's uniforms and get everyone dressed. I want the guards stripped, gaged and naked when I get back."

"Yes, Sir."

Within an hour I was dressed and shouting in the faces of the captured trainers, "What Mexican division are you a member of, soldier?" Of course they were gagged and could not say anything. "If someone does not respond I will be forced to march on Mexico City and capture your stinking capitol building!" I screamed. The good guys were enjoying this.

"Ensign Caldwell? When do you think Henderson and the others will be coming back?"

"Not until they find me dead in the desert. Let's get packed up and out of here before the trucks show up from San Diego."

"How do you know that trucks are coming?"

"Well, how else are they going to get us back in time for graduation?"

"No wonder you are an Ensign." Everyone began to police the whole area. We did not want to leave a single trace of our every being there. The trainers assigned to our capture began to issue orders as soon as the gags were removed.

"Look, whoever you are. You have no identification on your person. You had on a strange looking uniform. It is now at the bottom of the latrine. You are inside a federal reservation and I am the only US officer on this site. You will stop complaining and march with us or I will have you shot as a Mexican spy."

"You can't do that. I am a captain in the United States Marines."

"Marines, no wonder we had such an easy time of overpowering you guys. Marines are a bunch of pussies compared to United States Seamen."

"Then will you untie us and let us go?"

"Sure."

"Wait a minute, where are our clothes and weapons? You can't leave us naked and unarmed in the middle of nowhere."

"I told you, your uniforms and weapons are at the bottom of the latrine. See you back in San Diego."

3

Monterey Training Center

September 1, 1903

I graduated with the rest of the July recruits and boarded the train for the Monterey Training Center. I had heard of the war department's language school at Monterey. They accepted only those who spoke a foreign language already and wished to learn one or more additional. They reasoned if our brains already contained English and another language, it could learn to accept as many as were adequately introduced. I had passed my entrance exam in German and was there to learn French and all the others that I could absorb in twelve months.

I found my billet in the "old barracks building". The US Army was in the process of building new barracks for their detachments that would be training in some new form of cavalry which did not make use of horses. I had no idea how they were going to have a cavalry without horses. My roommate was already checked in, his name was Hans Becker. He had passed his test in German also and he spoke English with a slight accent.

"Mine name is Ensign Hans Becker. What is yours, please?"

"My name is Louis Caldwell. Are you native born?"

"JA, mine family has been in Pennsylvania for a long time."

"Do you speak German at home, Hans?"

"JA, how can you tell?"

"Just a wild guess, my grandmother Schneider spoke German to me all the time."

"Schneider, that is a good old German name from southern Bavaria, JA?"

"It is. You were not in my basic training session in San Diego, Hans. Where did you do your basic?"

"It was five years ago in South Carolina. That has to be the armpit of the nation, Louis. Do not go there unless you have to. The insects are so large there that three of them can suck you dry! I was a radio operator and I had to string wires at night through the woods on Pritchards Island. What a hell hole that was."

"My father was stationed at Port Royal during the last war. I know what you mean about the mosquitoes on Parris Island. Whenever I had a break from college I would ride the train as far as I could and he would come get me at a place called Yemassee."

"I know that damn place, too. Louis Caldwell. There was an Admiral Caldwell at Paris Island. He is your father, JA?"

"Afraid so, Hans. You got some really good training at Port Royal. Were you sent to Cuba?"

"JA, but the war was over before I got there. "

"Me too. I mean, the war didn't last very long. I was in college and missed it. But I am ready to 'go to war' whenever Uncle Sam needs me."

"You have an Uncle Sam in the Navy?"

"No, just an expression. You know, US stands for United States or in my case, it can also stand for Uncle Sam."

"What is your father doing now that the war is over, Louis?"

"He works for my Uncle Teddy."

"UT, what does that stand for, please?"

"My father's sister, married Theodore Roosevelt."

"So, you have friends in high places, Louis Caldwell!"

"My Uncle Teddy does not know I am alive, Hans. I have never been to the White House."

"But your father works in the White House, JA?"

"Yes, he does. I have been in college and then law school, I have not been invited to see where he works."

"Louis Caldwell, shame on you! See if you can get both of us an invitation to the White House during our Thanksgiving break, I want to meet the President, your Uncle Teddy!"

"I will see what I can do, Hans. My father likes to write and receive letters. You can help me write one to him right now."

We cleaned off a place on our study desk and got a piece of paper and a pen.

Monterey, California
September 2, 1903

Dear Father,

I arrived here from San Diego last night. My belongings still fit into one suitcase and I have gotten everything I own into a chest of drawers. My roommate is Hans Becker. He was one of the recruits that passed through Port Royal five years ago when you were in command of Paris Island. He says you should remember him, he was the one complaining of the rather large mosquitoes found in South Carolina. His family lives in Philadelphia and we plan on taking the same train back east for our Thanksgiving Vacation.

I have invited him to stop over in Washington with me for a few hours so we can tour the White House together. Neither one of us have ever been there and we decided that it might be nice to see the "People's House" up close. I hope that you will still be in your office on the 21st of November, so that Hans can get a peek at a real live Admiral at work.

We start our saturation in languages on Monday. I will write again next week and tell you how it is going.

Your Loving Son,

Louis

Hans and I forgot about my letter and it was nearly two weeks later that we got a reply from the White House.

THE WHITE HOUSE
WASHINGTON, D.C.

Ensign L. J. Caldwell
United States Naval Training Center
Monterey, California

Dear Nephew,

Your father shared your last letter with me. I remember how much I looked forward to letters from your Aunt Ruth when I was serving in Cuba. I will be looking forward to your visit with us here in the White House on or about November 21, 1903. I have no idea what will be on my schedule that day, but tell your roommate that he can stick his head in my office and see the commander-in-chief hard at work!

Save this and show it to the Marine guards at the east portico. They will admit you both and set up a tour for you.

T. Roosevelt

Theodore Roosevelt
President of the United States

Hans kept reading the letter over and over again.

"I am going to see the President." He repeated this to himself over and over again, also. We managed to get several weeks of study under our belts before the time came to board the train for Washington that November. Hans was in a talkative mood and asked me about the Judge Advocate General's Office.

"Louis, what is this *JAG* thing?"

"It started during the Civil War, Hans. Secretary Welles of the Navy, named a 'Solicitor of the Navy Department.' By the Act of March 2, 1865, Congress authorized President Lincoln to appoint, for service during the rebellion, a 'Solicitor and Naval Judge Advocate General'. The Congress maintained the billet after the war on a year to year basis until 1870. In that year it was transferred to a newly established Justice Department."

"Has it changed much in the last 33 years?"

"Yes, it has. In 1870, there was one office, located in the Washington Navy Yard. When this became overloaded with cases, Naval Legal Service Offices, called NLSO's, were established. They divided the area of Naval Responsibility within the US and world into the following branches; North Central, Mid-Atlantic, Southeast, Central, Southwest, Northwest, Pacific Coast, Europe and Asia."

"So which one are you headed for after you finish at Monterey?"

"You didn't let me finish how the JAG offices grew. After the NLSO branches were formed, RLSO offices inside each of the NLSO offices were formed. These Regional offices further divided the legal loads within the Navy. I hope to work in one of the trial judiciary offices. These are located in Washington, D.C.; Norfolk, Virginia; Camp Lejeune, North Carolina; San Diego and Pearl Harbor, Hawaii."

"You do not care where you are sent? These are really different locations."

"No, I do not care where I work. I still have officer's training to complete and I have no idea where that might be or how long it will take. You have to be patient if you are in the Navy. Right, Hans?"

"Right, Louis!"

"Tell me more of how you got sent to Monterey, Hans. How did a radio operator in Cuba get selected for special training?"

"It's a long story. Are you sure you want to hear it?"

"What else have we got to do during this cross country train ride?"

"I was a radio chief when we landed in Cuba at Guantanamo Bay. The Marines had established their base near there and needed help with captured messages. They had stacks of them. They had separated all the Spanish into one pile and assumed the others were sent in some kind of code. I picked up the first one off the coded pile and it read.

"***Opermerking***: *Zorg ervoor dat uw vingers droog en schoon zijin wanneer u met het keyer werkt. Zo houdt u het keyer zelf ook droog en schoon. Het keyer is gevoelig voor vingerbewegingen. Hoe lichter de druck, hoe beter de respons. Het keyer functioneert niet beter als u harder drukt.*"

"That sounds like German in some sort of code."

"JA, only it was Dutch sent in the clear."

"You read Dutch?"

"Of course, I am a graduate from Penn College!" He had a smile on his face that told me he did not learn Dutch in college.

"So, you are from Pennsylvania and you learned Dutch from a family member. Right, Hans!"

"Right, Louis!"

"Why were the Spanish sending messages in Dutch?"

"Do you remember the commanding general in Cuba?"

"The butcher of Cuba, Weylor, wasn't it?"

"General Valerano Van Weylor to be exact. The Valerano is Spanish from his mother and the Van Weylor is Dutch from his father."

"So these were messages from Van Weylor or to Van Weylor!"

"Right again, Louis!"

"What did you do with them?"

"I translated them."

"And?"

"And, I was no longer a radio chief. They promoted me to Navy Intelligence and sent me to Havana to be part of the American occupation forces in Cuba."

"So why did it take you so long to get more training at Monterey?"

"I could tell you, Louis, but then I would have to kill you." He was smiling.

"You continued to work in Naval Intelligence."

"You said that, Louis, I did not."

"Where did you get your officer training?"

"Lancaster, Virginia.

4

Lancaster, Virginia

July 1, 1904

LANCASTER IS THE NAME OF a county in eastern Virginia and the name of an estate that was taken under the Confiscation Act of 1861. It is now federal property and no longer the Fairfield family estate. The Fairfield estate was built prior to the American Revolution and they had an excellent view of the design and layout of Washington City. As the city was constructed and spread out from its center like a giant wheel it nearly engulfed the Fairfield estate. The 1100 acres of rolling forest and farm land was like an oasis just outside the capitol city. This was the ideal place for Commodore Rodney Lowe to establish his training center he called *The Farm.*

I had graduated from the language school and was about to enter my phase of training which would be similar to OTC for any other normal naval recruit with a college education. This Officer's Training Center would be one of 'dirty tricks' and 'staying alive in a foreign country.' Not every agent could, or should, be assigned to a US Embassy abroad. Since the founding of the United States, immigrants from all over the world came to these shores to seek their fortunes. My OTC class of 1904, contained at least one of these grandsons of immigrants. We had German, Italian, Japanese, Chinese, Philippine, Cuban, French, Spanish, African and Russian representation. I got to practice my German, Spanish and French every day.

The first day of orientation was an eye opener. I was walking into the morning breakfast and I noticed a wall of photographs. I stopped dead in my tracks, there was Hans Becker's smiling face. I took a step closer and read the information below the photograph.

ENSIGN HANS BECKER, COMMUNICATIONS INSTRUCTOR, 1899-1903.

A CONVERSATION, ON A TRAIN, IN NOVEMBER OF 1903 CAME BACK INTO MY MEMORY. *"I COULD TELL YOU, LOUIS, BUT THEN I WOULD HAVE TO KILL YOU."*

A voice behind me said, "I got a letter from Hans yesterday. He said your German was terrible and your Dutch was impossible to understand." I turned to face Rodney Lowe, Commodore USN and director of The Farm.

"Hans would know, Sir. His English is terrible and his Dutch is excellent!"

"How is your room?"

"On the top floor, a large bedroom with french doors that open onto a balcony that looks across a meadow and a stand of pine trees. Lancaster is a palace compared with the language barracks at Monterey, Sir. How long can I live at The Farm, Sir?"

"As long as you are a bachelor and assigned to the Washington NCI district, this is your home. I know what you mean about Monterey, a few months of language polishing and you are ready to leave there for greener pastures. We have not changed the inside of the Fairfield estate much, the bedrooms for example, are as they left them in 1861. Let's go in to breakfast and then I will take all the officer candidates on the grand tour of the place. I think you will like it, Louis."

AN HOUR LATER, Commodore Lowe took his fork and clanged it against his water glass and the dining room became very quiet. He rose and said the following. "Those of you who came down for breakfast this morning are a special breed of young men. Each one of you will be sitting in a foreign country one year from now or you will be dead. Look around the tables this morning, some of you will be sent to London, others to Berlin, Rome, Tokyo, Singapore, Manilla, Havana, Paris, Madrid, Marakesh or Moscow. The list of foreign capitols is almost endless, and we need to send at least two agents to each. The graduates of the Naval Counter Intelligence Training Center are prepared to do many things. For example, the young man on my right will be given a cover placement inside the Judge Advocates Regional Legal Services Office here at the Washington Navy Yard. He will not spend much time there, that is his cover assignment. He will be in charge of catching those foreign nationals who are in this country as spies. His language skills will permit him to travel unnoticed into Germany, Holland or France in pursuit of these individuals. If he ever has to travel to see another of you in your theater of operations, God help him to remain mute!" I looked up at the Commodore and smiled. He continued, "Not everyone is cut out for this type of Navy life. I sure as hell was not when President McKinley asked me to form this unit and to track down and kill everyone involved with the sinking of the *USS Maine.*" A few heads jerked towards him. "Don't look so shocked. You think that the United States never found out who sank the Maine. Not true, Admiral Caldwell turned everything he had over to me and I got the ones who attacked our vessel. I personally pulled the trigger of the pistol that I placed beside their heads. I was given a Presidential Warrant to be the one in charge of finding and finishing the guilty parties. There was no trial, the President wanted an excuse to enter Cuba and clean up the mess left by Spain. We clean up messes, Gentlemen. Your training begins today. You are all physically fit or you would not be here. You all have cover Naval assignments after you leave here, but you work for me. You will learn how to send a radio signal from inside a foreign country, contact foreign agents and retrieve sensitive information. That information can get you shot as a spy. You are not spies, however. Spies work for you gathering the data. They risk their lives within their home countries for you. These folks are called your assets. The training inside Lancaster is so specialized that once you have completed it, you have no option but to serve your country for the next thirty years. If you do not feel you can do that, I expect to see you in my office within the hour. That is all Gentlemen."

I spent the next five months training in "the spy school" as my Grandpa Schneider called it. I learned to send morse code with a key pad and how to string an antenna in the attic of an abandoned house or barn. We learned how to create a 'dead drop' and how to spot someone following us. We were sent to Montreal and Quebec on classroom missions that involved how to blend in with the local population. My French was not very good on those trips and everyone I talked to there assumed that I was from western Canada or the United States. I would be stopped on the street and asked directions, so I looked like a local, but the minute I opened my mouth, it was over. They would say, never mind, I will ask a local. I learned to use nonverbal communication as much as possible. A nod of the head, a shrug of the shoulders or the occasional, "Ca Va" was all that was needed. Or, this worked really well, I began to cough before uttering any French phrase.

Finally, by the beginning of the fall, I was released to my day time cover assignment as long as I continued to return at night to The Farm barracks and for weekend courses and refreshers. Louise kept her tiny apartment and I often stopped to see her after she completed a day in the classroom. Sometimes I took her out to dinner, other times she cooked something for us. She asked how I liked being a JAG lawyer, I did not have the heart to tell her I had no idea what a JAG lawyer did.

5

Assignment RLSO

WASHINGTON NAVY YARD

I REPORTED IN ON NOVEMBER 1, 1904. I found the office of Commander Sheldon Morton. He was my immediate supervisor and was unaware that my training at Lancaster was not complete. In fact, he had no idea that I still lived there while I completed some, but not all, the training at The Farm. My weekends were spent there taking what Commodore Lowe called his short finishing courses. I would take a day or two of 'on the job training' and other unmentionable exercises in how to eliminate a human being without a trace. I had taken one of these short courses at St. Elizabeth Hospital where I met Dr. Eli Waters, chief medical examiner.

"Lieutenant Caldwell, come in, sit down and take a load off. I have your file right here, let me open it. I have several notations that I made in it last night."

"Thank you, Sir."

"You graduated from William and Mary, pre-law, first in the class. Very impressive, Mr. Caldwell."

"Thank you, Sir."

"Law School from Georgetown, again number one!"

"Thank you, again, Sir." I smiled to relax him.

"Why did you join the Navy, Mr. Caldwell, you could have had your choice of any job on the east coast?"

"I am a Caldwell, Sir. My father is Admiral Caldwell, he works in the White House for a member of the family, my Uncle Teddy."

"You are the nephew of the President! I better make that notation in your file."

"My Grandfather was also an Admiral, the first superintendent of the Naval Institute after it was moved to Annapolis."

"Oh, my. That is missing also." He was busy with his pen adding notes here and there. "Now that you are assigned to me, I have the usual backlog of cases that I need to assign to you." He reached behind him and grabbed a stack of thirty or so manilla folders with a red strip running across most of them. "You need to sort these into those you will be defending and those you will be prosecuting. None of these are earth shaking and I imagine you can plea-bargain most of them. If you have any questions come see me or your senior partner that is shown inside each case folder. Bring these back one at a time when they are cleared."

"Thank you, Sir. Where can I see each of these men?"

"If they are in a holding cell, it is indicated inside each folder. If they have been released to return to duty, pending a hearing or trial, that is indicated, also. Good luck, Lt. Caldwell."

"Thank you, Sir." I rose to leave his office and hefted the stack of files. "Do I have an office or a work desk somewhere, Commander."

"Yes, let me show you where it is in the bullpen." He rose and walked with me into a large holding area with lots of gray metal navy desks, some of them pushed back to back. You are over there in the corner by the window, Lieutenant."

"Oh, good. An office with a window!" I walked over to it and threw the stack of folders into the corner, under the window. I really did not think I would like defending navy misfits who could not keep themselves out of the brig and I reached into the pile and took out the first red stripped folder. I placed it on my desk and began to read. The navy does not have a case here, this will never be brought to a hearing or a trial and I placed it on the right corner of the my desk. The left corner was for those interesting cases that I might like to defend. The losers in both piles were placed on the bottom of each stack. In a few minutes,

I had two stacks with the winners on the very top. I reached for the first red strip and I began to read it in detail. The crime was assault and battery with intent to kill, striking a superior officer and drunk on duty. Chief Malcomb Denny was being held in his cell pending a hearing to determine how he might plead. I saw that I had no partner assigned to this case so I tucked the file under my arm, found my briefcase and asked the lawyer next to me, "How do I find the holding cells?"

The holding cells were really the basement area of the RLSO building at the Washington Navy Yards, how convenient for the JAG defense and prosecution, I thought. I walked down the stairs to the holding area and asked to see Chief Denny. He was brought into a small interview room, handcuffed and chained through the wrists and ankles.

"Remove the chains and cuffs will you?" I looked at the SP who dragged him into the room.

"You do not want to do that Lieutenant, this is a real mean son of a bitch."

"What do you think, Chief Denny? Do you want to get out of those cuffs?"

"Suit yourself. I never laid a hand on that Ensign that they claimed I decked."

"Well, just so we understand each other, Chief, if you touch me I will put you in sick bay." I glared at him.

"Sure you will."

As soon as this was out of his mouth, I slapped him across the face as hard as I could. The SP had a shocked look on his face. I looked over at him and said, "To bad this man slipped and fell down the stairs on his way to this interview." I slammed by foot into the side of the chief's knee and heard a soft pop, a dislocation for sure. Dislocations are extremely painful but not permanent.

"I am a busy man, Chief. Make up your mind. Do you want to be released from your cuffs or not?"

"Yes, Sir." He said this through gritted teeth.

"Release him, and leave us alone." The SP was not sure what he should do. I asked him again and he released Denny and left the room.

"Chief Denny, I am here to get your statement on how you want to plead your case. I have read your file and I think you struck the Ensign just like it states here. I also think the Ensign was probably a prick and deserved every thing that you gave him. What do you say to my dropping the assault and battery charge and you plead guilty to striking a superior officer while you were drunk. You will serve some days in the brig, you may even get credit for time served. You have been here nearly a month. The Navy may give you a dishonorable discharge, but what do you care, you will be away from that Ensign for the rest of your life."

"Where do I sign?"

I fished the proper forms out of my briefcase and went through them with the Chief. He waved his rights to legal counsel. He pled guilty to striking a superior officer and to be intoxicated while on duty. He signed every thing in triplicate. I shook his hand and said, "I doubt this goes to a hearing, Chief, if it does I will see you again at that time. Please behave yourself in here, do not strike another officer or we will have to go through this all over again. Remember, some superior officers will take your lights out without batting an eye. You are very lucky you did not strike me or you would be in the morgue." I looked him straight in the eye and said, "Do you have any questions, Chief?"

"No, Sir. Thank you, Sir. I expected to be found guilty of the whole list of charges and spending time in a naval prison."

"You are welcome, Chief."

I packed up my things and headed back up three flights of stairs to my desk in the corner of the bullpen. I dropped off the paper work to Commander Morton.

"What is this, Lieutenant?"

"It is a plea agreement for Chief Malcomb Denny. He pleads guilty to striking a superior office and drunk while on duty, the case is cleared waiting processing on your end."

"That is marvelous work, Lieutenant. I met with him and I got nowhere, he even tried to strike me even though he was handcuffed and chained."

"I had the SP remove the handcuffs, Sir."

"You what?"

"He had slipped and fallen when the SP was dragging him from his cell and he was in no mood to strike me. Ask the SP how docile he is now, Commander."

During the next month, I cleared all of the red strip cases from my little corner of the world. I started on the plain defense folders. These were all awaiting hearings or trials and each had a partner assigned to them. I started with a manslaughter case and found the desk of my partner, a Lieutenant Commander Wentworth.

"Commander Wentworth, I am your second chair on the Dempsey case, do you have a minute?"

"Yes, Lieutenant, what is it?"

"I was wondering why we have not tried for a plea-bargain, Sir."

"Dempsey claims it was self defense not manslaughter, he will not accept a plea-bargain, he wants to go to trial."

"Can I talk to him?"

"Not without me and a member of the prosecution team present. Your reputation for strong arming defendants is now well known. I will not allow you to bully him into taking a lesser plea, he wants his day in court."

"Will he win?"

"Not a chance. He is guilty of killing his fellow shipmate with his bare hands."

"I want to talk to him with others present, or I want you to request another second chair, Commander. You can use the fact that I strong arm defendants after you see me break this guy's bones unless he accepts a plea." I was smiling.

"Okay, meet me and Commander Morton in the holding cells."

"Commander Morton is the prosecution?"

"Yes, he picks only the sure things as his case load. Only you have a higher percentage of cleared cases than he does."

Within the hour, the four of us were sitting in an interview room. I was sitting directly beside Seaman Dempsey, Commanders Morton and Wentworth were sitting across from both of us. Dempsey was not what I expected. He was smallish, almost like a young boy. I asked him, "How old are you, Mr. Dempsey?"

"I am thirty-one years old."

"Have you ever been trained as a prize fighter?"

"Prize fighter?"

"Yes, have you ever boxed in a ring for payment or as an amateur?"

"No, why?"

"Because your file states that you killed your shipmate with your bare hands. How did you do that? Did you choke him to death?"

"No, Sir. I have been telling these two officers here that we were involved in a pushing match, the deck was wet and his feet went out from under him and he fell back and hit his head. I never struck him, Sir."

"Seaman Dempsey, I believe you and the navy medical examiner agrees with you. Would you like to read what I found in the examiner's office? It was not in your file, I had to go and get a copy." Commander Morton was not happy.

"When did you get that report, Lieutenant? And why have you not given a copy to the prosecution?"

"I got it today, Sir. I did not know who the prosecution was in this case." I handed a copy to him. "I suggest that we drop the charges against Seaman Dempsey and clear this case."

"I will take it under advisement, I need to study the report first before we even consider dropping the charges. I have to get back to my office, I will need to see you sometime today, Lieutenant Caldwell." He rose from his chair and left the interview room.

"What does this mean?" asked Seaman Dempsey.

"It means that the prosecution is embarrassed, Mr. Dempsey. You will be released and returned to duty shortly." Commander Wentworth said with a smile on his face. "It also means that Lieutenant Caldwell will have to undergo a chewing out by his commanding officer."

"Thank you, Lieutenant. I am very glad you believed me and checked with the medical examiner's office."

"You are very welcome, Mr. Dempsey, I have no intention of being a whipping boy for Commander Morton. I will forget to go see him this afternoon, if he wants to see me, he can come to my little corner of the world."

A FEW HOURS LATER, he did just that. "Caldwell, give me the remainder of the files I gave you. A new man is being assigned to me and I want to give these really simple cases to him. I have something much more difficult for you." He held his hand out and I placed the stack of files from the left corner of my desk.

"That leaves me without any cases, Sir."

"Yes, I know. I am assigning you to one of the higher profile cases that needs immediate investigation. Have you completed your courses in forensic science at Lancaster?"

"Yes, Sir."

"Good, let me introduce you to your new, permanent partner."

My partner was named Carl Wallace. He was a few years older than me. He had attended law school somewhere in New York and finished near the bottom of his class. He took the bar exam a few times, failed each time and then finally joined the navy so he could practice law. It was a natural fit. The navy never expected more out of an officer than the officer could give and I had a feeling that Carl would always be an Ensign and that he would see the inside of every regional legal services office that the navy had here in the United States. He would always be assigned with another lawyer who would serve as first chair in any legal proceedings. Second chairs were important in any case work and Carl loved running down the "details" of case work. Give him something to do and point him in the right direction and you could concentrate on something else and be confident that the details would windup on your desk in a few days. Our cases were usually wrongful deaths within the RLSO, Washington Naval Yard. All that changed in late November of 1904 when we were handed the Hanson case.

6

Murder in Strange Places

RLSO, Washington, D.C.

THE WINTER OF 1904-05, PRODUCED a series of ritualistic style murders in and around Washington, D.C. All of these victims were active or recently retired US military members. My partner, Ensign Carl Wallace, and I were called to the home of Mark Hanson, the United States Senator from Ohio and retired US Navy Admiral. He was found in his study with the back of his head missing. The district police had found no blood in the study and concluded that the senator was murdered away from his home and the body was then placed in the study by persons unknown. The remains had been taken to St. Elizabeth Hospital for autopsy. We talked to the widow.

"Mrs. Hanson, we are all shocked by what happened to your husband. Do you feel like talking about who found your husband in his study."

"It was the housekeeper, early this morning. She thought he was asleep until she saw his head. Why would anyone take his brain?"

"I have no idea, Mrs. Hanson. I will find the guilty party and they will be brought to justice, I promise you that."

"Thank you, Lieutenant. I appreciate that more than you know. This is the third murder this year of a retired member of the military. Do you think there is a connection?"

"Very likely, Mrs. Hanson. Ensign Wallace will pull those two files and compare them for details. I am not familiar with either of them. Can you tell me where you were last night?"

"Yes, I went with friends to see a play, *The Scarlet Pimpernel.* It was late and Mark had not returned from his senate office and I went to bed. I heard the screams of the housekeeper and that woke me. I am still numb from seeing the body like that. I will have nightmares for years."

"We are sorry, Mrs. Hanson, we will let you get some rest. Where can I find the housekeeper?"

"She left with the district police to make a statement." I nodded to Carl to add that to his list of interviews.

"Do you have someone to stay with you, Mrs. Hanson?"

"Yes, my children are on their way here. Check back with me in a few days, will you Lieutenant, I may be able to remember some more details after I get over the shock of losing him."

"Of course, Mrs. Hanson, we will show ourselves out."

I CAUGHT A CAB TO ST. ELIZABETH and found the medical examiner, while Carl found the housekeeper and located the other two files. He would try to find the case investigators for the murders of George Phillips and Colonel Prentiss Ingraham. We were told by Mrs. Hanson that Phillips was a friend of the senator and only 38 years old. She had no idea who Colonel Ingraham was, except that she read about the horrible murder in the newspapers.

"Hey, Doc, what can you tell me about the death of Senator Hanson?"

"Hello, Louis, jumping right into it, as always, I see." He had the senator laid out on the autopsy table and he was making notes on his clip board. "You might like to see what I found lodged in the back of the senators skull." He handed me a bloody tip of what looked like an American Indian arrowhead.

"Is this an arrowhead? Was the senator shot with an arrow?"

"It is too large for an arrowhead, probably the tip of a spear of some sort."

"Can you clean this up and bag it for me? I need to take this over to the Smithsonian and see if anyone can tell me anything about it.

Can you tell me if the senator was alive or dead when his brain was removed?"

"I would say he was deceased. Notice the color of the white of the one eye that remained in the skull. See the tiny ruptured blood vessels everywhere. That information and the ligature marks everywhere on the arms and legs, tells me that the senator was probably wrapped from head to foot in a heavy rope and then a bag was placed over his head and he suffocated. A slow way to die, Louis."

"Then why mutilate the skull?"

"I have never seen this before, Louis, he was truly 'mutilated' as you say. Notice that the back of the skull looks like it was removed with a hammer and chisel."

"How was the brain stem removed, Doc?"

"Again, not by a surgeon or a medical person. It was pried out, almost torn from the body as though his attacker was angry or insane."

"I vote for the insane option, Doc. Send your report over to me at RLSO, I will compare it to the other two."

"What other two?"

"Mrs. Hanson believes that her husband was killed by the same persons that murdered Colonel Ingraham and George Phillips the Canadian-born US military hero of the Spanish American War in Cuba."

"I read about both of those in the newspapers, Louis. Where were the autopsies done? I would like to compare them with what I found here today."

"I will have Carl bring them over to you, Doc. I sent him to locate and get copies for us."

"How is Carl doing? He appears to be young and inexperienced, is he learning from you, Louis?"

"Age has got nothing to do with it, Doc. Either you have a feel for this type of investigation or you do not. I can not give Carl instincts, that is what keeps you alive when you arrest scum like whoever did this to the senator. I vowed that I would find the people who did this to the senator and that will surely find me knee deep among the scum of Washington, D.C."

I left Doc Waters standing over the body with a magnifying glass and tweezers still removing what he called trace evidence. I had the stone fragment that looked like an arrowhead and I stepped onto a streetcar and headed for the Smithsonian. I found my favorite person in the whole world in her lab, examining a pile of what looked like old bones.

"Hey, Madeleine, still love me?" Madeleine Barrias was a French beauty who came to this country from her native Paris. She was a doctor, a PhD not an MD. She was an expert in anthropology, antiquities and matters of the heart. I had first met her when I studied one summer at the Ecole des Hautes Etudes. She was my first venture into matters of the heart and my twin sister thought I had lost my mind. The affair was brief and white hot. I still had vivid dreams about her stepping out of a shower, dripping wet.

"Louis, what brings you to the bone yard?" I hugged her and whispered in her ear.

"Louis, you are terrible!" She was smiling.

"I have a mystery for you to solve."

"Good, I love mysteries, what is it?"

"A stone fragment recovered from a murder victim. I am hoping that you can tell me what it is." I handed the evidence bag to her.

"Do you need this right away, Louis? Or can I study it and return it to you over dinner tomorrow night?"

"You have a date, Madeleine. I will pick you up at six. Shall I get reservations at that poor excuse for a French café on Pennsylvania near the White House?"

"Hell, no. I want some real food. Let's go to the Hay-Adams!"

"This bit of information is going to cost me, Madeleine. I am just a poor Navy Lieutenant."

"Louis Caldwell, your family has more money than France! Do not poor mouth me, you can afford the Hay-Adams." I kissed her on the cheek and thanked her in advance for whatever she could manage to find out about the evidence that I left with her.

It was afternoon before I got back to the RLSO at the Navy Yard. Carl Wallace was sitting at his desk reading one of the autopsy reports.

"Louis, you are not going to believe this, both of the victims had their brains removed!"

"And, this did not raise a red flag and connect these two murders for either of the investigating agents? That is really sloppy investigation work, Carl."

"The autopsies were done in two separate districts, one in Maryland and one in Virginia. The information was probably never shared."

"Any stone fragments found in either case?" I asked.

"Yes, here are photographs of each piece." Carl slid them over the desk for me to examine.

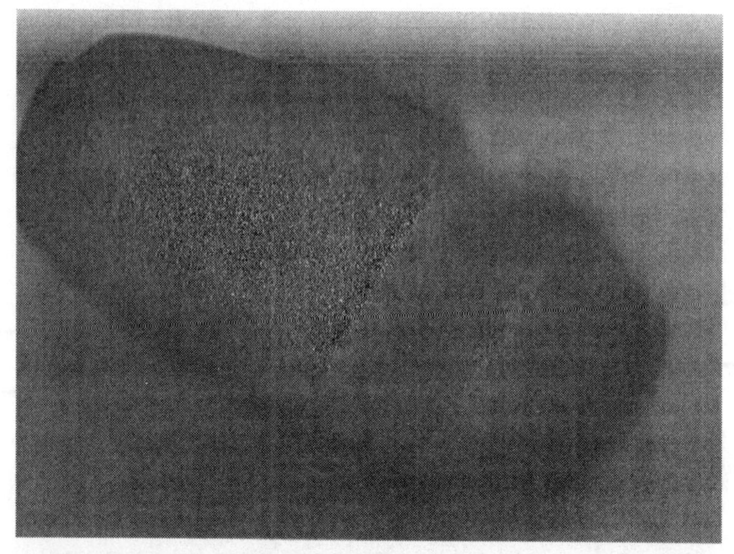

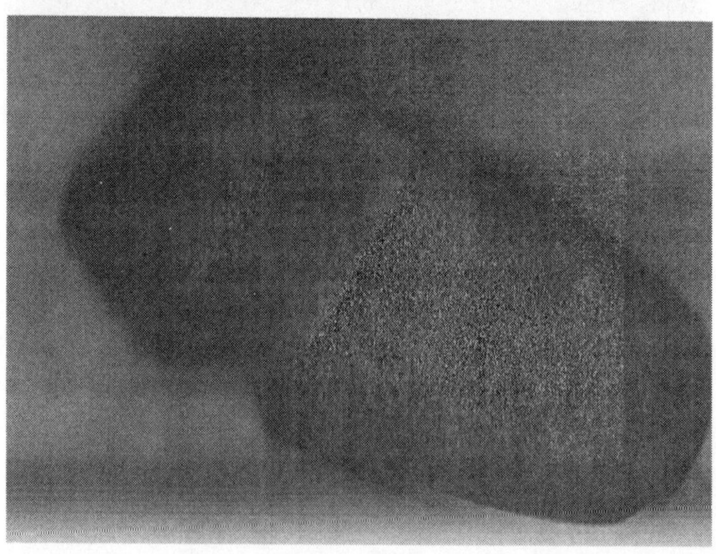

The first photo looked like a ancient stone hammer head. It was about five or six inches long and about three inches wide. I could not tell how thick it was. It was tear drop shaped with a groove about an inch from the right hand edge. I looked at the second photo. It was similar to the arrowhead fragment that Doc Waters found only it was larger. It looked like a stone chisel segment.

"Carl, we need to get both of these pieces and have my expert at the Smithsonian compare them with the fragment I gave her this morning. Have you located the investigating teams? We need to sit down with them and compare notes."

"Neither one was JAG, Louis. I will contact the two medical examiners and find out who investigated each case."

"You do that this afternoon, Carl." He picked up his phone and started his leg work. Carl was good at running down details. "I am going back to Doc Waters with these two reports, Carl. Are you through with them?" He nodded his head yes and asked a question into his phone.

Doc Waters was still writing notes as I walked in with the two reports for him to read. "Hey, Doc. Anything new?"

"Nothing more than I told you before. What did you find out?"

"I have a couple of photos that I think will confirm what you told me." I opened the folders and showed him both.

"The mutilation was definitely done by a hammer and chisel, Louis. I am ruling death by suffocation, you will get my report after I read the two that you just brought over, thank you, Louis."

My day was winding to an end. I decided not to go back to the RLSO and I caught a streetcar over to my father's office in the White House. The *Puzzle Palace*, as I liked to call the working parts of the people's house, was the west wing. My father was still the right hand and chief puzzle solver for his brother-in-law, Theodore Roosevelt. I could come unannounced to see either of them if they were free, sometimes I waited an hour or more to get inside to talk to them, but I never abused the privilege. It was usually to get a piece of information that I did not have access to in my little corner of the world. Besides it was closer to come here than run all the way out to The Farm. Commodore Lowe reported directly to my father.

"Hey, Dad. How was your day? Japan and Russia still trying to kill each other?"

"We are monitoring the situation, Russia will lose its entire army if they do not pull away from Port Arthur. What have you been doing?"

"I'm in charge of Senator Hanson's murder. Do you know that it is almost identical to two others? George Phillips and Colonel Ingraham were murdered last year in Maryland and Virginia. Both were heros in the last war, so was Senator Hanson. My question for you and Rodney is, are there any others that I should be looking at?"

"Recent homicides of Spanish American War veterans, that is an odd one. Who would want to kill veterans of a war that only lasted a few months?" He was talking to himself mostly, that was how his mind worked.

"If I knew that one, I would have my killer and I could arrest him." I was smiling.

"What?" I had interrupted his train of thought. "Let me call Rodney out at The Farm." He turned to his side desk and placed the call and asked the operator to connect him. We waited.

"Rodney, how are you? .... Good, Louis has an interesting murder case going ..... Yes, it is Senator Hanson ...... because he was a Navy Admiral before he was a Senator, I guess ...... Here is the thing, Rodney, did you know Colonel Ingraham and George Phillips were killed the same way? ....You did? ...... Who else? ....Jeremiah Farnham, Navy Captain and John Hayes. I knew Farnham he was a merchant marine captain who transported sailors and marines from Port Royal to Cuba. He would not have been investigated by JAG or NCI, the civilians would have handled that. Who was John Hayes? .... You have got to be kidding..... how old was he? ...... Sixty-seven that is too old to have been an active player in the Spanish American War......He was an American Diplomat assigned to Cuba .... That explains the tie in .... Louis has three and you have two ..... that is five in only a few months ..... all this winter..... I will have Louis get on an express streetcar and see you before you leave..... Thanks Rodney, that is a big help."

"Cuba is the common dominator, Dad."

"Yes, Cuba is the key, Louis. Every one of your victims has spent time in Cuba."

"Why did you ask Rodney if he was kidding?"

"John Hayes was the private secretary to Abraham Lincoln before he joined the diplomatic core and was sent to Cuba. Cuba is the connection - not Abraham Lincoln."

"I agree. All five were scattered among various jurisdictions and no one made the connection that it was a series of murders. But what is the motive? And why the mutilations after the victim is dead, usually revenge is completed by the killing of the victim, not the stealing of organs."

"Senator Hanson had one of his organs removed?"

"Yes, Dad. We kept that out of the news releases, his brain was removed."

"Not his heart?"

"No, what are you getting at?"

"Cuba is only one of the many islands that the Caribe Indians inhabited many years ago. They were cannibals and they ate the hearts of their enemies slain in battle. They believed that they inherited the soul of their victims in this manner."

"So, if there truly is a Cuban connection it might be cannibalistic in nature. Is that what you are saying, Dad."

"No, let's take it one step further. The Itza tribe were a warlike people from South America which came as far as north as Yucatan. They believed that in order to curry favor with the Sun God, a human sacrifice was to be offered up upon the temple altar. The beating heart of a human was removed and held up for the Sun God to accept."

"So, how do the Caribe Indians fit into this equation?"

"They were the only ones that the Itza could not defeat. The Caribes fed off the Itza until the Itza retreated back into Central America, they could not stand against the Caribes."

"Well, you certainly have given me some food for thought, Dad. I need to get going if I am going to see Rodney before he leaves for the day. Thank you, I now know that at least five Americans were victims."

AN HOUR LATER, I was at The Farm.

"Louis, here are the two files that you will need. Both Hayes and Farnham are still in cold storage if you need to see the bodies. The cases are still unsolved, NCI inherited the mess when the detectives found evidence of foreign involvement in the deaths."

"What foreign nation?"

"Mexico."

"No, it has to be Cuba."

"Why, because all your victims have been to Cuba? All of the victims have probably been to other common areas of the Caribbean, including the Yucatan. Mexico and Cuba have always been like two peas in a pod. Your answers are in the Yucatan, Louis. Find the missing organs and you find your killers."

"Assuming the organs were not eaten!"

After an hour, I took the two files and left my room at The Farm to go to Louise's apartment for supper. Most twins grow apart later in life. We were born in the winter and this winter we celebrated our twenty-fourth year together, twenty-five if you consider when life begins. She often finished sentences that I started. When we graduated from William and Mary, I thought, well, this is the separation. Louise is going to be a school teacher and I am going to law school. I was accepted into Georgetown and Louise took a teaching job in Alexandra, Virginia. We decided to find an apartment and share the expenses. After law school, I went off to San Diego and Monterey for a year and then I moved back to The Farm.

"Louise, are you home?" I dropped my briefcase on the hallway floor with a thud. JAG lawyers were not allowed to carry firearms on their person like the NCI agents, so I had a variety of personal protection items inside the briefcase that included a snub nose revolver which was not a technical violation since I did not carry it in a holster on my body.

"In the kitchen, Louis. What are you hungry for tonight?"

"It does not matter, you know Carl will show up before we eat so he can get a free meal and moon over you."

"Carl is a boy, Louis, I am looking for a man in my life that I can share with you."

"Louise! What would Mother say if she knew we were sharing a man!" She punched me in the chest, then gave me a big hug.

"I missed not talking to you today, Louis. What did you do?"

"Got a new case, Senator Hanson was murdered last night or yesterday sometime. Doc Waters can not give me an exact time of death. My briefcase is full of unrelated items that are pieces of the puzzle that Carl and I will try to fit together tonight. He has some files and we will sit down with you and you can help. You are like an extension ......"

"of your ability to solve problems." She was smiling.

"You just did it again." I smiled back at her and gave her a hug as the front door bell rang. "That will be Carl. You know he is older than us. He is twenty-seven."

"He acts younger, Louis. Find me another you and I will marry him."

I walked to the front door and let Carl in. "Put your briefcase down beside mine, Carl. We need to help Louise with the dinner fixings and bring her up to speed on the case. I already told her about the Senator."

"Good, I am starving!"

"There are now a total of five murders, Carl. I just picked up two more cases from The Farm; a John Hayes and Jeremiah Farnham."

"Both military?

"Neither one. Louise, do you remember Dad talking about a Captain Farnham from Port Royal?"

"Hello, Carl. No, Louis, who was he?"

"He was one of the transport ship's captains that took troops from South Carolina to Cuba during the war."

"We were in college, Louis, I did not pay attention to the war."

"Neither did I. I wish I had because we have five puzzle pieces to fit together that share a common denominator, they all spent time in Cuba during the war."

"What else do they share in common?" asked my sister.

"We have some of the bodies, not all of them have been released for burial because they are part of an ongoing investigation."

"Have you examined each to find common clues?"

"No, we need to do that tomorrow, Carl, can you contact The Farm and have their bodies delivered to St. Elizabeth, I trust Doc Waters to examine all of them. Did you find the other two examiners, Carl?"

"Yes, I will contact them and have the bodies sent to Doc Waters. I think the investigators will like to clear these homicides from their unsolved list."

"Your list gets longer because theirs is cleared." My sister was thinking out loud.

"I was just thinking the same thing, five cases will be solved or listed as cold cases unless we get a break."

"What else do the victims have in common?" She asked.

I was hesitant to mention the mutilation after the murder, so I said, "I think Doc Waters will determine that each victim was bound with a rope and suffocated with a bag of some sort."

"And each victim was mutilated after they died." Carl happily added.

"In the exact same manner?" She was on to something, we waited. "I would think that Doc Waters could confirm if these were random victims or they were selected to be punished for their time spent in Cuba. If the mutilations are exact in every detail - then these were ritual killings, probably in some sort of ceremony. The victim is really a sacrifice and it is not important that he be alive for the ceremony. A corpse is a very cooperative participant in the ceremony."

"The ceremony could have taken hours, not just a random bash in the head and snatch the brain and run, then." Carl was proud of himself but Louise was shocked.

"The brain was removed?"

"Yes, is that important?"

"Louis, you need to contact your French tart, she works at the Smithsonian now and can probably tell you the ceremony involved."

"She is not a French tart, she is a sweet tart from my childhood and I have a meeting with her tomorrow night. That reminds me, Carl, did you get the stone fragments from the two earlier murders?"

"Yes, I will put them in your briefcase so you can show them to Dr. Barrias tomorrow."

"Good, take out the two reports from The Farm and take them to Doc Waters and tell him that he should have all of the bodies soon. We would like him to compare all the skulls to see if the same procedures were used in all of the cases."

"Then what?"

"We look for the site or sites of the ceremony!" My sister said.

"No." Carl and I said together.

"I have to teach school tomorrow, gentlemen. I was using 'we' figuratively not literally." And she got up from where we were sitting and put the food on the table for dinner.

7

An Evening with Barrias

Hay-Adams Hotel

An evening in Paris with student Madeleine Barrias was not like what happened in the Hay-Adams the next night. A gentleman never kisses and tells so the important elements in my investigation were provided by the good Dr. Barrias from the Smithsonian. I picked her up from her apartment and met her roommate. We took a cab to the hotel and I handed her the new stone fragments that had come into my possession. She took one look at the chisel and said, "It is a match, Louis."

"What's a match?"

"The broken point that you gave me two days ago fits into the rest of the chisel. See." She placed the tip on the end of the chisel. A match.

"That means we have a mutilation weapon used in two different murders. What can you tell me about the other larger stone?"

"It is a stone hammer head."

"Where is the handle?"

"I have no idea, Louis. I can tell you that the original stone fragment you gave me is very old. I compared it with samples that we have in the Smithsonian. It is Mayan."

"Mayan, as in, Mexico."

"No, Mayan as in the religious belief, Maya."

"You lost me, I thought Mayans live today in the Yucatan of Mexico."

"Their descendants live there and all over that part of Mexico, Belize, Guatemala, El Salvador and Honduras."

"Tell me about the Maya belief."

"Maya is an artifice, illusion or unreality. In the Puranic mythology of the Hindus, it is the personified will or energy of the supreme being, who thereby created the universe."

"Hindu, are you telling me Mayans in Mexico came from India?"

"Hindu is a belief from all over Asia, Louis, not just India."

"Oh, go on, sorry I interrupted you."

"In this new world doctrine, the world is unreal or illusory, Maya assumes the character of illusion personified. Maya is the cause of all the phenomena of the world. It makes the unreal universe seem as if it really existed or was distinct from the one Supreme Spirit. In this sense, Maya also occurs in the later Vedanta philosophy and in some of the sectarian philosophies of India."

"Thanks for clearing that up for me, Doc." She ignored me.

"According to the modern Hindu view, Maya represents the limitations of time, space, and causation by which the absolute becomes the universe. It is then, almost, a synonym for the phenomenal world."

"Okay, thanks for filling me in on the Maya. How old is the stone fragment that you examined?"

"When you add the tip to the chisel, I would judge that this chisel was made some time in the early 1500's by a Mayan craftsman living on the island of Cozumel or within walking distance of a canoe trip to the coast of Quintano Roo."

"How in the hell do you know that?"

"Because the Smithsonian has stone samples from that area of the Yucatan and I studied them under a microscope. They are a match."

"I feel like I just dropped off the turnip truck. I am so ignorant about this stuff."

"You are going to have to be a fast study, Louis. I can give you, what you lawyers call a brief, of the civilized native race of the peninsula of Yucatan, Mexico."

"Please, I am listening."

"In 1511 the first landing was effected by the Spaniards on the coast of Yucatan, at the sacred island of Cozumel. Natives from the mainland arrived and killed every Spaniard on Cozumel. It took fifteen years, until 1526, for the rest of Mexico to fall to the Spanish. The Yucatan was held by the natives and the jungles were too dense to penetrate by men on horse back. It was not until 1539, when the Spanish commander, Montejo, entered Chichen-Itza and established a new city, called Merida. The Yucatan was divided into four tribute districts from west to east; Tabasco, Cameche, Yucatan and Quintana Roo. The missionaries from Spain began to Christianize the natives and, in their zeal, destroyed as heathen, the native temples and records that were not buried deep in the jungle. Mayan resistance was crushed by wholesale massacres and the Maya sovereignty was at an end. The Itza were much more warlike and they hid in the jungles until 1697 and then crossed from the Yucatan into Guatemala."

"Are the Itza extinct now?"

"Neither the Mayans nor the Itza are extinct. When the war with the United States broke out, the Mayans and the Itza saw their chance to rebel and they did by the thousands. They took one city after another, burning and destroying everything and consigning to indiscriminate massacre whole garrisons and Mexican populations. The Itza cut off the heads of the Mexicans and mounted them on poles that they carried before them into battle. The Mexican army was in ruin after the war with the United States and it took several years to mount a military response to the uprising in the Yucatan. The armies of Mexico finally signed a peace agreement with the northern Mayan tribes and they returned to their peaceful villages. The Itza, however, refused to make peace and they retreated into the jungles of the southern coast. They continued to make war on the Mexican army with aid from the English in Belize. Here they obtained their firearms and ammunition to continue the war. The end came on May 1901, when by means of a combined land and naval force made up of Mexicans and Cubans, the Itza were finally driven out of their strong hold at Chan-Santa Cruz and into Guatemala."

"They are still in Guatemala?"

"Yes, about 200,000 speak the Maya language and live throughout the area."

"Madeleine, you have started me on my quest. I need to spend some time in the library and find out as much I can about the present day peoples living in this area."

The next morning was spent in the national library, this what I found.

MAYAN CIVILIZATION

A group of cognate tribes or nations occupying the states of Vera Cruz, Yucatan, Campeche, Tabasco and Chiapas, in Mexico. Guatemala and El Salvador have also had mayan tribes. They exhibited the highest aboriginal development found upon the American continent. The civilization includes six languages, with nearly thirty dialects, the principal being the Huastec of northern Vera Cruz. The Itza and Lacandon is spoken across the Guatemala frontier. The present population is two million people. (Palenque anecdotes)

According to all historical evidence, the Mayan tribes emigrated from the far north at a very early period, probably near the beginning of the Christian

era. As they advanced along the shore of the Gulf of Mexico, they left the Huastec as a detached colony at the north of the Panuco river. The rest proceeded southward into chiapas, Yucatan and Guatemala. The date was 450 AD. (Quiche Chronicles)

Physically the Mayan peoples are dark, short, broad-headed and muscular. In pre-Columbian times they had attained a high grade of civilization. Agriculture was their main dependence, corn being the principle crop, along with beans, peppers and cacao. They mined copper, silver and gold and knew how to smelt it into pieces of standard value for commercial use. Bees were domesticated for their honey and wax. Cotton was spun for clothing and dyed and woven into fabrics which rivaled silk in delicacy. The lands were held in common by each village and were parceled out by the chiefs based upon family needs. The Mayan of the coast region had large seagoing canoes so they could carry on trade with islands as far away as Cuba.

The Mayan peoples were remarkable above all other cultured American nations for their architecture, calendar and hieroglyphic system. They had school systems that taught reading and writing. Books were written on folded sheets of maguey paper and bound together. The translation of these books by Abbe Brasseur de Bourbourg provided much about the Central American archaeology. The calendar system began on July 16th when the sun crossed the zenith of the heavens. It consisted of 365 days, divided into eighteen months of twenty days each. A week contained five days. At the end of the year, a special week of five days was celebrated for the coming of the new year. The years were grouped into Katuns of twenty years each. The completion of each Katun was celebrated by the placing of a commemorative stone in the wall of the principal temple of the city.

I practiced my Spanish by writing the last passage as:

El mapa de la region conocida el Mundo-Maya incluye los estados mexicanos de Campeche, Chiapa, Quintana Roo, Tabasco y Yucatan, asi como los paises centroamericanos de Belize, El Salvador, Guatemala y Honduras; en el se descatcan sus principlales carreteras, atractivos como sitios arqueologies, ciudades coloniales, communidades indigenas, reservas naturales, playas, etcetera y los servicios can que cuentan. El reverso lo ocupa un poster compuesto por una seleccion de fotos de elementos represntativos de las paises que integran esta enorme area cultural.

I packed up my research notes and headed for the US Senate Office Building to meet Carl Wallace and to talk to Senator Hanson's staff members. We needed to find the sites of the murders.

"I am Lieutenant Caldwell and this is Ensign Wallace from the RLSO JAG office here in Washington. We are investigating Senator Hanson's death. Did he come into the office two days ago?"

"No, I have his appointment book right here. He had an appointment at the Mexican embassy here in Washington."

"What time was the appointment?"

"8 am."

"Isn't that a little early for a diplomatic meeting?"

"The Senator got a telephone call the day before and he was upset."

"Did you hear his end of the conversation?"

"Yes, I did."

"Tell me what you remember."

"I answered the incoming call like I always do and screen his calls for him. When I knew it was the Mexican Under-ambassador to Washington, I put it through to him but stayed on the line to take notes in short hand. I have both ends of the conversation, you can have that copy."

"Thank you, miss, that would be very helpful to our investigation. Carl, do you have any questions?"

"Yes, what is your name and telephone number in case we have to contact you again in the future?" I glared at Carl.

As we left the Senator's office and caught a streetcar to the Mexican Embassy, Carl asked, "How did your date with Dr. Barrias go last night?"

"It wasn't a date. She gave me a brief on Maya Culture and informed us that the stone fragments found with three of the five victims came from the island of Cozumel or the coast line adjacent to it.

"Louis, how did you meet Dr. Barrias?"

"She is a doctor, a PhD not an MD. She is an expert in anthropology, antiquities and matters of the heart. I first met her when I studied one summer at the Ecole des Hautes Etudes in Paris. She was my first venture into matters of the heart and Louise thought I had lost my mind. The affair was brief and white hot. I still have vivid dreams about her stepping out of a shower, dripping wet."

"Why were you in Paris?"

"Louise and I had lived on the east coast, traveled to Bermuda and we wanted to spend a summer in Paris attending the Ecole des Hautes Etudes. We had asked our parents to send us there after our second year of study at William and Mary. They did not think it was a good idea, even though it was a sponsored summer course from William and Mary. We talked to our Grandmother Caldwell and she understood, she always did. After a twenty minute conversation with grandma, my father announced that my twin sister and I could go to Paris, on one condition! That condition was that we go in different summers. I went the first summer and Louise went the second.'

"So Louise never met this Dr. Barrias in Paris?"

"Madeline Barrias was not a Dr. In Paris, Carl, pay attention. She was a student, a red hot student, who dated more boys and men than carter has pills."

"Oh!"

8

Mexican Embassy

Washington, D.C.

The streetcar stopped two blocks from embassy row and we walked towards the front gate inserted into a brick wall which enclosed the entire property. We were stopped by two guardsmen in federallie uniforms.

"Buenas tardes, tenemos una cita para ver a los monores Ambassadoes. I am Lieutenant Caldwell."

"The under Ambassador is expecting you, Lieutenant Caldwell."

The gates swung open and we were allowed to enter. Ambassador Mendez, under secretary for foreign affairs, greeted us at the massive front door to the mansion purchased as the Mexican Embassy. Once we passed through the front gates, we were on Mexican soil.

"Buenas tardes, Mr. Ambassador. I am very glad that you could meet with us on such short notice." We extended our hands and he shook both as he said, "Buenas tardes, Senor Caldwell, Senor Wallace. Not at all. I only regret that Senator Hanson could not meet with me. I could have warned him that his life was in danger."

"You tried in your telephone conversation with him, Mr. Ambassador. I have a copy of the conversation if you would like to see it to refresh your memory. It is in my briefcase. I also have a loaded revolver on top of the copy. Can you take both out of the briefcase and find a safe place for them until we leave?"

His eyes widened and he said, "Of course, follow me into my office. I do not blame you for carrying the pistola. Caution can always save lives. If you two have read the conversation, then both of your lives may be in danger."

"Only the Senator's office staff and your office know of the conversation. Oh, I see, the staff have already told everyone they know by now. We will be careful in our investigation. If what you told the Senator is true, many more will die before we arrest the guilty parties."

"We have doubled the guards every where inside and outside the embassy, gentlemen. We are taking this threat to be genuine. General Valerano Van Weylor was not called 'The Butcher of Cuba' for nothing. Since his death, his lieutenants have vowed to destroy everyone who set foot on Cuban soil in 1898, that includes President Roosevelt."

"How did you come upon this information, Ambassador?" Carl had asked his first intelligent question of the conversation.

"Several sources. They were totally unrelated. The first was a report of stolen artifacts from our museum at Tulum. The second was an arrest of a man entering the State of Quintana Roo with a human brain in a glass apothecary jar. The jar contained a fragment of one of the stolen artifacts. When the man was subjected to rather rigorous and strenuous interrogation, he confessed to the murder of a man in Havana, Cuba, before he died. The man he killed was working in the American Embassy."

"John Hayes?"

"No, Simon Antido Juarez. He was a Cuban working as an interpreter." Carl and I looked at each other, the list was now six.

"Did you report this to the authorities in Havana?"

"Of course, I do not know what action they took."

"Why did you warn Senator Hanson that his life might be in danger?"

"The Mexican Embassy in Havana intercepted a list of names sent to the Spanish Embassy."

"Intercepted, how?"

"We have been monitoring radio transmissions from Spanish ships to shore and it was among the normal traffic. We did not become concerned until we found the name, Simon Antido Juarez."

"Do you have a copy of that list?"

"Of course, I was going to give the list to Senator Hanson because his name appeared on that list. He would contact the proper United States investigators. I give it you now so that you may do the same." He handed us the list. It contained nearly thirty names and our five names were among those listed. Two names jumped off the page at me, Theodore Roosevelt and Hans Becker.

"Mr. Ambassador, can someone in your office make copies of this list so that I can drop one off at the White House tonight? Has anyone checked to see if all of these names have addresses in the Washington area."

"Yes, we have. We assume that this is the target list for Washington and that there may be lists for other cities in the United States and elsewhere." He turned from his desk and spoke into a tube like instrument that reminded me of a ship's tube from bridge to the engine room. He asked for his assistant to make carbon copies of the original list presently on file.

"Is this list a copy, Mr. Ambassador?"

"Yes, it is rather good, isn't it. It is made by writing on a piece of paper and placing a carbon sheet between the first and second pages. Whatever you write is then transferred onto the second sheet."

"Can you use this in a typewriter?" Carl asked.

"Of course, but the second copy is somewhat smeared and it looks like a copy. Handwriting is much better."

We thanked the Ambassador for the copies and promised to keep him informed of our investigation progress. We put everything into my briefcase and noticed that it had gotten dark already, winter afternoons were not long in Washington. We stopped on the walkway to the front gate where the guards stood. We removed our revolvers from our briefcases and slid them in our jacket pockets. We stood outside the gate and looked for a cab. We did not want to risk walking to the streetcar stop two blocks away. A brand new Ford, Model T open touring automobile, with diplomatic plates was parked in the middle of the block. Two men got out of the back seat carrying umbrellas.

"Carl, watch these two, it has not rained for days in Washington. Why are they carrying umbrellas? To hide something, maybe." I moved my briefcase to my left hand and reached for the gun in my jacket pocket. Carl had not moved, he stood stock still while I took steps to close the distance between the two men and myself. I was two steps ahead of Carl when the men rushed us with their umbrellas raised at belt level. I stepped forward and brushed the umbrella aside and brought down my revolver on the head of my attacker. I heard a cry from Carl as his attacker pushed the tip of the umbrella into his thigh. I reached out and swung my gun hand again and hit his attacker in the temple. He staggered and I spun him hard, face first into the brick wall. Two were down and two were still in the Model T. I dropped to one knee, leveled the revolver and emptied it into the front windshield of the touring automobile. The automobile did not move. The men were no longer visible in the front seat. I opened my briefcase that was lying on the sidewalk and a reached for a speed loader and placed six more rounds into my revolver. I shouted to the guards at the Mexican Embassy to call the district police. I then called to the men in the automobile to come out with their hands above their heads. There was no movement. I crept up on the automobile with my revolver held in two hands to steady my shaking right hand. I reached the automobile to find two bodies on the floor with rounds in their heads and neck. Only one round had missed. Lucky shots, I thought. I reached out to get a pulse on the first, there was none. I walked around and felt the second man, no pulse. I turned to see the guards rushing to assist Carl. He was sitting up and holding his leg, his face was gray.

"Call an ambulance for my partner." One of the guards rushed back into the embassy. Ambassador Mendez returned with him and said, "The district police and an ambulance are on the way from St. Elizabeth, Lieutenant Caldwell."

"How are you feeling, Carl?" I shouted. He did not reply, his eyes rolled back in his head and he was foaming at the mouth. I felt for a pulse, it was rapid and thready. It seemed hours before the police or the ambulance arrived, it was a few minutes. I collected most of my belongings and Carl's, as well as the umbrellas. I handed them to Ambassador Mendez and said, "Keep these for me until I can come back and get them Mr. Ambassador, I do not want the district police taking these into custody. I think I know how the murders were committed. The answer is inside my briefcase. I am keeping it and the umbrellas with me."

The Ambassador hurried past the front gate just as a police automobile and an ambulance pulled up in front. Two policemen jumped from their open model T and began questioning the only conscious person at the scene, me. I showed them my federal ID and began to help load Carl into the ambulance. I had used my handcuffs and Carl's on the two unconscious umbrella carriers and said, "I am arresting those two in handcuffs for attempted murder of my partner, if he dies, then I will change the charge to murder. Can you two take them into custody?"

"They better go with you and your partner to the hospital, they might not make it either."

"The two in the automobile over there with diplomatic plates are dead, I killed them in self defense. I am charging them with attempted murder as soon as we get an ID. Why don't you start the paper work on them and I will catch up with you once I have these three in St. Elisabeth." They nodded and I jumped into the ambulance headed for the hospital.

All three men remained unconscious during the ride and I had a chance to decompress and think. Carl acted like he was injected with a fast acting drug. He could not talk or function within minutes of the attack. This was how the murder victims were taken from their homes or off the street. They were stabbed by a passerby with the tip of an umbrella. Before the victim could collapse a second man was nearby and the two of them carried the victim to a waiting automobile or van. It took a minimum of two men to overpower and transport the victim, therefore there were four men waiting for Carl and me. How did they know we were in the Mexican Embassy? Did someone inside the embassy telephone them? Were we followed? I had more questions than answers. I unsnapped the top of my briefcase and reached inside for one of the copies of the target list. The light inside the ambulance was poor and I could not read it. I pushed it back inside. Where were the drugged victims taken?

9

St. Elizabeth Hospital

Washington, D.C.

The ambulance arrived and we began to unload the three men. The driver and medic let me do all the talking for admittance.

"This man is a federal agent. His name is Carl L. Wallace, born June 7, 1877. He was stabbed with the tip of an umbrella. I think the tip contained a lethal drug, his reaction to it was almost immediate. His pulse is rapid and thready. You will need to check for the drug and any possible antidote. These other two, with handcuffs, are under arrest for the attempted murder of Carl Wallace. They have no identification on their person. I will need to talk to them, if they survive. They must be under restraint at all times, no exceptions. Do you understand?"

"Can I see some identification?" I showed them my NCI ID and not my JAG card. I did not have time for a sit down with Commander Morton.

"Do you have a telephone that I can use?" I dialed, from memory, the emergency number at the farm. "Hello, this is agent Caldwell on special assignment to JAG, Washington Regional Office. I have a valid threat to kill the President of the United States. Yes, I will hold." A minute later Rodney Lowe came on the line.

"Louis, what happened?"

"Carl Wallace is near death, if not dead already. We were attacked outside the Mexican Embassy by four men. Two are dead, two are here in St. Elizabeth with me waiting for them to regain consciousness."

"What is this about a threat to kill the President?"

"I obtained a list of nearly thirty names from Ambassador Mendez, the names of the six victims that we have identified are on that list."

"I thought our list was five?"

"It was, we added one an hour ago. That is not important right now, the names on the target list contain Theodore Roosevelt and Hans Becker. Both of these should be warned, as well as all the rest who are on the list. The list is for the Washington area only. Other lists probably exist. We need to contact all the police departments of the larger cities that provided troops for the Spanish American War. I would suspect that we have similar murders in New York, Boston, Philadelphia, etc."

"Slow down, Louis. What proof do you have?"

"I have two suspects in custody ready to interrogate, they should be transferred to Lancaster. This will break the case open as far as Washington is concerned, but NCI has responsibility for all the Navy and military personnel who served in the war, Sir."

"I agree, bring in your list and all other information pertinent to the case, Louis. Good bye." I sat looking at the phone, I can not leave Carl, I thought.

"Mr. Caldwell?"

"Yes, doctor."

"Your friend did not recover, he is on his way down to Doctor Waters, do you know where that is?"

"Yes, I do. Have the prisoners regained consciousness?"

"No, they are stable and should be fine. Apparently they were not exposed to the drug. They will recover fully."

"Doctor, this is now a murder case and a matter of national security. Representatives from Lancaster will be here shortly. Do not release the prisoners to anyone else under orders from Commodore Lowe of the NCI. Do you understand?"

"Yes, Mr. Caldwell. Will you be checking back with me to see if you can talk to these men before they are transported?"

"They will probably be transported before I get back to Lancaster. Tell your staff to be very careful around these two, keep them separated do not let them know the other is alive. Thank you, doctor."

I left the hospital with a heavy heart, I liked Carl. No one should have to die at age twenty-seven. The NCI automobile, that Rodney sent for me waiting for me at the curb.

"Driver, I need to go to the Mexican Embassy. Do you know where that is?"

"Yes, Sir. You look beat, Sir. Put your head back and catch some shut eye, I will wake you when we get there." I did. I felt the automobile come to a stop in front of the Mexican Embassy and I told the driver, "Wait for me, I will only be a minute. The next stop is Lancaster."

I was back in a couple of minutes with the guns and other items that I had left three hours before. Was it only three hours ago. I knew I would be up all night.

10

The Farm

Lancaster, Virginia

My driver informed me that he was assigned to me for the foreseeable future. I thanked him and asked him his name. He said that it was Tim Jacobson and that he was a sniper in Cuba before he was recruited to work on The Farm.

"That is good enough for me, Tim Jacobson, I hope you do not have to use your skills to protect me. I hope the last attempt on my life has just happened tonight and that I will live to be an old man." He laughed and left me standing in the hallway outside the "clinic" which formed part of the basement of the Fairfield family estate. I turned to see Rodney Lowe coming down the hall.

"Just in time, Louis. Your attackers are both awake and are extremely frightened."

"What have you done to them?"

"We stuck them both in the leg with one of the umbrellas you brought in."

"What? They will be dead in a matter of minutes!"

"Relax, Louis, Dr. Waters is here from St. Elizabeth, he has replaced the injection needle from both umbrellas with a new ones that contain a sleeping aid, it is harmless, but we have not told them. I think you walking in right now and asking them how it feels to die might help break them down."

We both entered the first of two rooms and walked over to the bed. I recognized the man as my attacker. I asked him, "Do you speak English?" There was no reaction. I tried the three languages that I knew with similar results. No reaction, this guy was good. I switched back to English and said to Rodney. "How long does it take for him to die? I want to watch him die for what he almost did to my partner." His eyes flew open and he tried to speak but his words were slurred from the sleeping potion. I turned back towards him and said, "We have an antidote and my partner will be fine – you are a piece of scum and you will die for what you tried to do to us."

"Please, Sir. I was only doing my duty to my commanding officer. Give me the antidote and I will tell you his name and location."

"Give me his name and location and then I might think about giving you the antidote. We will leave you for a few minutes to let you think about your answer."

"There is not time, the curari works too quickly. His name is Captain Manual Lopez Van Weylor and he is in the Spanish Embassy in Washington. Please, give me the antidote."

I turned to Rodney Lowe and said, " Have the doctor give him a partial dosage until I can check on the truth of this man's statement." I turned back to the man in the bed and said, "What is your name and diplomatic rank?"

"I am with the Cuban Embassy, my rank is of no importance, my name is Carlos Hernandez, please, give me the antidote." I nodded and Dr. Waters came into the room and gave him an injection of water. Rodney and I walked from the room to repeat our performance for the other attacker. He confirmed that the umbrellas contained vials of curari, a poisonous, blackish, resin-like substance obtained from certain tropical plants. It had been used for centuries by the jungle tribes of Central and South America. Near morning, Dr. Waters confirmed that the drug was actually curarine with the chemical compound C19H25N2O. The attackers had been told that it was curari from the Yucatan.

WITHIN TWO DAYS, we had the following information: the two men in custody were in fact with the Spanish Embassy, their names were Hernandez and Mendoza. They confessed to two murders inside the

Washington area, thinking that diplomatic immunity would protect them from prosecution. When I informed them that the Spanish Embassy did not acknowledge either of them, they became even more helpful. In exchange for early release they would give us the names of all other agents working within the Spanish Embassy and those embassies working in concert with them. They would provide detailed information on how to recover the various organs taken from the victims and sent to Mexico. This would give the relatives a chance to bury their loved ones and have closure. I finally collapsed into a bed in the clinic and slept for fourteen hours.

When I awoke, I was told that Marilyn Hanson wanted so see me.

"Who is, Marilyn Hanson?" I asked Tim.

"She is the widow of Senator Hanson. She probably has heard that we have made progress in the case."

"We do, but we are a long way from stopping the jigsaw murders and returning the stolen organs to the loved ones."

"Jigsaw murders, Sir?"

"Yes, once you think you have a handle on what happened, you get another piece to the puzzle. We still have no idea how many murders have been committed world wide. We don't even know how many have been committed in this country, let alone if the good General Van Weylor is alive or dead. The Mexican Ambassador said he was dead, but we have no confirmation of this."

"Who is, or was, this General Van Weylor, Sir."

"Our information indicates that his full name is Nicolas Valerano Van Weylor, the Marquis of Teneriffe. He was born in Palma, the island of Majorca, in 1839. He entered the army, was military attache of the Spanish Legation in the United States during the Civil War and accompanied General Sheridan on some of his campaigns. In the ten years' war in Cuba (1868-78) he held a command under Balmaceda and in 1873 he served in Spain against the Carlists, with some distinction. In 1879, he was made Governor-General of the Canaries and in 1889 Captain-General of the Philippines, where he amassed an illegal fortune. He was removed from the Philippines, with cause and sent to Catalonia in disgrace. In 1896, he was sent back to Cuba, in response to the demands of the Spanish advocates of severe methods.

He replaced Martinez Campos, who wanted to grant partial Cuban Independence. Van Weylor's ruthless policies earned him 'the butcher of Cuba moniker.'"

"Where is he now, Sir?"

"In 1897, he was recalled before the surrender in December so he could 'save face'. In 1900, he was made Captain-General of Madrid. He was minister of war in the Sagasta Cabinet, which held office from March, 1901 to December, 1902. He is, according to our records, in the present cabinet of Montero Rios."

"Would that be hard to prove, Sir?"

"No, we have agents in Madrid. It would be a simple matter to check."

"Have we done this, Sir?"

"I thought Commodore Lowe would do that, Tim. I bet he assumes that I would request it, thank you, Tim. I am on my way to the bathroom, then to see Commodore Lowe, then to see Marilyn Hanson. Get the automobile ready."

"Yes, Sir."

I FINISHED MY MORNING ROUTINES and headed for the office of the director of the NCI training center known as The Farm. Commodore Rodney Lowe was already past his morning routine, my days and nights were mixed up with my fourteen hour vacation trying to catch up on my sleep.

"Good morning, Sir. I am sorry that I have not been available for the last several hours."

"It is afternoon, Louis. You look much better. I left orders to let you sleep. Sit down and I will let you know where we are with the information that we have gained from the two suspects. First of all, it is, without a doubt, that the Mexican, Cuban and Spanish Embassies are working together to spread fear among the American population. The news of the *Jigsaw Murders* have hit the newspapers. We knew that we could not keep this sort of thing a secret for long. I see by the look on your face that you do not believe that it is possible for these three to be in cooperation. The Spanish were thrown out of both Mexico and Cuba. Think for a minute how the Cubans felt about how it was done. They tried three different times, in their history, to defeat the Spanish Army of Occupation and failed. Then the United States invades Cuba and in a matter of months the Spanish are defeated. At the same time the Spanish are thrown out of the Philippines, this had to make the Cubans angry because they now have traded one set of masters for another."

"What about Mexico, Sir? We did not come to their aid in 1824 when they defeated the Spanish."

"That is true. We waited until Texas picked a fight with them and then aided Texas with our navy and marines. Then we really made them feel good when we defeated them in the Mexican American War and seized the northern half of their country to add the southwestern states to the Union. Mexico is aiding the Spanish, 'because the enemy of my enemy is my ally.'"

"That makes no sense, Sir."

"Not to you, but it would to your grandfather, he fought in the Mexican War and it would to your father and me because we fought in the last war. This is your war, Louis. It will be one of night terrors that are inflicted on American citizens when they see their loved ones with missing organs. That is why the bodies are returned to the homes or offices or public places. Does that make sense to you?"

"Yes, it does!"

"Good, now on to my second point. The district police handled the paper work on the two men in the automobile that you shot. They were both unarmed and carrying identification as American citizens living in Washington."

"I killed American citizens?"

"Yes, you did. Citizens involved in the murder of Carl Wallace and the attempted murder of you. If they had lived the Justice Department would have tried them for Carl's murder. If you drive the get away automobile in a bank robbery, you are just as guilty as the men inside holding the guns."

"I know, but they were unarmed."

"That is not your concern, continue to do just as you did, or you will be on Doc Waters stone slab in St. Elizabeth. The newspapers have already reported that four men were killed outside the Mexican Embassy in an attempted murder of two JAG lawyers who were delivering briefs to the Ambassador. The State Department has already warned the Mexican Embassy that any further attacks at that location will result in deportation of the entire embassy. The State Department can not mention anything to the Spanish or Cuban Embassies until we have further evidence of involvement."

"We will lose the only contact that I have, under-secretary Mendez has provided our only leads in the case."

"Yes, and he now thinks that all four attackers are dead and he is clear of his involvement. I understand your situation, Louis. You do not want to lose this contact and you won't. Mendez will not be deported, he will probably be arrested."

"For what?"

"Providing false information in a federal investigation. We have already contacted every one on the target list. They have doubled security from the Secret Service on down. The President has said that he will increase his public appearances, not reduce them. He even has added new photographers to the White House. Both still and motion pictures will be released to the public showing the President hard at work."

"What is a motion picture?"

"You know the silent movies coming out of California. News events are shown before the movie with printed lines of information across the bottom of the screen."

"What will they think of next, Sir. I will have to take Madeleine to see one of these new movies."

"When the other murders have been solved and the suspects arrested, you do that, Louis. The public has to see that everything is normal."

"But we do not know that every thing is normal until we hear back from the other police departments that you have contacted."

"We are beginning to hear back from them, Louis. There is at least one in each of the cities that you mentioned, but no more. That is enough to spread panic. These isolated murders will stop once the network has been arrested, tried and put to death."

"Put to death?"

"Yes. Thanks to President Buchanan, it is a federal crime to threaten or take the life of any federal employee. The single murders in each of these other states are now federal offenses thanks to the target list given you by the Mexicans. They are up to their eyeballs in this mess, Louis, do not trust anything that is said or given to you by them. General Van Weylor is alive and on the job in Madrid. Did you know that your revolver that you left with them was returned with blanks? That was a mistake on their part and I think that another attempt was to be made on your life. Your revolver and blanks were taken into evidence to be used against them. Here is your new NCI issued hand gun, notice that it is not an American made revolver. It is German made and has a magazine of cartridges. I want you to go to the firing range and get familiar with it. Here is your new holster to be worn under your jacket. All JAG and NCI agents will now wear firearms on their person, no more fishing around in briefcases. The gloves have been come off, Louis. Your father has issued orders that from now on, 'We speak softly, but carry a big stick!'"

"My father said that!"

"No, actually the President said it to him, but he liked it and has used it as the motto for the NCI. I like it!".

"So do I, Sir."

"I understand that you are on your way to see Marilyn Hanson."

"Yes, Sir."

"Tell her the man who killed he husband confessed to the crime before he died and this has provided us with information to arrest others that may be involved. Do not mention any foreign contacts of any kind. Tell her that the United States thinks they have located the missing organs of all the victims and that you have requested permission to take a task force to Mexico to search for them."

"Is that true?"

"Yes, it is. While you were asleep the President has exchanged telegrams with the President of Mexico. Representatives from his government will meet you and your group at Playa del Carmen in ten days. Your ship, the *USS Hornet*, leaves in two days. Get all your things done here before then. Here are your written orders from the White House and a letter of introduction to the Mexicans meeting you."

"Can I take Tim Jacobson with me and can he be armed as a sniper? I feel better when he is watching my back."

"Good for you, Louis. You are beginning to understand that you are not a one man army!"

"How difficult will the search be in Mexico, Sir."

"It is a showpiece event, Louis. The Mexicans know where the organs are stored. They do not want to make it look too easy for you.

Besides, it may be a trap that is why we pried the information from our two friends downstairs."

"What will happen to them, once this is over, Sir."

"They will be processed at St. Elizabeth."

"Processed?"

"Don't ask, use your imagination."

"Sir, what has happened with the information about Captain Van Weylor?"

"That has been turned over to the Justice Department, he is under twenty-four surveillance. He is making trips between the embassies and giving orders to others. These others are being identified and arrested as they attempt to carry out his orders. They will be another source of information, just the like first two. By the time you get back from Mexico we should have the whole thing rolled up."

TIM WAS ASLEEP behind the wheel of the NCI automobile and I did not know if he had gotten as much sleep as I had in the last twenty-four hours. I woke him gently and said, "Tim, are you armed?"

"Yes, Sir."

"Good, the Commodore gave me a new hand gun and I am not familiar with it."

"Is it the new Sig, Sir."

"It is German, that is all I know."

"Where to, Sir."

"The Hanson home, back to mine and then I want to introduce you to a delicate french pastry."

"I do not like French food, Sir."

"I think you like this one, Tim."

11

Hanson Home
Georgetown

Tim and I got to the Hanson home and I asked him to come inside with me so he could meet Mrs. Hanson. I had decided that Tim could become my partner. He was better trained coming from The Farm, than a lawyer out of the RLSO JAG and he was not stuffy like Commander Morton.

"We will need to make another stop today, Tim. I need to check in with the JAG office. Do you know where that is?"

"Yes, Sir. It is located in the Navy Yard."

We continued to walk towards the Hanson's front door. We knocked and the housekeeper let us in. I opened my notebook and wrote down her name. She showed us into the sitting room.

"Good afternoon, Lieutenant. I hope you have good news for me."

"We do, Mrs. Hanson. This is my new partner, Tim Jacobson."

"Oh, yes, I was so sorry to read about Mr. Wallace in the newspaper is he recovering?"

"Carl Wallace was killed in the line of duty, Mrs. Hanson. The same man that was responsible for your husband killed him two days ago in front of the Mexican Embassy."

"Yes, too bad he died in the attack, I was hoping that you would get additional information from him." I looked sideways at Tim, but he kept his cool and did not tell Mrs. Hanson that our suspect was supplying us with information.

"We are making progress in the case, however. I have some additional questions for you and your housekeeper. Could you ask her to come and sit with us?" Mrs. Hanson left and I whispered to Tim, "Listen and learn on the job."

He whispered back, "Will do, Sir."

The two women returned and sat down with us. "I do not know what else we can tell you, Lieutenant."

"Mrs. Carmichael, you said in your statement to the district police that you found the Senator in his study. Did you see him leave for his office the morning before you found him?"

"Yes, he seemed preoccupied, I had to remind him to take his briefcase of papers."

"Where is that briefcase now?"

"I have not seen it, was it returned to you, Mrs. Hanson?"

"No, I had forgotten all about it. He was never without it. Many times it was chained to his wrist. He had a White House secret clearance and carried documents to and from the White House."

"Was it handcuffed to his wrist that morning when he left, Mrs. Carmichael?"

"Why, yes it was, Lieutenant."

"Do you think that is why he was killed? Someone wanted his papers, wouldn't it be easier just to steal them from the Senate Office Building or our home?" Mrs. Hanson was a very intelligent wife of a senator.

"Was there any evidence of a break-in here at the house?" I asked.

"No, nothing is missing from here."

"That is not what I meant. How did the persons who killed your husband return his body to the house? You said you locked the house before you went to bed when you came home from the play, Mrs. Hanson."

"I did lock it."

"And you said that you unlocked the house when you arrived the next morning to find the Senator in his study, Mrs. Carmichael."

"Yes, I told the police that."

"Tim, go and examine all the doors and windows on the first floor. See if you can find evidence of forced entry. If you find any, call our office and have a team come back out here and take photographs.

"Yes, Sir." He left the room and headed for the doors and windows."

"Mrs. Hanson?"

"Yes, Lieutenant."

"Let me find my place in my notes. Here it is. The last time I talked to you, you said, 'This is the third murder this year of a retired member of the military.' How did you know this fact?"

"Mark told me the last night we spent together that he had talked to someone at the Mexican Embassy here in Washington. That person told him his life was in danger and that Colonel Ingraham and George Phillips had already been killed."

"Those were the names given to him, not John Hayes and Captain Farnham?"

"No, I am sure he said Colonel, not Captain, and George Phillips."

"Did your husband know either Colonel Ingraham or George Phillips?"

"I have no idea, you could check with his office staff. They are in the process of cleaning his office out. I told them to bring everything here to the house. Would you like to look through those things?"

"That would be very helpful, Mrs. Hanson. Mrs. Carmichael, you have been very helpful. If my partner returns with no evidence of a break in, that means that the killers had a key to the house. You need to change the locks today before the papers are stored here." I did not mention that the killers could have taken the Senator's key and copies made.

Both women looked frightened when Tim returned and said that there was no evidence of a forced entrance.

It took a few minutes to drive from Georgetown to the senate office building. Tim and I informed the office staff that all the papers in the Senator's office were now sealed by a federal order and they were dismissed from further work in the office until notified by the

Department of Justice. I used their telephone to call The Farm and inform Rodney that an interesting twist had occurred in the case.

"Senator Hanson had top secret papers chained to his wrist on the morning he left his house, he was on his way to the White House. He had no intention of going to the Mexican Embassy. Those papers are missing."

"We need to find those papers, Louis."

"Any idea where to start?"

"Yes, I will get on it from this end. I will contact the Department of Justice and have the Senator's office sealed and all the contents, boxed as evidence."

"Good, I sent the staff home. They took no papers with them. Tim and I will stay here inside the office until you send someone to relieve us. Who are you sending?"

"Danny Middleton, he will be there shortly. Thank you, Louis."

We waited nearly an hour before Danny arrived and we left for my apartment, I needed a clean suit of clothes.

TIM WAS IMPRESSED THAT I KNEW ANYONE IN THE SMITHSONIAN, he could not take his eyes off Madeleine and she showed her interest by asking him if he was married. "Madeleine, we did not come here to expand your field of eligible bachelors. You have had a couple of days to examine the two additional fragments that I gave you in the Hay-Adams. What can you tell me about them?"

"Someone went to a lot of trouble to provide artifacts of such value to plant at a murder scene."

"What do you mean?"

"There is no evidence that the chisel has been struck since it was made."

"I don't understand."

"Microscope examination, Louis. When a stone tool is struck, there is evidence of internal stress fractures. This chisel has never been struck."

"Then why did you say it was a valuable artifact?"

"The stone is very old, but the strike marks are from when it was made a few years ago."

"Then this is not a Mayan tool from 450 AD. It was made recently?"

"Yes, this was made for a museum."

"And I know which one, the Tulum Exhibit. Artifacts were reported stolen by the Mexican Government."

"Pieces were broken from the point to be placed at the murder sites, Louis, but the stone came from Cozumel, Mexico. I would stake my professional career on it."

"What about the hammer head?"

"Same thing, it has never been used."

I kissed her and we left for the RLSO at the Navy Yard. Commander Morton would be interested in my whereabouts for the last couple of days.

Tim was like a sponge he wanted to know everything he could about his new assignment to JAG. And while he drove, he asked questions.

"Sir, what does JAG stand for?"

"JAG is the first three letters of Judge Advocate General's Corps, US Navy. It is the legal arm of the navy. Today there are about 350 Judges, 30 limited duty officers, which you are now one of, Tim, 500 enlisted members, which I am one of, and 275 civilian personnel."

"How long has it been around, Sir?"

"In 1775, the Continental Congress enacted the Articles of Conduct, governing the ships and men of the Continental Navy. The US Navy and Marine Corps was disbanded after the revolution, however. It was reinstated in July 1797 by Act of Congress."

"It is as old as the Marine Corps, I had no idea, Sir."

12

Cranson College

December 24, 1904

My grandmother's plans were coming together. When Uncle Teddy ran for re-election in November, she released his trust fund so that he could run a first class campaign. After his election, she released the Seneca Oil Trust Fund and the construction of Cranson College began. An architect from Pittsburgh was hired. The college site was to be designed with the Caldwell family house as the center point. My grandmother walked the site every day trying to picture what would be built. She estimated that it would take nearly three years for all the buildings to be completed. She was now age eighty six and she realized that she would probably not see the young women who would graduate from Cranson College. In fact this might be her last Christmas with her family. She wrote to everyone in the family and invited them to attend the final Christmas celebration at Seneca Hill. She still had a sense of humor, she wrote, "Most students leave college to travel to their homes for Christmas. I am asking each of you to leave your home to come to the future Cranson College, now under construction at the family estate. Carol Caldwell Cranson will host the event and I promise to come back and haunt any Caldwell who does not see fit to come home one last time."

We were all there. My sister and I rented a automobile and drove from Alexandria, Virginia. Our parents and Aunt Ruth had come by train from Washington to Oil City. My sister and I took the last team of four horses from the carriage house and hitched them to the largest carriage and met them at the train station. The secret service was not amused.

"The President can not be seen riding in a horse and buggy." Uncle Teddy said, "Snow is predicted for tomorrow and if my mother-in-law has a sleigh, these four fine animals will be pulling us all around the estate. Get used to it. We are in the country. One of you stay with all the baggage, you other two jump on the back where the footmen usually ride. Louis, take us home."

The carriage was full, the Roosevelt family numbered eight. They sat on each other's laps. My parents loved it. Twelve people crammed into a carriage from the nineteenth century.

"Who has arrived, Louis?" My mother asked.

"Brother James and his family, Busy is here with her family, of course, Aunt Carol and the Cransons. That will make a dining table of twenty-four, Grandma will love it."

"Has anyone come from South Carolina?" My father asked.

"No, they all sent their regrets, I guess Grandma's ghost is going to be busy in South Carolina." We all laughed.

When the carriage pulled up in front of the house and disgorged its passengers, Louise and I went back to the station for the baggage and the secret service man left as a guard. When we returned, Grandma was holding court. The President of the United States was the second most important person in the room and he was fine with that.

"I do not like the term 'freshmen' for first year students at a woman's college, what do you think, Teddy?"

"I like 'first ladies.'" He squeezed his wife's hand.

"That is because you are the only one in this room with a 'first lady'." She still had her sense of humor.

"Mother, Bill and I have a handful of early applications to Cranson College, would you like to see them?" My Aunt Carol handed some papers to Grandma and she adjusted her glasses, then said, "Hell, I can't see a thing with these new glasses, tell me about them."

My Aunt Carol, said that the applications were for the two year teaching option. She did not want to encourage two year students and see them graduate from *her* college. She said she wrote to each two year applicant and reminded them that a four year teaching certificate and a bachelor's degree was the desired goal. My Grandmother Caldwell then balked at the term *bachelor* and wanted Aunt Carol to find a more suitable label for women who had completed four years of education.

My Uncle Bill Cranson, was the college provost and his job was the placement of advertisements in the state newspapers for college faculty. He was trying to hire a few department heads and let them interview the faculty who would begin teaching in the summer of 1906.

Whenever I came to Seneca Hill in those years to visit my grandmother, I was amazed at her renewed strength and determination to see her life's goals completed. We always had a nice visit.

"Louis, what has happened with the Senator Hanson murder? Did you solve it?"

"We know how he was murdered, Grandma, he was injected with a poison from the tip of an umbrella."

"What kind of poison?"

"Curari, Grandma."

"Ah, yes the poison of choice for tribes of Indians from South America. They make it from the curare plant and dip their spears and arrows in it. Terrible stuff. There is no antidote, is there?"

"Yes, we use the antidote for curarine, the chemist's version of the same poison, it works."

"Well, you would know that, Louis, you are the smartest of my grandchildren. Why didn't you bring Madeleine Barrias with you for Christmas?"

"She is spending it with her Aunt and Uncle Louis Barrias in Washington. He parents are living in Paris and they have invited me next year for Christmas."

"Are you going?"

"Of course, Madeleine and I are very good friends and who could pass up a holiday in Paris?"

"You write to me too often, Louis, don't you write to your parents?"

"My father and I write to each other all the time. Mother is busy and she likes to read my letters home, but she rarely writes, why do you ask?"

"Your father and his father wrote back and forth all the time, it must be something special between the Caldwell men in this family."

"I think it was because Grandpa was a warrior first and a grandfather, father, husband, and company man second. Some men are like that, I found out from Grandpa Schneider that my Grandfather Caldwell hated injustice of any kind and he fought hard to make things right."

"In that respect, you are identical to your grandfather, Louis. Sometimes it skips a generation. Your father is not like that at all. Your father tried very hard to please his father so that your grandfather would try to be a father to him first. He knew that, that is why you have a very large collection of letters from your father over the years. Do you know that you have more letters than your sisters and me combined?"

"I had no idea."

"I know you saved them. When you get back to Washington, get them out and reread them. He is trying to make a connection with you, Louis. The connection he never had with your grandfather. Your father will continue to teach you life's lessons as long as he lives. He had your mother read each one and make corrections in his first draft so that his meanings were clear. If you reread them once a year you will always have your father and mother close to you. Maybe that is why your mother felt she didn't need to write, she already did inside your father's letters."

I did not tell her that I already figured this out on my own, I hugged her instead and went looking for Louise. It was beginning to snow and it was time to hitch up the sleigh.

13

JAG Offices

Washington Navy Yard

Commander Morton saw Tim and I enter the bull pen from our Christmas breaks and head for my desk in the corner. I had just laid my briefcase down on the top of my desk when he said, "Into my office, Lieutenant."

"Yes, Sir, Commander Morton." I winked at Tim and motioned for him to sit in my chair and unload my briefcase. I did not think I would ever have to carry it again. When he was inside his office with the door closed he asked, "Why have I not seen you for ten days?"

"I was on leave, Sir. I needed the time to clear my head about what happened to Carl and me outside the Mexican Embassy."

"Yes, that was terrible about Carl. I will need to assign you a new partner."

"I have a new partner."

"Why am I finding out about this now?"

"I was not allowed to leave the hospital, then I was on Christmas leave until now, I came right here to report to you." A partial truth, I was not bound by the military code of rank, hell, I didn't even know what rank I was today, it kept changing after each success and failure.

"Who is that man with you?"

"That is my new partner, Tim Jacobson."

"Who assigned him to you? I make all the pairings here in JAG."

"Since my life was threatened, I was assigned a bodyguard from NCI, Sir. I sort of gave him a promotion since he and I are now joined at the hip."

"He can not work out of this office without my approval. Where did he get his law degree?"

"He is not a lawyer, Sir. He is a Marine Scout, my bodyguard. Commodore Lowe assigned him to me. You will have to talk to him about removing him from my protection. I think I will need him in Mexico."

"Mexico, what are you going to be doing in Mexico?"

"On special assignment from the White House. I have the letter of appointment from the President in my briefcase. Would you like to read it, Sir?"

"Yes, I would, go get it for me." I stuck my head out of his office door and shouted for Tim to bring me the letter from the President of the United States. The entire bull pen turned to look at me. Commander Morton was not happy. He grabbed the letter from Tim's hand and read it.

"It says here you are meeting with representatives from the President of Mexico. It also says you are a Navy Captain, were you promoted in the last ten days?"

"I must have been, Sir. Uncle Teddy does not make mistakes."

"I know, but that means you jumped over three grades in a single promotion. Can that be correct?"

"You can check with the White House, Sir. Sir, does this mean I can stop calling you, Sir, all the time? Does it mean that you must address me as, Sir, when we are having a conversation?"

"I have no idea, Lieutenant Caldwell, I am going to get to the bottom of this."

"Captain Caldwell.'

"What?"

"You did not use my proper rank."

"You are dismissed, Lieutenant!"

"Shouldn't I be dismissing you Commander? How soon can we exchange office spaces, rank has its privileges, doesn't it?"

"Sit down Captain, until I can get someone on the telephone that can confirm your rank. What is your rank, Mr. Jacobson?"

"Major Jacobson, my rank is with the marines. I outrank both of you." Commander Morton was deflated. He reached for the telephone and connected with Commodore Lowe's office.

"Commander Morton, JAG, to speak with Commodore Lowe .... yes, I can hold....... he can not take my call? Can anyone there tell me the rank of Louis J. Caldwell, RLSO office Washington, D.C.? Who should I talk to ? ...... an Admiral Caldwell. Louis Caldwell's father ..... yes, I can wait while you transfer me to the White House.................. Admiral Caldwell's office, please ....No, I do not have a scheduled phone appointment. I was transferred form Commodore Lowe's office tell him it is about his son........ yes, I can hold.

We waited for fifteen minutes and the call was never connected through to the Director of NCI. Commander Morton placed the phone back in its cradle and said, "I will try later, Captain. If I wait two more days you will probably be busted back down to Lieutenant." He was smiling when he said, "Let's wait until you keep your *captaincy* for more than a week before we trade offices. Even with Uncle Teddy's help, it will take that long to get the paper work completed, making you the head of this regional office."

"You are probably correct, Commander. I will be gone twelve days to Mexico and that should be plenty of time for you to clear out of my office. Major Jacobson, do you have any orders for Commander Morton?"

"No, you are dismissed, Commander, I will need your office to make some telephone calls. I should not be more than twenty minutes. I will have Captain Caldwell come and tell you when I am done." The commander just sat behind his desk staring at Tim in disbelief. "Commander Morton, I will need your chair to make my calls."

"Of course, excuse me, I have to leave my office for a few minutes." Tim reached past him and picked up the telephone, "Connect me with the White House, special top clearance code, *Whitehorse*." Commander Morton's shoulders fell and he left his office. Tim dropped the telephone back in its cradle and said, "When are you going to tell him that your rank is temporary?"

"When are you going to tell him you were a sniper in the Marine Corps, but never made it above the rank of sergeant?"

"Sergeant Major to you, Sir. Sometimes I forget about the sergeant part." He had a giant grin on his face.

"How long should we sit in here?"

"Twenty minutes, that is what it takes to talk to anyone important in the White House with a Whitehorse clearance." We were both smiling.

"Tim, how good were you as a sniper?"

"Good enough to survive in the jungles of Cuba, on my own for two weeks at a time."

"Do you think you could do that in the Yucatan of Mexico?"

"With good maps of the area, yes. But the Commodore will never let me leave your side until he has this case closed."

"Do you have names of Marine snipers that could be assigned to the task force that I am taking to Mexico?"

"Yes, but I doubt you can get them in less than two days."

"Let's try anyway." I walked over to the telephone and placed a call to the Commodore.

"Commodore Lowe, please. ...... Yes, I will hold. ..... Commodore this is Louis again, sorry that Commander Morton bothered you a few minutes ago. Tim and I were just talking about the task force to Mexico....... Yes, do you think it is still a waste of time and just a showpiece event staged for us? .... Me too. If I hand the phone to Tim and he gives you the names of a few friends of his, can you arrange for them to be on the ship that will take the task force to Mexico? ....Yes, Madeleine is looking forward to it. I think she should remain on board the ship and any artifacts can be brought to you, it would be safer for her. ...... I agree. Here is Tim." I handed the telephone to Tim.

"Hello, Commodore .... I think he wants them on the ground ahead of the visiting party, so to speak, Sir........... I think it a very good idea, I wish I had thought of it .... They are all Marines, Sir .... I was in the jungle with them in Cuba, Sir....... They are very good, Sir ....They are all at Port Royal Training Center, First brigade, Sir.....Aye, aye, Sir." Tim hung up the telephone.

"What did he say?"

"We need to get our butts back to The Farm and write the operation plan for the mission."

"Mission?"

"That is what the man said!"

14

Task Force To Mexico

USS Hornet, Atlantic Ocean

It was like a three ring circus but we put together an operations plan that involved the First Brigade stationed at Port Royal Training Center in South Carolina. We left the Navy Yards, Washington, aboard the *USS Hornet,* a first class cruiser. I had never been on a war ship of any kind. The last ship I had traveled on was a transatlantic steam ship to Paris. Madeleine and I were assigned adjoining cabins. The rest of the task force members were scattered about the ship. A task force can mean a group of ships, usually a battleship and several escorts such as cruisers, destroyers and tenders of all kinds. This was not a naval task force, it was a group of experts making a presidential fact finding visit to another country. The *USS Hornet* was accompanied by the *USS Starfish*, a submarine commanded by my brother, James. The *USS Hornet* was the second ship commissioned with the same name. The first fought in the War of 1812 at San Salvador, off the coast of Central America, the present ship fought in the Spanish American War at Santiago, Cuba.

The operations plan called for the *USS Starfish* to travel, on the surface, at top speed, from the Naval Yard to Port Royal, South Carolina. The *USS Starfish* left a day before we left Washington. The US Marine snipers were taken aboard and the *USS Starfish* immediately left for the northern tip of the Yucatan peninsula. They would be landed at night south of Puerto Morelos and north of

Tulum, in the State of Quintana Roo, Mexico. The map coordinates were agreed upon between the two ship's captains and they were in constant contact with each by radio.

The task force members on board the Hornet ate our meals together and discussed the upcoming visit to Mexico. Madeleine was the PhD from the Smithsonian, her uncle, Dr. Louis Barrias, was a chemist under contract with the United States Navy. Dr. Samuel Langley was a Navy consultant also. Dr. Ernest Abbel had two degrees, one in medicine and one in physics. An odd combination until I learned that he was an expert in human body mechanics and brain stem functions. I felt like an idiot in the same room with these folks. I sat and talked to Tim about how the marine snipers were going to cover our "six" through the jungles between Tulum and Puerto Morelos. I was neither a trained warrior nor a highly trained scientist or medical doctor. I was Mr. In between, a lawyer who was willing to stick his neck out to catch a highly trained foreign national operating inside the United States.

"LT, are you engaged to Miss Barrias?"

The question caught me entirely off guard. "Engaged, are you out of your mind, Tim?"

"You have the cabin right next to hers."

"Tim, it does not have an inside door. Would you like to exchange for the trip?"

"No, mine is right next to yours on the other side. What good would that do?"

"Tim, ask Madeleine out on a date when we get back to Washington and you no longer have to babysit me. It would help if you were a Catholic, Tim. You know the French, it is alright to screw around with whomever you like, but you can only marry a Catholic."

"You are Irish, I thought you were Catholic."

"Close, Church of Ireland."

"And Madeleine will only consider another Catholic, I understand."

"No, you don't. Madeleine is not ready to settle down and find a husband. She wants to have some fun first. She asked you if you were married, remember?"

"Yes, I am through screwing around, I want to settle down."

"Sounds like you two are passing ships going in the opposite directions, Tim."

"Story of my life!"

"Tim, have you met my sister?"

"No, why?"

"She is as beautiful as Madeleine with a better temperament."

"What type of man is she looking for?"

"One exactly like me!"

"Will she settle for someone better?"

I sat and looked at Tim for a minute before I responded, "Have you made contact with any of the sniper scouts on board the Starfish?"

"Sergeant Riley, Shawn Riley, is on board for sure. I talked to him before he left Port Royal. I have not heard from them, maybe we should check with the radio room for any messages from the Starfish."

We walked down a flight of stairs and entered the radio room. I asked the chief radio operator if the Starfish had made contact with us.

"Several messages came for Captain Wainwright." Replied the chief.

"Are there any messages for either Captain Caldwell or Major Jacobson?"

"Here is one for Sergeant Major Jacobson."

"Close enough, read it to us, please."

"I have decoded it, Sir. This Sergeant Riley has a sense of humor."

> SERGEANT MAJOR JACOBSON
> USS HORNET
>
> CAPTAIN JAMES CALDWELL HAS FOUND THE IDEAL PLACE TO PUT US ASHORE. I AM NOT SORRY TO LEAVE THIS UNDERWATER TIN CAN. THE CREW OF THE STARFISH IS USUALLY ELEVEN. WITH TWELVE MARINES ADDED, THIS PLACE IS LIKE A SARDINE CAN. WE CAN NOT EVEN TURN AROUND IN SOME OF THE SPACES IN THIS THING. THE MEN WHO GO DOWN IN THESE THINGS ARE ABSOLUTELY CRAZY.

OPERATION IS AHEAD OF SCHEDULE, TIN CAN WILL RELEASE THE SARDINES TOMORROW AND MEET YOU AT THE NORTH POINT.

SERGEANT SHAWN RILEY
SCOUT LEADER AND DEN MOTHER

"Can we send a return to this message, Chief?"

"Of course, what do want to say?" He had his pad and pencil ready.

"Send, *good hunting*, please."

"Just the two words, good hunting, Sir?"

"That is all, Chief."

We left the radio room and headed for Captain Wainwright's cabin. We knocked and we heard, "Come."

Tim pushed the hand lever and the cabin door opened. We walked in and I said, "We received a message from the Starfish, Sir. The scouts are ready to land tomorrow morning."

"Good, that will give them an extra day to try and reach the map coordinates before you and your Mexican baby sitters show up."

"Can I ask what my brother sent you, Captain?"

"Just four updates, one each day since we left the yard. They are here somewhere. You can read them." He looked through the papers on his desk and found them.

CAPTAIN WAINWRIGHT
USS HORNET

DAY 1: LEFT PORT ROYAL WITH TWELVE OF THE ROUGHEST LOOKING MARINES I HAVE EVER SEEN. IT WAS A TIGHT SQUEEZE BUT THE MEN AND GEAR WERE PLACED OUT OF THE WAY OF THE OPERATION OF THE BOAT. THE SCOUTS HAVE OFFERED TO HELP IN ANY WAY THAT THEY CAN AND WHILE WE ARE ON THE SURFACE, I HAVE GIVEN THEM AS MUCH DECK TIME AS POSSIBLE. UNDERWATER SAILING IS NOT FOR EVERYONE.

Captain Caldwell
USS Starfish

Captain Wainwright
USS Hornet

Day 2: Still on the surface and ahead of schedule. If the situation presents itself I will let the scouts pick a landing sight in two more days. They are quite happy on deck but seem to become anxious whenever they have to come below to eat or sleep.

Captain Caldwell
USS Starfish

Captain Wainwright
USS Hornet

Day 3: The scout leader has asked me several times if the scouts are scheduled to return to the United States on board the Hornet. I think he will never volunteer for submarine transport again. We are twelve hours ahead of schedule.

Captain Caldwell
USS Starfish

Captain Wainwright
USS Hornet

Day 4: Sergeant Riley and his scouts have located a landing site and we have put rubber boats over the side. As soon as the last scout is in the water , we will not wait to retrieve the rubber boats, they are expendable. We will submerge and head for the north point.

Captain Caldwell
USS Starfish

The *USS Starfish* had landed twelve marines and would meet us the next day at the agreed upon meeting point. We would then sail into Cozumel and request docking space off the north light house at Punta Morlas.

15

Task Force

Cozumel, Mexico

The *USS Hornet* and the *USS Starfish*, minus the marine scouts dropped anchor at Punta Molas light house, Cozumel Island, as agreed in the letter of invitation from the Mexican President. The team of experts, a JAG Lieutenant promoted to a captain and a former Sergeant Major of the Marine Corps boarded a ferry and headed for the village of Playa del Carmen. From the ferry the coast line of Quintana Roo looked like it had sandy white beaches with coconut palm trees growing right down to the water's edge. I had not managed to keep Madeleine on the *USS Hornet*, she just laughed at me and said with two strong men to protect her, she would be fine. Dr. Langley was sixty-eight years old and I worried about him tramping through the jungle.

The ferry boat made a living by running visitors from Cozumel to Playa del Carmen. A large ship like the *USS Hornet* could not enter a harbor on Cozumel, there was none. There was a place to drop anchor at the north or south end of Cozumel and the ferry would come to either light house and shuttle guests to the mainland. The mainland was clearly visible from Cozumel and I judged the distance to be less than two miles. When the ferry bumped into the wooden docks at Playa del Carmen we could see under the palm trees and into the town. It looked modern. The streets were paved with red bricks, just like at home. The main shopping district was built around what we would call a town square, the Mexicans called it the "Plaza". There were probably a hundred shoppers in the Plaza, but not anyone who looked like they might be sent from the President of Mexico. I got my letter of invitation from the bundle of papers I was carrying and read the time and place of the meeting. No officials were here to meet us.

"I will ask someone." I said to no one in particular. I walked up to the first person that was crossing the plaza and asked, "Perdon, jha visto a los representates de la Ciudad de Mexico?"

"Si, Teniente. They await you in the Cantina Nueva."

"How did you know I spoke English?"

"It was easy, the US Army uniform gave you away." I was wearing marine fatigues for the hike into the jungle. We both laughed and I thanked him for his time. I motioned to the others to follow me across the plaza to the Cantina Nueva.

We entered a dimly lit cantina and I asked the bar tender the same question I had asked in the Plaza. He answered in Spanish and pointed to a doorway which led into a back meeting room. We walked in to meet our counterparts from Mexico City.

"Buenos dias, soy el Teniente Caldwell. Puedo introducir ...

"There is no need for Spanish, Teniente, we speak English."

"Thank you, I will be begin again. May I introduce my traveling companions? The beautiful Senorita is Madeleine Barrias, the ugly guy beside her, is Tim Jacobson, a member of my JAG office, next to him is Dr. Barrias, the senorita's uncle and a noted Chemist, beside him is Dr. Ernest Abbel, a medical doctor and next to him is Dr. Samuel Langley, an advisor to the United States Navy."

"Thank you, Teniente Caldwell, I am Teniente Jose Emanual from the Office of Military Justice, Ciudad de Mexico." He offered to shake all of our hands and we did so going around in a circle. "I have several guests with me this morning. The first is the customs officer who detained the man carrying the human brain into the State of Quintana Roo. He will meet and share information from his records with whomever you decide is best suited to hearing this information." I nodded towards Tim and they left and went back into the cantina. "The next is doctor Hernandez, he has brought the human brain for your examination and transport back to the United States." I nodded towards Dr. Abbel and Dr. Barrias and they left together.

"The next is Professor Perez from the museum at Tulum with the recovered fragments of Mayan stone." I nodded towards Madeleine and they left together. Dr. Langley and I sat at a small table and talked with Teniente Emanual. Dr. Langley had a detailed set of maps of the area between Tulum and Puerto Morelos, a distance of 68 kilometers along Mexican highway 307.

"Can you tell us where you were told the man carrying the brain was to delivery the organ?" Dr. Langley had asked a pin-pointed question.

"The man in question was carrying his diplomatic identification. He had landed at Cancun from Cuba. He was detained and questioned until a diplomatic representative from the Cuban counselor's office came for his release. We retained the glass jar containing the brain and told the representative that this was not allowed into the country, he could reclaim it from customs on his return to Cuba."

"During the questioning session, did the Cuban diplomat indicate where his final destination was located? Was he bound for Playa del Carmen or further south along 307?" Dr. Langley had re-asked the same question.

"Ah, I see. You want to know where to start your search. He indicated that he was to meet a man and a woman at the village of Punta Maroma, here on this map." He pointed to the coastal village.

"Did you or anyone else investigate to see if you could find this man or woman?"

"Si, we have driven the 307 from here to Punta Maroma and there are a few unpaved roads that head west at these locations." He again pointed to our maps. It was my turn to ask a few questions.

"Teniente Emanual, have you written to Ambassador Mendez in Washington?"

"I have not written to anyone in Washington, I was instructed to meet you and your team of experts and supply any information that you may require."

"Can you give us the name of the man you detained and released in Cancun?"

"Of course, Hector Castro."

"Do you know of a man named, Carlos Edwardo, who was arrested and taken to Ciudad de Mexico for questioning? He died during the questioning."

"Of course, this case is well known, he committed suicide rather than reveal any information. It was tragic really, there was no need for his death."

"Why do you say that, Teniente, he was also carrying a human organ in a glass jar, wasn't he?"

"I do not have the case file with me, but that was not the case. He was arrested for attacking his friend who later recovered from his wounds. Carlos Edwardo would have been released when his friend recovered, that is why it is so tragic."

"Is the case of Hector Castro, the only one that contained a brain in a glass jar?"

"Si, that is my understanding."

"Can you recommend a guide for our hike back into the jungle at the ends of each of these roads that you have shown us?"

"I will go with you to the Plaza and talk to the day laborers who will be there and ask questions for you. May I take this map with me to show the men I talk to?"

"Of course, Dr. Langley will go with you, while I check with the other members of my team."

We left the meeting room and I stopped at the tables where Madeleine, Tim and Doctors Abbel and Barrias were meeting with their counterparts. Madeleine and her uncle were going to Tulum to see the artifacts at the museum with Professor Perez. I told them to be back to the Hornet before nightfall. She said, "Yes, Mother."

Tim confirmed the information given to me that Hector Carlos was detained in Cancun and released to the Cuban Council. We thanked the customs official and he left the cantina. Dr. Abbel said he needed to return to the Hornet and begin the pathology on the brain given him to compare with the autopsy report of Senator Hanson. If it was indeed the Senator's brain, we would return it. If there was not a match, we would leave it in Mexico. I thanked everyone for their assistance and said, "Tim are you ready for a truck ride and then a hike in the jungle?"

"Please be back to the Hornet before nightfall." Madeleine was smiling at Tim.

Tim and I left the cantina and looked for Dr. Langley and Jose Emanual. They were standing talking to a group of men. It was an animated conversation with a lot of head nodding and arm waving. We walked over and listened.

"Si, there are trucks coming and going along this road west from the village of Punta Maroma." A worker was pointing to Dr. Langley's map.

"I think that confirms it then." Dr. Langley folded his map and turned to face us. "There is really only one chance in a hundred that there are additional organs in Mexico. But as long as we have come this far, it would be nice to investigate the most likely map location. Teniente Emanual would like to accompany us along with this local guide, Tomas."

"Where can we hire a truck?"

"I will show you." said Tomas. We all followed the local guide and he took us to a garage close to the Plaza. An hour later we had packed all our hiking gear we had brought with us into the truck and were headed north on highway 307. Sixty eight kilometers is about forty miles and it was not long until we came to the village of Punta Maroma. We turned west on an unmarked road that led into the jungle. Our guide drove slowly looking for evidence of a truck leaving the road, he found it a short time later. The bushes were broken by a wheeled vehicle leaving the road. We continued, the jungle closed on us completely. There was no evidence of further vehicle passage. We all left the truck and put on our back packs and carried our bottles of water. Tomas found much smaller wheel tracks, like those of a child's wagon that went off into the underbrush. We followed them. "This is way too easy." Tim said in my ear. "A boy scout could follow this."

The wagon wheel marks ended at a hillside beside a small stream. Into the hillside was a series of stone carvings. I turned to Tim and said, "Okay, it just got harder. Where do we go from here?"

Tim waded into the stream and looked at the far side. He looked up and down the stream. He returned and bent down to look at the tracks. "These end here. Whatever was in the wagon was carried from here. We must be close, fan out and search for foot prints, broken vines or anything that might indicate which way we are to proceed."

I asked Dr. Langley, "Can you take a photograph of these carvings before we move on?" He began to set up his equipment.

Before Dr. Langley was finished, Tim returned with one of the marine snipers. "Look who I found tramping around in the jungle. Everyone, this is Sergeant Riley. I served with him in Cuba." Sergeant Riley was one of the marines who had been inserted by submarine days before. Jose Emanual asked, "Are you from the US ships at Cozumel?"

"Yes, he is Teniente, I sent my scouts ahead of us before we met with you at Playa del Carmen. I thought it might save some time and it looks like it did. What did you find, Sergeant Riley?"

"Follow me, Sir. You are not going to believe this." He strode off into the jungle with Tim and the rest of us on his heels.

16

Task Force

Map Coordinates 7H-3

We could see the temple from a distance, through the tangled mass of vines and trees, it stood like a majestic tower above the green vegetation.

"The map coordinates you gave us, Lieutenant, were within a mile of this temple. We found several men camped here. They put up a short fight and we killed five, two are still alive.

"What did you do with them?"

"The two live ones are over there in that hut, the other five will never be found in this jungle. I thought it best not to leave any bodies for whoever came with you, Sir." We walked to the camper's hut to see if they could give us further information.

"This man is Hector Castro, Teniente Caldwell."

"I want you to translate for me, Teniente Emanual, I do not want this man to misunderstand what I am about to tell him." I reached for my new Sig automatic.

"Senor Castro, I have been sent from President Roosevelt to execute the man who killed Senator Hanson of the United States Senate. Do you have anything to say before I carry out that order?" I placed the barrel of the automatic against his temple. He jumped to his feet and began waving his arms and screaming. I smashed the gun into his temple and he fell to the floor of the hut, out cold.

"Take this man into questioning, Teniente Emanual, I have no authority in your country." I was smiling.

"You had me frightened. I thought you were going to kill him."

"That would be messy on your part trying to explain what happened to him. We already have the killer of Senator Hanson. I wanted to give you something to work with when you interview this man. Tell him you are trying not to let me take him back to the United States. He will not have someone from Cancun bailing him out this time. Do you think that this other man understands English?"

"I do not think so, he has peed his pants. Do you want to do the same thing with this man?"

"Of course, you draw your weapon and be the 'bad cop' and I will translate into Spanish what you say to him." We got a confession in less than two minutes. His name was Emilio Cantez. He had taken Simon Juarez, who worked at the American Embassy off the streets of Havana similar to the abduction of Senator Hanson in Washington. He and his companion had taken the unconscious Juarez to a hospital in Havana where his brain was removed for transport to Cancun. He then led us out from the hut and up a short flight of steps on the temple's east side to a holding room where the glass jars of human organs were stored. I counted eleven jars with labeling on each.

"Which one is Simon Juarez?" He pointed to jar and I carefully lifted it from its stone shelf. I read the label "Havana 18-4-1904- QC". "What does the QC stand for?"

"Point of entry for Mexico, Quintana, Cancun."

"These other labels are marked, QIC, BC, HD, YIC, CIP, and TPZ, what do they stand for?"

"Other points of entry; Quintana, Isla Cozumel, Belize City, Honduras, Yucatan, Isla Cerritos, Campeche, Isla Piedra and Tabasco, Punta Zacutal."

I turned to Jose Emanual and said, "Continue to work with this man and see if you can indicate a name and country for each of these jars, I need a breath of fresh air." I left the store room and signaled to Sergeant Riley. "We have eleven organs to recover and take back to the ship for transport. Not all eleven will be Americans, we have already identified a Cuban by the name of Simon Juarez. Do you have a presidential warrant for this operation?"

"Yes, Sir."

"Assign two of your best men to take that jar to the Cuban Embassy in Cancun. Place it outside the front gate or door just before day break. When whoever comes to retrieve it, put a bullet in his head. Do you understand the symbology here, Sergeant Riley?"

"Yes, Sir. If you kill someone working at an American Embassy, then someone dies at your embassy. It is from The Bible; an eye for an eye and a tooth for a tooth. Too bad we do not have the time to take it to Havana."

I looked into Sergeant Riley's eyes and said, "If you ever get tired of the marines, Shawn, you come and see me in Washington. There is a job waiting for you there that pays ten times what you make as a marine."

"Sir, I will remember, thank you."

"Shawn, the Hornet sails in a few days, please have your men back on board before we shove off. I would miss their ugly faces."

He waved as he walked away and sought out two of his men to deliver a package. I walked back into the storage room and found Jose working with the jars and sorting them into groups.

"Made any progress?"

"Si, this group goes back to Ciudad de Mexico with me, they are all foreign nationals, the second group goes back to the United States with you. They are all labeled; Hanson, Hayes, Farnham and Phillips."

"So the brain Dr. Abbel is working on may not be Senator Hanson."

"Correct. The third group are, sadly, all Mexican Nationals who lived here in the Yucatan. That will be the saddest delivery for me, Louis."

"When this is all over, Jose, come visit me in Washington. I would like to give you a tour of our Office of Military Justice." We shook hands and started to assign scouts for the jars to be carried back to the truck.

"Two of your scouts are missing, Louis."

"I sent them on a side trip with the Simon Juarez jar. They will meet us in Playa del Carmen."

"Do they have transportation?"

"Just the horses they rode in on, Sheriff!"

"Sheriff, I don't see no stinking badges?" We began laughing. "You, Norte Americanos, always with the jokes!" He shook his head and walked slowly to the loaded truck.

The truck was heavily loaded. When we arrived we had our equipment and five men. Three men were in the cab and two were in the back. When we left we had three men in the cab; Tomas, Jose and Samuel Langley. The fourteen in the back were composed of ten marines, two prisoners, and Tim and me.

"Well, does this end our beautiful relationship together, Captain Caldwell?" I had forgotten that I had a temporary advancement in rank.

"That depends on what happens in the next few days If the two embassies involved want to stop this thing right here, I think it is over. If they continue, then you and I will be sent to hunt down and eliminate the problem."

"Cut off the head, not just the arms and legs – that may mean a trip to Madrid."

"That is correct, Sergeant Major, first the Captain Van Weylor and then the general."

17

Task Force
Playa del Carmen

I could not get the storage room out of my mind, I would have nightmares for many years, I was sure. We arrived back in Playa del Carmen and I thanked Jose Emanual and gave him the assistance of two of my scouts so that he could move his items to the Cantina Nueva. He was undoubtedly going to meet the members of his team for their debriefing, as I saw some of them come across the Plaza. My team was to meet at the ferry in order to get back to the Hornet. Once aboard, Tim and I got some of the scouts to carry our jars of remains to sick bay where Dr. Abbel and Barrias had examined the jar given to us in the cantina this morning. Tim and I walked into sick bay.

"What was the result of your examination of the jar?"

"These are not the remains of Senator Hanson. They are not a match with the autopsy report from Dr. Waters."

"Do you have the remains back in the jar?"

"Yes, they are ready for you to return them to Lieutenant Emanual."

"Teniente."

"What?"

"Nothing. Were there markings of any kind on the outside of the jar?"

"None."

"Thank you. Has your niece returned from Tulum with you Dr. Barrias?"

"Yes, she is in the mess, waiting to talk to you and Sergeant Jacobson." I took the unknown jar and headed up several flights of stairs to the mess.

"Hello, Madeleine, did you miss us?"

"Louis. Tim. What did you find at the site?"

"The scouts beat us to it. They found seven men and had a fire fight with them. It was all over by the time we got there."

"Did you recover the American remains?"

"Yes, this is not one of them, I am returning it to Jose Emanual before he leaves the cantina. Tim will fill you in on what happened."

"I would love to, Madeleine, but where he goes, I go. President's orders."

"Did you find anything unusual at Tulum?"

"No, the reproductions are common in Mexico. Some are even sold to tourists."

"Has the museum sold any to Cuban tourists?"

"Yes, they have. They are their biggest customers."

"I bet those are all from Cancun, not Cuba." We left Madeleine sitting in the mess and headed for the shuttle in order to get ashore. Tim and I talked on the way over.

"So what is the real purpose of all this window dressing?" Tim asked.

"I believe it is a side show to coverup the real purpose of the murders. Senator Hanson was carrying top secret papers to the White House. We need to concentrate on the others now. What were Hayes, Farnham and Phillips doing at the time of their deaths. Did they have state secrets and are they missing, also. We need to talk with the Commodore and find out if he has the network rolled up."

"Why did they attack you and Carl outside the Mexican Embassy?"

"That was really not thought out, Tim. That broke the case wide open. It gave us the cause of death in all five murders. The side show to make the killings look like a ritual was a clever idea, but it backfired on the two embassies involved. It drew attention to them. They are not immune, they can not hide behind diplomatic immunity. We will seek them out, one by one, and bury them in the jungle if need be."

"We are here, Captain Caldwell, let me go first."

"Aye, aye. Sergeant Major!"

We found Jose Emanual and his team in the Cantina Nueva.

"Teniente Emanual, I have the last of the evidence jars for you. This is not Senator Hanson's, the jar marked Hanson is now being looked at on the *USS Hornet*. If it matches the autopsy report, we will return it to Washington and release the body for burial. We also brought the reports for Hayes, Farnham and Phillips and we hope to confirm these so those remains can be released to the next of kin. It has been a successful visit."

"Si, we all agree. Without your scouts we would not have the evidence to take back with us to Ciudad de Mexico. It will take us some time to solve these murders. Why were they killed? What did they know? Who thought they were in danger? Many questions, my friend."

The same unknowns on my end. If I find any of these answers, I will telegram you at your office, adios Amigo." Tim and I left the cantina.

"Now what?" Tim seemed uneasy. His eyes darted around the Plaza.

"Now we wait for our two scouts to return from Cancun and we head back to Washington. I expect a reaction from what happened today."

18

Task Force
USS Hornet

Doctor Langley had developed his photographs from the site and he was showing them to Madeleine and her uncle. One caught my eye.

"What is this photograph, Dr. Langley?"

"It looked like an altar of some sort, so I decided to make a photo for your report.

"Madeleine, what does this look like to you?"

"That is the altar of sacrifice. It should have been on the east face towards the rising sun."

"It was. It was above the room where we found the jars with the remains."

"Dr. Langley, did you look at the surface of the altar?"

"Yes, I did. I took a photograph of the surface, it is here somewhere."

"Here it is." Tim had found it and handed it to Madeleine.

"These are probably human blood stains, I will not know until I examine the surface tomorrow."

"No." Tim and I said together.

"We will send a 'ship to shore' and see if Jose Emanual is staying for the night in Playa del Carmen. He can go back up in the morning."

"Yes, Mother."

"Madeleine, Louis is trying to protect you. Five men have been killed at that site today. You seem to think this is some kind of treasure hunt that we are on." I had not seen Tim this angry.

"I am sorry, Louis. Tell me what Jose finds in the morning." She left the mess and I headed for the radio room.

"Can you telephone from the ship?"

"Sure, what number did you want?"

"I do not have the number, I am trying to contact a Mexican officer who is presently in the Cantina Nueva."

"I can do that, Sir. Someone will answer at the cantina and you ask to speak to the officer." He put through the call and I talked to the bar tender. I asked him to call Teniente Emanual to the phone.

"Amigo, I did not expect to talk to you so soon. What have you found for me?"

"Jose, I think I have found the murder site for the Mexican nationals on your list. Dr. Langley was taking photographs of the site, remember?"

"I remember."

"He has a photograph of the surface of the altar of sacrifice above the storage room. It has blood on it. If you go back up there, with troops, I think you will find that the blood is human and it matches the blood in the jars that you have."

"A reasonable assumption, Amigo. I will start back as soon as I can find local troops. I am staying at the Casa del Sol, Playa del Carmen. Do you have something to write with? I will give you my number there."

"Jose, you can telephone or telegraph me here on the ship. The radio room will deliver the message."

"I will let you know what I find, Louis, adios."

"Adios, Jose." I left the radio room and went back to my cabin. I wanted to talk to Madeleine. I knocked on her cabin door, it was locked and she did not answer. I knocked on Tim's cabin and it was locked also. I headed for the sick bay.

"Any comparisons on the specimen jars, doctors?"

"They are matches for the autopsy reports, Louis, we need to take these jars home with us."

"I will be in the mess having coffee if you need me for anything."

I walked up the flights of stairs that I had descended and entered the mess. Dr. Langley had a hand held magnifying glass and was examining the photographs that he had taken.

"Anything new, Doc?"

He looked up and said, "I think I know why the Cubans and Spanish selected this site for the storage of the remains."

"You are ahead of me then, Doc, I do not have a clue why they removed the brains and took them thousands of miles from the murder sites to store them in an ancient ruins where anyone could stumble on them."

"I overheard what you said to Sergeant Riley. It is symbology. The defeated Cuban and Spanish Armies can now claim small victories. A senator who declared war on Spain, is defeated. An ambassador from the United States sent to Cuba, is defeated. A Navy Captain who transported United States troops to Cuba, is defeated. A Canadian born hero of the war, is defeated. They were defeated in such a way as to bring horror and shame on the United States for not being able to protect its heroes. The removable of the brains indicate the complete domination and defeat of the enemies. The brains were not meant to be found. They hid them in the most remote corner of the Spanish speaking world."

"I agree with him, Louis!" Madeleine and Tim had been listening from across the mess.

"I do not, Louis." Tim was smiling. He had obviously made up with Madeleine.

"I think the Spanish are stealing government secrets and selling them to the highest bidder."

"And who do you think the highest bidder is, Tim?"

"Germany, they have the most money in Europe."

Everyone began to speak at once. The conversation lasted until the evening meal was served in the mess.

19

Task Force
USS Hornet

TWO DAYS LATER, DR. LANGLEY was still examining his photographs. He was pouring over the photograph of a hut where the scouts had held the captives for us to talk to. It was long after most of us decided to return to our beds before the ship sailed for the United States. This might be the last night the boat did not rock. The marine scouts still had not returned from Cancun and I feared that they had been arrested before they managed to get to Cancun, let alone deliver the package. I could not sleep and I got up, dressed and went for a walk on deck. Madeleine and Tim were huddled together under a blanket, winter nights could be chilly even this far south. I smiled to myself and thought, good for you two, why not share some body heat? I unwrapped a cigar I had been saving and struck a match. A shot rang out from the darkness and I dropped the match at my feet. I felt Tim crash into me and we were both laying on the steel deck.

"What the hell are you doing, Louis? Are you trying to get yourself killed by lighting a match?"

"It was only a match."

"A good sniper can kill you at 200 yards from the light of a match, Louis, tell him Madeleine!" There was no answer. Madeleine did not stir. Madeleine was dead. A hole the size of dime was in her forehead and blood continued to pour from it because she had such a young, strong heart.

"Tim, get the marines, that sniper did not shoot from shore, that is two miles away. He is in a small boat, we can get that bastard, pull the fire alarm over there, that should wake the ship. Get boats lowered so we can get underway, I want a complete search of the water around this ship!"

Tim just looked at Madeleine and did not move. I leaped to my feet and jerked the fire alarm. Emergency lighting came on all around the ship. The marines grabbed their rifles, their most valuable positions, and came on deck near us.

"Spread out around the deck. Sniper in a small boat. Try not to kill him." I was screaming out my orders. Tim still sat and looked at Madeleine

"Port side, 200 yards away." I heard a marine scream.

"Shoot the oars men, not the man with the rifle." I screamed back.

Shots rang out and cries of pain were heard over the water. Several lifeboats were lowered and the men in the sniper boat were brought on board the *USS Hornet*. There were three of them and two bloody jars. Our scouts were home.

The entire ship was in a state of shock. An American citizen on a war ship of the United States was murdered while in a friendly country.

I telegraphed the White House, *attention Admiral Caldwell.* I reported the deaths of two marines while in the jungle of Yucatan and a member of the Presidential Delegation, Dr. Madeleine Barrias. We have captured the individuals involved and are transporting them back to Washington for trial. Mission is now complete.

I found Dr. Langley and asked him if he had taken any photographs of the inside of the storage room at the temple.

"No, there was no natural light in there, Louis. I have some of Jose Emanual bringing the jars outside and placing them in groups."

"Good, make up a press release kit that shows the location of the temple on a map, the temple itself and the jars outside. These photographs should be supported by a brief description of each. Include a statement that indicates that the Cuban Counsel's Office in Cancun was responsible for the transportation and storage of human remains taken from victims in the United States. Indicate that Mexican citizens have been arrested and detained by Mexican authorities. Do not mention who these authorities are or where the arrested individuals are being held. Do not mention that we have detained three suspects in the murder of Dr. Madeleine Barrias. I think the intended target was me, so does Tim Jacobson, now that he has calmed down."

"What do you want me to do with this package after I have it together?"

"What I am asking you to do, is a violation of protocol, Dr. Langley. Our State Department will have a fit that this information about a foreign embassy is made public. My concern is this, the damn Spanish will continue to hide behind the Cubans. They will continue to bring their mutilations to the Mayan Temple we located and the Mexicans will continue to arrest them and return them to Cancun. Nothing will be done to discourage the practice. I want to expose the Spanish ring leaders for what they are, common murderers."

"I would be honored to do this for the memory of Dr. Barrias. Do you think this will end the killings?"

"No, I think they will escalate, that is why I have asked for personal protection for you, Dr. Abbel, and Dr. Barrias." He had an uncontrollable shudder.

20

USS Hornet

Washington, D.C.

Dr. Louis Barrias led the procession off the *USS Hornet* with the body of Madeleine. He had tears streaming down his face as the newspaper reporters clamored for information. I saw Dr. Langley hand a folder to one of the reporters. Tim pushed his large fist in the mouth of one reporter and they backed off. A large black hearse was waiting and her body was gently placed inside and the rear doors closed as Tim and I watched. Her uncle was placed in the back seat and the hearse left for St. Elizabeth. Dr. Barrias would meet his bodyguard at the hospital after he talked to Dr. Waters and had signed some release forms as the next of kin in this country. Her parents would want the body embalmed and returned to France for burial.

Tim and I were met by Commodore Lowe and we drove out to The Farm. Rodney was unaware of the attachment between Madeleine and Tim. I could not tell him with Tim sitting right beside me, so I decided to take a sideways approach.

"Both Tim and I were very fond of Dr. Barrias. We are both to close to her to be the ones assigned to the prosecution of this case." Rodney Lowe spoke for the first time. "There will be no prosecution of this case. We will wring everything we can from the suspects and they will follow the first two into St. Elizabeth's for processing." He turned to face both of us. "The President is not pleased with how this Jigsaw series of murders has evolved. He has ordered the elimination of Captain Van Weylor of the Spanish Embassy here in Washington. Tim, I want you to be extra alert in your protection of Louis. The attempts are not going to stop over night and before we can eliminate Van Weylor with no traces. I have ordered that he and whatever protection detail he has, be taken off the streets and taken to St. Elizabeth. He will simply disappear."

"Thank you, Commodore." Tim had spoken for the first time. "I want to check with you to see if we can bury the remains of the two members of Sergeant Riley's detail."

"The next of kin have been notified that their loved ones are missing in action. There has been no pathology on the jars that you brought back with you. I doubt that these are your two marine scouts, Tim. They are being wrung out in Cancun as we speak. That is why Louis' father has ordered a black Ops raid on the Cancun Counsel's Office. This team is local and will find the location of the two scouts before the week is ended."

Tim and I looked at each other in disbelief. "How often does this type of thing happen, Commodore?" I did not want Tim to have false hopes.

"All the time, Louis. Usually they are traded for two men that we are holding. We have not heard anything from the Cuban Embassy, because the Spanish are really the ones pulling the strings."

"Did you roll up the network of operatives during the last ten days while we were gone?"

"Yes, a total of twelve have been taken from the streets."

"How many of ours have been taken, Commodore?"

"Ah, you are beginning to see how the game is played, Tim. None, so far and that concerns me."

"Why?"

"The Spanish are not interested in trading to get back Cuban surrogates."

"Tim and I are wondering if anyone has found the papers that Senator Hanson was carrying, or at least found out the contents of those papers."

"The contents are known, classified, sorry, can't tell you."

"Can you tell us the contents of the papers that were stolen from Hayes and Farnham?"

"Who told you about those papers?"

"You did, just now."

"Louis, you are too smart for your own good. All five, Hanson, Hayes, Farnham, Ingraham and Phillips, were working on government contracts or projects. The information stolen has shown up in Germany."

Tim and I looked at each other in disbelief again! "Sir, you are aware that Dr. Abbel, Barrias and Langley are both under Navy contracts, that is why they were chosen to make this trip with us."

"Yes, Louis. We will do our best to protect them, now that we know the real plot."

"The real plot, Sir?"

"Yes, Spain is an ally of Germany and is selling American plans and projects to the Germans."

21

JAG Offices

Washington Navy Yard

Commander Morton was waiting for Tim and I to enter the bull pen and head for my desk in the corner. I had just laid my briefcase down on the top of my desk when he said, "Lieutenant Caldwell, I understand that your rank of Captain has now been reduced to Lieutenant Commander."

"Yes, Sir, Commander Morton." I winked at Tim and motioned for him to sit in my side chair and unload my briefcase. I was wrong about the briefcase, it was still with me, full of assignments and meetings to be concluded in the next few days.

"Do you have a report for me on the arrests made in Mexico?"

"No, Sir. My report was taken by NCI and marked, Top Secret, Eyes Only, White House."

"When will I see the information contained within it? It is hard to assign your case load when I am left in the dark."

"I would think that the censored report will filter down in a week or so. In the meantime, the newspapers have an interesting take on what happened in Mexico, Sir. It should be in the Washington Post tomorrow. I also have a letter of assignment from the White House. Would you like to read it?"

"That will not be necessary. What will you be assigned to complete in the next few days?"

"Tim and I have to take a final status report and the papers for the release of Senator Hanson's body to his wife. Would you like to accompany us, Sir? I think she would like to talk to a higher ranking officer than a Lieutenant."

"She will, you are now a Lieutenant Commander and the Major here, should be able to comfort her. Report back here when the NCI assignments are complete. I will show you as 'joint resolution'." He returned to his office and began to shuffle some papers.

"What in the hell is joint resolution?" Tim had a quizzical look on his face.

"I have found, Major Jacobson, that 'joint resolution' is when neither NCI nor JAG know where I am or what I am doing."

"You are on 'joint resolution' most of the time Captain Caldwell."

"Lieutenant Commander, please, let's keep this rank business current, shall we?"

"Aye, aye. Sir."

The door opened to Commander Morton's office and he stuck his head out and said, "Major Jacobson, I can not find you listed as a member of the marine scouts assigned to NCI. Can you bring your file with you the next time you are back here in JAG?"

"If you have the time, Commander Morton, I will call the White House and have the Director of NCI talk to you about my present assignment." Tim was going to get nailed, it was only a matter of time.

"That would be Admiral Caldwell? He is the Director of NCI, I have a call into him. I will ask him to forward a copy of your file, Major."

"Very kind of you, Commander Morton. You are dismissed."

"Thank you, Sir. Just trying to run a tight ship here at JAG."

We left JAG and headed for our first stop of the day. "I will bet that pompous SOB has never been on a war ship, Louis."

"Can't say without reviewing his file. But this pompous SOB, that you hang around with, was not on one until I stepped foot on the *USS Hornet.*"

Unknown to us, my father was planning a little surprise for Commander Morton. He had before him, the promotion papers for Sergeant Major Jacobson from Commodore Lowe, director of the NCI training center located in Lancaster, Virginia. He had made a number of red lines changes already. He took his pencil and crossed out the word Sergeant on the form. The form now read that Major Timothy Lee Jacobson was recommended for promotion to Warrant Officer, he crossed out "to warrant officer". My father was not known for his sense of humor or fair play.

He wrote the following recommendation to the President. "Request for promotion denied. Timothy Lee Jacobson should remain a Major for at least seven more years, until he has proven his worth to the agency." He then sent a blind copy of this recommendation to Commander Morton, RLSO JAG headquarters, Washington Navy Yard.

The next day, when we reported for work, Commander Morton was all smiles towards Major Jacobson. With insincere looks, he told Tim how sorry he was that his request for promotion was denied at the President's level and that Tim would have to remain a major for at least seven years.

"Major Jacobson, I am sorry I doubted your rank within the Marine Corps, Sir. You look so young, Sir. I am glad we got that cleared up, Sir. You are a member of NCI and not in my division here at JAG, Sir. You do not report to me or I to you, Sir."

"Thank you, Commander Morton. I admire what you have managed to accomplish here at the RLSO with so many inexperienced lawyers here in the bull pen. I will also put a good word in for you at NCI. You are dismissed."

"But, I do not report to you."

"That is correct, Commander, but I out rank you, and rank has its privileges. Don't you agree?"

"Oh. Yes."

"Oh, yes. What?"

"Oh, yes, Sir."

"That will be all, Commander Morton."

22

Hanson Home

Georgetown

Tim and I got to the Hanson home and I told him this part of the job was the most difficult for me. Mrs. Hanson would receive closure and she could begin her husband's funeral arrangements. The body would probably reach Ohio about the time that Madeleine reached France. I had decided the last time we were in the Hanson home, that Tim could become my partner. He was better trained coming from The Farm, than a lawyer out of JAG and he was not stuffy like Commander Morton, he was a breath of fresh air.

"We will need to make similar stops today, Tim. I need to check on the Washington addresses for Hayes, Farnham, Ingraham and Phillips. Do you know your way around Washington? You are driving."

"Yes, I have a map right here with the addresses marked."

We continued to walk towards the Hanson's front door. We knocked and the housekeeper, Mrs. Carmichael, let us in. I opened my notebook and marked off the name, Hanson. She showed us into the sitting room.

"Good morning, Lieutenant. I see you two have been promoted."

"Yes, I am still a Lieutenant. This time a Lieutenant Commander. I have been every kind of Lieutenant that you can be in the Navy, Mrs. Hanson. Tim has just recently been promoted to Major. You remember my partner, Tim Jacobson."

"Oh, yes, how are you, Major?"

"Fine, Mrs. Hanson, have you seen the morning Post?"

"Yes, I was so sorry to read about Dr. Barrias. You arrested the people who did that, didn't you?"

"Madeleine Barrias was killed while advising the Navy, Mrs. Hanson. The same group of men that were responsible for your husband, killed her, also."

"Yes, too bad she died in the attack on your ship. I was hoping that you would get additional information from your trip to Mexico." I looked sideways at Tim, but he kept his cool and did not break down in front of Mrs. Hanson.

"We have made all the arrests necessary to close your husband's case. The missing organs were found and identified in Mexico. Each organ has been returned to each victim's family. I had Dr. Waters place Senator Hanson's in his casket in Lancaster, Virginia. You may now make arrangements to have your husband moved to his final resting place, Mrs. Hanson. The horrible ordeal that you went through is now at an end." The shock of what I said was apparent, but Mrs. Hanson was a strong lady and she would survive. Tears were rolling down her cheeks as she asked, "Are the other cases closed now, also?"

"Every one of them, Mrs. Hanson. We have the killers and the missing organs. We are out today contacting each of the families, this was our first stop."

"I do not envy your jobs today, Commander, Major. Thank you for finding and arresting those animals who did this to these fine families."

It took the entire day to visit the homes of the closed cases. Our next stop was at the address of R. Jeremiah Farnham. I checked my notes. Cpt. Farnham was born in 1829, Boston, Mass. He was a graduate of the U. Of Vermont in 1849. He taught school, studied law, and was admitted to the bar in 1869. It took him twenty years because he served in the Civil War as a volunteer from Vermont. He was a member of the State of Vermont Senate in 1868. He was Governor of Vermont from 1880 to 1892. When the war broke out in Cuba, he volunteered for service, but he was told he was too old, so he agreed to captain the ships transporting the troops from South Carolina to Cuba.

"We should find Mrs. Farnham, a senior citizen at this address, Tim." We knocked and a middle aged woman answered the door.

"Is Mrs. Farnham at home?" We asked.

"Yes, I am."

"Mrs. Roswell Jeremiah Farnham?"

"Yes, are you here about my husband?"

"The final pieces of evidence have been gathered and the men arrested, Mrs. Farnham. Your husband's remains are ready for your undertaker at St. Elizabeth Hospital. Ask for Dr. Eli Waters, he is in charge of the transfer."

"Thank you, anything else?" When we did not respond, she slowly closed the door.

The third stop was at the home of Colonel Duncan Ingraham, the son of a famous naval officer who faced down the Austrian Navy at a port in Turkey to rescue Martin Koszta. His father was later a commodore in the Confederate Navy. His grandfather served under John Paul Jones on the Bon Homme Richard. This marine colonel had come from a long line of navy men. We found his widow at home and passed the information that funeral arrangements could now be made.

"I am sorry you had to make this trip out here, Commander. My husband has been buried, his body was not held like the others. When he was killed, no one knew it would be a series of murders. Are you in the process of notifying all the families?"

"Yes, we are."

"Please check your information, Commander, some of these widows have already buried their husbands."

"Thank you, Mrs. Ingraham, that will be a great help to us." I crossed off the name Ingraham and we started for the Phillips home. His body would also already be buried and we simply notified his children that the case was solved and those responsible were now in custody awaiting trial. That left only one name remaining, John Hayes. When we arrived at the address, we found another family living there. They had bought the house from the Hayes estate. He left no widow and his estate was now in probate. There was no one to notify.

We had ended our day and Tim drove us back to my sister's apartment.

"Louise, are you home?" I dropped my briefcase on the hallway floor with a thud. "Tim and I have had quite a day." JAG lawyers were not allowed to carry firearms on their person, like the NCI agents. Today I was working from the JAG office and I had left my Sig in my room at The Farm, locked in a gun safe. I did have a variety of personal protection items inside the briefcase that included a snub nose revolver which was not a technical violation since I did not carry it in a holster on my body. When I worked out of NCI, I wore a shoulder holster with an automatic tucked neatly away.

"In the kitchen. What are you men hungry for tonight?"

"It does not matter, you know Tim will eat anything that does not eat him first." Tim punched me in the arm and made a face.

"Tim is a growing boy, Louis. Aren't you, Tim" She stood on tip toe and gave Tim a kiss on the cheek.

"Louise! What would Grandma Caldwell say if she knew you were kissing a man?" She punched me in the chest, then gave me a big hug, something she did regularly.

"I missed not talking to you two today. What did you do?"

"Closed the Senator Hanson case and notified the other four widows that their husbands were ready for funeral arrangements."

"That does not sound like fun."

"Your brother handled it with his usual gentleness, Louise. Where does he get the ability to shoot a bad guy and console his widow?"

"I have no idea. Maybe it came from his childhood when he would catch an insect, pull off its legs until it died and then give it a 'decent' burial in our flower garden." She was smiling, she did not think I had a disturbed childhood. Tim was not so sure, he kept looking from one to the other of us until we started laughing and he got it.

"My briefcase is full of unrelated items that are pieces of the final puzzle that Tim and I will try to fit together tonight. He and I have some files and we will sit down with you and you can help. You are like an extension ......"

"of your ability to solve problems." She was smiling.

"You just did it again." I smiled back at her and gave her a hug as Tim was looking at the two of us.

"Remember when you told me that I should meet your sister, Louis? I had no idea she was an extension of you!"

"We need to help Louise with the dinner fixings and bring her up to speed on the closed cases."

"Good, I am starving!"

"There are now a total of five closed cases. Madeleine's is still open, but that is a technicality." Tim's face paled and his shoulders dropped, he was still not over Madeleine.

"Madeleine's death is really a new case, it may be the first of many revenge killings for the exposure of the Mayan Temple storehouse of horrors."

"Yes," Tim added, "Lancaster has kept your brother's protection in place, but they have given the rest of the Mexican Presidential party the option of a body guard. I think it is too early not to have protection for Dr. Abbel, Barrias and Langley."

23

Black Operation

Cancun, Mexico

The office of NCI is headed by my father, Admiral Caldwell, and I was surprised when he called me into his office for a briefing of what took place in Cancun. The special team was assembled from the US Embassy, Mexico City and sent to Cancun. It seems that NCI was having many more difficulties inside Mexico than the case that I was working on. During the last four months, special purpose agents were added to our embassy for black operation assignments. This was just one of many that they had successfully carried to a conclusion. My father smiled as he began, "Louis, I am happy to report that your two marine scouts, Corporal Adam Smythe and Corporal Harold Davis were located and they are safe in Mexico City awaiting transport back to South Carolina."

"When did this happen?"

"Last night. They were found in the basement of the Spanish Embassy in Mexico City."

"Mexico City?"

"The Cuban Counsel in Cancun shipped them to Mexico City for interrogation after they found them carrying a glass apothecary jar near the front entrance."

"Then, no one was shot in Cancun by the scouts?"

"Yes, if that had happened, the scouts would be facing a murder charge. Whoever gave the scouts an order to kill a civilian is guilty of attempted murder. I assume that was your bright idea, Louis. You know the law. An illegal order does not clear the scouts, they would be guilty of murder, just like you."

"Wait a minute, who gave the order for agents to enter the Spanish Embassy in Mexico City during the dead of night?"

"That would be me, Louis. I did not order anyone to kill anyone. A rescue was underway."

"A rescue on Spanish soil."

"Yes, it was. The next order I will give is for the elimination of Captain Van Weylor here in the United States."

"Elimination, isn't that kidnaping and murder, Father?"

"Yes, I suppose it is. My time in hell will certainly be as long as yours, Louis. Not to change the subject, but how are you handling the loss of Madeleine? I know you two were close since your days together in Paris."

"Did you ever live with someone before you married Mother?"

"Yes, I did."

"Can you tell me about it?"

"Yes, but your mother has strong feeling about this woman, Louis."

"No doubt. Did you love her?"

"I thought I did. I had just finished my third year of study at the academy and the course entitled, 'Naval Engagements'. It was taught by your grandfather. It was also time for the summer cruises to begin. This summer cruise was to be a transatlantic adventure that consumed the entire summer break. The purpose of the cruise was, of course, to give experience to the cadets at Annapolis but it also allowed the *USS Castor, Monongahela* and *Nispsic* to complete their crews and make port of calls in Europe. Both the English and American navies were perennially short of men, but with this difference, American war ships lacking crews stayed in port, while English ships had to go to sea. The safety of Britain depended on it.

The US Navy had decided to send these three vessels on a transatlantic cruise to the European ports of: South Hampton, England; Copenhagen, Denmark; Oslo, Norway; Stockholm, Sweden; Helsinki, Finland; St.

Petersburg and Tallin, Russia; Danzig, Prussia and then back to South Hampton. In order to get to South Hampton, the three ships needed to complete their crews. They cruised from three different locations. The three ships arrived in Annapolis on June 7, 1876. All officers and hands were given 24 hours shore leave and on the morning of June 9, 1876, we left Annapolis and sailed south back down the Chesapeake and into the Atlantic Ocean. I had spent many hours aboard ships inside the Chesapeake and across the middle Atlantic to Bermuda and back to Annapolis. I was fairly comfortable with the Nispic, she was, after all, classified as a 'gun boat' and I was the ordnance officer in charge of every gun on board.

We had smooth sailing to Philadelphia, two short days, then left for Yarmouth, Nova Scotia. The temperatures dropped fifteen degrees during the five day sail. We were given 24 hours leave again, but I was assigned to ship duty because during the rougher water of the North Atlantic, some gun mounts needed adjustment and realignment. June 17th was the day we were to begin heading across the North Atlantic to Reykjavik, Iceland. Here we found bright green fields, steaming hot water pools alongside the roads and summer like temperatures. It was a long day and a short night on to Scotland. We docked in Orkney. Because they were so far north on the short hop route, Admiral Hagood decided to skip the courtesy call in South Hampton and sail directly to Copenhagen. Shore leave was granted in Copenhagen and several hundred American sailors descended upon the city. The Danes may be the most playful people in Europe. Even the capital has a 'look' about it; coppery green towers alongside gingerbread houses, inlets and millponds surrounded by willows, dozens of bicycles along cobblestone streets. Copenhagen was not used to drunken sailors, however, and we began to be arrested and returned to our ships. Admiral Hagood had seen enough, he ordered us to set sail for Ganzig, Prussia.

Prussia was not Denmark. The Danes spoke fluent English. The Prussians spoke only German. There were exactly seven Americans who spoke German and they were used as interpreters for small groups of well behaved sailors who toured the city. Two days later we docked in Tallin, Russia. Again, there were no English speaking natives and no Americans with Estonian language skills. The seven

German speaking interpreters sought out those Estonians who also spoke German and in this manner they toured Katherine the Great's summer palace and the city of Tallin. The next day we docked in St. Petersburg as the midnight sun was just beginning to catch the gold on the spires and domes throughout the city. By design, it was to be the world's most beautiful city, and the capital of its largest empire. Peter the Great, Czar of all Russia, had commanded that a "window to the west" be built to replace the old capital, Moscow. His wife, Katherine I, succeeded him and continued the construction of the city. She was succeeded by her two daughters Czarina Elizabeth and Katherine II. The city gained its most beautiful buildings after Peter's death.

It was not until we docked in Helsinki, that we learned that Finland and Russia had been at war since the days of Adam and Eve. They are not ethnic related even though they share a common geographic border. Finland was settled by nomadic tribes from central Asia.. Their language belongs to the Finno-Ugrian group, which is distinctly related to Hungarian and Turkish. It is not comparable with their closest neighbors; Swedes, Russians or Prussians, who over the centuries had ruled them. I found out that Finns are known for their sisu, which is untranslatable to English, but means tenacity or stubbornness. I learned this first hand when I met a beautiful young woman in a shop where I was trying to buy a piece of jewelry for your grandmother.

'For Mother, not wife?' She asked.

'No, I am not married.'

'Why you wear ring?'

'That is my class ring.'

'Can see? It say USNA 1877, it not 1877.'

'USNA is the United States Naval Academy and 1877 is my date of graduation.'

'You school boy? You virgin?'

'No, I am twenty-one years old, an adult, not a boy.'

'You look like boy, act like virgin.'

'Do you like virgin boys or men?'

'I like you, so must like boys.' She had a beautiful smile.

'You are not wearing a ring, are you married?'

'None of business for you to know, nice boy. You try pay for jewelry with US Gold coins, you not have real money?'

'Gold is real money.'

'Yes. Gold Krone is real money. Not sure about this gold from America.'

'Do you want me to go to the bank and exchange it for Krone?'

'If I come too. Noon meal time come soon. You wait on sidewalk outside.'

I considered walking on to the next shop, forgetting about trying to buy anything from this impossibly wild girl. I hesitated for just a few minutes trying to make up my mind what to do and heard from behind him, 'Hey, virgin boy from America, you miss me?' She was smiling again. 'Bank not open for lunch, we hurry or you not get Krone.' She grabbed my hand and we raced down the street and around a corner.

'Bank right here, I go with you to talk so they no cheat you.'

'My name is James, by the way. I do not know your name.'

'My name Ingrid. Not from Helsinki. I am from Sweden.'

We walked into the Bank of Helsinki and Ingrid spoke fluent Finish, too fluent to be from Sweden. She motioned for me to put two five dollar gold pieces on the counter and the teller returned several gold Krones. 'We go now, business finished.'

'Ingrid, what is your real name?'

'What you care, you not come back to Finland to see me again. You just have good time and forget about me.'

'What if I paid for a ferry for you to come from Helsinki to Stockholm tomorrow? We could spend the entire weekend in Stockholm. Are you from Stockholm?'

'No, my name is really Helga and I am from Norway.' Her eyes were sparkling and she was having fun. 'We rent a room in Stockholm?'

'I am an officer and a gentleman in the United States Navy, Helga. Of course I will rent us a room.'

'Make up mind. I thought you were virgin school boy?'

'I am both, I guess. I am sorry I asked you to come to Sweden with me, Helga. You would not have fun with a virgin.'

'I not say, I not come. I say, I am afraid to stay in same room with you. I am virgin, also. Can you show me what to do?'

'How would I know, Helga?'

'Do you want to try?'

'Yes, I want to know you better!'

In Stockholm I did not see a public building, a park, or anything that a typical tourist would see, I was looking into Helga's eyes. The weekend passed and Helga asked, 'James, would you like to buy me another ferry ticket?'

'Yes, we must get you back to Helsinki so you can open the shop tomorrow.'

'I have a holiday for the next two weeks, James. Where do you stop next on your cruise?'

'Helga, I am not sure that you should go to Oslo with me.'

'Why not? You can meet my parents in Oslo.'

'Then your name really is, Helga? Show me your passport.' She reached into her purse and withdrew a Norwegian Passport. She held it close and said, 'Do you really want to know my middle name? It is hideous.'

'No, the Norwegian Passport has convinced me that you are who you say you are. What is your last name?'

'Runden. Helga W. Runden.'

'Might as well go the whole way, Helga. What does the W. stand for?'

'Wilhemena. Is that not hideous?'

'Wilhemena, Wilhemena. That is as beautiful as you are. We will have to name our first child, William.' She burst out laughing, 'That is English, James. I hate the English.'

'You do? What did the English ever do to you?'

'Not a thing. Come on buy me a ticket to Oslo and I tell you what I think of the English.'

In Oslo, the adventure with Helga continued. I met her parents and they thanked me for bringing their daughter home for her holiday. They tried to repay me for the ferry tickets and I refused saying that Helga was like a breath of fresh air in my life. All I had ever thought about was the US Navy and now all I ever thought about was Helga. I stayed with Helga and her parents, we slept in her bedroom and I was positive that I would marry this girl."

"Wow, Dad, I had no idea!"

"Neither does your mother, let's keep it that way."

"Do you miss Helga?"

"No, you never forget your first, but your mother is the love of my life, first and always."

24

Death of Van Weylor

Spanish Embassy

The next logical step in the case was the arrest or detainment of Captain Van Weylor of the Spanish Embassy. We had testimony from six different men that Captain Van Weylor had paid them cash for murder of American citizens. In a normal situation the embassy member would be sent home. We felt that additional information could be obtained from an interrogation. The interrogation of suspects was a speciality of The Farm. It had been our experience that no one could remain silent when the proper method of interrogation was applied. It was not a matter of if the suspect talked, it was when he talked. The plan was to take him from his home or on the street. He was under constant surveillance and his whereabouts were always known to us. My father decided to take him off the streets when he and his bodyguards were leaving his home and heading for the embassy. The bodyguards, themselves might provide some useful information as well.

The detainment did not go well and a fire fight with hand guns resulted. . Two federal officers were wounded and all of the Van Weylor party were killed. The evening edition of the Washington Post had a field day reporting the shooting. The headlines read.

SHOOT OUT AT THE OK CORRAL

The location was given as, 16th and Maryland Avenue, Washington, D.C. But little else was correct, as usual, the newspapers had what the federal government let them have. The bodies had been whisked away for disposal at St. Elizabeth and a cover story was released to all the local papers.

"Yes, there was a shooting at a downtown location. Two federal agents were wounded by persons unknown. The agents were being questioned by the district police who think the two off-duty men were part of a holdup gone bad. The would-be robbers had no idea that the two men were armed. The crime rate after dark is increasing and this broad daylight attempted robbery is appalling to those of us who live and work within the district." The story was continued on page A3.

I laid the paper down and drank the rest of my supper. My sister looked across the kitchen table and said, "What?"

"What, what?"

"You know, Louis, you want to ask me something or tell me something about our father."

"Did you know that dad had a girl friend in Norway?"

"Yes, before he and mother were married."

"Why didn't you tell me?"

"Mother was crying one day and I asked her why she was crying and she told me 'about that Helga person'. I was sworn to secret status never to reveal the details."

"So why are you telling me?"

"I am not telling you the details, Louis. I am telling you I know about our father's Norwegian Tart."

"Everyone who has sex is not a tart, Louise."

"Oh, yes they are!" She laughed and threw the evening newspaper at me.

The meal would have been perfect if the telephone had not rung and Tim's voice said, "It is not over, Louis. I have been reassigned as your bodyguard. The district police found the body of Dr. Barrias across from the White House. Meet you there in twenty minutes."

25

Death of Dr. Barrias

Washington, D.C.

In thirty minutes I met Tim and explained that I could not catch a street car from Louise's apartment at this time of night and I had to hire a cab. Tim and I had been called to the scene of the murder when the victim was identified as Dr. Louis Barrias. His body was found in an alley behind a fashionable café across from the White House. There was no sign of a bodyguard, alive or dead. His body had not been mutilated, shot or stabbed. I assumed that he was injected with curarine, when I found an umbrella in the trash bin. I placed the umbrella in an evidence bag and told Tim to call St. Elizabeth, we would be accompanying the body to Dr. Water's lab.

The district police released the case to us and handed me their paper work. I slid it into my briefcase and we waited for the morgue van to arrive from St. Elizabeth. We walked back into the café and took a table by the window so we could see anyone coming or going from the alley. Tim began to ask his normal questions about why I was doing this job which required me to work at The Farm and at the Navy Yard.

"Why did you decide to become this hybrid cop, Louis?"

"What you and I do is a lot like what a police detective does, Tim, I will grant you that. I am a lawyer and you are a skilled marine scout watching my back. Together we make a great team."

"I know, you have told me that before. When did you decide to do this job?"

"Let's see, it was 1901, and the country was still unsettled from the assassination of President McKinley and my Uncle Teddy was now the President of the United States. My twin sister and I were home all summer and it was time for her to start her teaching career. She and my mother left to set up her apartment near her school. Louise and I had decided to rent a tiny apartment for the both of us. I would be in law school and she would begin teaching in Georgetown. The plan was to make our home in the Washington area. Neither of us had a close friend and neither of us was considering marriage anytime soon. My father and I drove to Georgetown and he was to drop me off at the Schneider's brownstone. General Schneider was retired and I think he missed out on his own children growing up and he wanted to spend time with those grandchildren that were left. I liked to humor him and I spent any free time with him, I think he missed my Grandfather Caldwell."

"You decided way back then you wanted to hunt killers?"

"Yes, I had decided to try to do that. On the drive over to Georgetown, I asked a lot of questions of my father. I asked him why he decided to apply to Annapolis. He answered that it was in his blood. My grandfather spent a lot of time with his children. He was older when he adopted my father in '57. My father was born in '55 and was about 18 months old or so when they took him home from the orphanage."

"Your father was adopted?"

"Yes, I asked him what month and day he was born. He answered he had no idea, my grandmother chose the date she first laid eyes on him, all covered with chicken pox."

"He had chicken pox when they first saw him?"

"That is what he told me. My father does not remember anything about coming home to the White House or even the years that he lived there with my Great Uncle James Buchanan. He was the fifteenth president. He was followed by Lincoln, the 16th, Johnson, the 17th, Grant, the 18th, Hayes, the 19th, Garfield was killed but he was the 20th, Arthur took his place just like Uncle Teddy did in 1901 and he was the 21st, Cleveland, 22nd, Harrison, 23rd, Cleveland again for the 24th, McKinley must have been our 25th president and Uncle Teddy is our 26th."

"Why were you concerned about the progression of presidents?"

"I was not. It just got me to thinking about presidential protection and the large number of criminals that go unpunished."

"What did your father say to that?"

"He asked if that was something that I might like to do after law school, be a prosecutor like my Uncle Teddy. He went to law school, also. His military career was very short. He is seen as a reformer. He began his career in New York City trying to fight the political corruption that was rampant."

"So, you patterned your life after Teddy Roosevelt?"

"No, I told my father I had not decided about what field of law I might like, but I had been talking to my Grandfather Schneider. Mr father said he knew and he thanked me for that."

"Why were you talking to your grandfather?"

"I asked my father if he knew that Grandpa Schneider killed an unarmed man because he refused to do what Grandpa told him to do. My father answered that he thought that was a tall tale repeated so many times that grandpa thought it was true."

"What did you say to that?"

I said, "I don't think so, Dad. Grandpa says he still has nightmares about it. I don't think he has told anyone about it, except me."

"Why did he tell you?"

"I asked him if he had ever killed an unarmed man when he was in the marines. He said once, he had to. Grandpa Caldwell had sent him into Mexico to get a handle on the strength of the French in northern Mexico."

"I remember my granddad, telling me stories like that, Louis."

"Anyway, Grandpa Schneider needed horses to transport crates of guns that he stored in a warehouse. He asked my Grandfather Caldwell to take him and his men down the coast a ways and up a river and wait for him to return. On his march to find horses Grandpa Schneider came across a troop of French cavalry coming down the road. He had his men hide and then ambush them."

"The men he shot were probably armed, Louis."

"No, wait, this is the interesting part. One of his men said he knew French and that they would capture the troops by making them stop along the road to help some wounded Mexicans. He passed the word that the French phrase, 'Ferma La Fenettra' meant surrender your arms."

"That means 'close the window', Louis."

"I know, the French had dismounted and were totally confused when they were captured without a shot."

"So, why did your Grandfather Schneider shoot an unarmed man?"

"He wanted the horses and was going to let the troopers go."

"What happened?"

"Grandpa Caldwell had ordered him to take all dead, wounded and live prisoners back to the boat so he could 'make them disappear at sea'".

"What?"

"That is what Grandpa Schneider said. My Grandfather Caldwell made French soldiers 'disappear' during the Civil War. Grandpa Schneider had his Mexican troops, that he was training, take the horses overland to the warehouse and he started marching the prisoners back to the ship that was 'up-the-river' so to speak. These cavalry troops were used to riding and they refused to march on foot. So Grandpa Schneider pulled his gun and pointed it at the head of the French Officer and motioned for him to walk. The captain laughed and sat down on the ground. Grandpa shot him in the head and had his body loaded on a wagon. He then walked to the next trooper and that trooper said in perfect English, 'Please sir, we need to rest'. Grandpa shot him in the foot and threw him along side the officer. The rest of the French hot footed it back to the waiting ship."

"Louis, do you believe your grandfather was a killer?"

"Which one?"

"Both. No, I mean either one."

"I think it is a true story, Tim. My question to you, is this. Do you think what they did was murder?"

"I have no idea, Louis. It was war time and it could have happened, but shooting an unarmed man is never justified. And if your grandfather threw live French soldiers over the side of his ship, then that is murder. Now, I am going to have nightmares."

"Sorry, Tim. I did not mean to upset you."

"I am not upset. Why not ask your Grandfather Caldwell what happened?"

"He is gone and we can not get any answers from him, but my Grandfather Schneider is alive and well, we will ask him."

"Louis, the van just arrived from St. Elizabeth."

We went into the alley and helped the driver lift the remains into the back of the van. Tim and I got in the cab with the driver. We continued on traveling in silence until we reached the underground entrance to the morgue at St. Elizabeth. It was amazing how many automobiles were on the streets of Washington. We pulled into the unloading bay and two lab assistants removed the body. We found Doc Waters and the three of us sat down to have a conversation, medical examiner, lawyer and marine scout.

"Doc, you see death every day. Tim and I were just discussing the legal, moral and ethical questions when one man takes the life of another.

Dr. Barrias just buried his niece and his death was a foregone conclusion on our part. We have the umbrella that we think he was killed with. His death is a revenge killing. Can you help us understand what we are facing? It is almost like serving in the military during a war."

"What about in war time? There are times that a helpless prisoner of war is simply executed so that the captors do not have to feed him, and that, gentlemen, is murder, pure and simple. It happened all the time during the last war on both sides." A light went on in my head!

"Doc, you are brilliant! Something triggered the Van Weylor's and that must have been it. Tim and I have a lot of research to do before we can solve all the pieces to this puzzle. If the Commodore brings in Captain Van Weylor's replacement at the Spanish Embassy, please notify us, we have some ideas that might bring this string of murders to an end." I jumped up and said, "Tim, I told you that in 1901, I was about to enter law school and I wanted to focus on deaths in the military during peace time. Did they happen? Were they required for service? Were there times when the President or a superior officer ordered his troops to kill people, to stop a riot, for example. Yes, yes and yes. I have what motivated the Van Weylor's."

"What the hell are you talking about, Louis?"

"General Van Weylor has former troops who served with him in Cuba, an endless supply of them. We can not capture or kill all of them. We have to take away the motive for killing."

"Which is?"

"They are killing murderers of the troops under their command in Cuba. Don't you see, killing a murderer is justified."

"What about the motive of stealing state secrets and selling them to the Germans?"

"That fits perfectly, Tim. It costs money to support an army of killers that need to come to this country from Spain. The money that comes from the sale of secrets, funds the killing. Cut off the money and the army dies from lack of funding."

Of course the only flaw in the logic was, how much of a war chest already existed in Madrid. The funds could last for years and the Van Weylors of the world would be thorns in our sides forever.

26

Working the Barrias Case

RLSO Washington

We needed to talk to Mrs. Barrias, two members of her family were murdered in a ten day period. We had caught the man who shot her niece but we had no clue who the man was that was sent from the Spanish Embassy to revenge the death of Captain Van Weylor. I did not see how anyone who had access to military or state secrets would remain safe in this town. The sale of secrets was worth millions of dollars and it would not stop until the supply of killers was exhausted. We had cut off one of the heads of the monster in Washington, D.C., but another still was alive in Madrid. General Van Weylor had made millions doing the same thing in the Philippines. He had no motive to stop. The anger in Spain had built from 1899 until it spilt over in the United States in November, 1904, with the first Jigsaw murder.

Tim did not want to go with me to interview Mrs. Barrias. He had dealt with the death of the niece and now he had to assimilate the death of the uncle. He let me do most of the questioning.

"Mrs. Barrias, we are very sorry for what you have gone through the last ten days. Can you tell us who your husband was meeting at the Café Olay?"

"No, he seemed excited about getting a new contract from the Navy and he was to sign it in the Café Olay. It was near the Army Navy Building and he was to read and sign it before going to his lab."

"Where was your husband's lab, Mrs. Barrias?"

"In Lancaster, Virginia. Somewhere called the Fairfield Institute. I think it was a government think tank. I was never there." Tim and I nodded our heads and thought 'The Farm'. I wrote in my notebook, *call the Commodore.*

"Did your husband carry a briefcase to and from his lab?"

"Oh, yes. He was never without it."

"This is important, Mrs. Barrias, did he sometimes have a chain that he used to fasten the briefcase to his wrist?"

"Yes, he did that before he left the house that day. He said he would have a new contract that he would lock in his safe at the Institute."

Tim asked a very important question. "Mrs. Barrias, did your husband have a safe at home?"

"Yes, it is in the study. Do you want me to open it?"

"Would you, Mrs. Barrias? There may be a clue to who he was meeting at the Café Olay. You know, a follow up name or time of the meeting." Tim was smiling to put the widow at ease.

"Let's go look, Major. I want to help put a stop to these senseless killings before I leave for home."

"Home?"

"Yes, I have the house for sale and as soon as it sells, I am returning to France. I never wanted to move here. If it had not been for that large German chemical company grant to conduct research in the United States, Louis would never have come to this country."

"Did Louis keep a copy of that grant in his safe, Mrs. Barrias?"

"Yes, he kept a copy of Madeleine's grant, also."

"Madeleine had a German contract to conduct research in the United States?" Some of the pieces of the puzzle just clicked into place.

"Why, yes. Not a chemical grant. Her specialization was anthropology and antiquities."

"What German company offered her the grant?"

"It was not a company, Lieutenant, it was from the German Government." Another piece just clicked into place.

We emptied the safe and separated the personal papers for Mrs. Barrias to keep. I noticed that the deed to the house was in the safe, it did not have a mortgage. The German grant must have been sizable, I thought. We thanked her for all the information that she had supplied and we headed for The Farm. We could not discuss what we had over the telephone and its party line connections. It took us an hour in the city traffic to reach the Commodore's office.

"We have just returned from the Barrias home with the mother lode, Sir. We need to discuss some things before we proceed with this information."

"Good. What did you find?" We laid all the documents on his desk and he went through them one at a time. The name Hans Becker and a telephone number was written on a single piece of paper.

"We did not recognize the number, Commodore."

"That is a number in Berlin, Tim. I have used it to alert Hans that something very important is in the pouch."

"Pouch, Sir?" Tim looked puzzled.

"Diplomatic Pouch. Hans is our station chief in Berlin." I gave a gasp of relief.

"You two are going to learn some things that are above your pay grade. Louis Barrias was a double agent working for us. Madeleine was an agent working for the Germans. Her death had to be an accident, the target was you, Tim." I glanced over at Tim and he was embarrassed by his attraction to a German spy.

"So, the jigsaw murders are over. This is the beginning of a whole new round!"

"That is right. You and your sister are in danger now, you know too much and anyone associating with you is marked also. Can your sister move to a new location?"

"We will move her tonight, Sir." Tim was tight lipped and steely eyed.

"Not to your apartment, Tim. That is the first place they will look. It has to be out of the line of fire. We have a safe house on the estate."

"Sir, what is the Fairfield Institute?"

"It is a building here at Lancaster, Louis Barrias was working on a battlefield weapon called 'mustard gas'."

"Oh, My God!"

"If the Germans get their hands on this weapon, the balance of power will change in Europe."

"Do you know who Dr. Barrias was meeting from the Army Navy Building, Commodore?"

"No, but I will find out, that's for damn sure!"

"Do you have an idea who killed Dr. Barrias?"

"The Germans, they must have discovered he was cooperating with us."

"Are the Spanish out of the loop? Can we concentrate on the German aspects of the case?"

"No, not as long as the Spanish are selling items to the Germans, they are both embassies of concern for us."

27

Message to Berlin
US State Department

THE STATE DEPARTMENT WEASEL-WORDED A soft message of complain to the capitol of the German Empire. It warned of trade sanctions against the Klienhorst Chemical Works of Frankfort, Germany. When I read a copy sent to The Farm, I said, "All this will do is alert the German Government that we are watching their spies in this country. We need to send a strong message of 'hands off, dumbkopfs.' This does not sound like the policy, 'speak softly but carry a big stick'."

"It certainly has the *speak softly* part down pat." Tim was smiling. "Commodore?"

"Yes, Louis."

"What has Hans Becker found out in Berlin?"

"They have sent someone to Frankfort to find out if the Klienhorst Chemical Works is manufacturing mustard gas."

"How are they going to check that?"

"Hans has two men working inside the chemical works. The formula that Dr. Barrias was working on was C4H8CI2S. This is a colorless, or brown, oily liquid which evaporates slowly to a poison gas that causes burns, blindness and death. They are looking for the liquid compound, if they find the gas, we will not hear from them."

"How many forms of the compound are there?" I asked.

"The Germans are working on phosgene and lewisite, a variation of what Dr. Barrias was developing here at the Fairfield Institute."

"What if some of the Barrias papers were sold to Berlin from someone in Spain, someone who is beyond question? The papers containing the formula would immediately be sent to Frankfort for testing. Suppose the papers contained some rather exciting short cuts to the production of the formula? Suppose, further, that in the process of reproducing this formula short cut an explosion took out the entire Klienhorst Chemical Works?"

"Louis, what do you have in mind?"

"I need to talk to the Barrias team members still at Fairfield and see if what I have proposed is possible. If it is possible, how many months or years, will it delay the German version of mustard gas?"

"That would depend upon how many other sites are working on the same project." The Commodore was thinking how he could take out multiple sites.

"Louis, you and Tim get over to the Fairfield Institute, here is a hand written pass to get you in to see Dr. Barrias' partner. Ask for a Dr. Ernest Abbel, you both know him, he went to Mexico with you."

"How many Germans do you have working for you?"

"As many as I can find in this country who do not agree with the Kaiser and his plan to dominate the whole of Europe. In fact, I would love for you to bring back as many scientists and engineers who would like to escape the German war machine."

"Back, I am going to Germany?"

"If a highly unstable version of C4 mustard gas can also be made into an explosive, then you will devise and carry out the termination of Klienhorst Chemical Works."

"How much time do we have?"

"We?"

"Yes, I am not leaving here without Tim."

"Tim has no language skills, Louis."

"Yes, that is why we are going to have a lanyard that reads, *I am a deaf mute,* printed in both Spanish and German. Tim and I will use a form of sign language to communicate when in the presence of those in Madrid or Berlin. What do you think, Tim?"

"I think you are going to get me killed." But he was smiling and he gave me a thumbs up.

"Let's find out if the lab here can make us some C4 explosive before we decide if Tim is a deaf mute. Get over to the lab and talk to them. Call me if it is possible and I will write a black operation request and send it to your father."

AN HOUR LATER we were talking with Dr. Abbel in his office.

"We have already done exactly what you propose, it was an accident, of course, one of the steps was reversed and we produced C4 liquid which exploded here in the lab. It was a tiny amount and that is why I am still alive and talking to you."

"Can you reproduce that mistake again? Only this time, I would like you to produce a very heavy liquid or a paste."

"Yes, with some safeguards, we could do that."

"How many days will it take you to produce a paste?"

"It would depend on how much you would need and how you might wish to detonate it."

"We would like an electrical current detonation. If, for instance, we have a copper wire and we wrap the paste around it then the current passing through the wire should detonate the paste. Is that possible?"

"It would be easier if we made a semi- solid so you could just push the end of the copper wire or small copper tube into a block of C4."

"That would be great, Dr. Abbel, when can we expect to see a sample?"

"In a couple of years."

"We need something in less than a month, Doc."

"For that, I would need written instructions from the Commodore. The Commodore would have to request that the work on the mustard formula be halted, temporarily, because all our efforts and liquids would be used in the distillation of the liquid into a semi-solid."

"Let's call the Commodore!"

28

Message to Madrid

US Embassy, Madrid

The message sent to Madrid was of a different nature entirely. The US Embassy in Madrid was like all foreign embassies that the United States maintained throughout the world. The message from NCI was received on May 1, 1905. It stated that a sanction was to be performed in the next twenty days. The sanction was for the Spanish Minister of War, General Van Weylor. The terms of the sanction were standard. The general should meet his death by accident or natural causes. There was always the mishap with an automobile, but the general did not drive, he had a driver. The usual skiing accident was not on the table, it was May, not skiing weather. Death in a public place was always preferred, there should be plenty of witnesses to the fact that the general had a tragic accident. The accident could be in a café or restaurant, choking was always a dramatic sight to behold.

The cabinet of Regent Montero Rios met every Friday at a different restaurant in Madrid. It was an opportunity to discuss, in a relaxed atmosphere the current matters of state. One of the matters for discussion was the boiling situation in Washington, D.C. There was open warfare between the Spanish Embassy and the United States federal government. The military attache assigned to the embassy was missing and the newspapers had not reported his death. They did report that he had been recalled to Madrid, this was a lie. General Van Weylor had not recalled his nephew. He would be forceful with his Regent, the personal representative of King Alfonso XIII, and demand that the whereabouts of his nephew be explained by the Americans.

In 1905, each of the US Embassies abroad contained an infirmary and pharmacy. The pharmacy, of course, contained a number of drugs. The combination of drugs caused a variety of reactions when introduced to the human body. Some of these drugs were traceable, others were not. The drugs chosen to introduce to the general were *fexofenadyne* and *levetiracetine*. Both of these leave the stomach within thirty minutes of ingestion and are untraceable after one hour. Unless the Regent of Spain ordered an autopsy within an hour of death, the accident would be believed. The plan was simple. Locate the restaurant in Madrid, insert a dessert cook into the kitchen, lace all of the food with fexofenadyne and contaminate a second dish that only the general would be eating, the dessert. It was the combination of the drugs that would induce the coughing, choking and finally death. A first attempt was attempted the first Friday of May. A simple ruse was used to locate the restaurant. Each of the most probable restaurants within walking distance of the Royal Palace were entered on Friday morning. An official looking diplomat with a clip board entered and started writing notes. When the head waiters saw this they rushed to the side of the diplomat and asked what they could do for him. The clip board carriers simply said they were checking the restaurant in advance of the noon meal being prepared for the Regent's Cabinet. If the head waiter confirmed that the Regent was coming, the clip board carrier asked if the special desserts cook had arrived. If the head waiter said that a mistake must have been made, then the man carrying the clip board apologized and quickly left the restaurant.The single restaurant was identified, and a sequence of events began to unfold. Extra kitchen help was always employed to prepare a Regent's cabinet meal and the new dessert cook was not questioned. The impostor would appear to assist in the preparation of the desserts and other dishes preferred by the Regent. In his apron was sewn the vials of the two drugs. Once the orders were placed in the kitchen, then the first drug was introduced to each plate that would be served. General Van Weylor loved his flan, his dessert would contain the second drug. An additional drugged dessert would also be prepared in case the general would send back his dessert, a practice he was known for throughout Madrid.

The general ate all of his main courses and had a running conversation about the American problem. The general's dessert came, he took one bite and spat it out on his plate. He complained to the waiter and asked for a replacement, the second drugged dessert was brought to him and he consumed the entire thing and he commented on how delicious it was to the Regent. In ten minutes he began to cough and a minute later he was choking. His face turned blue and an ambulance was called. He died on the way to the hospital.

In Port of New York, Tim and I were about to board the Star of the East, transatlantic steam ship. Louise had come as far as New York to see her brother and her brand new husband off. It had taken Dr. Abbel and his team longer than the month to distill and stabilize the C4 explosive. I had asked him what the German inspectors would find in the remains of the explosions in the chemical factories that were targeted for elimination.

"Louis, the traces of C4 will be assumed to be part of the C4H8CI2SO4 formula that they are producing. They will assume that a leak occurred and that they better find the leak before it happens again. They will know there was not a leak if all the factories explode on the same night. I would stagger the explosions to make it look like the problem is getting worse and the leakage has not been found."

"That is the smartest approach, Doc, but the risk to the men who have to set the charges is too great. All the factories have to go up in the same night. We can stagger the times of detonation though, it would really send up a red flag if every factory producing mustard gas is exploded at 20:24 hours."

"It is still risky, the Germans will retaliate when they finally figure out what happened."

The Star of the East docked in Corunna, the seaport for the Provence of Coruna, Spain. There would be no record of Tim or I entering Germany. We had blocks of C4 sewn into the lining of our suitcases and copper tubes inserted into our belts and the bands of the hats that we were wearing. These were in plain sight for anyone to ask about the strange ornamentation. No one asked, however. Coils of fine copper wire were inside the hat bands and inside our pant waists out of sight. Inside our brief cases were letters from General Van Weylor to us and carbon copies of letters sent to him. All of these were careful forgeries, of course, courtesy of The Farm. We were to use these to convince the Spanish that the sale of documents was pending and we were to receive payments and return home. If we could not get admittance to the Royal Palace and the office of the Ministry of War, then the papers would be planted in the deceased ministry's office during the dead of night.

We bought tickets to Madrid and rode the train overnight into the capital city. We rented a room in a four star hotel and we got some sleep until the noon hour arrived. We started our day during the normal siesta period in all of Madrid. The offices within the Royal Palace would not be fully staffed and those that were there would not be diligent. We stopped at the front gate and I practiced my Spanish asking to see the acting Minister of War. I told him we had a letter of appointment and I handed him one of the forged letters from my briefcase. The time was cleared typed and he nodded his head and said something to Tim. Tim reached for his lanyard which said, "I am a deaf mute." The guard read it and shouted the same phrase he had said before. Tim looked at me and did the "It's bitty spider" with his fingers and I nodded and said to the palace guard.

"He is deaf, thank you for your concern." We entered the palace and found the office of the Ministry of War. I again pulled the same letter to show to a man sitting at a desk, obviously the minister's secretary. He would know he had not typed the letters, but was he replaced when the new minister took the general's job. We would have to chance it. I handed the forged letter to him. He read it, nodded his head and showed us into the minister's office. I tried my Spanish again and the minister recognized my accent.

"I speak English. Please sit down. General Van Weylor died suddenly last week, I am now the acting minister. Do you have something from the general to prove who you are and why you have come to Madrid?"

"Of course, we both work in the Fairfield Institute." At the mention of the Fairfield Institute his eyes lit up. I handed him the short cut for the formula that Dr. Barrias was working on.

"We also have copies of the letters sent from Minister Van Weylor to your embassy in Washington and passed on to us. We have stolen the formula and can not return to the United States. But with the final payment due us, we can retire in Spain and my Spanish will improve over time." I was smiling.

"I am new and my secretary is new. I will phone Berlin and find out what they are willing to pay us for this formula. I will, of course, not give them the full description, otherwise we will receive nothing. Do you agree to the normal split of the payment from Germany?"

"Of course, I speak German. It is better than my Spanish. If you would place the call to Berlin and introduce me, I would be happy to get the best possible price for us." His eyes lit up again. We had traded one corrupt minister for another.

"Of course, I will place the call and the operator will ring us back. I will have some refreshments brought into us."

Tim memorized the name and location of the man whom the minister contacted in Berlin. This name and location would be forwarded to Hans Becker for elimination or turned into an asset. The phone rang and the minister answered it and read part of one of the letters, as soon as the short cut for the production of C4H8CI12S was mentioned the phone was handed to me.

My German was better than my Spanish and a price was decided upon. I asked if the normal split between the American finder and the Spanish transfer was in place. I indicated that I would like him to hold my split and I would pick it up in Berlin as I delivered the stolen documents. I indicated that there were more documents than the short cut. He agreed to see us at the first of the week and I wrote down the address and telephone number. I handed the phone back to the Minister of War. Something remarkable happened then. The minister said, "You two were lucky that you left when you did. The Institute is scheduled for destruction, our agents will place explosives inside the traitors offices. Abbel's and Barrias' work will be destroyed. The United States will be set back at least five years in their ability to produce quantities of mustard gas.

29

Warning Sent

Madrid, Spain

We left the Royal Palace and hurried to our hotel and checked out. We needed to catch the train to Paris. I bought two coach class tickets at the Madrid station while Tim removed our diplomatic passports hidden inside the suitcases. We needed to travel with our suitcases, if we bought first class tickets, the suitcases would be checked in the baggage car. The train made many stops on route and the first stop inside France we left the train and walked to the telegraph office.

"I would like to send a telegram to my father in the United States."

"Certainly, Monsieur. What is the address for delivery?"

"James Caldwell, 2167 Woodland Way, Washington, D.C."

"What is the body of the message, Monsieur?"

"Having fun, wish Uncle Louis Barrias were here. Tell his partner that his job is a killer and he needs a vacation. Paris would be lovely this time of year."

"And the signature, Monsieur?"

"Your Son and partner OPS."

"OPS, Monsieur, I do not understand."

"It means I will get an immediate reply."

"But Monsieur, the telegram must be sent to London, then through the cable, it will not arrive until tomorrow."

"Is there another, faster, way to send the message?"

"Not that I am aware of, Monsieur."

I thanked him, paid him for the telegram and we bought two more tickets to Paris. Tim looked at me and said, "We forgot to have a neck tag made for French, Louis."

"Take that off and leave it off, you have just been cured."

"How did that happen?"

"Direct orders from a superior officer. When we get to Paris let's find the American Embassy and show them our passports and credentials. I fear that tomorrow will be too late to warn Dr. Abbel."

THE TRAIN ARRIVED and we took a cab to the American Embassy. We were already too late, news of the explosion in the Fairfield Institute had already reached the American Embassies in Madrid, Paris and Berlin. A detailed message in code was waiting for Tim and I.

1nmd4 l96mf Lotp9066 m4o per57nfoe:
(FIELD AGENTS CALDWELL AND JACOBSON:)

JIDKLFI HT 2KDLR. FKOSLW9 2EG HRR4B INP RET IWOKL
(PROCEED TO BERLIN. DELIVER THE GOODS FOR THE WORKS.)

DKEOP CDMOSQNO NR PQT NR DVK PERT QWERTYUIOP ASDE
(SUPERVISE, DO NOT DO THE WORK YOURSELVES. HANS)

QWE QWERT AS DFGHJ ISE ZXCVBNMKGFRD.
(HAS UPDATE OF PLANS FOR IMPLEMENTATION.)

ZXCVBNM ASDFG
(ADMIRAL LOWE)

"The Commodore got a promotion, Tim. Look, he is an Admiral now."

"I thought you were not rank conscious, Louis."

"When it is my boss, I am. When it involves me, I never know what type of Lieutenant I am."

"Do we take the overnight again to Berlin?"

"It will not take overnight, Tim. That is what I like about Europe, every thing is much closer than at home. I will wire Hans to expect us in the morning. This afternoon we need to call on Madeleine's parents here in Paris."

"Madeleine was a German agent, Louis. I do not want to spend time with her parents."

"Let me put it this way, Sergeant Major, where I go, you go."

"I can't argue with that, Lieutenant."

"Lieutenant Commander!"

"See, you do know what rank you are, some of the time."

TIM WAS RIGHT, the meeting with Madeleine Barrias' parents was a disaster. They blamed me for the death of their daughter and told me so in direct words that stung to hear. Tim said he was going to ask Madeleine to marry him and they burst out laughing at him and ridiculed him until he rose from the chair he was sitting in and told me that he would wait outside until I was finished with the meeting. I looked at her parents and said, "You know I loved your daughter and would have done anything for her, including the conversion to become a Catholic, but she threw the offer back in my face and slept with my partner you just insulted. Tim Jacobson is a man of honor, your daughter was a whore." It went down hill from there until I left the house and found Tim with red eyes and a set jawbone that twitched.

"You were right, as always, Tim Jacobson. This was a total waste of time. You can not convince a parent that their little saint was really a sinner."

"You did not tell them she was spy, did you?"

"No, I forgot to add that to the list of sins for them to think about, Tim. We need to get organized and on our way to Berlin. The Germans are going to be sorry that they ever decided to escalate the Jigsaw murders with murders of their own. The entire US delegation to Mexico is dead except for you, me and Dr. Langley. One of the three of us will be next."

"Pleasant thought, let's go blow up some chemical plants in Germany!"

WE SLEPT THE NIGHT in the basement of the American Embassy, Paris. In the morning we boarded the first train headed for Berlin and arrived to meet with the man I had talked to in the Minister of War's office in Madrid. We found the address, Tim put on his lanyard printed in German and we entered to find our contact.

"Heir Weiselman, this is my partner from the Fairfield Institute." Tim bowed shook the man's hand and clicked his heels like a real Prussian. He raised the lanyard so Heir Weiselman could read it and bowed again. We all sat and I started handing the forged documents to our contact. He really wasn't interested in reading anything until we showed him the fatally flawed document for the short cut to producing mustard gas. If anyone tried this, the plant would go up in a giant explosion. Our contact was not a chemist and he quickly agreed to pay us the amount requested. He walked over to a wall safe and began to pile stacks of British pound sterling on his desk.

"May I inspect one of the bundles, Heir Weiselman?"

"It is not counterfeit, Dr. Wenten." He said to me. Dr. Wenten was the cover name for me that Tim and I had decided upon before entering the office.

"I see that, Heir Weiselman, one can not be too careful these days. This is our retirement, we can not return to the United States."

"My government is dealing with the Spanish in this matter. This is the first time that we have met with any Americans."

"German Americans, Heir Weiselman."

"Of course. Thank you for delivering these documents, Van Weylor was a greedy pig, I am very glad not to have to work with him again."

We left the office and proceeded back to the train platform to see Hans Becker waiting for us. I had not seen Hans since Monterey language school. We had written and talked on the telephone, of course. He was the same old Hans.

"Louis, mine friend, vos is los width ja?" I turned to Tim and said, "In English, that was, Louis, my friend, what is up with you."

"That was in English, dumbkopf!" Hans would never change.

"Not in any English I know, Hans. I have been practicing my Dutch. Do you want to hear the same phrase in Dutch?"

"Got, no. Your Dutch is worse than mine English." We both broke out into laughter.

"This is my partner, Hans, his name is Tim Jacobson and he understands me as much as you do."

"Dat, is quite a complement, Tim. I had to babysit him all da way through language school. Are you da babysitter now?"

"Ja, mine job is never done!" Tim was smiling.

"I like dis, Tim Jacobson, Louis, let's keep him."

"Right, Hans!"

"Right, Louis!" Hans put his arm around Tim's shoulder and whispered something to him.

"I heard that!"

30

Operation Berlin

American Embassy

Hans drove like a maniac through the streets of Berlin and I thought that we were all dead twice before we reached the American Embassy. We took our suitcases to the ops center and unloaded the blocks of C4 and the pound sterling. I broke off a tiny pinch of the corner of one of the blocks and inserted a fine copper wire. I twisted it to a pencil timer made out of copper tubing. I placed the tiny charge under the waste basket that I had placed on the table of the briefing room. Hans had called all of his assets in for a briefing on the new explosive from the United States.

"Now, gentlemen, when I place the end of this wire into any electrical outlet, such as we have here the timer is activated. Set your watches and let's time the detonation fuse." I stuck the end of the wire into a wall outlet with my bare hands, I had forgotten that European household voltage was 220 not 110 as in the United States. I burned my finger. "Be sure to wear gloves when you set your charges." I said through gritted teeth. In exactly three minutes, the charge exploded and the waste basket was flattened against the ceiling and came crashing down on the table, which now contained a giant flash burn mark about two feet across.

"Ja, you paying for dat table, agent Caldwell." Hans was smiling, he was enjoying the show. I reached across the table and grabbed a bundle of pound sterling.

"Keep the change, Hans." There was laughter from his men he had assembled.

"The point is, the time can be adjusted by using a longer or shorter pencil fuse. I will not be going into any of the chemical plants assigned to you. I wish I could go into each one and set the fuses personally for what they did to my friend, Dr. Abbel. The President of the United States wants to send a message to the Kaiser. Each plant will explode at the same time, there is no way the Germans can not put two and two together and come up with sabotage. They will be unable to detect what blew up the plants, however. All they will find is some copper wire."

Tim turned to Hans and said, "The message is, if you fuck with us, we will bring the whole load of horse shit and make you eat it."

"I would have used less colorful language, gentlemen, but, yes, the President has gotten away from 'speak softly and carry a big stick' to 'here is how the big stick feels up your ass.'"

"Ja, I like bode of dos sayings, can I use dem?" Hans had everyone in tears from laughing at him.

"What?" Hans did not have a clue that everyone in that room would have followed him off a cliff if he was their leader. I wished I would have team members like that some day. Then I looked over at Tim and realized that I already had one.

THE RAIDS WERE SET for the following Monday night. Hans' assets needed travel time to get to the five locations in Germany. The demonstrations and training were over. Tim and I had divided the blocks of C4 into five groups. We handed out the copper pencil fuses from our hats and pants. The copper wire was tested and exchanged for a heavier gage to handle the 220 voltage that would be in each of the chemical plants. We were to say goodbye to Hans and leave Berlin before the first plant went sky high. I would have loved to be present at one of the plant sites, but we knew that all travel would be restricted after the massive attack at five chemical plants. Here is what happened at each of the sites as reported to Hans in the after action reports.

Frankfort: *The Klienhorst Chemical Works is one of several war production plants inside a larger industrial complex. After we set the C4 blocks and inserted the timers, we ran outside the fence and walked as quickly as we could, so as not to attract attention to ourselves. There was only a skeleton crew on the third shift, but all of these workers perished in the chain of explosions that followed the first C4 blast. The tanks of mustard gas producing liquid began to explode one by one in a chain reaction until the entire plant collapsed upon itself and sent balls of fire into the adjacent munitions plants. These plants exploded and sent flames and red hot debris into adjacent warehouses. In four hours the entire industrial complex was in ruins. As an observer, I am lucky to be alive.*

Hamburg: *The Wassinhaver Chemical Works is outside of Hamburg and closed during the night. Only a night watchman had to be avoided when we broke a window and entered the factory. We placed our charges under the mustard tanks, set the fuses and ran for our lives. In three minutes the Wassinhaver Chemical Works was a smoking hole in the ground. Not a single brick was left, it seemed that most building materials melted in the extreme heat of the explosion.*

Dusseldorf: *This is a beautiful old city with a classical cathedral across the square from Muching Chemical and Pharmacy Company. No one was present at the time of entry, not even a night watchman. We taped the C4 charges to the sides of the mustard tanks, set the fuses and casually walked across the square. The explosion blew out all the stained glass window of the front of the cathedral, while burning my eyelashes and eyebrows off my face. I had never seen or experienced anything like it in my lifetime.*

Hanover: *The Villhelm Processing building is no more, it was standing one minute and gone the next. The debris is in small pieces the size of a shoe or smaller and is scattered over four city blocks.*

Leipzig: *The Leipzig Petrol-chemical plant is near a refinery and it will burn until it is extinguished by fire fighters. The estimated time to control the fires are one week. The economic loss to the Leipzig area is massive. I doubt that the gas manufacturing facilities will ever be rebuilt in a populated area again.*

The reactions in Madrid and Berlin were immediate. In Berlin, the orders went out to stop the short cut method of producing mustard gas to the remaining plants still in production. The orders arrived too late and these plants exploded during the production runs. In Madrid, orders went out to the Spanish Embassy in Washington, stop all killing of American citizens. The big stick was beginning to have an effect. The German government broke all contacts with Spain and demanded that reparations be paid for the destroyed mustard gas plants. They also demanded the whereabouts of the two Americans, Dr. Wenten and the 'deaf mute' in Spain. A contract was written for the termination of these two as soon as they could be located in Spain. In the off chance that this might be American agents and not defectors hiding in Spain, a cable of instructions was sent to the German Embassy, Washington, D.C.

Military Attache Von Wurtemberg
Embassy of the Greater Prussian and German Empire
Washington, D.C.
United States of America

My Dear Von Wurtemberg:

It pains me to tell you that the two American agents known as Dr. Wenten and the deaf mute have escaped to France. They have changed identities and are booked aboard the French Ocean Liner *Enceintes des Philbus.* They are posing as brothers returning from business in Paris. We have two agents booked on the same passage. They are to identify, eliminate and dispose of the bodies at sea. The Enceintes is sailing from Calais, they are scheduled to dock in New York. They are not traveling under their real names, but we have determined that Wenten is really the son of Admiral Caldwell, the director of the Naval Intelligence unit within the White House. His companion is probably his driver, a Timothy Lee Jacobson.

Because of the mass destruction to our war facilities, war with France and the expansion of our empire has been delayed at least two years. The death toll of workers within these plants must be avenged. We must show the

> Americans that it is not their concern what happens in Europe. I, therefore, ordered that the two individuals be eliminated before they reach Washington, D.C. Should the two agents reach New York, you are to have agents waiting at the docks to resolve the problem. Supreme headquarters does not want any of the details of how or where this is accomplished. Notification of the deaths is required.
>
> Otto Von Bulow, Prime Minister of Prussia and Chancellor, German Empire

THE DAY BEFORE, Tim and I boarded our train in Berlin and headed for the Port of Calais in northern France. Hans and I had left a rather sloppy trail for the Germans to follow. Hans had purchased two train tickets in the names of Lenard and Walter Steeve to the Port of Calais. Then he also booked passage on the "Enceintes des Philbus" in the names of Lenora and Walter Steeve to New York City. When Tim and I reached Calais the first explosion had not occurred and we purchased ferry tickets to Dover, England, in the names of Lord and Lady Edward Turnbull. Tim was costumed as the lord from a party shop in Calais, the French loved their costumed balls. I, unfortunately, was much smaller than Tim and I spent nearly an hour getting into my corset and makeup for the short trip across the channel. A channel ferry took nearly half a day and we got some rather odd looks from the ferry passengers. I was never so glad to see the white cliffs of Dover and the seven sisters appear on the horizon.

At the ferry terminal I went into the woman's dressing rooms with my suitcase and found an empty stall. I peeled off everything and stuffed it into my suitcase. I removed my men's clothing and dressed. England had never provided a combination restroom and toilet in the same space. The toilet and wash basin were always separate, so I timed my escape from the dressing room when no other women were present and headed for the men's toilet to remove my heavy makeup. Again, with the strange looks, have they never seen a beautiful man with such long eyelashes! I smiled and entered the toilet and finished my preparations for the train ride to South Hampton.

31

Death Takes a Holiday

Enceintes des Philbus

A French ocean liner is not like the transatlantic steam ship that we boarded in South Hampton for our transportation to Washington. The *Enceintes des Philbus* was like a floating hotel and the two decoys from the American Embassy, Berlin, were going to enjoy our tickets to New York, stay on board and then return to Calais. If the Germans had managed to pick up our trails from Berlin, they would be following two other agents to New York, where they would appear to vanish.

The two German agents, one Heinrick Hemmler and one Karl Witenshon, showed their false passports and purchased last minute tickets to New York. They asked the ship's Purser where their business partners, the Steeves ,were cabined for the cruise. They were told that they could be paged to meet them in the Schooner Bar. The agents were sure that this was not a good idea and said, "That is quite alright, we are dining with them tonight at the same table, we will see them then."

The purser watched the two German men walk away from his desk and thought this was odd and checked to see what the evening dining reservations were for Lenora and Walter Steeve, an American couple returning home from a holiday in France. He found no such names as those on the passports of the two German business men and picked up his ship's telephone and placed a call to the Emerson Suite.

"Allo, Monsieur Steeve?"

"Yes, this is Walter Steeve."

"Monsieur Steeve, do you know a Heir William Carltonburg or Otto Von Whittenberg?"

"No, we do not know these German gentlemen."

"They were just at my desk, inquiring about your cabin location. Since you are preferred suite guests, I told them you could be paged and you and Frau Steeve would meet them in the Schooner Bar."

"Are you sure that they showed you the proper passports? It sounds like a practical joke to me. Why not have both of them paged to meet their party in the bar, anyway and we will observe from a distance to see if we know them and the joke will be on them."

"Oui, Monsieur, as you wish."

Walter Steeve hung up the telephone and said, "Lenora, my dear, the act is about to begin."

"So soon, I am not unpacked." She dropped what she was doing and pinned on her rather large dress hat, batted her eyes at her co-worker from the American Embassy, Berlin, and said, "Frederick, my dear, Frau Steeve is prepared." They left the Emerson Suite and headed for the ship's bar when they heard the announcement for Heir Carltonburg to meet his party in the Schooner Bar. The two German agents froze in their tracks, "What has the idiot Purser done?"

"We will split up, you go and I will watch."

The agents separated and headed for the ship's bar. The three entered the bar at the same time. They did not recognize each other and the watcher did not look twice at the elderly man and woman in the huge hat. Both partes ordered a round of drinks and waited for the other party to arrive. When an hour passed, the Steeves left and the watcher sat down beside his partner and said, "We will need to find someone else working in the purser's office and offer him 100 pounds sterling to obtain a passenger list. That will tell us where everyones cabin is located and we can isolate the cabins with two men traveling together."

"Yes, we have the physical descriptions, it should not be hard to locate and then identify the two Americans for the their elimination before we reach New York." He was smiling, after all, it took nearly a week to sail from Calais to New York, there was plenty of time. The agents began to relax. They returned to their cabin and changed into casual touring clothes. They began having conversations with the desk clerks outside the Purser's office.

"I was sent here from Paris to locate two American brothers sailing on this crossing. I know it is against the ship's policy to reveal any cabin assignments. I want to make it worth your while to give me this information and he handed a tri-folded 100 pound note so the desk clerk could palm it.

"What is the name of the parties you wish to locate, Monsieur?"

"Steeve."

"One moment, Monsieur, I will need to look up the information for you." He left the front desk and entered the Purser's office.

"We have another request for the location of Mr. and Mrs. Steeve. Can you come to the window and see if this is the same man that requested this information from you, Monsieur Le Purser?"

The Purser looked through the small window and nodded his head. "Oui, it is the same man. Make a note of this request, keep the money he gave you and return with the information that he requested. I will notify ship's security that we have a problem with two men and they are to be watched for the remainder of the voyage. It would be bad for our image to have trouble with these two German pigs."

The desk clerk returned with the information that Mr. and Mrs. Steeve were in the Emerson Suite.

"There must be some mistake. The Steeves are brothers traveling together. Do you have other Steeves as passengers?"

"I can check for you, Monsieur, and he held his hand out for another note." He left the desk and entered the office again. This time the Purser was watching and wondered what was next.

"Monsieur Le Purser, he is not requesting information about the Emerson Suite guests. He is looking for brothers with the same last name. Do we have guests aboard with the last names of Steeve, that is a very unusual American name, is it not?"

"Something is not right here, Marcel. Look, we have three unoccupied inside cabins all registered to Steeve, none of these persons came aboard to occupy the cabins. They were paid for but not used."

"I think the two men you talked to are German Secret Police or worse, Monsieur Le Purser. Let's have some fun with them. They can not harm anyone by observing empty cabins, nes pa?"

"Return for now and tell the gentleman that we have three more Steeves aboard. See what his reaction to that is."

Marcel returned to the front desk and said, "Monsieur, we have four cabins with the last name of Steeve, what are the Christians names that you are seeking?"

"Lenard and Walter." The desk clerk held out his hand again and again a note was placed into it. The desk clerk retreated again into the Purser's office.

"He is seeking a Lenard and Walter, Monsieur Le Purser."

"I have alerted the Captain via ship's phone that we have a problem with these two men. He has agreed to have the empty cabins filled with security men and unpacked suit cases so the borsch will have a difficult time arresting anyone. You may give the man the locations of the cabins after an hour. That should be enough time for us to set the trap." The desk clerk returned with a frown on his face.

"Monsieur, I do not know what to say. All four cabins are reserved with a variation of the same names. The Emerson Suite is reserved by a Lenora and Walter Steeve, a married couple. The cabin on the fourth deck is reserved by a Mrs. Lenard Steeve and a Mr.Walter Wenton, a man and a woman. The cabin on the third deck is reserved by a Leonard Wenton and a Walter Steeve, two men. The cabin on the fifth deck is reserved by a L. Wenton and a W. Steeve, sexes unknown. Can you give me a physical description of your two male friends and I can have a porter contact them with your name. What is your name, Monsieur?"

"My employer in Paris did not think it would be this difficult to locate two brothers. Perhaps I should send a wireless to Paris and inquire what to do in this situation."

"That is an excellent idea, Monsieur, you should have your answer within the hour. Return to me when you have further instructions. It has been a pleasure to assist you, Monsieur, I am sure." The German agent asked for directions to the radio room and departed. The desk clerk picked up the ship's telephone and rang the radio room.

"This is Marcel, I am sending a German gentleman to you so he can send a wireless. The Captain would like a copy of whatever is sent."

It took a few minutes to find the radio room and the agents assigned to find and eliminate the Steeve brothers knocked and entered.

"May we send a telephone message to our employer?"

"Mae Oui, Monsieurs. What is the location of your employer?"

"Paris. The number is Regent382."

"Merci, Monsieurs. One of you may use the private booth over there." He was pointing to a glass door in the side wall.

"Merci." Heinrick walked to the door just in time for a man with headphones to listen to the conversation on the other side of the ship's bulkhead.

"German Embassy, who is calling please?"

"This is Otto1."

"What is your report, please?"

"We have located four male suspects traveling under the name Steeve, please advise us what to do."

"Hold one moment." More than a minute passed.

"Your superior says to terminate all four and report to the company representatives waiting in New York. Do not contact this number again." There was the sound of a disconnect on the Paris end of the conversation.

WITHIN FIFTEEN MINUTES the Captain of the *Enceintes des Philbus* was reading the transcript of the telephone call. He thanked the porter and walked from the bridge to the Purser's office. He entered without knocking and handed the transcript to the Purser.

" Marcel is a good man, Pierre, he did this on his own, without instructions from you?"

"Oui, Mon Captain. He is a fine staff member, what do you make of this call?"

"Obviously, the two German's were sent to kill the Americans traveling in the Emerson Suite. No one has broken any laws of the sea and can not be arrested. But that does not stop us from contacting the nearest American Embassy and alerting them that four Americans are being followed and may be killed at the first opportunity."

"But, Sir, we do not have four Americans with the name of Steeve on board. The Emerson Suite is occupied by a wealthy, older American couple. The three inside cabins are reserved but not occupied at this time. We are in the process of having security move into them and make them look occupied for the benefit of the Germans, as per your suggestion."

"This is what we shall do, Pierre, contact the American Counsel in Calais and say that two German agents are interested in the two Americans in the Emerson Suite. They can not be interested in empty cabins."

"Oui, Mon Captain."

"Ask the Counsel for assistance in identifying the two German agents, send the physical descriptions. We can provide time for the sending and receipt of messages by having the two Germans explore the empty cabins, tell security to stay out of the cabins. We will continue to observe the two Germans, tell security to be obvious that they are being watched."

"Oui, Mon Captain."

THE INCOMING MESSAGE from the French ocean liner just departed from Calais was forwarded to Paris. The time constraint of one hour was forwarded as well. The Paris Embassy knew nothing of this matter and contacted the American Embassy in Berlin. Berlin sent two messages, one back to Paris and one to Captain Du Pont aboard the ocean liner.

PARIS

THANK YOU FOR THIS INFORMATION, MISSION PRESENTLY UNDERWAY ABOARD THE *ENCEINTES DES PHILBUS*. PLEASE FORWARD ALL MESSAGES FROM CALAIS.

HANS BECKER

ENCEINTES DES PHILBUS
OFF THE COAST OF FRANCE

DEAR CAPTAIN DU PONT:

THE TWO PHYSICAL DESCRIPTIONS MATCH THOSE OF GERMAN AGENTS HEINRICK HEMMLER AND KARL WITENSHON OF THE SS. TAKE CARE NOT TO CONFRONT THESE AGENTS, THEY ARE KNOWN KILLERS.

OBSERVATION IS RECOMMENDED, NO ARREST ACTION IS RECOMMENDED, UNLESS JUSTIFIED.

HANS BECKER
MILITARY ATTACHE
AMERICAN EMBASSY, BERLIN

The first day of the cruise ended in frustration for every one.

First: Heinrick Hemmler and Karl Witenshon had paid for the three inside cabin locations and picked the locks to each of the cabin doors. They were occupied, but not by two professional spies. As soon as they left the third cabin two security members of the *Enceintes* followed them wherever they went on the ship. This was highly unusual and they locked themselves inside their cabin. When ever they checked the peep hole in the cabin door, the security men were watching.

"We are supposed to be terminating the brothers, Karl. We are forbidden from contacting Paris, what will we do?"

"We shall shake the security men and enter the Emerson Suite, we must decide who of the Steeve travelers to terminate. If we can not decide, we will terminate them all."

Second: The two American agents in the Emerson Suite, who were posing as the Steeves, had not seen the German agents.

Third: The Captain was certain that a murder would occur on his ship before the Port of New York was reached.

Fourth: The security detail was jumpy, they had been ordered to make three unoccupied cabins look occupied. They were told to observe two passengers and to make it obvious that they were being watched.

DAY TWO BEGAN . The German agents decided to split up the various tasks that they were required to do. They were walking on deck, talking casually and suddenly went in opposite directions. The two French security members were taken off guard and one of the agents disappeared in the crowd who had gathered to hear a ship board lecture about the Azores Islands. The *Enceintes* was scheduled to stop at the Port of Ponta Delgada, Azores. Passengers could leave the ship to see the sights for two hours. It was feared that the German agent might go ashore and send a message that would not be monitored. He did. The second agent, Heinrick Hemmler, remained in plain sight watching the passengers leave the ship. He was searching for the Steeve brothers. No one left the ship with the physical descriptions of either suspect. He took special note of the husband and wife in the Emerson Suite as they left the ship. Neither one of them fit the description but they were involved in the concealment of the real Steeves. He could feel it in his bones. When all the passengers left the ship he went back to all four cabins and searched them. He started with the Emerson Suite in plain sight of his security observer. He found nothing unusual except what looked like stage makeup and a woman's wig. He went to each of the remaining inside cabins and found everything exactly as he and his partner had observed the day before.

"*This was impossible. An inside cabin was exactly two feet wider than a double bed or two singles placed together. In order to walk between two singles, each one had to be pushed against the bulkheads. A wash room the size of a normal shower stall was in one corner of the cabin, he looked in and found everything as it was yesterday. This was truly impossible for two people sharing such a small space. This cabin is unoccupied! His thoughts raced ahead to the conclusion that all the inside cabins were unoccupied. I better check each to be sure.*"

An hour later he was sure, the only Steeves aboard were the older couple, they would have to be terminated before they reached New York. He smiled as he thought of Karl having to send a coded telegram to Supreme Headquarters in Berlin confessing his failure to identify and terminate the targets. He would also implicate Heinrick in the failure and knew he had less than a hour to get off the ship and send a message – unless he could use the radio room again. He found the radio room with only one person working, his tail was still with him so he asked the radio operator if he could use the keypad to send a message to his ill wife in Germany.

"I am sorry that your wife is ill. Tell me your message and I will send it for you, Monsieur."

"Merci. The telegraph office closest to Haus Frau Anka Munson is the Elder hostel, Mien Yodest. The telegraph code there is GRM414. Send only the following please, "I am sorry that you have fallen ill and am leaving the ship to return to you." He waited until the key operator had sent the entire message and he left the ship to find Karl. His tail was still in tow. Heinrick met Karl two blocks from the ship and the surprise on Karl's face was apparent.

"What are you doing off the ship?"

"All inside cabins are unoccupied and the Emerson Suite contains a husband and wife. I sent a coded message to the Elder hostel."

"What are our options at this point?"

"They are simple, find the Emerson Suite couple and terminate them here in the Azores. Or and this is risky, we inform Berlin that neither suspect is on board the *Enceintes.*"

"The second option can be given to the agents in New York, I vote for termination of the man and woman and letting the New York agents sort it out."

They walked back to the ship, convinced that they were protected from the wrath of Berlin for failure.

DAY THREE BEGAN. IT was now better for the ship's security. The day before, they had let the Germans split and followed both of them. One went off the ship and one explored around the various parts of the ship. When Heinrick Hemmler entered the radio room, the key operator was a member of the security detail and he had unplugged the antenna which sent the wireless message from the ship. The sound of the keypad was normal but no message was sent to Germany.

The Steeves had not returned to the *Enceintes*, instead they booked into a resort hotel and waited for the return leg of the cruise from New York. They had reported to the ships's Captain that two strange men were following them and they were afraid. They would spend a few days in the Azores to be rid of the problem.

Heinrick and Karl ignored the three empty cabins and watched the Emerson Suite. Two security detail watched them in plain sight.

"How are we going to get near this couple? We are watched day and night."

"We shall wait until the shift change and terminate the watchers and then enter the suite and terminate the agents posing as man and woman."

"We will be arrested for the killings, Karl. That is not an option. We will have additional manpower waiting on the docks in New York. We will follow them and terminate in New York City."

On the morning of the landing, the Steeves suite door was still locked. Heinrick Hemmler and Karl Witenshon were two of the first passengers off the ship and located the waiting agents by a prearranged signal. Five German agents now stood close to the gangway waiting for the Steeves to leave the ship. When the married couple did not appear after all the passengers had exited something was amiss. The waiting agents in New York asked them what had happened.

"I thought there were four persons, three men and one woman."

"There was only a man and a woman."

"Your call to Paris confirmed that four people were involved."

"Yes, but our telegram indicated that there was only the man and woman."

"What telegram?"

"The GRM414 dead drop."

"That telegram was never received."

"Our orders were to eliminate the four. Since you have failed to do this, we will inform Berlin of your failure. Are you two returning to Calais?"

"Yes, we have to find the ticket master on the docks and purchase our returns."

32

Return to Washington

Navy Ship Yard

Tim and I returned to Washington aboard a transatlantic steamer from South Hampton and reported for our debriefing at The Farm. We read the after action reports forwarded from Hans. Admiral Lowe indicated that all activity from the Spanish Embassy had ceased and the Jigsaw murders were now solved. The German Embassy was another matter. Agents were seen coming and going. Three were followed to New York where they met two more who came off the French ocean liner *Enceintes des Philbus*.

"It will not take the Germans long to figure out what happened and they will come after you two and your families. I will alert your father and the White House about the added risk level. The world is ready to explode because of what Otto Von Bulow considers manifest destiny. The German Empire began in Prussia and he envisions an empire that has seaports which stretch from the Gulf of Danzig in the north to the port of Cherbourg in the south. This would include all of the coast line of what is now northern France, Belgium, Holland, and Denmark."

"Prussia is already half way up the peninsula of Denmark and they have taken the Frisian Islands which used to belong to Holland. How much of Europe does Von Bulow want?" I asked.

"All of it, piece by piece. Austria and Hungary are giving way in the south, France has given Lorraine in the west, Poland has given territory in the east and the Baltic Sea is now a German Sea." Admiral Lowe was foreseeing the great war of Europe that he was sure to come.

Tim and I needed to get back to the safe house and get some clean clothes, we stunk. Louise was teaching in Alexandria and we had the house to ourselves.

"Did the Admiral say that we needed to report to RLSO, Louis?"

"Yes, sometime today, when do you want to drive over to the Navy Yard?"

"Let's get it over with, Morton is a pain in the ass." We were dressed in civilian suits and ties. We each had a shoulder holster and our hand guns, extra clips in our suit jacket pockets. We were not expecting any sort of trouble this soon after landing back in the United States. We got in the navy gray model T Ford and backed out into the street and left The Farm. It took us less than forty minutes to drive and find a place to park outside the RLSO building inside the Navy Yard.

We entered the JAG office and headed for my desk in the corner. Commander Morton's door was closed and his office light was off. We both breathed easier until I saw the pile of case files stacked on my desk.

"It never ends, Tim. Look at all these sailors who have managed to get their ass's caught in some sort of legal crack. I am not going to sit here and read all of these, let's take them back to the safe house and we can go through them with Louise. She always has good ideas." I scooped them up into my arms and we headed back to our gray colored Ford. Tim opened the back door and I crawled into the seat still holding a hundred or so files. We could not have been inside the RLSO more than ten or fifteen minutes. We were not very diligent about our surroundings and we had jumped into the Ford without thinking. Tim pushed the starter with his foot. The motor did not turn over, the entire front of the Ford exploded in an giant orange ball of flames. The last thing I remember seeing was a cloud of paper ascending all around me and then total blackness.

The next weeks of my life, I do not remember. I must have spent them in the navy hospital in Maryland, because that is where I am now. When I am awake I see light and dark patches with wet shinny stalagmites hanging from the top edge of my vision. They never go away, when I turn my head, there they are, wet and shinny. I can not hear anything except a dull roar. I talk but nobody answers me. I see my sister standing at the foot of my bed crying. When I ask her what is wrong, she can not hear me. When I try to raise my voice, my head aches. I am not hungry. That is odd because no one has brought me any food in several days. I sleep really good, I am tired again from being awake and trying to talk, I will go back to sleep.

"Has there been any change doctor?"

"No, your son is still in a coma. He is responding to stimulation so he should be regaining his consciousness within a few days."

"Thank you doctor." My father left the room. Only my sister remains at the foot of the bed rubbing my feet. Cut that out, Louise, you know how ticklish I am. She does not hear me. Why doesn't she hear me, I am shouting her name and telling her how much I love her. My head hurts again. I think I need some more sleep.

"How long will my son be in this coma, doctor?" Oh, hi Mom. Where is Dad?

"He is semi-conscious now Mrs. Caldwell. He can hear you, he can not respond to you, but he can hear you. Say something to him and watch his non-verbal responses, they appear before full consciousness." What a quack! A am fully conscious of what is going on around me.

"Louis, darling can you hear Mommy?" How old am I? She has not called herself Mommy in a hundred years. I wish she was not so upset.

"Did you see that Doctor? He moved his eyes back and forth and squeezed my hand!" I said, no, I am having trouble hearing anyone mother. Can't you hear either?

"Yes, I did Mrs. Caldwell. He will start his long way back today and the rest of his life." The rest of my life! Are you kidding me, you quack. I could get up and go back to work right now, if only I was not so tired. Why hasn't Tim come to see how I am doing?

"Doctor, how is my brother today?" Hey, Louise. How come you are not in school? Wait a minute who got rid of the wet shinny stalagmites? Why is it so bright in here?

"He is awake. He woke up last night and tried to fondle a nurse." Why are you telling my sister that, I did no such thing. I am now an officer and gentleman in the United States Navy. Oh, my. God! They replaced my brain, I hate the Navy and everything it stands for, I am a spy. A Yankee Doodle Spy – That is me!

"Louis, I am so happy to see your eyes open!" Me too that must be why it so damn bright in here! A spy, I spy, we spy.

"What did you say? Louis, oh Louis, talk to me!" I am, listen to me. I am a spy. I work for Uncle Teddy. He is a big bag of wind with that carry a big stick shit. It is too bright in here I am going to close my eyes for a minute.

"What happened? Why is he asleep again doctor?"

"He has spoken his first word in two months. His left temporal lobe is working, Ms Caldwell. Go tell your parents while he takes a little nap. Come back for evening visiting hours and I think he will say a few more words."

Ring, ring, ringaling, ringaling ..... Someone answer that telephone, wherever it is.

"Room 307." There is a telephone in my room?

"Yes, General, he said his first word today to his sister." I did? What did I say?

"Of course, General, he can hear every word." Why are you placing that telephone by my ear nurse?

"Louis, they tell me you woke up, son. I want to finish our chapter today." Oh, yes. Grandpa Schneider loves Charles Dickens and he is reading me Oliver Twist.

"We had just started Chapter 5, Louis, you know where Oliver mingles with new associates. He goes to a funeral for the first time and he forms an unfavorable notion of his master's business of undertaking." Yes, I remember.

"*For a second or two Oliver glanced up the street, and down the street, and over the way, impressed with the belief that the unknown, who had addressed him through the keyhole, had walked a few paces off, to warm himself' for nobody did he see but a big charity-boy sitting on a post in front of the house, eating a slice of bread and butter, which he cut into wedges, the size of his mouth, with a clasp knife, and then consumed with great dexterity.*"

"General?" Don't take the telephone away. I can not hear if you take the telephone away.

"Yes, nurse Williams." Oh, this is great what happened to Oliver and this charity-boy eating his bread and butter?

"He has fallen asleep sir." I am not asleep.

"Louis, can you hear me?" Hello, father. Hello, mother. Hello, sister. Hello Grandpa. The whole gang is here, let's have a party!

"Look he is smiling!" Oh Mom, don't cry I will be fine.

"I'm fine." Wow was that me? Why am I whispering?

"Oh, Louis, you can talk, Louise did not image it!"

"Don't cry Mom."

"Why is he whispering?" I am not whispering, am I?

"He has not used his vocal chords in two months, Mrs. Caldwell. He is a little rusty and probably a little dry down there, let's give him some shaved ice. He may not be able to swallow yet. The tubes have been out for only a day. He needs time, that is all." What a quack, I am doing all the work and he is taking all the credit. I am a spy, a sleepy spy, good night to all.

"Let's let him sleep. He is back. Thank God for that."

"Father, what will happen to Louis?"

"He will recover and return to the Navy. Why do you ask?"

"Because he nearly died in that explosion with Tim. I can not go through that again." Tim is dead! Oh my God, Tim. I must be alive, but you are gone. Tim, my body guard, and best friend is dead. I am going to get the bastards that did this to us, Tim. I promise.

"Get the doctor, father. Louis is trying to get out of bed!" That quack can not keep me in this bed. I am going to find the persons who set that bomb for us and I am going to tear off their heads with my bare hands.

"What happened, why is he so excited?"

"He was asleep and we were talking and he just started to thrash about."

"What were you talking about? He can hear everything you say."

"Then he knows about his partner, Tim."

"I will prepare a syringe so he can sleep. Listen family, be careful what you say in this room. He hears and understands, he is not a mental patient. Do not say anything you do not want him to hear. Do you understand?"

"Yes, doctor, I am sorry, it was my fault." Oh, Louise do not cry. I am sorry I am such a hot head. I am sorry I got Tim killed, that was my fault not yours. Oh that feels really good like honey toast and something mixed ....

A WEEK LATER, I was up and walking the halls of the hospital. Not by myself, of course, a man in a white coat came in everyday and tied a flat cloth belt around my waist and lifted me over the side of the bed. I stood and nearly fainted every time he did that. My legs had a mind of there own. They moved up and down and my feet had trouble keeping up with them. We walked the halls and then tried a few steps. That really hurt my legs. Everyday I could go farther and soon the doctor, who turned out not be a quack, released me to come home provided I signed up for out patient rehabilitation once a day. The hospital gave me crutches to leave and I handed them back to them on the front sidewalk and asked for a cane. The cane and I went every where together. My new driver, I did not want to know his name, I called him driver, drove me to the RLSO office and helped me up the flight of steps. We walked towards my desk in the corner and someone was sitting there.

"Hello, what can I do for you Commander?"

"I am Commander Caldwell and that used to be my desk before my automobile was blown out from under me."

"Sir, it is still your desk, should you be back at work so soon?"

"You sound like my mother, Lieutenant, where is Commander Morton?"

"Right behind you, Louis. Congratulations on your promotion to Commander."

"Thank you, Sheldon, when I make Commodore, I want you to come work for me." We both had a laugh.

"I came back to work but I see you can get along without me."

"Nonsense, Louis, you are going to need a bigger desk and an office. Lieutenant Henderson here works for you now."

"He does? What is my new title?"

"Chief prosecutor of the NLSO office next door. You are in the wrong building."

"I can still give orders to the LT here, right."

"Louis, the Lieutenant is just using this desk until you reported back. He will be moving with you today." Sheldon Morton had changed, where was the prick we all loved?

"Go ahead, Sir." Lieutenant Henderson was smiling, my God he is young. Was I ever that young?

"LT, I want you to start three open files. Label the first one Heinrick Hemmler."

"How do you spell that, Sir?"

"H, e, I, n, r, I, c, k H, e, m, m, ,l, e, r"

"And the second one? Sir."

"Karl Witenshon."

"Karl with a K, Sir?"

"Yes, then W, I, t, e, n, s, h, o, n"

"And the third, Sir?"

"Label that the three bad guys last seen in the Port of New York."

"I can't fit that on a label, Sir."

"Just label it 3 bad guys."

"Where do I find the contents of these files?"

"Telephone Admiral Lowe at the NCI training center and he will fill you in. But before you do that, would you walk with me and my driver over to my new office. What is your name? I can't keep calling you my driver."

"It is Tim, Sir. Timothy Caswell." I cold shiver went up my spine.

"I will call you Timothy. Tim is not formal enough for a Marine Scout and an expert sniper."

"How did you know that, Sir? My file has not caught up with me yet, it is still at Pendleton."

"Timothy, I have this sixth and even a seventh sense about people, you look like a sniper!"

"I do? Thank you, Sir."

"You are welcome. Lieutenant Henderson show us the way."

We began walking to a down stairwell.

"I notice that you carry a cane, Commander. How many weeks until you can get rid of it?"

"Timothy my boy, I never plan to be without it." We stopped while a grabbed the heavy brass head and turned it ninety degrees. It was spring loaded and popped about two inches above the shaft of the walking cane. I continued to pull and an eight inch stiletto came out of the cane.

"That is amazing, where did you get that?"

"I could tell you, but then I would have to kill you." I put my mean face on. I put the stiletto back and showed my two young admirers the tip of the cane.

"It is hollow."

"That is right, 20 gauge shotgun barrel."

"How do you fire it, Sir."

"You pull this trigger built into the brass head. See it is right here."

"Amazing, how do you load it?"

"See this brass band under the head. I twist it like so and the cane comes apart."

"It is loaded, Sir. Are you allowed to carry a loaded weapon in JAG?"

"It will be our little secret, gentlemen, what Commander Morton does not know will not hurt him. Besides, my doctor has instructed me to carry this until my rehabilitation is complete."

"Really, Commander Caldwell?"

"Lieutenant Henderson, do not believe everything you hear and only half of what you read."

"Didn't President Lincoln say that, Sir?"

"No, I did just now, pay attention." His face dropped. "LT that was a joke. President Lincoln said you can fool some of the people some of the time and all of the people some of the time; but you can't fool all the people all the time – unless you work for NCI."

"He did? I don't remember that last part."

"Then, maybe that last part is not true, or NCI was created after he left office and he would have added it, if it existed. The point is, in our jobs we fool all the people all the time or we are dead. I am walking proof of that statement. Now, let's get next door and start to fill those folders and recruit some foot soldiers."

"Foot soldiers?"

"Yes, I would like you to pull the files on three Marine Scouts. I do not want Timothy, here, to get lonely. I need the files of Master Sergeant

Shawn Riley, Corporal Adam Smythe and Corporal Harold Davis on my desk in the morning, understood."

"Understood, Sir."

"Good, how far is my office? I do not want you two to have to carry me."

"Not far, Sir."

We walked for what seemed like hours, but it was only a few minutes and I had to sit down behind my desk. My office was nice, not too big, not too small, it had its own telephone and I picked it up and a voice said, "Yes, Commander Caldwell, can I place a call for you?"

" Who is this? Where are you?"

"I am the switchboard operator, Commander. I answer whenever you pick up your hand set. My switchboard is in the basement."

"Can I make a call without going through the switchboard?"

"Of course, use the rotary dial."

"Is that this thing below the hand set?"

"Yes, Sir."

"What is the number for The Farm?"

"Which farm is that, Sir?" I knew then, that this girl did not have a clue what I did for a living.

"The one in Alexandria that has all the turkeys at Thanksgiving, I forget its name."

"Well, without a name, I can not look it up for you, Sir."

"If I think of it, I will call you back. What is your name?"

"It is, Miss Hattie, Sir."

"Thank you, Miss Hattie, I am sure that we will be hearing a lot from each other, now that I have moved into my new office."

"I am sure that we will"....click.

"She hung up on me! Sit gentlemen, LT, open my brief case and get the number for Admiral Lowe's office."

"It is, PENN473, Sir." I stuck my finger in the dialer and made my first person to person telephone call. "How did you know that number, LT?"

"I talk to that office at least once a day, Sir."

"What about? I already know, you could tell me but then you would have to kill me." The three of us burst out laughing. The voice on the other end of the connection said, "What's so funny?"

"Hello, Admiral. Lieutenant Henderson made a funny remark, Sir."

"How is Tim Caswell working out?"

"Timothy Caswell is the best retread from the Marine Corps that I have ever seen, Admiral. That is why I am calling you. I want to see if Master Sergeant Shawn Riley and the two Corporals are available for training at The Farm and assignment to me."

"Their names are Davis and Smythe, Sir." Again the LT surprised me. But then again, he had their names on a piece of paper in his hand. I motioned for him to put the files down and get a note pad and a pencil. I held the hand set away from my ear so that the two of them could hear the Admiral.

"I know you want to go hunt down the people who did this to you, Louis. You are not cleared for field work, give it some time."

"That is what I need Shawn Riley for, Sir. I do not plan on hunting anyone down, now or in the future. We have specialists in the Navy who do that for us. My assistant prosecutor, who I understand you talk to ever day, is going to gather enough information on the ones who did this to Tim. When I get this information, I want you to go to the President and request a Presidential Warrant for them."

"Just forget that your father is the Director of NCI, my boss, and go over his head, directly to the President? I have never gone outside the chain of command, Louis, you know that."

"Of course not, Sir. We need everyone to sign off on this operation I am suggesting. It will take weeks, maybe months, but the evidence will prove, beyond a shadow of a doubt, that these German agents entered this country illegally with intent to kill Americans. They are not protected by diplomatic status. The Chancellor of the German Empire will continue to send these agents unless he gets the message that it is a death sentence to do so. I want to be able to eliminate them before they have a chance to complete their assignments, that is all I am proposing. I can not hunt down these scum, but I know some people who can and these people are United States Marine Scouts, Sir."

"At ease, Commander, you have just convinced me. I will go to the White House and present your idea to your father and your Uncle Teddy. I will suggest a permanent force be assigned to NCI to deal with foreign assassination attempts in this country. You will be hearing from me."

"Sir, before you ring off, can your people assist Lt. Henderson if I send him out to The Farm?"

"Assist him with what?"

"He has five persons of interest, Heinrick Hemmler, Karl Witenshon and three to be named later. You know the three that were tailed from Washington to the Port of New York.

"Good idea, have your people speak to my people, Louis. Louis, welcome back to the game! Now that you know where you will be working take the rest of your medical leave and let us get to work on catching the bad guys. I understand that Louise is trying to purchase the house from Dr. Barrias' widow. She can move out of the safe house here as long as we assign security to the Barrias house that she will purchase. Let me know the address before you move."

33

Rehabilitation

Bethesda, Maryland

Bethesda Maryland is so close to The Farm that you could walk to it in twenty minutes. Timothy drove me every day. I had him pull open the spring loaded fasteners on the hood covers and pull them up so I could look inside the engine compartment. Timothy had no idea why I had him do this, but I was sure that it would be a routine for me the rest of my life. He was billeted at The Farm and he had other duties besides babysitting me. Louise and I had left the safe house at The Farm and had bought a small house. We did not want to go to back to the apartment.

"Louis."

"Yes, Louise."

"Do you think our parents have forgiven us?"

"That we told them to quit hovering over us and that we could take care of ourselves, yes, I think so, Louise. I am glad we told them that we are adults now, living without the co-dependency."

"I know, Louis, I feel the same way. Can we decide something right now?"

"Sure, what is it?"

"You have just lost someone close to you. Until you heal and find that person that you want to marry, let's you and me spend as much time as we can together at my new house."

THE NEXT DAY I was sitting in the rehabilitation center waiting to see my doctor. Louise and I were holding hands and talking about what we would do with the rest of her summer vacation and my medical leave.

"Mr. and Mrs. Caldwell, the doctor will see you now." Because I had listed Louise as my next of kin and we had the same last name, the Navy Hospital made an assumption that they should not have made. We looked at each and grinned. We could still read each other's minds.

"Well, how have you two been getting along?" My doctor asked us.

"We have just purchased our first house, I can't wait to get us moved out of that apartment." Louise had decided to answer all the joint questions.

"Very nice, Mrs. Caldwell, when do you plan on starting a family?" He looked at me and said, "Everything all right in that department, Commander?"

"It certainly is." Louise responded, "He was caught fondling a nurse during his recovery in the hospital." The doctor blushed and said, "Well, that is a normal response from a healthy male, I am glad to hear that."

"Yes, but I was hoping that he would wait until he got home to me." The doctor just smiled and looked at his file that he was keeping on my condition.

"Do you still have pain when the therapists take you through your exercises, Commander?"

"No pain, mostly stiffness. My reflexes are not what they used to be. My Grandfather has promised to work with me as soon as you release me, Doctor."

"What does your grandfather do for a living, is he a physical therapist?"

"He is retired from the United States Marine Corps and he has offered to exercise and run with me."

"Running short distances would be a good thing, Commander, walk when you feel tired. Be sure and exercise before running. I want to see you every month for six months. I am signing your release from Bethesda."

"Thank you, Doctor."

We left the hospital to continue our discussion of summer vacations and medical leave.

"You have 60 days leave, Louis. What do you want to do?"

"I want not to be afraid of my own shadow, Louise. Before that Ford was blasted from under me, I thought I was made of iron. Nothing would hurt me. Now, it hurts to walk."

"You told the doctor you did not hurt, only some stiffness."

"I lied. Maybe Grandpa Schneider has something that will help. I would like to spend the time with you in your house. You know, doing what normal couples do."

"We are not a normal couple, Louis."

"I realize that, Louise. We are related, not husband and wife related, but you are the best friend I have ever had. I have told you about all the first times in my life. I have held nothing back and I never will. You are me in another body. People who are not lucky enough to be twins, have no idea what we share. If you or I never find someone to marry, I will still be the happiest man alive."

"I know, Louis, I am looking, but not very hard, for another man in my life. No one can ever measure up to you, in my eyes." She began to cry.

"It is too soon, honey, give it time. There may be someone waiting out there for both of us. With the burns from the explosion down the side of my neck, it will take a special woman to even look at me twice."

"What burns?" She placed her hand over the burns on my neck and pulled me to her and clung to me again. When she finally let me go, I said, "I did talk to someone that really sounded exciting the other day."

"Who is she and where did you meet her?"

"I have not met her yet. She has the sweetest voice you have ever heard. She is the switchboard operator in the basement of my office building. I want you to go there tomorrow and ask where my office is located. Ask her a lot of questions, get to know her. Check her out."

"Shouldn't you be doing that, brother?"

"Not if she is not sister-in-law material, sister!"

"What is her name?"

"Miss Hattie."

"Sounds like an old maid school teacher to me. You do not even know her first name?"

"I love old maid school teachers." I wrinkled up my nose and hugged my sister again.

"Don't you be calling me an old maid!"

"Relax, Mrs. Caldwell, you will never be an old maid!

LOUISE AND I WERE IN THE PROCESS OF PACKING all her belongings from her apartment when the real estate broker stopped by to give her the bad news.

"Louise, I am sorry, your house evidently had a gas leak and the workmen there must have lit a cigarette and the explosion leveled the house. They are all dead. I am so sorry. You have not taken possession, so the insurance will pay to rebuild or find a replacement. Which do you want to do?"

I looked at Louise and she said, "Neither one, I have changed my mind about purchasing in the immediate area. I will look elsewhere." He left us and we finished our packing, there was only one box left. She called the moving company and told them she needed storage for a few months because fire destroyed the house that she was planning on moving to. She did not tell them that this was the second attempt on our lives since I returned from Germany. We each had a personal suitcase that was allowed on the streetcar system of Washington, D.C. and we headed for Forest Heights.

"Did you lock the apartment, Louis?" Louise was shaking.

"I think so, I don't remember. I think you need to write your letter of resignation to the school board?"

"Yes, I am scared, Louis. This is not over. I do not want another attempt at the school."

"Louise, you need to call Seneca Hill and ask Aunt Carol for a job at Cranson College in the next few days. When you find a place there, I will have your things moved to you. Let the bastards try to locate you then."

"They will, you know."

"Yes, I know. But it gives us time to get them off our backs. Rodney Lowe needs to be taking the fight to them. He needs to arrest, eliminate or deport the threat. Otherwise, our days are numbered, I will not live the rest of my life looking over my shoulder."

The streetcar stopped two blocks from our parent's property and we walked slowly down to the lane that entered the wooded estate. I looked to see if anyone else got off the streetcar. I was clutching my cane like it was my best friend. A navy grey model A Ford came up the lane from the estate and stopped. Our father cranked down his back window and said, "Looks like you kids had quite a morning. How do you feel, Louise?"

"I am scared, Daddy. Can you and Mommy take me to Aunt Carol's place?" By this time, our father's driver had gotten out of the automobile and opened the trunk. He loaded the two suitcases and he turned the automobile around. We drove back down the lane through the woods. I had always liked this place ever since my folks found it right after the last war in 1899. There was no sign at the beginning of the lane as it merged into the highway, nor was there a locked gate. The idea was to make it look normal, like any other medium priced property south of the nation's capital. There was an old milk can, like dairy farms used, about 3 feet high and two feet around, it was filled with concrete and painted flat black. A mail box was mounted to the redwood 4 x 4 which extended through the milk can cap. The lane ran for two or three hundred yards and then took a sharp turn to the right. A set of stone pillars were built on either side of the lane and a small, stone, gate keepers house connected all three with a heavy iron chain similar to the harbor chains used a century ago. My father liked that nautical touch. A gate keeper with a shotgun slung over his shoulder came out and unfastened the chain between the pillars and let the Ford drive across it, it was too heavy to drag out of the way.

When my parents first saw the place that Teddy Roosevelt had said had possibilities, it was a working farm in financial distress. It had many acres of woods and open fields in which to plant grass for hay and field corn for the dairy barns, which at one time held scores of milk cows. As they looked at the giant farm house with four brick chimneys, two at each end, they knew they were looking at something built between the Revolutionary and Civil Wars. It reminded them of their Beaufort home. They walked around the house and decided that would be the center of a much larger house to be completed whenever they might have the time and energy to undertake such a large endeavor. They decided to offer cash on the barrel head, as my father described it, so much an acre, forget about the barns and house. The owners took the offer and the farm land was immediately rented out, on shares, to local farmers. Each year the income was 'plowed' back into the construction of the main house. The purchase was made in 1899 and six years later 'Bellawoods' was a masterpiece. It was three or four times as large as the original Virginia farmhouse, with the additions now complete. The center retained its four massive brick chimneys and the eight fireplaces on two floors. A large front porch, two stories high, was added to the center. It had exact copies of the columns that supported the portico at the White House. The left wing was a single story, white clap board, framed structure built to match the west wing of the White House, only smaller. The east wing was made of brick, painted white to match the east wing of the White House. The White House had 135 rooms, my parents settled for 29 rooms, four inside bathrooms, one outside bathroom attached to the swimming pool and patio, which ran along the back of the house. The main barn was converted to a very large garage where my father kept his collection of antique steam automobiles and his modern cars. There was even a trap range and small office where a small barn had once stood. It over looked a small valley. My father had said, "Now that Seneca Hill is a woman's college, we need a family gathering place."

The Ford stopped in front of the house and my mother came running out the front door to meet us. A butler and a maid followed along in her wake.

"Reginald, get the bags from the trunk. Maria, help my daughter into the house and help her get settled in her room." My mother had taken command. "James, I want the property guards doubled, see to it today. Louise, telephone your moving company and have them deliver your household goods here. Louis you are home for the summer and your medical leave will be spent here. Your sister does not have to start at Cranson College until September. We are going to be a family again, so help me God." I looked at my father, he looked at me, Louise looked at both of us.

"Oh, Mommy, it is so good to be home." My sister was crying again.

"If the German agents follow the moving van, they will know where we are, Dad." He looked at me and said, "Your Uncle Teddy has a detachment of marines on their way as we speak, I hope the dumb fuckers try to break in here, they will all be dead. Their orders are to take no prisoners, even if they surrender."

I had never heard my father say more than damn or shit in my whole life, he must really be angry. And, more importantly he probably hoped that all the agents assigned to the German Embassy would converge on 'Bellawoods' and the matter could be settled once and for all.

THE NEXT DAY a moving van arrived with the household belongings of the Caldwell twins. It was admitted to the estate after twelve marines inspected the undercarriage, motor compartment and crawled into the rear storage areas. Louise and I were lying next to the swimming pool soaking up the sun rays. Within a few minutes of the moving van, a model T Ford came as far down the lane as the stone guard house and stopped at the harbor chain blocking their entrance. The same guard, with the shot gun, came to see what they wanted. They claimed they were lost and asked directions to the main road into Washington, D.C. The driver had a local accent that sounded normal, but the three others did not speak. The guard reported this to Captain Merfield of the United States Marines on special assignment, "Bellawoods". He trotted up to the house, found my father and said, "Contact with four suspects at the front gate, Sir."

"Good hunting, Captain. You understand your orders from the President?"

"Yes, Sir. No prisoners, no survivors. Remains to St. Elizabeth Hospital for processing. You can sleep safely in your beds tonight."

The woods around the house were salted with anti-personnel mines by the marines. They would be impossible to see at night and a single detonation would sound the alarm that an assault on Bellawoods was underway. The family was on edge, we ate a somewhat normal meal and went to bed around midnight. At 1:30 in the morning, the first mine exploded under the foot fall of an intruder. We heard small arms fire for about ten minutes and then nothing. Captain Merfield ordered his men to stay clear of the mined area and check for bodies. In two minutes the small arms fire began again. At sunrise, four bodies were recovered and identified as the four men in the model T Ford. The automobile was found parked on a side road adjacent to the property. They had walked from the automobile directly into a mine field and a cross fire from Captain Merfield's marines.

"Are any of these men the five agents that you were looking for, Louis?" My father was hopeful.

"Yes, I believe this man is Gunther Hesse from the German Embassy, NCI had him under surveillance, he must have slipped away. I do not recognize any of the other three."

"There is no identification on any of these men, Sir." Captain Merfield's men had checked each of the bodies.

"Check the clothing labels, sometimes they forget to remove them." I said. I reached down and looked for labels on Hesse. He was a pro, nothing at all.

"Here is one, Sir." A marine had found a German language label.

"Let's get these bodies to the morgue, Captain." My father walked away towards the house.

"Are all the mines clearly marked for daytime safety?" I asked Captain Merfield.

"Yes, Sir, Commander, you can walk in the woods, but I would not suggest that until this is over."

"You think this is not over?"

"No, sir. It has just started. It will continue until they run out of agents in Germany, not the embassy. The embassy is just a stopping off place, until they come to this site and meet their deaths. Spies are not equipped to mess with troops, the troops will win every time, Commander." He was smiling, he liked this.

THEY CAME BACK THE NEXT THREE NIGHTS, the first group contained five men who met their deaths from mines, small arms fire, and rifle fire. The second group contained ten men who met their deaths from mines, grenades, rifle fire and machine guns. The final group contained fifteen men, ten were killed and five had surrendered to Captain Merfield. He placed them in handcuffs and sent them off to St. Elizabeth Hospital for processing. It was a suicide mission on the part of the intruders, but the emotional damage inside the house had taken its toll. My father had not been to work in the last four days and he left early the morning of the fifth day and headed to the White House. A marine patrol went ahead of his automobile and behind it and returned to the house.

The President, his brother-in-law, was waiting for him, my father handed him a piece of paper with the body count and the names of those who we knew were dead or captured.

29 Dead   5 under interrogation at The Farm

1. Kreis Nauheim	Helmut von Graffenberg
2. Gunter Hesse	Otto Schmidt
3. Unknown (27)	Unknown (3)

The president picked up his phone and asked to speak with Admiral Lowe. He hung up. He picked up a second phone and asked to speak to the German Ambassador to the United States. He waited a few minutes and the President spoke very slowly, he did not wait for any responses.

"Mr. Ambassador, this is the President of the United States. You may inform your government that I have issued the following orders to my military police. Your embassy is considered German soil and I will not send someone onto that soil. I have instead, asked the police to stop all persons from leaving or entering the German Embassy until further notice. I have also closed the American Embassy in Berlin and have asked that all consul offices be closed throughout the German Empire and for those officials to return home. We have broken all diplomatic ties with your government. If you, or anyone else, leaves the embassy you will be arrested. Do you understand everything that I have told you? Good!" He hung up.

His first phone buzzed. He picked it up. "Hello Rodney, do you have any names for me? You do, bully for you old man. I will give you to James and he can write the names down on our list. I have some more calls to make. Good talking to you again too." He handed the phone to his Director of the NCI. He picked up a second telephone and called the Washington Post.

"Hello, I assume my secretary has given you the proper code words and you know that this is the President of the United States speaking. I have an interesting story for you." He visited for about twenty minutes and hung up. He placed another call to the New York Times.

"Hello, I assume that my secretary has given you the proper code words......" He spent the rest of the entire day speaking with newspapers across the country. He wanted to let them know that he had recalled all US diplomats from the German Empire. This total recall, a defacto declaration of war, was in response to the terrorist actions coming directly from the German Embassy in Washington, D.C. A total of thirty-four murder attempts had occurred in the last four days. He had given the Governor of Virginia and his state police permission to fire upon any vehicle carrying German diplomatic plates. He hoped the German Government in Berlin would come to their senses and make contact with their Embassy in Washington. He had also said that he would welcome the closing of all German Embassies and consul offices and the recall of all diplomats within a 48 hour time limit. After that time, all diplomats trying to enter the US would be arrested and deported. All diplomats within the United States would be placed under arrest to face charges of murder and attempted murder of American citizens. The German Empire is a rouge nation without honor of any kind whatsoever and as President of the United States, he considered it an insult to see his name appear upon an assassination list taken from one of the those already involved. He was taking this method of informing the people of the United States of the actions already taken. And, those actions that might be needed in the near future, that was why he was now ordering the Secretary of War to place the country upon a war time footing and to begin calling officers that had served in 1899 to return to active service. He was sorry that he had to take this action, but unless changes were made in Berlin, war was certain to follow.

It took a day to print and distribute over 65 million newspapers across the country. Twenty-fours after that, things began to happen. The Ambassador of the Austro-Hungarian Embassy asked for an emergency meeting with the President. He came to the White House with a telegram from Emperor Franz Josef and Kaiser Wilhelm II informing him that OttoVon Bulow was no longer the Chancellor of the German Empire, he was replaced by Bethmann Hollweg. The entire diplomatic staff from Germany, now serving in the United States has been recalled and would be replaced as soon as the Americans return to their embassy in Berlin. The Kaiser had also included a personal hand written letter to Theodore

Roosevelt that included an apology for the actions of his late Chancellor. He wrote that it is not the policy of his Empire to engage in terrorism of any kind, we meet our enemies upon the battlefield with respect and honor. My respect for you and the United States has not changed and my offer to exchange college professors is hereby reaffirmed.

34

Hunt for Missing Pieces

NLSO, Washington Navy Yard

My father and I rode together from Bellawoods and I returned to the NLSO office after my recovery leave. My father dropped me off and continued on to 1600 Pennsylvania Avenue. I wanted to see what progress my assistant prosecutor had made with the five cases that I had asked him to open. He reported that Admiral Lowe had determined that Heinrick Hemmler and Karl Witenshon had tried to return to France on the Enceintes des Philbus using another set of forged passports. The ticket master had collected the fares, but as soon as the ship's security saw them trying to board, they stopped them and took them back to the ticket master for a full refund. They had simply disappeared into the New York population.

The three agents that met with Hemmler and Witenshon had come from the German Embassy, Washington, D.C. They were followed and long range photographs were taken and placed in their files. They were identified as Helmut von Graffenberg, the head of embassy security in Washington and two of his foot soldiers, Gunther Hesse and Kreis Nauheim. All three had diplomatic passports, and therefore, The Farm had marked them for elimination once they left the United States. An accident at sea on a vessel other than American manufacture would be ideal. The events at Bellawoods had been recorded and the word DECEASED had been stamped across the face of each file.

The German agents at large in New York City were not protected by diplomatic passports and I was determined to locate them. The bomb set in the Washington Naval Yard could not have been Hemmler and Witenshon. This was done on orders from someone in Germany through their embassy in Washington.

"Let me see the reports on our three Marine Scouts that are going through The Farm, Lieutenant Henderson."

"They will be finished tomorrow and they will report to you with Admiral Lowe's blessing. He says use them wisely, there are no more to follow. The President of the United States has made peace with Germany. No more arrests are to be made by NCI."

"What were the latest reports of the observation team on the comings and goings at the German Embassy, Lieutenant?"

"Agents from The Farm have reported that both Hemmler and Witenshon have been seen entering and leaving the embassy. Heinrick Hemmler likes the ladies, Sir. He parties well into the night in and around Washington, sometimes with Karl Witenshon and sometime without him."

"Starting in two more nights, let's give them something to think about."

"Sir? NCI can't arrest them."

"They are professionals, Lieutenant. They know that they are under constant surveillance. It is their insurance policy. As long as we are keeping tabs on them, they know we will not take action against them. Now that the matter is considered closed by the federal government, what will be their reaction when no one has them under surveillance?"

"They will think that they are to be eliminated within a short time. What can we do that Admiral Lowe's agents can not?"

"We can divide and conquer, Lieutenant. We can't be blamed if the Germans shoot and kill each other by accident."

"I don't understand, Sir."

"When we have all of us on board, Timothy can be the wheel man, you can be the lookout and the three scouts can be the invasion force. We will begin by placing a device that looks exactly likes a bomb inside the embassy automobile that Hemmler takes for his evening ventures. He or his driver will not be able to start the automobile. When they check under the hood, they will find a working bomb that did not detonate. They will contact either the local police or they will have their embassy staff remove it and examine it. It must be convincing to them that an assassination attempt was made upon their lives."

"I don't understand, Sir."

"Every item inside the device will be a German made bomb part, Tim and I brought several of these training devices back with us from Berlin. What else can they think? They are being marked for elimination by their own people. You know, loose ends that need to be taken care of, Lieutenant."

"I am not sure it will work, Commander."

"Following the non-explosion of the embassy automobile, the embassy itself will have a bomb scare and when the embassy is evacuated and the search begins, they will find a tiny German made charge on the incoming gas line. Wrapped around the gas line will be small canisters of mustard gas. It might be interesting to see what type of reaction the newspapers might create when it is known that German mustard gas was found in Washington, D.C. I have at least twenty other little items that will be designed to have the two agents and those who report to them, shooting and asking questions later."

"Sir, that sounds like a game we can not win."

"We must send the message to the German Embassy that it is not business as usual. They can not replace faces and continue the same policy of murder and mayhem. Hemmler and Witenshon are already on the elimination list. Why wait until they are outside the United States, why not have them kill each other?"

THE PLAN WAS SUBMITTED AND REJECTED. We redid it and submitted it again. Admiral Lowe turned our first version down flat as being hair-brained, ill-conceived and against current White House orders to have a "hands off" policy with the German Embassy. We sent him a second plan and he rejected it as wishful thinking, with too many ifs and what ifs throughout the length of the operation. I finally indicated that we were no longer considering a plan to kill anyone or have anyone killed by accident in any manner what-so-ever.

Timothy and I began to work in secret with Shawn Riley and his two scouts, we left Lieutenant Henderson out of the loop, he would report everything to NCI, he was required to do so. I had given the bomb making elements to Shawn and asked him to follow Heinrick Hemmler and Karl Witenshon the next night to one of the "night spots" in Washington. It was called the Marlon Rouge, obviously a tongue in cheek jab at the French. Shawn raised the hood of the imported automobile from Germany and cut a single wire to the push starter button on the driver's side of the floorboard. He twisted the dud in place and attached two wires and carefully lowered and fastened the hood. They watched from a safe distance and waited for the Germans to return to their car. They waited until closing and the Germans walked towards the automobile with a Fraulein each. All four got into the automobile and tried to start the engine. Nothing happened. They sat in the auto and did nothing. Hemmler left and entered the Marlon Rouge and thirty minutes later, a tow truck pulled behind the embassy auto and pulled it away. Shawn Riley, looked at his two scouts and said, "Follow that tow truck, Davis. Smythe and I are going to get in the other auto and stay here with the four party goers."

Corporal Davis followed the truck towing the embassy auto to a repair shop and watched it being locked inside an enclosure for the night. The truck drove off and Davis returned to the Marlon Rouge. The four people under surveillance were gone and so were Sergeant Riley and Corporal Smythe. No one had found anything.

An automobile with German Embassy plates was stopped at a house, the Fraulein's home, obviously, and all four people got out and the auto drove off.

"Do we follow the embassy auto or stay here, Sir?"

"Get some sleep, Smythe, I will take the first watch."

The next morning, both Sergeant Riley and Corporal Smythe were both asleep when a German Embassy automobile stopped and picked up Heinrick Hemmler and Karl Witenshon. When they awoke, it was nearly noon. They knew the coverage was blown when no one answered the knock on the door at the Fraulein's house.

"We need to report back to Commander Caldwell and see if he wants to go through with the bomb scare. This part certainly did not work." They drove to the Navy Yard and entered the NLSO building and found the Commander hard at work. He was talking with the telephone switchboard operator downstairs.

"Has the Commander seen Miss Hattie? Her face would stop a train, she is so ugly! It is not fair, the rest of her is Miss America."

"Shut up, Smythe. He likes her voice. I don't think he has even seen her."

"Hello, Sergeant, Corporal. Harold has already checked in. He has the device to wrap around the gas main at the embassy. Do it tonight."

"Aye, aye, Sir. Is there any news of our first plant?"

"No, I have called the repair shop that Harold trailed them to. I spoke to them in German and asked when the automobile would be returned for service. I was told, in perfect German, that the auto was repaired already and the extra part that was used to increase the starting voltage was replaced with a new one."

"Then they knew you were not from the embassy, Sir."

"Yes, and now they know that our fake was not planted by someone inside the embassy. All they know is that someone is having fun at their expense."

"So, why go through with the rest of the plan, Sir?"

"I want to change it a bit. I will call the newspapers and the local police and tell them someone is poking around outside the embassy. I will do this as soon as you three are safely away."

"What will that do, Sir?"

"The Germans can not hide it from the public."

"The Admiral will know it was you, Commander."

"Yes, he will. I may be given a temporary assignment outside the United States for punishment, but nothing ventured, nothing gained. Let us hope tonight is more successful, Gentlemen. Go back to your rooms at The Farm and get some sleep, you will be been up all night."

THAT NIGHT THE FIASCO CONTINUED. My men waited until after midnight and parked two blocks from the German Embassy. They were carrying all their equipment in a tool bag. They had driven past the embassy several times and decided that a wrought iron gate in the brick wall, near a rose garden, would make an ideal point of entry. They stopped before the gate and took bolt cutters from the bag. They cut the pins in the hinges and pulled the pins out. This allowed them to swing the gate in a reverse motion, just enough for two of the them to sneak through and locate the gas main. A gas main is a two inch wrapped steel pipe, everywhere in Washington, D.C. I thought my men understood this, but I must not have mentioned this to them. They found a pipe coming through the brick wall of the embassy and placed all the necessary elements in place; two small tanks of fake mustard gas, one fake bomb constructed of genuine German bomb parts and one real timer. They retreated through the iron gate, swung it back and replaced the pins. Covert operation complete and they called me at Bellawoods.

"Commander, it was easy, it only took a couple of minutes."

"Did you take the wrapping off the metal gas pipe before you attached the package?"

"Sir, there was no wrapping around the pipe. It was a bare metal four inch pipe."

"Sergeant, you just placed an explosive device on the roof drain pipe. You are looking for a two inch or smaller metal pipe that is coated with tar and wrapped with a paper like material."

"Do you want us to back and see if we can find the gas pipe, Sir?"

"That would be a good idea, Sergeant. Call me when it is done."

"Aye, aye, Sir. Sorry, Sir."

I fell asleep waiting for the Sergeant to call. When the phone rang, it woke me and I had no idea how long it was since I talked to him last.

"Sir, you are not going to believe this. When Davis and I went back to move the package, it was gone."

"Where are you now, Sergeant?"

"At the public telephone two blocks away, Sir."

"They knew we were coming, Sergeant. Come back in and call it a night. Our plan is out the window." I hung up and my father was standing in my doorway.

"Your operation run amuck, Louis?"

"Yes, how did you know?"

"Rodney showed me the two plans that you forwarded to him. I rejected both of them, Louis. The German Embassy is no longer a threat to us. The spying will continue, just not from the embassy as its head quarters. Hemmler and Witenshon are a couple of stumble bums. They are window dressing for us to watch at the embassy. Find where the real agents are operating, Louis. Rodney tells me you are the brightest and the best he has. Use your head and think about the problem. I will see you in the morning and we can talk some more on our ride into the offices. Good night, Son."

"Good night, Dad. Thank you."

THE NEXT MORNING, I was ready for another discussion with my father, but he never mentioned anything about our conversation the night before and my wasted efforts for the last week. He talked instead about what he was doing as director of NCI and what Uncle Teddy expected of him, Rodney and me.

"You know, Louis, I am the one who hands the President the results of our efforts. The effort begins with you and Rodney. The Farm is a huge expense to the federal government. It is worth that expense because for the first time in our history, we can shape our future, not just react to things after they happen. The world is at war, Louis, and it always will be. Humans are what they are and that makes us our own worst enemies. Murder is justified because the 'Nation' wills it. Germany is a perfect example. Otto Von Bulow was a Prussian. Prussia was a small military state and today it has become the German Empire, by killing its neighbors and claiming their lands for the building of the empire. This is not new. Nation building has been going on inside the United States since 1780. How many American Indians, Canadians, Mexicans and others have died because we wanted the land upon which they lived? The answer is hundreds of thousands."

"When does it stop, Dad?"

"When every human being upon this planet is extinct, Louis."

35

A Word With Admiral Lowe

NLSO Office Building

My father's words were burned into my memory, "*When every human being upon this planet is extinct*" It kept replaying in my mind as I walked up the stairs to my office in the NLSO building. Admiral Rodney Lowe was sitting in my office.

"Good morning, Sir. Did I miss a meeting with you at The Farm?"

"No, Louis, I am here to reassign you."

"I know, my father has already lectured me about having my head up my butt, so to speak. He is a great one to talk, he has never been behind enemy lines."

"Louis, for a smart man, you can be stupid at times. Has your father ever told you about his early career?"

"I know he was never put behind enemy lines."

"You would be wrong about that too, son. Sit down, I want to tell you about your father." This most incredible account followed.

The *USS Yantic* docked at the Potomac Dockyards and your father, Commander Caldwell, caught a cab to the Army Navy Building next to the White House. He had not been there since his first assignment after graduation in 1877 when he worked for me. Fifteen years had certainly changed the look of the place. He entered the building and handed his orders from Secretary Tracy. The seaman, converted to a desk clerk, opened them and began reading them. He came to rigid attention, saluted and blurted out, "Commander Caldwell, it is an honor to meet you. Everyone has been talking about you the last few weeks. The secretary will return from the Yantic and he wants to visit with you after your formal debriefing. Let me store the sea bag that you brought with you, behind this desk. It will be waiting for you when you leave today."

He was shown to a long narrow room with windows along one side, where I was waiting for him. It was completely empty except for me, a long table and four chairs across from it on one side and a single chair opposite. We shook hands and he sat in the single chair. Within a few minutes additional officers, way above his grade, began filing into the room one at a time. None of them looked at him, they seemed to be more interested in the stack of papers before them.

"You will stand, Commander Caldwell, place your hand upon the bible and swear that you will tell the truth and only the whole truth about the incidents of October last, in the Port of Valpariso, Chile. Do you so swear?"

"I do."

"Please, be seated."

"Commander, I am Admiral Davidson. The Rear Admiral on my left is David Whiteside. The Commodore on my right is Rodney Lowe. I think you served under Commodore Lowe when he was a captain. Is that right?"

"It is, Sir."

"You will note that a court steno is recording everything said in this debriefing. Do you object to that?"

"No, Sir."

"Commander, I am going to read you a report sent to us from a Senor Emanuel Matto of the Chilean Senate. It has been translated into English so you can understand it."

"I can read Spanish, Sir. Would you like me to read the Spanish version?"

"That would be very kind of you, Commander. Where did you learn Spanish?"

"At the Academy, Sir. It was not required, per se, only a foreign language requirement. I took four years of Spanish as electives. I still have trouble with rapidly spoken, slang Spanish, but reading is fine."

"Would you read this document carefully, Commander, and tell us what you think of it?"

"Yes, Sir." He handed your father a single page of Spanish. He read it and handed it back to him.

"Well, Commander?"

"It is the preliminary findings of the Chilean investigation. It says that my escort was not attacked by an angry mob. It claims that a fight broke out between the two escorts groups – American and Chilean. It states that the police were called to stop the fight between the groups. The two deaths had already occurred when the police arrived. That is the end of item one.

In item two, it states that the American minister and consul at Valpariso kept back testimony which would have cleared up the matter.

Item three indicates that the reports sent to Washington from the *USS Yantic* made by myself and Captain Bertram, were false.

Item four indicates that the Secretary of the Navy has broken several Chilean laws.

Item five indicates that the President of the United States may be mentally unbalanced in his illegal detention of Chilean citizens serving in the embassy in Washington."

"Are you paraphrasing the items that you stated for us?"

"No, Sir. That is what the items said to best of my ability to remember them."

"You have a remarkable memory, Commander, that is pretty much what the translation says, also. Item one. Is it true?"

"No, Sir. There were about 180 men in the central plaza of Valpariso on the day in question. 40 American escorts, 40 Chilean escorts and the rest were men dressed in civilian clothing."

"Could these 100 men have been Chilean Army members?"

"I have no way of knowing that, Sir."

"So it is your contention that these were civilians?"

"Yes, Sir."

"Item two. Is it true?"

"I did not know that there was an American minister in Valpariso. I have never seen him or talked with him."

"Item three. Is it true?"

"My report is as factual as I remember the events happening."

"What about Captain Bertram's report?"

"I have not seen that report."

"Item four. Is it true?"

"I have no knowledge of what the Secretary of Navy has done."

"Item five. Is it true?"

"I was not aware of anything happening in Washington, Sir."

"Thank you, Commander. We would like to ask some questions about your after action report that you sent to Washington at the request of the President."

"Yes, Sir."

"Do you remember that report? Would you like to see a copy of the report?"

"I remember it, Sir."

"Can you tell us what was in that report?"

> *"It was October 16, 1891, when I left the USS Yantic with my escort. Admiral Brown had asked for volunteers. Everyone was in uniform, except me, and we left the Yantic to meet the Chilean escort waiting on the docks. A Chilean naval officer saluted and said in perfect English, 'Mr. Caldwell, it is an honor to escort you to Santiago. My name is Edwardo Concepcion.'*
>
> *'Thank you, Sir. How far is the depot?'*
>
> *'It is a short walk, Sir. Just enough time to tell you about the city of Valparaiso. It is the capital of the Province of Valparaiso, Chile. It is the chief seaport of the republic, situated on a bay of the Pacific, 68 miles west-northwest of Santiago. We will travel about 116 miles to get there by rail, however. The older and business portion of the city extends along the bay, while on the slopes of the surrounding hills are the finer residences. Vina del Mar, a few miles to the east, is a noted suburb and seaside resort. It enjoys a mild and equable climate, the average temperature being*

58 degrees. The hottest is January with 63 degrees and the coldest is July with 53 degrees."

'I have gotten used to winter and summer being reversed, since my assignment in the South Atlantic.'

'I thought you came from Washington?'

'No, I was brought here from the Falklands. President Harrison has decided that I could get here much quicker than someone from Washington. He considers this matter with Chile to be very serious and we need to get the situation calmed down before it escalates into something that neither country desires.'

'We are entering the main plaza with many monuments. That one over there is a statue of Columbus. We also have statues of William Wheelright, who built the first railroad in Chile and Thomas Cochrane who organized the Chilean Army. Over there is a statue of Admiral Prat and .....'

He never finished his sentence because a mob of men, about a hundred in number, came rushing across the plaza and attacked his escort. The mob was trying to fight through the Chilean Naval escort and kill the American sailors. The mob pushed through the thin line of Chileans and the unarmed Americans fought back with bravery, but they were at a fatal disadvantage. Charles Riggins, a boatswain's mate of the Baltimore, was killed and William Turnbull, a coal-heavier, had his neck slashed before the 80 man escort could drive the mob away.

'It looks like two of your escort are dead, Mr. Caldwell, and several others need medical attention. The depot is a block away. I will leave a guard detail with the dead and wounded and the rest of us will put you on the train to Santiago. You need to select a body guard from your remaining escort, we will arm them for you.'

'Excellent solution, Sir.' I began tapping men on the shoulder and said, 'Get a rifle from a Chilean Marine and walk with me to the depot.'

No one refused and within a few minutes we were on the train. I had no idea how many of the wounded men would survive - but I needed to send a telegram to the USS Yantic and report what happened. I knew that the survivors would be taken back to the ship, but I and an armed body guard detail had to continue on.

Our first stop was Vina del Mar and I left the train and entered the depot with a Spanish speaking seaman from the San Francisco. 'Tell the telegraph operator that we need to send a telegram to the Valpariso dockyards, pier six.' I wrote out my telegram in Spanish.

The train continued on into Santiago without further incident and we left the train as a group. I had some money with me for emergencies and I had seaman Lopez hail us a cab. All seven of us squeezed into it and Lopez asked if he could drive by the American embassy that was now under house arrest. He laughed and said he could for five extra pesos. Lopez handed him the money and we were there in a few minutes. Lopez asked the driver to stop, handed him another 100 pesos and said, 'We were never here, understand?'

We showed our diplomatic papers and we entered the embassy grounds. We walked over to the Chilean guard at the door to the embassy building. I handed him my papers. He examined them and opened the door. He said something in Spanish, I nodded my head and kept walking. I asked Lopez what he had said to make sure. The guard was leaving his post. We entered the embassy and found Patrick Egan. He and the others were hungry, as they were rationing food and water. Nothing was allowed in or out of the building.

I told the Ambassador that the guard at the door had left and I thought it was over. We had to figure out a way to get the embassy personnel to the train station. I asked if the embassy had emergency funds, transportation and armed guards.

The Ambassador began shouting orders to everyone in sight and within twenty minutes the wagons and carriages were loaded with departing embassy members and we were on our way to the train station. The next two hours before the train left, I expected the Chilean Army to appear and arrest all of us.

We arrived in Valpariso and Captain Bertram had taken no chances. He had ordered two deck guns mounted on wagons and nearly all the Marines on board to meet us. We walked slowly back to the ship and looked down each street that entered into the plaza. We were on board before the Captain explained what had happened to my escort. He informed me that my escort was arrested for inciting a riot."

"Do you always include direct quotes in your after action reports, Commander?"

"I have never written an after action report before, Sir."

"Well, it is damned refreshing to read one like yours!"

"Thank you, Sir."

"Alright, we can stop the dictation now, thank you, seaman, you are excused." The steno got up and left the room.

"James, we are off the record. Do you want to change any of your statements?" I was smiling as I asked your father this, Louis.

"No, Commodore Lowe." He was smiling at me, Louis.

"Well, for what it is worth, that Senator Matto is a liar as well as a 'son-of-a-bitch.'" Commodore Whiteside spoke for the first time.

"Commander Caldwell, you are not to speak of anything that you have testified to at this hearing to anyone, especially your father. Do you understand?"

"Aye, aye. Sir. You can count on my silence."

"You are entitled to know what we are going to recommend to the President, James. Our recommendation shall be that the President give the Chilean Government the following choices, a state of war will exist between our two countries unless the following terms are met:

1. An apology for the attack on the sailors of the Baltimore,
2. An indemnity to the sailors killed and injured, and
3. The recall of the insulting report by Senator Matto.

Your father and I left the interview room and walked to Secretary Tracy's office. He was in and asked us to come through the outer office and have a seat on a soft leather coach. He sat beside us.

"So, how did the debriefing go, Gentlemen?"

"Fine, Sir." We both said at once.

"Can you summarize for me, James?"

"Of course. I have been asked by Admiral Davidson to not repeat anything I said under oath in his presence. You will read his report before it is forwarded to the President and the sworn statement is contained inside that document. Before I was sworn, I met the other members of the board. I served under Commodore Lowe, here, when he was head of the Hydrographic Office. That was '77. After the steno left we visited for a short while and Admiral Whiteside said a rather interesting thing, 'Well, for what it is worth, that Senator Matto is a liar and a son-of-a-bitch!"

"That sounds like 'Stormy Whiteside'. He is a man of few words and when he speaks, you should listen, he is always on target. Those are my feelings about the Chilean Senator, also, by the way. James, I have a question to ask you?"

"Yes, Sir."

"Have you ever thought that maybe engineering is not for you?"

"Absolutely not, Sir. I am an Hydrographic Engineer, graduate of the Academy, author of the only modern textbook on the subject. I was allowed to practice my profession for the navy for only eight years, the last seven have been a total waste of time, in my opinion."

"You speak your mind, Commander. I like that. Why did you think that it has taken fifteen years for you to get so few promotions?"

"I did not complete my two years of sea duty required after graduation in '77, Sir. I reported to the *USS Quinnebaug* in Philadelphia as its Hydrographic Engineer, but the ship was under quarantine and the insides were finally burned out to get rid of what ever was aboard."

"I remember that. What did you do?"

"I came here for reassignment and Secretary Hagood assigned me to the USCGS office. I was stuck with the rank of Ensign and I never progressed much beyond another promotion stage, I guess. I did get to write and edit my first book there, however."

"How many books have you written, Commander?"

"The manual used by the USCGS, a marine surveying field manual and a textbook for John Wiley and Sons. It is used at the Academy."

"Are you familiar with what we do at the Naval War College in Newport?"

"The navy provides additional study beyond the normal bachelor's degree programs at the Academy. My father got his master's degree in Naval History there."

"James, your family is very good at keeping secrets given to them. Would it surprise you to know that your father never took a history course at Newport, he took his history courses at Georgetown. We do not offer history courses at the Naval War College. We train our very best officers at either Monterey, California, if they show a talent for languages or at Newport if they have the capacity to become 'stone cold killers.'"

"My father is not a killer, I doubt he has ever even seen anyone killed in action."

"You would be wrong, James. Your father was a warrior and warriors kill people that are trying to kill them or the troops under them. That is what war is all about, in its simplest terms."

"I have read that exact statement at the Naval Institute, Sir. It was somewhere in the Grant papers regarding his upper Mississippi and Ohio river campaigns."

"Yes, and it was made by your father about Colonel Grant, who he was trying to get promoted to brigadier."

"My father never talks about the Civil War, Sir."

"I know, you Caldwells can keep secrets. The question I have for you, is this. Do you want to go to the Naval War College and teach there?"

"Teach there?"

"Yes, I do not think you are a stone cold killer, James, or that the Navy could or should make you into one. You have the unique ability to sort vast amounts of information from many sources and formulate it into a concise, short form. The Navy better begin to tap that ability and pass it on to others that desperately need it. I am putting a Presidential Order into your 'Navy Jacket', James. It states that you have performed behind enemy lines with distinction, you are privy to information of national security importance and therefore are restricted to assignments only at the Department of the Navy, Washington D.C., Monterey, California, Newport, Rhode Island, or the Academy."

"Thank you, Sir. I was considering a letter of resignation and joining my father as the director of CI."

"What do you think now?"

"I think I have a career in the USN, Sir. But I doubt that I will ever be able to talk about it to anyone, not even my wife."

"Correct, you will be lucky to retire on a Captain's pay, James. Naval Intelligence is unseen, but critical to the nation. This president and future presidents are asking a lot of you, James. The PO does not get pulled by the next president, it remains in your file until your death – not your retirement. You are NOT free to write another book about your adventures in the Navy."

We, all three, burst out laughing. "I understand and accept this, Sir. The Navy is not about promotions for me, it is about a family feeling of pride. Can I ask a question, Sir?"

"Yes."

"Is there a similar PO in my father's file?"

"I can not answer that, James. You already know the answer to that, do you not?"

"Answer a question with a question, a classic Jason Caldwell response. I am beginning to understand my father better and better."

Admiral Lowe was standing at my office window as he finished his story. He turned and looked at me. "Do you have any more questions or comments about your father?"

"No, Sir. I feel like an ass."

"As I said, when this meeting started, I am here to reassign you, Louis. You are leaving NLSO and getting an office at The Farm. I have notified Commander Morton that you will be returning to JAG - RLSO on a use as needed basis. He may request your services for any high profile case that he desires, but he is not to assign a daily work load. You will be out of the country too much for that.

36

Ships at Sea

Atlantic Ocean

I was in transit to deliver a coded set of operations to Hans Becker, station chief, Berlin. Admiral Lowe was using me as a high level "errand boy" until I could learn something about the NCI, its director and the head of The Farm. I had been given a berth on the *USS Vixen* which was part of group of ships in route from the Washington Navy Yard to the Baltic Sea and the port of Danzig, Germany. I met the ship's, white haired, captain my second night on board.

"Hello, my name is Captain Bertram."

"Not Captain Hiram Bertram, the skipper of the *USS Yantic*?"

"I was much younger then, son. You are too young to have been a member of my crew aboard the Yantic."

"My name is Louis Caldwell, my father was James Caldwell who served under you in Chile."

"Did your father tell you what happened to him in Chile?"

"No, my boss, Admiral Lowe, gave me a heads up when I happened to say that my father was never behind enemy lines." He began laughing and he spent the next several hours telling what happened before Rodney Lowe's account.

I was in the radio room with your father when the message was decoded. My ship, the Yantic, San Francisco and Baltimore were ordered to break away from our South Atlantic stations and cruise at top speed to the port of Stanley in the Falkland Islands.

"Where are the Falkland Islands?" My radioman asked me.

"Off the coast of Argentina, I think. We need to check our maps and charts. Take this message up to the chart room and find out."

"Aye, aye. Sir."

They checked our maps and found the Falklands Islands. I checked our port information handbook and learned that the Port of Stanley houses the largest ship repair facility in the South Atlantic. Like Bermuda of the Middle Atlantic, Great Britain built a shipyard at the Port of Stanley. We would undoubtedly receive further orders upon arrival.

The three ships entered Port Stanley. We docked and were met by the United States Minister to the Falklands. He requested a meeting with me, Admiral Brown of the San Francisco and Captain Schley of the Baltimore. The meeting lasted several hours and when I returned to the Yantic I had an officer's mess with junior officers like your father.

"Gentlemen, it appears that the Presidente of Chile has requested assistance against a group of rebels who have attacked the Capital at Santiago, Chile. The closest seaport to Santiago is Valpariso, Chile. We are ordered there to show the flag in support of Presidente Balmacceda. I do not anticipate any trouble what-so-ever from the Chilean Navy. The Chilean Army and Navy are presently supporting the government of Chile. The Secretary of the Navy has ordered us to leave Stanley and sail through the Straight of Magellan, which is entirely within the country of Chile. We are requested to make port calls at Punta Arenas, Puerto Montt, Concepcion and north to Valpariso. It is spring in the South Atlantic but we may encounter ice flows from winter this far south. Mr. Caldwell, are our charts up-to-date for those waters?"

"Yes, captain."

"Admiral Brown will issue orders for all three ships during the passage through the Straight and the port stays during the next three months. That will be all. Return to your normal routines and await my orders."

As I walked back to my cabin, I thought this could turn out to be another year away from home and family. I hated a police action and this was setting up to be just that. The Marines aboard the San Francisco and Baltimore might see action before this is all over. In a matter of minutes we had a message from the San Francisco. "Fire boilers."

The cruise through the Straight was uneventful and no ice flows were blocking our passage. We entered Punta Arenas and docked with the other two American vessels. I was called to the San Francisco for a briefing from the Admiral.

"It seems that 'Presidente Balmecceda' has asked for political refuge in the American Embassy in Santiago. Ambassador Patrick Egan has granted his request. The Army has joined the rebels and the Navy of Chile has remained neutral. I do not have to tell you that Chile is one of the most powerful and warlike countries in South America. Your mission may become one of rescue for the Americans and Presidente Balmecceda from Santiago through Valpariso. Please brief your ship's company on this new development."

We sailed for Puerto Montt the next day. We docked with no objections from the Chilean Navy and got further information. The insurgents had charged that US Ambassador Egan had given aid to the Balmaccedists and allowed many to find refuge at the Legation in Santiago.

We sailed for Concepcion. We again docked without any Chilean Navy notice. It was now October and the insurgents had prevented many persons from entering or leaving the US Embassy. They arrested Americans working at the Embassy when they left and then held the Embassy in a state of siege. Matters were so threatening that the United States Department of State closed the embassy in Santiago and sent word to the new Chilean Government to end the siege, release the Americans working there and transport them to the Port of Valpariso. A telegram from the Chilean capital was sent to Washington stating that the embassy employees were persona nongrata and expelled from Chile for giving aid to the Balmaccedists during the revolution. The embassy members could be transported from Santiago to Valpariso by train, but someone above the rank of Admiral would need to travel to Santiago and sign for the release of those being held. Admiral Brown of the *USS San Francisco* was to be relieved of command as he had given secret information to the Balmaccedists during the revolution. A charge which, I thought, was ridiculous on the face of it since the ships were not in Chilean waters until the revolution was over.

The Secretary of State, James Blaine, presented the demands to President Harrison. The President laughed and said, "I wonder if they would release Patrick Egan to me?"

"Mr. President, I have an idea."

"Yes, Mr. Blaine, what is it?"

"I wonder if they would release them to the former vice-president, Caldwell?"

"Caldwell is past seventy years old and retired in Pennsylvania, he can not go there!"

"No, but his son is there."

"Where?"

"On board the *USS Yantic*. He is the third officer."

"What is his rank?"

"I have no idea, but I know it is not an admiral."

"Fine, make him special assistant to the Secretary of State and send him to Santiago."

"Sir, would it be alright if I sent a telegram stating that the terms of the Santiago Mission are acceptable to our government. The *USS San Francisco* and the *USS Baltimore* will be ordered to leave Valpariso. We are asking J. Jason Caldwell to head the mission to Santiago. He will be leaving Valpariso as soon as he gets there to take charge of the release of the Americans being held at the Embassy in Santiago. We request that a detachment of Chilean Marines be assigned to Mr. Caldwell for escort. If Chilean Marines are not available, then we request that a detachment of American Marines be allowed to escort Mr. Caldwell."

"I like it, this tin horn Chilean General, will think we are sending the former Vice President and we are taking his little revolution seriously. The Chilean Navy is still sitting on the sidelines, correct?"

"Correct, Mr. President."

"Good, send the telegram and orders to Captain Bertram of the *USS Yantic* and let him break the bad news to James, the son. Oh, and if the son survives this mission, promote him in rank."

Your father was in the radio room when the orders from the Secretary of the Navy were decoded. His radioman said, "LT, you have been given a temporary promotion."

"What?"

"The orders to Captain Bertram indicate that you are to be released from your present command aboard the Yantic and you are to be assigned to the Department of State. Once this has been done, you are to travel directly to the Capital of Chile. You are to locate Ambassador Egan and others being held inside the Santiago Legation Compound and return them to the Yantic for transport to Washington."

"How the hell am I going to do that?"

"There are more coded messages following, LT. That must be the 'how' of the mission. Wait a few minutes and you can take the whole lot up to the Captain."

In a matter of minutes, he was at my cabin asking for permission to enter.

"Enter."

"Captain, here is an 'urgent' from the Secretary of the Navy, Tracy."

"Did you read it when you decoded it, Mr. Caldwell?

"I did, Captain. It sounds like a hair brained scheme to me, Sir."

"Let me read it." I finished with a smile on my face. "Having the last name Caldwell, got you in hot water with this one, James. I doubt it will be dangerous, especially with the US escort unarmed and the Chilean escort clearing the way for you from the docks to the train station. It is only 68 miles to Santiago, but you never know, I would tell your marines to carry personal weapons, like knives or concealed hand guns, if I were you. I will contact Admiral Brown and see if he was copied on these orders and if he will provide his best marines for your escort to the train station. You will need civilian clothes, do you have any on board?"

"No, Sir. Just my navy gear."

"Well, we are about the same size, go over to my wardrobe and see if you can get into my business suit. I want it returned without bullet holes, James."

It was October 16th when he left with an escort of 20 marines from the San Francisco and 20 volunteers from the Baltimore. Admiral Brown had said that he could not order his men to complete a Department of State mission to Santiago and he asked for volunteers. Only the truly adventurous or mentally incompetent ever volunteer to go unarmed behind enemy lines, he had told me. The seamen from the Baltimore included coal-heavers and boiler makers. These were some of the largest men I had ever seen. Everyone was in uniform, except your father, and he left the Yantic to meet the Chilean escort waiting on the docks. A Chilean officer saluted and said in perfect English, "Mr. Caldwell, it is an honor to escort you to the train depot for our trip to Santiago."

"Thank you, Sir. How far is the depot?"

"It is a short walk, Sir. Just enough time to tell you about the city of Valparaiso. It is the capital of the Province of Valparaiso, Chile. It is the chief seaport of the republic, situated on a bay of the Pacific 68 miles west-northwest of Santiago. You will travel about 116 miles to get there by rail, however. The older and business portion of the city extends along the bay, while on the slopes of the surrounding hills are the finer residences. Vina del Mar, a few miles to the east, is a noted suburb and seaside resort. It enjoys a mild and equable climate, the average temperature being 58 degrees. The hottest is January with 63 degrees and the coldest is July with 53 degrees."

"I have gotten used to winter and summer being reversed since my assignment in the South Atlantic."

"I thought you came from Washington?"

Your father realized his error. He was speaking like an American seaman, not a diplomat. He tried to recover, "No, I was brought here from my diplomatic assignment in the Falklands. The President decided that I could get here much quicker than someone from Washington. We consider this matter with Chile to be very serious and we need to get the situation calmed down before it escalates into something that neither country desires."

The Chilean officer looked doubtful but continued his description of Valpariso. "We are entering the main plaza with many monuments. That one over there is a statue of Columbus. We also have statues of William Wheelright, who built the first railroad in Chile and Thomas Cochrane who organized the Chilean Army. Over there is a statue of Admiral Prat and .....

He never finished his sentence because a mob of men, about a hundred in number, came rushing across the plaza and attacked the escort. The mob was trying to fight through the Chilean Naval escort and kill the Americans. The mob pushed through the thin line of Chileans and the unarmed Americans fought back with bravery, but they were at a fatal disadvantage. Charles Riggins, a boatswain's mate of the Baltimore, was killed and William Turnbull, a coal-heavier, had his neck slashed before the 80 man escort could drive the mob away.

"It looks like two of your escort are dead, Mr. Caldwell and several others need medical attention. The depot is a block away. I will leave a guard detail with the dead and wounded and the rest of us will put you on the train to Santiago. You need to select a body guard from your remaining escort, we will arm them for you." He looked shaken.

"Excellent solution, Sir. I began tapping men on the shoulder and said, "Get a rifle from a Chilean Marine and walk with me to the depot."

Not a one refused and within a few minutes, they were on the train. Your father had no idea how many of the wounded men would survive - but he needed to send a telegram to me and report what had happened. He knew that the survivors would be taken back to the ship.

His first train stop was Vina del Mar and your father left the train and entered the telegraph depot. He told the telegraph operator that he needed to send a telegram to the Valpariso dockyards, pier six.

> Walk to depot interrupted by well wishers – party got wild and two are drunk – the rest will have hangovers – I have members with me – names are Easterbrook, Howard, Williams, Nelson, Carson and Lopez – hope my tour guide will bring all home to you.
>
> JJ

The train continued on into Santiago without further incident and he left the train as a group. He had some money with him for emergencies and he had seaman Lopez hail a cab. All seven of them squeezed into it and Lopez asked if they could drive by the American embassy that was now under house arrest. The driver laughed and said he could, for five extra pesos. Lopez handed him the money and they were there in a few minutes. Lopez asked the driver to stop, handed him another 100 pesos and said, "We were never here, understand?"

He nodded and pulled away. "Now what, LT?" Seaman Nelson asked.

"Now we get to show our diplomatic papers and enter the embassy."

"We may not get out again." Nelson was smiling.

"I thought you were the adventurous type, Nelson!"

"No, Sir. Mentally incompetent!"

They all began to laugh and they walked over to the Chilean guard at the gate to the embassy grounds. Your father handed him his papers. The guard examined them and opened the gate. The guard said something in Spanish, your father nodded his head and keep walking. "What did he say, Lopez?"

"He said finally he could get back to his barracks and get a bath."

"Has he left his post?"

"Yes, he is packing up."

They entered the embassy and found Patrick Egan. He and the others were hungry, as they were rationing food and water. "Nothing was allowed in or out, Mr. Caldwell."

"Well, the guard at the gate is leaving, I think this is over. We have to figure out a way to get your people to the train station. Does the embassy have emergency funds, transportation and armed guards?"

"Of course."

"Get all the money together. We will eat on the train. Get everything that can be used to haul people to the train depot. We need to get out of here in a few minutes."

"I am not sure that we can do that."

"Let me put it this way, Mr. Ambassador. I am not a member of the State Department. I am a member of the United States Navy, I and my men are leaving in ten minutes. I hope that you and yours will accompany us."

The ambassador looked shocked and began shouting orders to everyone in sight. Within twenty minutes, the wagons and carriages were loaded with departing embassy members and they were on their way to the train station. They left the horses attached to their wagons and bought tickets to Valpariso. The next two hours before the train left, your father expected the Chilean Army to appear and arrest all of them.

When they arrived in Valpariso, I had taken no chances. I had ordered two deck guns mounted on wagons and nearly all the Marines on board to go with me to meet them. We walked slowly back to the ship and looked down each street that entered into the plaza. We were on board before the your father explained what had happened to his escort.

I had to tell him, "James, you are not going to believe this. Your escort was arrested for inciting a riot."

"All forty of them, including the Chileans?"

"Yes, except for Riggins and Turnbull. They are all locked in the city jail in two separate cells, one for the Americans and one for the Chileans. Not a single member of the mob was detained."

"What? How can that be?"

"I think the locals recognized men in the mob and let them go."

"Have we lodged a formal complaint?"

"First, we cabled Washington asking for orders and then we sent a shore patrol to the jail to await the release of the sailors."

"Has Washington responded?"

"Not yet. I think we will hear something tonight or tomorrow."

IN WASHINGTON, President Harrison was meeting with his Secretary of State, War and Navy. "What happened in Valpariso, gentlemen?"

They read the messages from the Yantic and said, "We have not heard from Lieutenant Caldwell, Mr. President."

"Go down to the basement and send a message to the Yantic. I want to hear from Caldwell, Egan and Bertram, in that order."

"Yes, Mr. President."

ON BOARD THE YANTIC messages were decoded. I was asleep when my radio man woke me and said, "You have a request from the President, Captain."

"Quit kidding me and let me go back to sleep."

"No kidding, Sir. You are required to respond immediately."

I was out of my bunk, and dressed, sort of, and on my way to the radio room. I had the radio man code an answer to all the president's questions and Patrick Egan walked in. He sat down and responded to the president's questions and left. Your father sat down and did the same. We sat looking at the radio receiver expecting it to come to life.

It remained silent. Finally, I said, "Sounds like Benjamin Harrison is upset, I wonder what he will do."

In Washington, the Ambassador from Chile, Jose Florentino, was sitting in the Oval Office. He was uncomfortable because the President of the United States was yelling at him.

"Listen, Mr. Ambassador, I understand that your country has just gone through a revolution and your new dictator, General 'what is his name' may not understand what the killing of American diplomats in his country will mean."

"General Peron, is the new Presidente, Sir. I am unaware of any killing of American diplomats in my country."

"Well, you are behind the times, maybe tomorrow you will get word of what has happened. In the meantime, I have ordered a brigade of United States Marines to surround the Chilean Embassy here in Washington. I have ordered that no one is to be allowed in or out. That includes food and water. You will not be allowed back inside. I suggest that you use the telegraph services here in the White House to notify your government of what has happened here. There have been deaths in Chile. We will arrest the same number and drag them from your embassy if there is no response from your country in twenty-four hours. These persons are not US Citizens and they will be treated as spies and shot by firing squad."

"Sir, I understand that you are upset. But that is ridiculous. We have diplomatic immunity."

"Not if the two countries are at war. I will arrest the entire legation and exchange them for those Americans being held in Chile. They did not have diplomatic immunity, you killed two of them. I will respond in kind to every action taken in Chile. If you kill Americans, I will kill Chileans. If you fire on US ships in Chile, I will order the entire Atlantic and Pacific fleets to hunt down and sink every Chilean ship afloat. War can be avoided, but it is really up to you, Mr. Ambassador. You need to tell your government that I have ordered the Secretary of War to place our country on a wartime footing. Do you wish to send messages to Chile?"

"Yes, Mr. President."

On board the Yantic, in obedience to orders from Washington, your father and I were preparing a complete report to be sent to the War Department. We reported that the diplomatic delegation was attacked in the Plaza by a mob of men. One of the escorts for Mr. Caldwell had been shot in the head with a pistol (seaman Riggins) and another bled to death from a knife wound (seaman Turnbull). Mr. Caldwell was an eyewitness to the murders.

According to eyewitness reports of the arrest of the Chilean and American escorts by Valpariso Police, the result was brutal. A number of wounds were made by bayonets, proving that the police over- reacted and there was no cause for the arrest of the escorts, the mob should have been arrested instead. It was coded and sent to Washington, along with Egan's report of the rescue by your father.

In Washington, Ambassador Florentino had returned to the Oval Office. It was now forty-eight hours since the death of seamen Riggins and Turnbull. The conversation began anew.

"Ambassador Florentino, have you forwarded the reports that I gave to you from the *USS Yantic*?"

"Yes, Mr. President, all of the Americans have been released from jail in Valpariso and have been returned to their ship."

"Thank you, Mr. Ambassador. What about the reparations called for in the Egan report?"

"My government has given no weight to the Egan report, as he was not at the scene of the riot, Mr. President. I have been told that the riot is under investigation by my authorities, who have promised to judge and punish the guilty. Since judicial investigation under Chilean law is secret, the time has not come to make known the result. The demands made by Ambassador Egan can not be agreed to."

"I would like you to return to the basement and send the following information to your new Presidente, not to an underling. You will tell him that I find his reaction to this affair insulting. You will use those words. Do not use some other diplomatic substitute. If the word insulting is not included in your message, my radio man will not send it. Do you understand my request?"

"Yes, Mr. President."

"You may also include that I have released the members inside the Chilean embassy except for two foreign ministers. They will be shot by military firing squad unless this matter is resolved."

"Thank you, Mr. President, I will return to my embassy and send the message as you indicated."

"No, you will not. You, Ambassador, are now under house arrest here in the White House. You will be released when the matter is settled."

THE RADIO ROOM aboard the Yantic had incoming messages from the White House.

> 1. RETURN ALL AMERICANS TO WASHINGTON AS SOON AS POSSIBLE.
>
> 2. INFORM LIEUTENANT CALDWELL THAT HE IS NOW A COMMANDER IN THE UNITED STATES NAVY – JOB WELL DONE.
>
> BENJAMIN HARRISON, COMMANDER-IN-CHIEF

THE RADIO ROOM aboard the San Francisco and Baltimore had incoming messages from the Secretary of the Navy.

> 1. ADMIRAL BROWN, RETURN THE SAN FRANCISCO AND BALTIMORE TO DOCKAGE IN VALPARISO.
>
> 2. REMAIN ON STATION UNTIL THE INQUIRY INTO THE DEATHS AND INJURIES OF AMERICAN SAILORS HAS BEEN RESOLVED.
>
> 3. IF FIRED UPON, RETURN FIRE TO POINT OF ORIGIN. DO NOT RETURN AN EQUAL RESPONSE. FIRE FOR TOTAL EFFECT. IT IS THE PRESIDENT'S WISH TO SINK AS MANY CHILEAN SHIPS AS POSSIBLE, BOTH MERCHANT AND WARSHIPS. IT IS ALSO HIS DESIRE TO LEVEL THE SEAPORT OF VALPARISO.
>
> 4. THIS MESSAGE IS SENT IN THE CLEAR. COPY IS SENT TO USS BALTIMORE AND USS YANTIC. YANTIC IS RETURNING TO WASHINGTON THIS DATE.

I radioed Admiral Brown off the coast of Chile and offered to exchange pier locations with him. He radioed back that he preferred to keep the San Francisco and Baltimore free to maneuver in case of a declaration of war. He then added something that surprised us. He had received messages from the *USS Maine* and *USS Texas* that they were in route to Valpariso to take up station with him. Both of these ships and their escorts would enter from the South Atlantic. He warned us that these newest ships were both battleships of immense size and to please be careful in the Straight of Magellan. He then added that the ten other ships joining him from Hawaii were much smaller, 8000 ton class. He sent his response in the clear so that the Chilean Navy could hear and forward this information to Santiago.

It was late in the evening and Captain Bertram and I were still talking about my father when he was a Lieutenant Commander assigned to the radio room on the *USS Yantic* in October of 1891..

"Commander Caldwell, I have served in the US Navy most of my life and survived two wars. What your father did, unarmed, in Chile was the most remarkable thing I have ever witnessed."

"Thank you, Captain. I am just now beginning to understand my father and how he sees the world around him. My commanding officers would never trust me with the responsibility that was given to my father in Chile."

"They must. I have forgotten why I came looking for you tonight, Louis. Here is a radio message that informs you that you have been promoted from Lieutenant Commander to Commander. Let me be the first to congratulate you on your promotion."

"Thank you. Coming from you, that is greatly appreciated, Captain. Can I tell my father that I met you aboard the Vixen?"

"Of course, tell him this is my last duty before retirement. The Navy has agreed to promote me to Commodore, if I will agree to hang up my uniform."

"May I be the first to salute the new Commodore, Sir?"

"That would mean a lot, son. Thank you."

37

American Embassy

Berlin

The *USS Vixen* docked in Danzig and I took the train to Berlin. Hans Becker and two men were standing on the train platform. I had not seen Hans since before the death of Tim Jacobson. We had written and talked on the telephone, of course. As I gazed out the coach window and waited for the train to come to a complete stop I remembered the last time I was in Berlin.

"Louis, mine friend, vos is los width ja?" I turned to Tim and said, "In English, that was, Louis, my friend, what is up with you."

"That was in English, dumbkopf!" Hans would never change.

"Not in any English I know, Hans. I have been practicing my Dutch. Do you want to hear the same phrase in Dutch?"

"Got, no. Your Dutch is worse than mine English." We both broke out into laughter.

"This is my partner, Hans, his name is Tim Jacobson and he understands me as much as you do."

"Dat, is quite a complement, Tim. I had to babysit him all da way through language school. Are you da babysitter now?"

"Ja, mine job is never done!" Tim was smiling.

"I like dis, Tim Jacobson, Louis, let's keep him."

"Right, Hans!"

"Right, Louis!" Hans put his arm around Tim's shoulder and whispered something to him.

"I heard that!"

I was brought back to reality when I heard, "Over here, Louis!" Hans was waving his arms. I had a chained embassy brief case fastened to my left wrist. I walked over and shook his hand with my right hand.

"How have you been, Hans?"

"Mine life is a mess, Louis, I have met the love of mine life here in Berlin!"

"Which of these two is he?" Hans looked confused and the two body guards began to laugh. They said something in German to Hans and he glared at me and said, "The one on the right, dumbkopf." I began to laugh, it was a long time since I had really laughed at anything.

"Can I meet her, Hans?"

"Ja, only if you behave yourself and you are here a week. She is on a holiday with her parents in Switzerland."

"Is she Swiss?"

"Nein, dumbkopf, she is visiting her money in Switzerland, no one trusts German banks anymore."

"Let's get my baggage and you can tell me all about her on our drive into the embassy. Right Hans?"

"Right Louis."

The ride into the American Embassy was a revisit of the train ride Hans and I had taken from Monterey, California, to Washington, D.C. nearly two years ago. We sat in the back seat and one of the body guards drove. The last time I was in Berlin, Hans had driven Tim and I into the embassy. When we arrived that time, I got out of the car and dropped to my knees and kissed the ground. Hans said, "Ja, you must really like Germany, Louis."

Tim replied, "I think he is thankful to be alive, I know I am!"

I was smiling at my memory when Hans said, "So, what was so important that Admiral Lowe sent you to Berlin?"

"I have no idea. We will open the sealed orders when we get in your deluxe, basement facilities, Hans."

"We can use the table with the huge burn mark, if you like, Louis." We laughed at my little demonstration of the C4 used to destroy mustard gas factories throughout the German Empire. It would be the last laugh either one of us had for several months.

LATER INSIDE, WHAT HANS CALLED THE SAFE ROOM, we opened the case fastened to my left wrist. It felt funny having the metal bracelet taken from my wrist. It was attached in Washington and I had worn it aboard the *USS Vixen* and the train from Danzig to Berlin. I broke the seal in front of the American Ambassador to the German Empire. He would store the documents for us after we had read them. The first document was a letter from the President to the Ambassador.

THE WHITE HOUSE

WASHINGTON, D.C.

Ambassador Woodrow Wilson
American Embassy
Berlin, Germany

Dear Dr. Wilson:

This is to introduce the courier of this letter to you. He is Lieutenant Commander Louis Caldwell, Presidential Envoy to Kaiser Wilhelm II. You will seek an audience with the Kaiser at his earliest convenience. Commander Caldwell is carrying a letter from me to the Kaiser. You should find that letter below this missive to you. Remove it, read it and give it to Commander Caldwell for delivery. The letter is meaningless on its surface, it is a device to grant the Commander an audience with the Kaiser where he will deliver a personal oral message to the Kaiser.

Lieutenant Commander Caldwell is on a mission from the Director of the Office of Naval Counter

Intelligence at my request. His time in Germany will be determined by the rate of success he experiences. He will make use of all of the personnel assigned to our embassy, including your services if necessary. Please burn this letter, after you have shared the contents with Lieutenant Commanders Becker and Caldwell.

T. Roosevelt

Theodore Roosevelt
President of the United States

The second letter was to the Kaiser.

THE WHITE HOUSE

WASHINGTON, D.C.

Wilhelm Hesse-Cassel
Kaiser of the German Empire
Kaiserslautern, Bavaria

My Dear Wilhelm,

Your hand written message was greatly appreciated. I remember with fondness your visit to Ruth and myself in 1902 and your gifts to the American people. Your brother, Admiral Prince Henry of Prussia, continues to be of great assistance to my Secretary of the Navy. Your proposal to exchange college professors has been approved by the following American Colleges and Universities: Harvard, William and Mary, Princeton, Cambridge and Dartmouth. I am sending my personal representative, a graduate of William and Mary and my nephew to visit with you further on this matter.

Give my best to your wife, Princess Victoria Schleswig-Holstein-Sonderburg-Augustenburg and your son, Prince Frederick William.

T. Roosevelt

Theodore Roosevelt
President of the United States

The third letter was to Hans Becker from Admiral Rodney Lowe.

Fairfield Institute for International Studies
Office of the Director

Professor Hans Becker
American Scholars Abroad Program
Berlin, Germany

Dear Professor Becker:

It is my desire that you meet President Roosevelt's envoy when he arrives in Berlin. He is carrying a letter of introduction to Kaiser Wilhelm II. He may ask you to accompany him to Kaiserslautern, Bavaria. Please give every assistance in his quest to arrange professorial exchanges with the German Empire. He is interested in air travel and I would like to have him travel from Berlin to Kaiserslautern, a distance of 298 miles, in the new zeppelins now serving all of the German Empire. In addition, the aeroplane is now a modern form of rapid transit between remote points inside the empire. Please request a visit to the nearest place where the President's representative may witness or even fly in one of these machines. Thank you for your consideration.

Rodney Lowe, Dean

Woodrow Wilson was the President of Princeton University when President Roosevelt asked him to take a temporary leave of absence from his office and travel to Berlin. The tensions between the two countries were at the boiling point. The Kaiser was a champion of higher education within the German Empire and Theodore Roosevelt wanted to insure him that the United States was not seeking a war with Germany. He persuaded the foremost educator at the time, Woodrow Wilson, to pour oil upon the troubled waters in Berlin.

Wilson was born in Staunton, Virginia. He graduated from Princeton in 1879, then studied law at the University of Virginia, and for two years, in 1882-83, he practiced law in Atlanta, Georgia. In1884, he entered the newly opened John Hopkins University where he was awarded the degree of PhD, presenting as his thesis, *A study of Congressional Government* which won him a reputation as a scholar and a clear, original thinker. He was an associate professor of history at Bryn Mawr, 1885-88. He moved to Wesleyan University as department chair until 1890, when he returned to Princeton as professor of law. In 1902, when President Patton left Princeton, he was elected president as his replacement where he was serving until 1905, and the visit from the President of the United States.

The total number of letters, diagrams, maps, and other documents totaled 37 in number. It I used all of them, it would take me more than a month in Berlin and the surrounding estates, airfields and military installations. In my orders from Admiral Lowe he was very particular to point out that I was to go and see everything that the Kaiser suggested and everything that he was particularly proud to show me. I was, after all, the nephew of his friend, Theodore Roosevelt. I began my quest my asking Ambassador Wilson to tell me what he knew about Count Zeppelin's airships.

"I am not the one you should ask about this, Commander. There are military experts assigned to the embassy besides Commander Becker, one of them can bring you up to speed on the 1905 Zeppelins in service."

"What about the history of airships, Sir?"

"That, I can help you with, Count Zeppelin's or all airships?"

"I have to write report about the effectiveness of Zeppelins in support of ground troops, so I suppose you better brief me on the Zeppelin, Dr. Wilson."

"The Zeppelin is a notable airship, both for its size and design. In 1900, Count Zeppelin made several voyages to London, Madrid and Paris. The 1900, model consisted of a row of seventeen balloons, confined like a row of lozenges in a package. The package was placed in a cylindrical shell 420 feet long and 39 feet in diameter, with pointed ends. These balloons were filled with hydrogen to lift the structure in the air, where it was driven forward or backward by means of large screw propellers operated by benzine motors. A pair of rudders, one forward and one aft, serve to steer the airship. The crew and passengers occupy two aluminum cars suspended forward and aft, below the body of the shell."

"Dr. Wilson, I am also to report on how the Germans manufacture their metal you just called aluminum. Can I interrupt you long enough to take a side trip into aluminum?"

"You are referring to Zeolites, a family of minerals including hydrated alkalies or alkaline earths, usually containing aluminum and sometimes magnesium. Magnesium is highly flammable and combined with hydrogen, it would be a death trap for anyone inside the Zeppelin. Therefore the refinement of aluminum from the Zeolite ore must as pure as they can make it. Zeolites are all secondary minerals and are found largely in cavities and fissures in basic igneous rocks such as Basalt, Diabase, and others."

"Thank you, Dr. Wilson. I will tell Washington to forget about aluminum frames."

"Or stay away from hydrogen, use helium instead, the western United States is full of helium. That is one of the items that the Kaiser, or one of his aides, will ask you to make a commitment about."

"I don't understand."

"Germany has been trying to buy liquid helium from the United States since 1900. We have feared that it would be used in the Kaiser's war efforts and not for commercial travel."

"I see, I will inform the Kaiser that I will pass his request on to Washington. I may not even get an appointment to see the Kaiser."

"Yes, I have a feeling all three of us will travel from Berlin to Kaiserslautern within a few days of receipt of my letter to him."

"I am sorry, Dr. Wilson, continue about the history of the Zeppelin."

"The cars which are hung from the aluminum frame of the Zeppelin have a speaking tube that runs between them. From the crew's car a ladder runs up into the Zeppelin where the machinery is located. A crew member can move a large weight along a cable. When the Zeppelin is in level flight, the weight is in the center of the ship. When the weight is moved forward, the nose starts to tip down. When the weight is moved backwards, the tail tips down. The rudders cause right and left movements during flight. The Daimler benzine engines, one below each car, are 16 horsepower and weight 700 pounds each. The propellers, two for each engine had four blades on the 1900, model."

"What was the ground speed of the older models, Dr. Wilson?"

"It was not very good, depending upon head winds or tail winds, it averaged 12 to 13 miles in an hour. None of the 1900 models are in service."

"Tell me about the 1905, models used for commercial travel. Why would anyone take a Zeppelin when a train is so much faster?"

"Because, the Zeppelin you will ride in this week will not need a set of tracks and its ground speed is 45 mph from start to finish. A train can not average 45 mph because of all the stops necessary on a crowed railroad and the need to pick up additional passengers at every railroad station. Have you ever ridden in a dirigible, Commander?"

"No, why do you ask?"

"You are in for a treat. The ride is smoother than a train or a ship at sea. The furnishing are very luxurious, indeed!"

"What changes were made to too make the speed so much faster?"

"The 16 horsepower engines were replaced with 170 horsepower and the propellor design changed to be similar to an aeroplane. Do you have any more questions, Commander?"

"No, Sir. There are 37 pages inside that brief case and we have looked at the first three. Hans, flip through the rest of the pages, are they in code?"

"Ja, these all have to go down to crypto in order for us to read them."

"Then I will leave you two gentlemen and retire to my office to write a letter to the Kaiser, informing him that two representatives from President Roosevelt have arrived in Berlin with a reply to his request for university professor exchanges beginning next year. Hans, I would carry your letter from Fairfield with you on our visit, Hans."

"Yes, Sir, Mr. Ambassador I will."

THE NEXT DAY, Hans and I had a decoded version of the next 34 pages contained in my delivery from Washington, D.C.:

1-5. Data sheets for observations of Zeppelin airship passage from Berlin to Kaiserslautern.

A. Description of airfield in Berlin used by commercial zeppelins.
B. Photograph of zeppelin loading passengers if possible.
C. Interview with crew members on board if possible.
D. Tour of zeppelin if possible.
E. Weight and amounts of luggage allowed on flight.

6-10. Data sheets for observation of Kaiserslautern.

A. Photograph of zeppelin airfield at Kaiserslautern if allowed.
B. Description of Kaiser's compound and working offices.
C. Description of troops stationed at Kaiserslautern.
D. Photograph or description of aeroplanes and/or airfield at Kaiserslautern or nearby locations.
E. Interview with Kaiser and aides at Kaiserslautern.

11-15. Report format for visit to Valkyrie aeroplane factory.

A. Photographs of processes if possible
B. Description of assembly process
C. Description of wing design
D. Gun mounts and number placement
E. Part inventory if possible

16-20. Report format for inspection of armored tracked vehicle factory.

A. Photographs of processes if possible
B. Description of armored vehicles
C. Description and/or photograph of MAV
D. Photograph of steel tracked vehicle
E. Part inventories if possible

21-25. Report format for summary of professor exchange conference.

A. Names of certified professors and universities
B. Names of persons who might be possible agents
C. Speech by the Kaiser
D. Speeches of interest by German University Professors
E. List of names who might want to immigrate to the US

26-30. Report format for visits to Lorraine, Wurtemberg and Baden.

A. Description of the extensive arsenal built in Strassburg
B. List of manufacturing facilities and those toured
C. Tonnage produced in a normal production run
D. Division of rounds into army, navy and other
E. Estimate of numbers of workers employed

30-34. Berlin to London courier instructions.

A. Contacts within the embassy, Berlin
B. Contacts within the embassy, London
C. Contacts within the British War Department
D. British reaction to the massive buildup of war materials within the German Empire
E. Diplomatic passport for Louis Jason Caldwell

38

Count Zeppelin Airfield

Berlin, Germany

It took ten days for the Kaiser to answer Ambassador Wilson's letter. His response contained an invitation to visit his retreat in Kaiserslautern. He had arranged a university exchange conference for Professor Hans Becker and I to attend while we spent the week with him. His letter also included two tickets from Berlin to Kaiserslautern, and factory passes for the various other sightseeing requests in Dr. Wilson's letter of introduction. Obviously, the Kaiser did not want to see the American Ambassador after the actions from the White House last month.

Hans and I decided to leave most of the coded instructions inside the American Embassy in Berlin and travel with a minimum of documents. We had our passports, of course, but neither indicated that we were diplomats. We could be stopped, questioned and even detained while traveling inside the German Empire. We hoped the letter of invitation from the Kaiser to meet him would be our safeguard. Hans had his bodyguards drive us to the Aerodrome in Berlin. It is hard to describe a set of buildings and a site large enough to hold a 480 foot long and 60 foot diameter dirigible. The repair hanger, next to the airship terminal must be longer than 500 feet, contain the necessary equipment to deflate and inflate the hydrogen cells, do the necessary repairs on the crew and passenger compartments, and resupply the zeppelin after each long flight across Germany. The height of the hanger must provide for the 60 feet of the dirigible plus the height of the two compartments below the dirigible. The Berlin Aerodrome was a showplace for visitors to Germany, the Kaiser wanted to show the world how advanced the Empire had become in such a short time. I was impressed.

We showed our tickets and the letter of invitation to visit the Kaiser at the ticket window and the man inside fell all over himself when he looked at the letter.

"Welcome to Berlin Aerodrome, Professor Becker and Mr. Caldwell, we have been expecting you. Come with me to the VIP lounge." His high German was perfect and I had trouble understanding him, but Hans babbled on and on to him as we followed him down a hallway and around a corner to the lounge area. One wall was entirely windows and there was the *Count Zeppelin III* tied to its mast awaiting the boarding of passengers. We stopped dead in our tracks and gazed at the giant, silver cigar before us. Our ticket master smiled and said, "When someone sees the *Count* for the first time it is awesome, yes?"

"Yes, it is! Dirigibles in the United States are 100 feet long and twenty feet in diameter. That is a monster." Hans said.

"Yours are experimental, carrying two or three people, the *Count* is more comparable to a small ocean liner, while yours is like a row boat."

"That is a very good comparison, Sir. Can I use that when I see my Uncle Teddy?" The ticket master looked confused and turned to Hans. Hans repeated my statement in high German and the ticket master smiled and said, "I think the President of the United States would like you to say exactly that, young man."

The ticket master never left us and I wondered who was at the ticket window. We were given a small meal of bread, cheese, sausages, Rhine wine and a dessert. We watched as a load of suitcases were loaded into the crew compartment, we saw ours among them. The ticket master told us that the luggage was placed above the crew's compartment inside the *Count.* He explained that to balance the airship, weights were divided between the crew and passenger compartments. A small group of passengers came walking out on the surface of the landing pad and walked up three sets of stairs onto a platform that looked like it was twenty feet above ground level. A door slid open and they entered the passenger's compartment.

"I will walk with you gentlemen, if you are ready." He opened one of the windows, which was really a door cleverly disguised and we began walking towards the *Count*. It got larger and larger. The shadow cast by the *Count* was immense. We got to the top of the three flights of stairs and stood on the platform. The door of the compartment slid open again and we stepped inside the passenger's compartment. We were standing on two inch thick carpet that ran between a double row of opera seats. These seats allowed the passengers to look out of the windows that were on either side of the compartment car. The compartment car was about twenty-four feet long with a doorway which, I supposed, provided crew access to the overhead storage space inside the *Count*. The door was locked. A voice came out of a grill work at the front of the compartment.

"Good Morning, welcome aboard the *Count Zeppelin*. I am Captain Nedimeyer speaking to you from the flight deck directly above you. Our flight to Kaiserslautern is about 4 hours and ten minutes. You will need to find a comfortable seat and remain seated until I announce that we have reached our flight altitude. Matches, lighters and open flames are not permitted while you are aboard. This is a non-smoking flight."

"Four hours? That can not be right, Hans, it is 298 miles to Kaiserslautern."

"Kilometers, not miles, Louis." He had just gotten that out of his mouth when the cable was released from the mooring mast and we floated twenty feet above the ground. I could hear the sound of the propellers turning and I felt the tail sink slightly and we moved forward along the ground. We picked up speed as we traveled parallel to the ground, I heard a hissing sound and the *Count* slowly began to rise vertically at a steady rate.

"That must be the full inflation of the hydrogen cells, Louis." Hans was enjoying this. The hissing stopped the tail dipped nearly ten degrees and the *Count* roared into the air at a high rate of speed. I asked the steward who had appeared from the locked door, "How fast are we going?"

"You must be one of the Americans on board, I can tell by your accent. We are traveling about 30 kilometers per hour during the assent. When we reach our flight altitude, the captain will level the *Count* and increase speed to 80 kilometers per hour."

"80, I had no idea!"

"Kilometers, not miles, Louis." Hans wrote 48 mph on his note pad. In a few minutes, the voice through the grill spoke again.

"Good morning again. This is your captain speaking. We have reached our flight altitude of 650 meters and we have increased our forward thrust to 90 kilometers per hour. We have increased our flight speed today because we will have a military escort. In a few minutes you will be able to see a flight of four Valkyrie, German made, aeroplanes. Two will be on our port side and two will be on our starboard side. These new German fighters are in honor of our two guests who are representing the President of the United States. Professor Becker, please raise your hand so the rest of the passengers can meet you. Professor Becker is a language professor and he is fluent in German, his mother tongue, English and Spanish. Please feel free to visit with him in your native language. Accompanying Professor Becker is President Roosevelt's nephew, Louis Caldwell. These two representatives will be attending the same conference that you ladies and gentlemen will be attending. Please feel free to get acquainted before the conference begins. If you have any questions about the *Count* or the newest German fighter aeroplanes, please ask the steward who has just entered the compartment. He will take your dinner orders shortly and we will be changing the compartment from opera seating to tables and chairs. Please take a seat on one of the couches provided on each side of the compartment. Thank you."

"So much for keeping a low profile." Hans was smiling.

"It is better to hide in plain sight, Hans. You are the expert, I am just the retarded nephew of the war like Roosevelt."

The flight of German Valkyries appeared outside our windows. I had seen the English Valkyrie, a small, one seat aeroplane about twenty five feet long with a wing span of about the same length. The Brits called them "mosquitoes." These valkyries were much larger, two seats, one forward and one facing rear. The pilot, of course, faced forward to fly the aeroplane and to operate two machine guns forward. The rear seat was manned by a gunner who had a single machine gun mounted on a swivel. No more sneaking up on the pilot's rear, I thought.

They obviously had radio communication with the *Count*. The pilot's voice came through the grill work.

"Good morning, passengers on board the *Count.* I am Captain Ludwig Schmitz of the hundred and first fighter wing out of Leipzip. You are about a fourth of the way to Kaiserslautern and it is my honor to escort you for the next hour. You will then be met by another group who are stationed at Frankfort. That flight is made up of our newest single seat Valkyrie model, they will be with you for about an hour and a half and then they will leave and you will be accompanied by the final escort from Kaiserslautern. If you have any questions about our Valkyrie aeroplane, please ask the stewards in your cabin and they will forward your request to Captain Nedimeyer who will radio your question to me or one of the other pilots in my group. Have a good flight."

"Are you impressed, Louis?"

"Not until I see the toilets on this monster, I am going to ask the steward where they are."

"Ja, while you are gone, I am going to ask the steward why a fighter is called a Valkyrie."

Since I had known Hans, he always took the opportunity to expand his understanding of other cultures and peoples. What he learned from the steward, was that a Valkyrie was a mythology maiden of the God Odin. She was adorned with golden ornaments and she rode through the sky in brilliant armor. She delivered death according to Odin's commands. Death was by light streams from the points of her lance and a flickering brightness announces her arrival in battle. Valkyries travel in threes, sometimes nine and are said to represent storm clouds. The folk-lore of Valkyries says that whoever gains possession of their feather robes, has them in his power. Valkyries were made famous in Richard and later Siegfried Wagner's Der Ring des Nibelungen, second act "Die Walkure".

He also learned that there were two Wagners. Richard the father and Siegfried the son, the father was the famous German composer (1813-83), while his son is the famous conductor. Hans learned that Siegfried wrote several comic-romantic operas. His present opera is *Bruder Lustig* (1905) and is presently playing in Berlin. Hans made a note of attending upon his return to Berlin. Others still in production are Der Kobold (1904), Herzog Wildfang (1901-1903) and Der Barenhauter (1899-1901).

It is really nice that your partner can get a cultural education while you are looking for the toilet on an airship 650 meters in the air and traveling at the speed of 90 kilometers per hour. When I returned, Hans was surrounded by most of the college professors who were on their way to the conference at Kaiserslautern. He was trying his best, but he was not a college professor and it would be apparent soon to the others, also. I decided to rescue him.

"I am sorry, I was looking for the toilet. You have to ask the steward for directions. Did you know that this floor covering is not carpet? It is a rubberized covering to reduce static electricity. If you leave this compartment, you have to take your shoes off. Less chance of a spark, you see, the hydrogen cells, you know."

No one was impressed with my German except the two professors from Munich, they understood every word, while those from Hamburg looked at me like I was an idiot. In so small a country, why are there three different dialects for one language? Then I remembered living in Beaufort, South Carolina, low country English and low country German verus Maine English and high German. Middle German was spoken in Austria and Saxony, thankfully we would not be traveling in either. Hans looked relieved that the attention was now focused on me.

"My Uncle, the President of the United States, has accepted the Kaiser's proposal for a university professor exchange. I was sent here to interview candidates for positions at William and Mary, Harvard, Yale, Princeton, Dartmouth and Cambridge. The applications are in my luggage, otherwise you could begin filling them out. I will ask the steward if a crew member could locate my luggage." I found the steward and asked him if I could be escorted to the flight deck, up the ladder into the hold of the *Count*, across the cat walk and into the luggage compartment. He looked at me and said, "Is your handbag clearly marked, Mr. Caldwell?"

"It is."

"It will be brought to you after the dinner is served, you and the passengers can begin your paper work then." This proved the stewards were listening to every word. I was about to mention this to Hans, when the voice out of the grillwork began again.

"Attention, ladies and gentlemen, the 101 fighter wing will now be leaving us to land at Leipzip. We are leaving Prussia and entering Saxony airspace. We will remain in Saxony twenty minutes, until we enter Thuringia airspace and meet the escort group from Frankfort. Thuringia is a picturesque region of Germany, traversed by the Thuringer Wald, lying between the Prussian Province of Saxony on the north and Bavaria on the south and between the Kingdom of Saxony on the east and the Prussian Province of Hesse-Nassau on the west, our 201 fighter wing is stationed in Hesse. The entire region below us consists of a number of duchies and principalities. The so-called Thuringian States are; Saxe-Weimar-Eisenach, Saxe-Coburg-Gotha, Saxe-Meiningen, Saxe-Altenburg, Schwarzburg-Rudolstadt, Schwarzsburg-Sonderhausen and the two Reuss principalities. The largest city is Erfurt, in the Prussian Province of Saxony. The region took its name from the Thuringians, who at the time of the great migration of nations, established a kingdom near the center of the present German Empire. In the early part of the sixth century the Franks overthrew this kingdom and joined it with Franconia. This name applies to the region between the two rivers, Werra - Saale and the two mountain ranges, the Harz-Thuringian. In the tenth century, the region was ruled by the dukes of Saxony. In the twelfth and thirteenth centuries, the landgraves of Thuringia held a prominent place among the German Princes who lived at their Castle of Wartburg. After the War of the Schmalkald League in 1547, the princes were stripped of their possessions and the lands were returned to the various dukes. The area we are flying over today in 1905 has not changed much since 1547."

"Did you hear that, Hans? The North American Continent was discovered fifty-five years before the War of the Schmalkald League. This region has remained stable while the North American Continent has under-gone remarkable changes."

"Louis, these people are trying to impress you with how long they have been a civilization. That is why this is called the 'old world' and we live in the 'new world'. Why do you think so many people left this region to immigrate to other parts of Europe and America? Do you think it was because this was such a wonderful place to live, work and raise a family?

Your Grandfather Schneider's family left this area of the world to come to America, so did the Beckers."

"I am glad they did, Hans, otherwise we would never have met! Right, Hans."

"Right, Louis."

The flight of four, single seat, Valkyries buzzed around the *Count* like it was standing still. The two seaters had left and landed at Leipzig. They had left Leipzig and flown northeast to meet the *Count* shortly after we had taken off from Berlin. They kept pace with us until we crossed into Saxony. The new flight had come from Frankfort, Hesse. Hesse is shaped like a figure eight on the map of the German Empire. The city of Frankfort is at the intersection of the figure. Upper Hesse, north of Frankfort is mountainous, and is identified with the basaltic Vogelsberg, situated in the east, rising to a height of 2500 feet. We could see the mountain top off to our right hand side in the distance. We were flying at the height of 1950 feet and I understood why there were no night time flights allowed across Germany. The Hesse Province was typical of the German Empire states. A single mountain top dominated the physical features and climate, from this mountain top, groups of smaller peaks would radiate spurs and outliers west and north through the provinces. This left the southern edges with a Wetterau, extensive, undulating and arable tracts of farm land. We were flying over the southeastern part of the Hesse and towards the northern end of Mount Taunus when the voice through the grillwork announced that the stewards would now be rearranging the cabin for dinner.

Dinner on the *Count* was the mid day meal, not the evening meal, thank God. I had decided that flying was for the birds and I was a land creature. The stewards pulled a pin in each opera seat and rotated them to form groups of four. In the center of each group, a brass ring was located. I never noticed that they were there before. From the locked door appeared brass poles about two feet long and they were inserted into each ring in the floor. Next the table tops were snapped into place and rotated until tight. White linen table cloths were placed on each. There was no silver wear. We had our choices of wooden chop sticks or small wooden spoons. Bottles of German wines were placed upon each table and opened to breathe. The meals were placed on board before we left Berlin, cooking was not allowed on the *Count*. The paper plates contained what we had already eaten in the VIP lounge and I picked at my plate and drank a paper cup of white wine.

I asked one of the young women stewards if I could get my brief case from the luggage compartment and she offered to escort me. We left our shoes inside the locked door, put on special shoe like socks and climbed up past the flight deck and into the hold above the flight deck. No one on the flight deck paid any attention to us. We were on a cat walk. It was about 18 inches wide, made out of a grid-like metal, I guessed it was aluminum. The hold of the *Count* was over 400 feet long and it was a mass of crisscrossing metal strips and cables that made up the shape of the zeppelin. We walked nearly 200 feet and were in a storage area above the crews compartment. I spotted my brief case and pointed to it. She picked it up and carried it for me. We retraced our steps and were back outside the locked door and I put on my shoes to enter the passenger compartment. The steward handed me my briefcase and smiled, "Will there be anything else I can do for you, Mr. Caldwell?" The use of English threw me at first because I responded in German.

"Your English is very good. Where did you learn it?"

"Most of the employees for the Zeppelin Company are from foreign countries. I am Danish. In Denmark we learn English from the first grade."

"How did you know my name?"

"All the stewards were shown a photograph of you and Professor Becker before we left Berlin. This is a common thing for all VIP passengers. In fact, every person on this flight was interviewed a week before the scheduled flight. University Professors and their wives were invited to Berlin to be screened and selected for the conference. Only those likely to be selected by you and Professor Becker were put on the *Count*. The rest left four days ago by train."

"So, the couple from Munich traveled all the way to Berlin where they were selected for this flight. Munich is a short distance to the conference site, Kaiserslautern. That does not seem like a very efficient, German-like system of selection." I smiled at her.

"You must have some German ancestry, Mr. Caldwell. I am Danish, I do not pretend to understand the German mind set."

"My mother was German, a Schneider."

"Ah, the German name for 'Cutter', you must come from a long line of small boat builders."

"No, mine were butchers." I was feeling uncomfortable. My Grandpa Schneider had told me all about the Schneider Cutter Plant in Rosenheim, Bavaria. My Grandfather Schneider had written letters and received replies in order for us to schedule a visit to that plant next week. The hair was standing up on the back of my neck, when I noticed that my brief case had been opened and searched. When you are in the spy business, you become paranoid. You never leave a personal item outside of your immediate eyesight, if you do, make sure that the procedure for opening and closing that personal item is rigidly followed. At The Farm, we were trained to check for trip wires to make sure that someone had not put an explosive device inside. This was a sloppy job. There were no trip wires, but someone might as well have written a note and placed it inside the brief case saying, "Thank you, your luggage has been searched and no items hazardous to a flight in a hydrogen filled death trap have been found. Have a nice day!"

Hans was visiting with the couple from Munich and I joined them. I placed my brief case on the dining table that had been cleared and left in place so that the passengers could fill out forms, play cards or engage in writing letters home.

"Professor Schlozer and Frau Schlozer, I have the information forms for you to look at, they are in English. You speak English very well, if you need Professor Becker to assist you with anything, please feel free to ask him any questions that you would like."

"Are we required to complete these forms?" The Professor's hands were shaking as he tried to hold the papers steady. Something was not right here.

"Professor Schlozer, did you and Frau Schlozer travel from Munich to Berlin last week?" The look of surprise was evident on both of their faces. He struggled with his answer, "We were ordered to Berlin by the Chancellor's Office. We could not refuse the order, we would have been arrested, as enemies of the State of Bavaria."

"I understand, Professor. Would it be of assistance if I marked your application 'hold for review' for the exchange program at this time? I could also write that Professor Schlozer is exceptionally qualified in the field of experimental Physics and that the United States would like for him and his wife to apply again as soon as an American Physics professor can be located." The look of relief was apparent on both of their faces.

"Am I assuming that no American professor will ever be found?"

"Your assumption is correct, Sir. How many other couples on this flight are in your situation?"

"We have no way of knowing. We do know that not all of these couples are university professors."

"Professor Becker and I were sent to filter out those that are not. Would you turn your forms over and draw the table layout for the compartment, Sir? Number each, beginning with our table as number 0, use lower case for those tables that you think have university professors and upper case for those tables that you are sure are not university professors." Hans and I watched as Professor Schlozer did as I asked and continued to write information for us on the right side of his sketch. He was convincing and the hovering stewards did not act like they knew what we were attempting to do. When he was finished, I thanked him and asked for him to talk to the table next to us and offer to exchange seats with the next couple that we assumed were husband and wife.

"Good afternoon, we are part of the selection committee for your application to enter the United States as an exchange professor. How did you hear about the exchange program?"

"A notice was posted at the University of Heidelberg, Department of Physics."

"So you contacted your department head and filled out an application?"

"No, we have a large family and it would be a hardship for us to leave Heidelberg for such a long time. The notice said husbands and wives only."

"You had no intention of making application until you were summoned to Berlin by the Chancellor's Office." Hans was a fast learner.

"How did you know about that, Professor Becker?"

"You are not the only couples in that uncomfortable situation. We have no intention of accepting your application. We will, instead, indicate to the Chancellor's Office that no exchange professor has been located in the United States and until one has been located, you will be on a 'waiting list'."

"Will we have to wait long?"

"For the rest of your lives." I was smiling. They were relieved. Hans asked them to do the same thing that Professor Schlozer had done with their application. In this manner we talked to the university professors first. Not one of them had volunteered to leave Germany. We met with each of the other couples. They were eager to fill out all the forms that we required. We sat and watched them as the they completed them and then we told them, "We see no reason why you will not be approved by the United States Colleges and Universities that we represent. Do you have any preference where you will be located?" None had a preference, which was odd. There is a big difference between the climates and living conditions of Dartmouth, and William and Mary. I looked at Hans and nodded. We both understood that these couples were trained agents.

The stewards entered from the locked door and began to remove the tables and reposition our opera seats for our gradual descent across lower Hesse. The voice came through the grill again.

"Attention ladies and gentlemen, the 201 first fighter wing will be leaving us and landing in Frankfort. They will be replaced by four, long range, scout aeroplanes from Friedenhoffen Airbase, Stuttgart, Wurtemberg. They will escort us across lower Hesse and on into Kaiserslautern, Palatinate. Hesse is a grand duchy of Germany, the eighth largest German State in size, lying between latitudes 49 degrees, 24 minutes and 50 degrees, 50 minutes North. The longitudes are 7 degrees, 51 minutes and 9 degrees, 39 minutes East. The State consists of two divisions and eleven enclaves. We have left Oberhessen, the upper portion and are entering Unterhessen. The two division's area is approximately 2965.5 square miles. The Rhine traverses for about 55 miles inside Hesse during its journey from its head waters in Switzerland and its final destination to the Zuider Zea in Holland. The Unterhessen consists of the provinces of Rhine-Hesse and Starkenburg. Five of the enclaves border on, or are inclosed by Baden and Wurtemberg. The remainder of the enclaves are within Prussian territory."

"Did you hear that, Hans? Only a German would say that the area is approximately 2965.5. An American would say approximately 3000."

"Ja, but then the term 'approximately' would not be used correctly. You see, you rounded the figure, you are an American. We Germans use slide rules and the use of the term 'approximately' is to indicate that there are no decimals on the slide rule scales, therefore, the half square mile must be approximated. Right, Louis!"

"Right, Hans. You are not going native on me, are you?"

"Nein, I am simply pointing out that a German is more precise than an American. Did you know that there was a Professor Otto Hesse who taught at the Universities in Halle, Heidelberg and in the Polytechnic School at Munich?"

"No, is he on our list to interview at Kaiserslautern?"

"He is retired now, but he continues to contribute to the theory of determinants by his publications in *Vorlesungen aus der analytischen Geometrie der geraden Linie des Punktes and des Kreies.*"

"I could have lived without knowing that, Hans." I closed my eyes, leaned back in my seat and tried to take a nap. I had not returned the application forms to my brief case. I had folded them length wise and placed them in my inside suit coat pocket, they had sketches on the backs of some of them. I closed my eyes for a few minutes and I heard the Danish Steward ask if she could return my brief case to the luggage compartment. Hans nodded his head that she could. The voice in the grill was at it again.

"Attention ladies and gentlemen. We are now making our descent into Kaiserslautern. We have just passed over the upper Palatinate known as the Oberpfalz and have entered the Unterpfalz where the city of Kaiserslautern is located. Palatinate is one of the oldest states within the German Empire. It is composed of an irregular and disjointed territory on both sides of the Rhine, included roughly within the space marked by the ancient city states of Mainz, Worms, Heilbronn, Heidelberg, Mannheim, Landau and Zweibrucken. This German State is composed of the former Principalities of Simmern, Deux Ponts, Veldenz and Lautern. The Count of Palatine of the Rhine appears in the eleventh century as holding a leading position among the hereditary of German princes. In 1214 the Rhenish Palatinate was acquired by the House of Witttelsbach in the person of Louis I., Duke of Bavaria and remained there for four hundred years. In 1356, Emperor Charles IV designated the Count of Palatine as one of the seven Imperial Electors.

Count Rupert I founded the University of Heidelberg in 1336. The Reformation changed Palatinate from Catholic to Calvinism. Count Frederick extended his protection to the French Huguenots living in Alsace and Lorraine in 1563. During the wars of Louis XIV, the Palatinate was mercilessly devastated by the French armies and the Alsace Lorraine territory was returned to France.

Today the population is over 1.5 million people living on the farm lands, swelling hills and wooded mountain sides. The mountains are located along the western side and are called the Hardt ranges. This region yields bountiful crops of cereals, potatoes, tobacco, hemp, flax and it noted for its wines. The capital is Speyer. The Danube flows along the southern border. Enjoy your conference here in Kaiserslautern. We will be docking in just a few minutes."

I looked out my window and the ground was very close. We had slowed to a standstill and I heard the hissing sounds of hydrogen being released from the cells above us. The Count Zeppelin began to sink slowly into its docking location at the Kaiserslautern Airfield.

39

Kaiserslautern

Palatinate, German Empire

Kaiserslautern airfield was a rather crude affair compared to the Count Zeppelin Aerodrome in Berlin. There was no hanger or terminal building. Hans and I watched as lines were dropped from the crew's compartment and ground workers began to fasten each of these lines to a capstan. Once the aft lines were fastened, a similar set of lines were dropped from the flight deck above us. The ground crew began turning the capstans forward and aft. These appeared to be powered by two small steam engines. Slowly, the Count began to approach the grass field below us. The capstans stopped turning when the two compartments were within a foot or two off the ground. A porter brought two small sets of steps like you might find at a train station and placed them below the sliding doors of the compartments. Luggage began to appear from the crew's compartment and passengers began to take two steps off the Count. A small stone office building stood beside the mast where the Count would be secured for the night. The office doors opened and the Kaiser's entourage appeared. First came the Imperial Guard, marching in formation, to form a pair of columns about 400 yards long. Next, a huge roll of carpet was rolled out between the columns of guardsmen. We had all stepped off the Count and began walking towards the end of the carpet. The grass had been clipped and sprayed a dark green for the occasion. The university professors and their wives let Hans and I walk forward to meet his royal highness, Kaiser Wilhelm Cassel II. He stood midway of the carpet length and waved to us. It was obvious that he had seen our photographs along with a thick file of information. I wondered if he knew that we were spies sent to gather as much information on the German Military as we could find.

Hans took matters into his own hands. He stopped three feet in front of the Kaiser and said, "Kaiser Wilhelm Cassel II, it is an honor to meet you." He clicked his heels and bowed from the waist. "I have the honor of presenting Commander Louis Jason Caldwell of the United States Navy and nephew of the President of the United States, Theodore Roosevelt. I am Professor Hans Becker of the Fairfield Institute, Washington, D.C., assigned to the American Embassy, Berlin. We have letters of introduction from President Roosevelt and Ambassador Wilson."

He handed the letters to an aide standing beside the Kaiser. The Kaiser nodded his head in acknowledgment of the receipts.

Hans continued, "Ambassador Wilson regrets that he will not be able to attend the conference. His tenure as Ambassador is over and he will return to his post as President of Princeton University. He is very excited about receiving the first of the German Professors at his university. I have another letter from President Wilson to you, Sir." Hans handed the letter to the same aide. The aide standing on the other side of the Kaiser stepped forward and began his welcoming statement in English. "The Kaiser of the German Empire welcomes Professor Becker and Commander Caldwell to the conference for the higher education exchange. In honor of our American guests, the entire conference will be available in both English and German. Refreshments await at the Schloss Cassel. Please follow me inside and through the terminal. A motorcade awaits us at the front entrance." He clicked his heels bowed to the Kaiser and was off at a brisk pace. The Kaiser smiled, extended his hand to Hans and shook it. He extended his hand to me and shook it. Then he did a strange thing for a king.

"Come, my two American friends, let me show you my home." He stepped between us, turned 180 degrees and placed his arms around the shoulders of each of us. "I understand that both of you speak excellent German and that your great grandparents came from greater Germany. Is this true?"

"It is your highness." Hans spoke in perfect high German.

"While you are in my home, Professor Becker, please call me 'Willy', Wilhelm Hesse-Cassel is so formal."

"Yes, your highness, it would be a pleasure!" Hans was smiling from ear to ear.

"And what about you, Commander? Do you think that you could call me 'Willy'?"

"My Uncle Teddy warned me about you. He said,'The Kaiser will completely disarm you with his considerable charm.' I would be pleased to call you what ever my Uncle Teddy calls you." The Kaiser threw his head back and began a genuine belly laugh.

"Your Uncle is no fool, Louis. He gave you good advice. You can call me Uncle Willy, if you like."

"Thank you, your highness."

We had walked through the stone building and onto the parking area in front. Twenty-two brightly shined new Daimler automobiles awaited our arrival. A uniformed driver stood beside each. The second aide began directing the university professors and their wives into the waiting motorcade. The first aide had opened the first Daimler with the Imperial Seal and the three of us got into the two back seats that faced each other. Hans and I sat on one and the Kaiser introduced us to his wife, Princess Victoria Schleswig-Holstein-Sonderburg-Augustenburg.

"Please call me 'Vicky', Willy can be so formal at times. We spent a very enjoyable week with your Uncle Teddy. Did you know that Teddy and Willy got along famously? I have never seen Willy warm so quickly to anyone that was not German. It was amazing."

"My wife is somewhat of a historian, would you like a short tour of the town before we go up the hill to the house?"

"That would be wonderful. My Grandfather Schneider has told me so much about this part of Germany, I can not wait to see it, feel it and eat its food." The Princess did an imitation of her husband and began her own belly laugh.

"You are as charming as your Uncle Teddy, Louis. Isn't he, Willy?"

"The best way to avoid misunderstandings and conflicts is to know and understand the people and nations that you deal with, don't you agree, Louis?"

"Yes, your highness, that is the reason that my uncle sent me to see and meet with you and Vicky. It is his hope that we can become familiar with each other and can trust each other in future dealings. The higher education exchange is just the beginning of the cooperation that my uncle seeks with you and the German people."

"Oh, Louis, that is our hope also. We are now entering the city center, it is a prominent and thriving town of the Bavarian Palatinate. The town was chosen by Willy's father, Kaiser Wilhelm I, as his summer residence away from Berlin. We also have enjoyed the summers, and now the falls, here. We have left the political considerations of the Empire to the Chancellor, Von Bulow."

My thoughts were somewhat different. '*It appeared to me that the new Chancellor had taken up where the old one had left off. Agents were not only sent to every embassy and consul office in the United States, they would appear in some American colleges and universities after January,1906. Hans would identify each one that he could through his office in Berlin, attached to the American Embassy, but known as the office of American Scholars Abroad Program (ASAP).*'

The Princess continued," For now, we are spending the summer and fall months of 1905, in the Waldlauter, 42 miles by rail west of Mannheim. Because it is the town selected for the Schloss Cassel, or castle of Kaiser Wilhelm Hesse-Cassel, it has fine schools, hospitals, an industrial museum, a municipal theater, and all the modern improvements known to man."

"What are the industries of the town and surrounding area?" Hans asked the Kaiser.

"The principal industries are spinning factories, not cotton or wool, but metal. Large aluminum and other metal discs are spun on a lathe to produce all sorts of parts for dirigibles, aeroplanes, motorcycles and motorcars. Military motorcars, trucks and motorcycles are assembled in nearby Stuttgart. You have asked to tour that factory later in the week and you shall see the assembly process then. There are also extensive railway shops and iron works which produce parts of Germany's trains, trucks and steel tracked vehicles which are used in the lumber harvesting. Enclosed cabs are sometimes added to the tops of what you and Louis would call bulldozers and machine guns are mounted to these tops. We are in the process of offering these for sale to any country that would like to purchase them. They were called mobile armored vehicles, MAVs for short. MAVs are used together with armored motorcars, trucks and motorcycles to replace the German Cavalry horses. I disbanded the cavalry in 1899, and replaced it with the Panzer Corps. Instead of horses, my troops ride motorcycles, trucks and their MAVs into a battle 100 times faster than the traditional cavalry."

As Hans and I were driven around the town, we could tell that it was of ancient origin. The Princess continued, "In the twelfth century, Frederick Barbarossa built a fine palace here. It was demolished during the Spanish War of Succession. It was rebuilt as the Schloss Hesse-Cassel and Kaiserslautern became a free Imperial city under the protection of the Kaiser."

She smiled at her husband and patted his knee, he continued, "Kaiser comes from Latin and means Caesar or Emperor. Under the Holy Roman Empire the acknowledged heirs to the throne, added the name Caesar (Kaiser) to their own. From Otto the great to Francis II, the Kaiser chosen by the German nations became Emperor of the Holy Roman Empire, at first by consecration at Rome, but later through the act of election. Charles V was the last German King crowned in Italy. In 1806, a hundred years ago, the Holy Roman Empire was dissolved, but the Imperial title was retained by the House of Hapsburg, the head of which has borne the title of Kaiser of Austria. On January 18, 1871, Wilhelm I of Prussia assumed the title of German Kaiser as head of the newly created German Empire. I am his son, Wilhelm II, who has called the scholars to the conference." His wife continued her description.

"From the town center, we can see the Schloss Hesse-Cassel situated on the hill about 600 feet above the town. The present site has contained at least three separate palaces or fortified manor houses. The first was begun in 1070. At this time in history a Schloss was a fortress, a rather crude affair with a ditch, dike, fosse, or moat, surrounding the fort. You crossed the ditch via a draw bridge that could be pulled upward into the outer walls or curtain, 20 to 25 feet high, with towers and bastions, it had a terraced walk with single or double parapets. Inside the outer walls was the gate-house flanked by towers, leading into the outer bailey court with buildings for feeding, organizing and lodging the garrison used to defend the Schloss. A second layer, like a wedding cake, came next. A repeat of the ditch, draw bridge, inside walls with walks and parapets to include a second set of gate houses usually called the castle keeps. The inner bailey contained the great hall, chapel, and accommodations for the Count or Baron of the Schloss. This concept of stacking the layers was repeated more than twice in some of the later Germanic castles of the twelve hundreds. The site of our home was the residence of the Landgraves of Palatinate, attaining its greatest splendor under Frederick Barbarossa II (1190-1217). It was destroyed beyond repair by war and it sat for years until the second Schloss Rheinfel was built in 1247. Instead of giant earthen works stacked in layers, the existing earth was removed and replaced with giant stones to form the baileys. Also, the rear of the Schloss was placed into the rock of the mountain behind it, as you see it today.

Willy's grandfather began the restoration of the Schloss Rheinfel in 1847. He renamed it *The Kaiser's Lair.* It was designed by Ritzen, who was responsible for the restoration of Wartburg Castle in Saxe-Weimar. The Hofburg wing of the castle, by means of mural paintings and antique furnishings, has been made as near a duplicate as possible to what must have been its appearance at its prime in the thirteenth century. The Vorburg wing, in the same manner, has been refitted in the style of the early sixteenth century, when Luther spent nearly a year (May 4, 1521 to March 6, 1522), at work on his translation of the Bible."

"We are almost there. In a mile or two you will see the castle garrison. I keep a battalion of the Imperial Guard in those barracks you see on the right." Uncle Willy was smiling as Hans and I remembered that a battalion of guards was slightly over a 1000. He had brought 400 to the local aerodrome. If you could transport 20 men to a truck, it took 20 trucks just to bring his honor guard from the barracks to the aerodrome.

We drove past the garrison barracks and turned sharply to the right. There stood *the Kaiser's Lair*, a superb example of a feudal structure commanding a great city sized town. Its narrow rocky setting gave it not only a strong walled advanced work toward the town but a double encircling wall. Three successive baileys, on ascending levels, were divided by deep ditches which had been planted with grass, flowers and shrubs. This was in sharp contrast to the heavy stone walls and towered entrance gates. The draw bridge was gone, replaced by a modern concrete overpass that allowed us to enter the Schloss. Like so many other German castles, the palace takes the place of the keep in the inner bailey. This was the work of Uncle Willy's grandfather no doubt. The two modern wings, the Hofburg and the Vorburg had been joined to the main palace. The original palace formed a quadrangle in the center of a long and fairly fortified enceinte and double outlying baileys were built to construct the two new wings. The result was breathtaking. The Daimler stopped in front of the palace and the Kaiser said, "My simple house on the hill compares quite nicely to Schloss Marienberg of the Teutonic Knights. Don't you think so, Hans?"

"I have no idea, your highness, I will let you know after I visit Marienburg on the northen German, Polish border."

"You do know your history, Professor Becker." The Kaiser gave another of his belly laughs.

We were out of the Imperial Daimler in time to begin a receiving line for the next black Daimler to arrive. The professors and their wives were greeted by the Kaiser, the Princess and two American guests. Like clockwork and a credit to German efficiency, the Daimlers kept arriving four minutes apart and were greeted until all twenty-two automobiles had deposited their passengers from the aerodrome. When the last guests to the Schloss had arrived, a servant passed out invitations to dinner in the great hall. They were small white cards with gold lettering with our names and room numbers on one side and our placement at dinner on the other side. Our luggage was already in our rooms, dinner would be formal. We had a minimum of luggage, we were wearing business suits and I had brought a dinner jacket and dress slacks from the Embassy in Berlin. When everyone excused themselves and located their rooms in what ever wing of the Schloss, Hans and I had a chance to talk in private. We were standing outside our rooms in the Vorburg wing.

"I will check for recording devices in both of our rooms, Louis. You need to burn the folded pieces of paper in your jacket pocket. How can we write down the names of those we think are the agents from the zeppelin?"

"I will make up some sort of code, and use a laundry pencil that I brought with me in my suitcase. I will write the code on the waist band of my undershorts. No one will ever think to look for information on dirty underwear and if they do, it will look like laundry marks. Right, Hans?"

"Right, Louis! I will check your room first. Be careful of what you say inside either of the rooms, though."

Hans went about his 'treasure hunt' while I went through my brief case and suit case. They had both been searched. I jerked out my dinner jacket and slacks and took them into the bathroom. I hung them on a hook close to the shower and turned it on full blast, hot only. Soon the small room was full of steam and the wrinkles began to disappear, an old trick that my sister had taught me. I took the jacket and slacks into the bedroom and replaced them with a formal dress shirt and some badly wrinkled shirts. Hans was gone checking his room when I returned from the bath. I found the laundry pencil and took the folded papers from my jacket. I sat down at a small desk and devised a code for each name. I had just finished when Hans came back and nodded his head yes. He watched me crumple the papers and place them in an ashtray. I struck a match and watched the papers burn. I carried the ash to the toilet and flushed it down. Hans followed me into the bath and wrote on the steam coated mirror above my sink.

"Both rooms bugged" He toweled the message off and shrugged his shoulders. I motioned for him to follow me into the bedroom.

"Well, Professor Becker, what did you think of the Kaiser and the Princess Victoria?" Hans immediately understood that I was giving the listeners something to report to the Kaiser or the Chancellor.

"We have just met, Commander, but the trip in the zeppelin was most exciting and I thought nothing could top that, but I must confess the Kaiser is not what I expected. He is truly a leader of his people, not anything like what Ambassador Wilson had described. I am impressed by the professors and their wives that we visited with on the flight. I recommend that they all be accepted for placement. What did you think, Commander?"

"I agree, they were most impressive. I am just a navy lawyer, not a college professor, but I think we will have a hard time matching the quality of those professors we met. The United States is way behind the German Empire on dirigible design and construction and those Valkyries that we saw make the Wright brothers aeroplanes look like toys. Even the Curtiss fighter would be outclassed in a dog fight with them."

"What time is dinner in the great hall?"

"Seven."

"I need to get back to my room and get my tuxedo pressed, see you at dinner, Commander." Hans left and I decided to take a nap.

In the basement of the Vorburg wing, the recording devices continued to turn on their reels. A technician was transcribing the conversation in the navy commander's room. He finished and handed it to a messenger who carried it to the waiting Kaiser and his wife. They read it and said, "It is either an act for our benefit, because they know they are being recorded, or they have just met at the American Embassy. I wonder which it is?"

40

Kaiserslautern University Conference

Palatinate, German Empire

The two day conference began that evening with dinner in the great hall. I found the great hall in the main palace a few minutes before seven and began shaking the hands of some of the people I had met on the zeppelin. The train load of professors from Berlin were anxious to met Hans and I. They had found him and were pressing him with questions. I worked my way across the giant room, which dominated the older, center, section of the Schloss. It was three stories high and you could enter from any of the floors. Inside staircases came down from each story until you were on the floor which contained three long tables. Maximum seating was 180 dinner guests. On the ground floor there were four fireplaces, two at each end of the room. It was fall and the nights were chilly. The servants had built a fire in each fireplace. The firebox openings were as tall as my head, I could have walked into the fireplaces. Above each of the fireplaces on the second story was a balcony. On the east end was a library with leather bound first editions, on the west end was an opening space large enough for a three piece string group and they were playing some German compositions. On the third level, a ringed walkway provided easy chairs, reading tables and more books of all types and descriptions.

Guests were gathered around each of the four fireplaces with a crystal wine glass partly filled with the last years harvest from the local vineyards. It seemed like a scene out of the silent movie that I had taken my sister to see many weeks ago during my rehabilitation from a botched assignation attempt. My thoughts were interrupted when a soft voice said, "Guten abend, Commander, sie genieBen Ihren aufenthault?"

I turned my head to see the Danish stewardess from the Count Zeppelin. She was not in uniform, she was in the most beautiful evening gown I had ever seen. My mouth ran away with itself, "Good evening, Fraulein. I am sorry, you know my name but I do not know yours. I usually do not forget to get the names of beautiful women that I meet."

She frowned and said, "You sound like my brother always trying to impress the ladies, but then he opens his mouth."

"I apologize, Fraulein, may we start over?"

"But of course, Monsieur!" She was mocking my use of 'may we'.

"Hello, you beautiful creature. Have we ever met before? Was it a thousand feet in the air over part of southern Germany?"

"It was, Monsieur. I am your stewardess for your flight today, my name is Elska Van Mauker." She gave me a small curtsy and a large beautiful smile. "I have taken the liberty of changing our seating cards for tonight, I noticed I was sitting between two old German Barons and I traded with the lady that was sitting beside you. Shall we find our seats, the Kaiser and Princess will be here promptly at seven. It will give us a chance to visit.

I forgot all about Hans as she took my hand and led me to the card locations. I pulled her chair away from the table and placed her wine glass in the proper place within the 20 pieces of silver, china and crystal that occupied the table in front of us. She noticed that I was at ease with the European arrangement for dinner settings.

"Do you know what to do with all these pieces? Watch me if you need help, Commander."

"My first name is Louis, not Commander, we dine in America also Elska, would you like the German names for each of these pieces, since you live in Denmark?" I was smiling and she giggled. She squeezed my hand and I realized that I had never let loose of it. We were holding hands under the table.

"So, Elska, what brings you to the Schloss von den Adlern?"

"Castle of the eagles? Is that what the Kaiser calls this outdated pile of rocks?"

"It is not as nice as my castle in the United States, Elska, but it is much older. You have to make allowances for antiques."

"That is what the two Barons said when I moved my seating card." I began giggling and it was contagious, we could not stop. Our visit was cut short when the butler entered the great hall and announced the arrival of the Kaiser and the Princess. The entire audience began clapping and we had to stop holding hands. We looked at each other and she gave me a slight nod of her head.

The banquet was served and all 180 seats were occupied. It took two hours and ten minutes and I was eager to continue a private talk with Elska. My hopes were dashed when the Kaiser announced that he had a short speech prepared for the opening of the conference.

Welcome to our home. Princess Victoria and I will not see much of you in the next two days because of your busy schedules. The conference is designed to better understand the relationship between the university systems of the two nations. The German system is based upon the Prussia identity as a nation. Prussians, both men and women, have been raised in a military system for centuries. The power of that system rests on two elements: the material strength and its moral strength; the former depends on the character of its leaders and followers, and its organization. The latter being determined by its discipline, the system of military education, and the national spirit. Organization, in a military sense, comprises, in general, all the measures taken to insure the institutions of higher learning, a regular and normal working of all of its parts. This conference will examine those parts common to both the United States and Germany and those unique to the German system.

This conference hopes to provide a means whereby professors of both nations can provide proper education to their students while at the same time protect the rights and prescribe the duties of each individual by suitable regulations, to supply the personnel and material necessary, and finally to provide a means whereby nothing may be wanting to enable them to teach under the most favorable conditions....blah, blah.

I was not listening any longer, I had found Elska's hand again under the table. I was tuned into her breathing, the front of her gown rising and falling with each breath. Suddenly there was clapping and I realized the dinner guests were rising from the table. I had to let go of her hand again. She stood and said, "*The Count* leaves for Hamburg in the morning, but we have tonight, Louis."

"When will I see you again, Elska? Tonight is not enough."

"I am stationed in Berlin. I will see you when you return to Berlin, Louis." I gave a sigh of relief and we walked out of the great hall arm in arm to explore the rest of the rooms open to guests. Outside the great hall was a large, open plaza-like space, with tropical plants and three giant sky lights to let natural light inside the Schloss. It was nine-thirty at night under a clear mountain sky and the stars shown down upon us. We were staring straight up at them, when Hans found us.

"There you are, Commander. We have been looking all over for you." He had four professors in tow. "These fellows have questions I can not answer, would you care to try?"

"Fraulein Van Mauker and I were just looking for the salon in order to have a nightcap. Would you gentlemen like to accompany us?"

"We would be most delighted," they all said at once. Then two professors remembered they had wives with them and they excused themselves to go and fetch them.

It was ten-thirty and Elska and I were still not alone.

"When are all these older citizens going to bed?" Elska whispered in my ear. I returned her smile and said, "It has been a long day and we must retire, ladies and gentlemen. We will see you early in the morning, I will be taking Elska back to the aerodrome and then attending the first and second sessions in the library. Guten Abend." I clicked my heels and bowed. I took Elska's hand and we walked hand in hand out of the salon and into the Vorburg wing.

"Elska, we can not use my room, it is a mess." I was thinking about the recording device.

"So is mine, it is also crowded, I have a roommate and she snores." We laughed and continued walking around the Vorburg wing until we came to a small sitting alcove where no one would interrupt us and we talked, it was after midnight when she yawned and said, "I really have to get up early tomorrow morning, Louis."

"Where shall we meet?"

"Were you serious about taking me back to the aerodrome? We do not have an automobile."

"I will borrow one of Uncle Willy's Daimlers."

"You call him Uncle Willy behind his back?"

"No, he asked me to call him Uncle Willy because I call the President of the United States, Uncle Teddy."

"That is not very respectful, Louis."

"The Uncle Willy or Teddy?"

"Both, you are not related to either one."

"My father's sister married Theodore Roosevelt. That make me related, Elska."

"Oh, my, God. Do you really have a castle?"

"Yes, I do. Every man's home is his castle in America. They were all built after 1609, however. My grandfather built more than one castle. He used his income from Caldwell International to build a 135 room estate in Pennsylvania, a state in the US settled by the Germans and Dutch. Later he became interested in the settlement of the western US and he built a larger lodge in the State of Nevada, settled by Mexicans and Confederate States of Americans fleeing the US in 1865. My family owns a large plantation in South Carolina, a conference center in Bermuda, a shipping business and other side interests."

"Side interests?"

"Small business ventures, you know, like American Motors, International Business Machines and American Telegraph and Telephone."

"My, God. You are wealthier than the Kaiser. Why did you choose a career in the United States Military Command?"

"I am a navy lawyer, I went to law school, Elska. I am not in the US Military Command, that would be my Uncle Teddy. Uncle Willy and Uncle Teddy are roughly at the same level of command. I hate the military and every thing it stands for."

"I don't understand."

"I don't either, Elska, are you going to stand there all night or are you going to kiss me?" We had walked to her room in the Hofburg wing.

"I lied about having a roommate, Louis, let's get inside before someone sees us and my reputation is ruined for what I am about to do."

THE NEXT MORNING OUR REPUTATIONS WERE RUINED as we were seen coming from her room. I did not care. The experience was totally different than with Madeline Barrias. I was twenty-four years old and had been with two women, my whole life. Madeline was French, aggressive and I could not satisfy any of her needs. Elska was gentle, shy and cried when she was happy. I wondered if she was anything like Helga Runden that my father met so many years ago in Finland. I left her to get some breakfast being served in the great hall and returned to my room to change into my business suit. Hans was waiting for me.

"Louis, what did you find out from the Danish muffin?"

"I grilled her all night and she would not confess to being a German spy, Hans, now what?"

"Are you happy?"

"Very."

"Good, now it will be alright to introduce you to Greta when she returns from Switzerland. I have a car and a driver waiting for the two of you to return to the aerodrome, Louis. You better change quickly and get back to her before someone else butters your muffin." I glared at him but did as he said and I was back for breakfast as fast as possible.

THAT SAME MORNING, the basement of the Vorburg wing was busy.

"Are you sure there is no sound track from the Caldwell room? Not even some tickling and giggling, I saw them leave the great hall together."

"The recording was made. There was no one in that room all night. A few minutes ago the following was recorded."

"Louis, what did you find out from the Danish muffin?"

"I grilled her all night and she would not confess to being a German spy, Hans, now what?"

"Are you happy?"

"Very."

"Good, now it will be alright to introduce you to Greta when she returns from Switzerland. I have a car and a driver waiting for the two of you to return to the aerodrome, Louis. You better change quickly and get back to her before someone else butters your muffin."

"That confirms what the Chancellor has suspected. The two Americans know each other from before, they have not just met. We now have three possible American agents to track, Elska Van Mauker, or whatever her name is, Hans Becker and Louis Caldwell. All three will meet with unfortunate accidents. Send a message to Greta Gerbrells in Switzerland. Tell her she is needed in Berlin to keep track of the head of the NCI at the American Embassy."

In the Daimler on the way to the aerodrome, we continued our conversation.

"Elska, tell me about your family."

"You really don't know anything about the history of Denmark, do you Louis?"

"I confess, I am ignorant of the entire history of your country, Elska. My Grandfather Schneider got me interested in Bavaria and I have studied mostly Prussian history, it is violent."

"So is the Danish history. Denmark is the smallest of the three Scandinavian kingdoms of Europe. Our King, Christian Van Mauker, is very old and ill. When he dies my great uncle is next in line to become King. He, too, is very old. Denmark's glory days are behind her. She still has some of the colonies, Iceland, Greenland and the Danish West Indies."

"Elska, why didn't you tell me you were that *Van Mauker*. And what are you doing working in Germany at one of the most dangerous jobs one can have?"

"The royal line has many members in front of me, Louis. I am not even a Princess, never will be. Our branch of the family is poor as church mice. My father lives off of a very small stipend from the King. Why is my job the most dangerous in Germany?"

"Elska, your job is the most dangerous in the world. You know what happens to hydrogen when it comes in contact with a fire or even a spark. There are no survivors. I was scared as hell riding from Berlin to Kaiserslautern. The first two Count Zeppelins exploded with no survivors. I fear for your life, Elska."

"What do mean?"

"Elska, honey, we just met. The Count Zeppelin is doomed, it is just a matter of time. I don't even want you to go to Hamburg."

"You don't? But I have a contract, I will have to refund the advance payment they gave me."

"Elska, I am a lawyer. Do you have a copy of the contract that you signed?"

"Not with me. It is in my apartment in Berlin. And what about the apartment? I can not just quit my job, Louis."

"You can be sick and unable to make the short hop from here to Hamburg. That would put you on a train to Berlin, much safer."

"Then what? The next flight out of Berlin is to Munich."

"Elska, first things first. What was the advance payment to you?"
"A thousand German marks."

"Gold or silver?"

"I don't know. My father deposited it in his bank in Copenhagen."

"If it was gold marks then it is worth $0.238 in US currency, if it was silver then it is worth $0.138 in US currency."

"I don't understand, Louis." I reached into my suit coat and removed my wallet. I removed a hundred dollar bill, a twenty, a ten, a five and three ones."

"This is what you are risking your life for, Elska, pocket money. Do you want to be sick or do you want to purchase your contract?"

"Louis, I can not let you do that. How will I ever repay you?"

"You can get a safe job that pays the same salary and you can repay me over the next fifty years. Let me see, 138 American dollars divided by 50 equals 2 dollars and 76 cents a year. If you would like monthly payments than it would be twenty-three cents a month."

"You are being silly, Louis, we won't even know each other in fifty years, I will be seventy years old." I smiled and she realized that she told me she was twenty years old.

"Elska, I care for you and I care what happens to you. Do you have a Danish passport?"

"Yes, why?"

"After we purchase your contract at the aerodrome, I am buying us train tickets to Copenhagen. I would like to talk to your father about your employment with Caldwell International. It would mean you would be working in one of the Caldwell European offices, you can have your pick of London, Rome or Copenhagen."

"You have an office in Copenhagen?"

"Yes, Caldwell Shipping. Is that where you would like to work?"

"Oh, Louis, my head is spinning, first last night, then this morning a new job in Copenhagen!"

"I take that is a yes?"

"Yes, oh, yes, Louis, I am so happy. I was always scared to death in the airship." She began crying again.

I WAS LATE TO THE FIRST PLENARY SESSION in the library of the Schloss Hesse-Cassel. I had sent the Daimler back to the Schloss because I did not know how long it would take to re-purchase her contract. It turned out that the station master was happy to have the payment and he gave us a receipt and said that the cancelled contract would be mailed to Elska's apartment in Berlin. We hired a cab to the railway station to purchase train tickets from Kaiserslautern to Berlin and on to Copenhagen.

"What do you have in this suitcase, Elska, it weights a ton!"

"An evening gown takes up most of the suitcase. I noticed you enjoyed looking at it last night."

"Elska, are you sure you are only twenty years old? Hans and I will be making side trips to Stuttgart, Munich, Rosenheim and Strassburg before we can use the train tickets to Berlin. You do not have a room at the Schloss, would it be alright with you if you stayed at a nice hotel in town?"

"Are you coming back to Kaiserslautern during any of the side trips? Will I see you?"

"No, we leave Kaiserslautern after the conference is over with a day and night in each of the stops."

"Why don't I go to Berlin today and tell my room mate that I am moving to Copenhagen. I will meet you in Berlin. Let me write down my address."

Elska Van Mauker
768 Zellin StraBe
Berlin, Deutschland

The hair on the back of my neck was standing on end. This was always the sign that danger, immediate danger, was at hand. I had a habit of placing my hand on the back of my head and rubbing the hair. The cab pulled into the railway station and I bought Elska a one way ticket to Berlin.

"Louis, this is not on to Copenhagen."

"No, we will need two tickets to Copenhagen from Berlin. I will see you in seven days at your apartment. I am very glad we met, Elska, you have renewed my faith in young women throughout Europe. Please be careful." I kissed her goodbye and left her at the train station.

THE THIRD PLENARY SESSION WAS IN THE AFTERNOON at one o'clock. I was standing, waiting in line, to get into the library when I felt a gentle hand on my arm. It was the Princess, she had been crying.

"Commander, I do not know how to tell you this. The Count Zeppelin has exploded between Kaiserslautern and Hamburg. All aboard have perished. It has been confirmed that your friend, Elska Van Mauker was on board. I am sorry, I know you were fond of her." My mind was reeling, okay, the zeppelin is gone or is it? How can I find out? Elska is safe on a train to Berlin, or is she? How can I find out?

"That is really a shock, Your Highness. It could have been me on my trip yesterday. Thank you for telling me, I appreciate it very much. I will not attend this session, tell Professor Becker that I have gone to the telegraph office to send a cable of condolence to the royal family in Denmark."

"Why would you want to do that?"

"Elska was the grand niece of King Christian V of Denmark."

"What was she doing working on a zeppelin in Germany?"

"I have no idea. I would like to find out. See you in few hours with some answers." I left the Schloss and walked towards the train station. Item 1, talk to the ticket master and find out if Elska, or whatever her name is, returned a one way ticket to Berlin for cash. Item 2, if she did, take a cab to the aerodrome and get your money back from that station master, right after you rearrange his face. Item 3, report back to Hans that you are stupidest, dumb shit on the planet.

I entered the train station and walked up to the ticket window. I asked him if my companion had changed her mind and decided to take the zeppelin to Hamburg.

"No, she did leave the station for a half hour and then returned. She wanted to change her ticket to Copenhagen. She tried to pay me with American money, a twenty dollar bill, I had never seen one before. I asked her go across the street and exchange it at the bank."

"Did she show you her passport, because the ticket was out of the country?"

"Of course."

"Did you notice the name on the passport, or the date of birth?"

"Yes, I wrote it down for my records. Her name was Elska Van Mauker, born 1885 in Frederica, Denmark.

"Thank you, you have been very helpful." I walked out of the rail station and hired a cab to take me out to the aerodrome. I entered the aerodrome station master's office with blood in my eye.

"Do you remember me? I have lost my wallet and I wonder if someone might have found it here." He seemed amused.

"I think Elska is up to her old tricks, Sir. She must have picked your pocket."

"How much money did you give back to Elska this morning after she returned from the train station?" I grabbed the front of his shirt and hauled him out of his chair. "When someone cheats me, Mister, I usually kill them. In your case I will make an exception and only break both of your legs. Give me what is left of the 138 dollars that I gave you a few hours ago and you will live."

"Yes, Sir. It is in my top desk drawer, a hundred dollar bill."

"Elska, did this to me for thirty-eight dollars!" I began to laugh so hard that tears began to run down my cheeks. "You keep the hundred, pal, you earned it. Did Elska return here and get on the Count?"

"No, she is on her way to Copenhagen to start the scam all over again."

"Is her name really Elska?"

"Yes, of course, Elska Flensburg."

I released him from my grip and smoothed the front of his shirt and said, "I came to Germany from America to learn as much as I could about the German people and I was taken in by a Danish muffin called Elska."

41

Valkyrie Assembly Plant

Stuttgart, Wurtemberg

I was still feeling like a jackass when Hans and I said goodbye to the Kaiser and the Princess and boarded the train for Stuttgart. I kept running the last forty-eight hours through my mind. I met the stewardess on the Count Zeppelin and I thought she was English because of her speech. She did not have the sing-song accent of someone born in Denmark, who had learned English in school. This was something she had told me, not a fact. She was a member of the crew of the Count Zeppelin that was certain. But there may or may not have been a contract advancement in the amount of a thousand German marks. This was something told to me, not a fact. She could have been hired at the last minute as a replacement. I wonder if the Zeppelin Company has a habit of doing this?

Her suitcase was way over weight for someone traveling on a dirigible. Fact, I had carried it for her. Where did the extra weight come from? Was she really planning on returning to Hamburg on the next flight out, her suitcase would never be allowed on the Count and it would be searched. No, she was planning all along to travel by train to Copenhagen. I was a means to an end for her. If she could convince everyone in the Schloss that she had fallen in love with me, it would only be natural that I would want to protect her and whatever was in the suitcase. She was desperate to get to Copenhagen. No, stupid, she was desperate to get what was in the suitcase, to Copenhagen. If this were an American operation she could travel by ferry to Sweden or by ship to France, England or anywhere in the Baltic once she reached Copenhagen. Her cover story of a distant Danish royal family member was perfect. I accepted it without question. She had never spoken Danish, only English and German. She is definitely not Danish or French or Russian or German, she had stolen something from the Germans. She would be marked for death as soon as the stolen items were identified and recovered.

"Hans, I have done something stupid!"

"You are young, Louis, young people think they are in love all the time."

"Not that. I think I may have gotten us involved with a British covert operation."

"What? How?" I told him what I had been thinking and he said, "There are two possibilities, Louis. She was working alone and needed a partner to get the suitcase to Copenhagen, or she already had a partner and she used you as a smoke screen. If they recover her body from the wreckage of the zeppelin, then she had a partner and the partner took the suitcase to Copenhagen by train. If there is no body, then she was working alone and she took the suitcase to Copenhagen. Either way, they think we are part of that operation. Our operation may go unnoticed. If it does, we have to be aware that the Germans are now trying to nail us for what happened to the zeppelin and the missing items that were stolen. We are in more danger from Elska's operation than we ever were from our own."

"What do we do, Hans?"

"Protect ourselves and continue on with our operation. Someone is certainly following us on this train, Louis. We need to keep them in tow, we can not afford to lose them. It will cause a panic and that is when people can get hurt."

"I agree, let me get our letter of introduction from the Kaiser and read it again, it will outline the sections of the plant that we are allowed to visit." I reached into my brief case and withdrew the letter. "It says we are going to get a guided tour of the frame building section, wing assembly area, elevators and rudder sections. There is no mention of the roll control, keel and propulsion, and landing gear assembly points. We will not ask to see them."

"Good idea, Louis. The photographs that I took of the Valkyries from the zeppelin windows should be enough for our report. I wonder how the new 'idiot proof' hidden camera will work? I can not get a very good photograph with a regular camera."

"We are here to take photographs and write a report of what we have seen on our trip, Hans. We do our best, we keep out of trouble and we get back to Berlin as soon as possible."

"We need to keep to the schedule laid out for us by the Kaiser. If we suddenly cut our trip short, that would send a signal to Berlin that we are in some sort of trouble. Let's lull them to sleep and hope that they do not wake up and bite us in the butt!"

It was a short distance from Kaiserslautern to Stuttgart and the train was entering the station. We waited for our luggage to be brought from the baggage car, we were in first class. We did not notice anyone watching us. We picked up our bags and walked slowly through the train station. We hailed a cab and asked for the hotel that the Kaiser and the Princess had recommended to us. Our driver said he could take us, but it is only one block over and two up. We thanked him and we began walking. I noticed a clothing shop and stopped to look in the window. In the reflection, I noticed two men at the end of the block.

"Hans, let's go in here, I need some new underwear, I can't risk sending my undershorts to a laundry."

He began laughing and said, "Ja, they will think that they have scared you and you need new underwear. One of them will ask the tradesmen what we bought for sure!"

"Then let's use our expense account and get a full outfit. I always wanted a Hamburg hat!" We both entered the shop and told the tradesman that we on our way to our hotel and that we would like to buy a new suit of clothes. The suits would be off the rack, but the alterations should be done in a few hours and delivered to the hotel. He indicated that it was no problem. Hans and I each bought a high quality German made, three piece business suit, a dress shirt and several sets of underwear. I paid the full amount in German marks for each of us and thanked him for his ability to help us in the short time frame.

We left his shop and continued slowly up the street towards the hotel. One of our followers went into the shop and the other kept us in view. We entered the lobby of the hotel and showed the front desk our letter from the Kaiser. Our room was waiting for us. Once inside, Hans motioned to me that a recording device was probable. I nodded my head, yes, and opened my suitcase so that it could be examined later after we left our room, this we expected, anything we did not want to have seen by a German agent was placed in my brief case, including my dirty undershorts. I placed my new underwear in a chest of drawers. We checked our watches and picked up the hotel telephone in our room.

"Hello, has the automobile arrived from the Valkyrie assembly plant? Thank you, we will be right down."

A black Daimler was waiting at the curb. Our driver introduced himself and we were there in a few minutes. The plant manager was waiting to greet us as the Daimler stopped outside the factory.

"Welcome to the Stuttgart Valkyrie Assembly Point, SVAP is stamped on every part made and assembled in this plant." He handed us a black leather covered notebook with gold letters SVAP on the cover. I opened it and it contained an outline of the visit. Photographs of all the assembly points, starting with the FRAME POINT were clearly identified.

The Frame Point

A very fine quality of Honduras mahogany is used almost exclusively in the framework. The main members of the frame are two long skids, upon which the rest of the frame is built. These skids are wide apart and take the place of a central chassis. The joints of the frame are made up of aluminum and are very easily bent. All aluminum joints are wire wrapped to increase their ability to withstand the forces of take offs and landings.

As we walked around the framing point, I realized that this plant did not believe in Henry Ford's assembly line. Each assembly point was set up like a giant checker board throughout the plant. Workers moved from point to point rather than have the item moving. Henry's moving assembly line started with a model A frame and ended with a finished automobile. In this German plant, all the frames were started at the same time and workers brought items to be mounted to the frame in a few days all of the checker board locations had completed aeroplanes. These were rolled out and filled with fuel and the engines started and the process started all over again. A different concept to be sure.

The Wings

The wings and rest of the body of the Valkyrie are made in three sections, the one between the frames and back of the propeller has a similar chord and less incidence than the other sections because of its position in the slip stream of the propeller. The two outer sections of the plane are turned up slightly, giving a dihedral angle effect. The surfaces are made of one layer of Egyptian cotton fabric stretched tightly over the numerous wooden and aluminum ribs. The plane is braced by cables to the struts and frame of the central section. The spread is 32 feet, the chord is 6.5 feet and the surface area is 190 square feet.

We had walked from the Frame assembly point and watched the workers assembly the wings and the remainder of the fuselage. I read the description in my notebook and examined the photographs provided for us. There was no need for Hans to practice with his brand new super secret spy camera.

The Elevators

Out at the front, under the horizontal front fixed keel plane, is the single surface elevation rudder. This is operated by wires leading to a

LEVER WHICH IS MOVED TO AND FRO, AS ON THE H. FARMAN MODEL BIPLANE. THE ELEVATOR IS 8 FEET WIDE, 2.5 FEET DEEP AND 20 SQUARE FEET IN AREA.

Hans and I stood and watched the workers come to this assembly point with their tools and parts to be placed at the front of the aeroplane. I wondered why the Germans were using this system of assembly, it was exhausting for the workers. We walked on to the next assembly point.

THE DIRECTION RUDDERS

TWO IDENTICAL SURFACES AT THE REAR SERVE AS DIRECTION RUDDERS. THEY ARE CONTROLLED BY A FOOT PEDAL OR BY THE SIDE TO SIDE MOTION OF A LEVER.

I began to see the logic of this method of manufacture. It took about an hour at each assembly point. There were eight assembly points, in eight hours the workers had assembled eight Valkyrie fighters that were ready to fly. The plant was producing 40 aeroplanes a week, that was more than the entire inventory of aeroplanes in the United States Military in the fall of 1905. This was just one model being assembled throughout the German Empire. Hans and I had seen three different models on our flight from Berlin to Kaiserslautern.

THE ROLL CONTROLLER

AILERONS FIXED TO THE TRAILING EDGE OF THE MAIN SURFACE AT EITHER END CONTROL THE TRANSVERSE BALANCE. THEY CAN BE OPERATED BY PEDALS OR BY SIDE TO SIDE MOTION OF THE LEVER, AS DESIRED. THESE AILERONS ARE 5 FEET WIDE AND 2 FEET DEEP.

Hans looked at me and smiled. He was thinking the same thing that I was thinking, this is not spying, the whole plant is open for anyone who wants to tour the plant and purchase an aeroplane. This is not a military secret, it is a commercial enterprise to improve the economy of the German Empire.

The Keel

The Valkyrie has a large horizontal keel placed well out in front and called the "leading plane", it is 14 feet wide and 3 feet deep. It exerts a considerable lift and is set at a greater incident angle than the main surface, thus employing the principle of the dihedral angle for longitudinal balance. The incident angle of this plane can be altered at will. There is no rear tail.

At this assembly point I understood the genius of the German design. The rear seat of a two seated Valkyrie would machine gun off a rear tail when in a dog fight. I wondered how the pilot fired his forward machine guns without destroying the propeller.

The Propulsion

A 30 horse power Benz engine, placed at the center in front of the main plane, drives a 7.5 foot propeller at 900 rpm. The position of the propeller is a curious one, working as it does in a slot in the framework. The rotation of the propeller is timed so that the firing pin of the machine guns does not engage when the propeller is vertical to the ground.

All I had to do was read my notebook, this was the secret of how the forward pointing machine guns worked.

The Landing Gear

The landing gear is purchased from the United States Wright factory and attached directly to the skids. This combination of serviceable skids and the Wright gear make this

THE SAFEST AEROPLANE IN THE WORLD. ON EACH SKID AT THE FRONT, BELOW THE SEATS, IS FITTED A PAIR OF WHEELS ATTACHED BY SPRINGS AND AT THE REAR ARE TWO SMALLER WHEELS.

I noticed that the seats were very conveniently placed out in front of the motor. In case of an accident, this position appeared to me to be extremely dangerous for the pilot. The center of gravity appears to me to be very far forward and would necessitate a considerable lift on the part of the leading plane.

I closed my notebook and handed it back to the plant manager.

"You may keep that with the Kaiser's complements, Commander."

"Thank you Sir. I assume that these fine aeroplanes are for sale."

"They are."

"I would like to purchase a two seater. Do you accept bank drafts?"

"We do, Sir. What bank are you planning to use, Sir."

"My bank in London, or if you prefer, The Bank of Copenhagen. I would like the certificate of ownership to be made out in the name of Caldwell Trading and Shipping, Copenhagen. I would like the plane delivered to our airfield in Copenhagen next month. Do you see a problem with that?"

"None, Sir. You may have it next week, if you like. You have not asked the price of the Valkyrie, Sir."

"I will not pay over a thousand German gold marks."

"Then you have just purchased one half of a Valkyrie, Commander."

"That will never do, I will write the check for two thousand gold marks, Sir."

"You understand that the Danish will not allow an armed aeroplane to land in Copenhagen. The aeroplane will be flown to your airfield and the guns will be sent separately in crates marked *spare parts*."

WE LEFT THE VALKYRIE ASSEMBLY PLANT with the notebooks under our arms and a bill of sale for a two seater Valkyrie to be flown to Copenhagen next week. Hans was shaking his head and said, "Louis, NCI just wanted photographs and specifications, not the whole aeroplane."

"I think Admiral Lowe will be overjoyed when we ship him the plane in large wooden crates to be reassembled and test flown in the United States. It is time that our military sees what they are up against from the Europeans."

42

Panzer Assembly Plant

MUNICH, BAVARIA

THE TRAIN RIDE FROM STUTTGART, Wurtemberg, to Munich, Bavaria, was passed in conversation with Hans. Our followers were still with us. There was a US Consul's office in Munich and we needed to find a way to get my "dirty underwear" to this office so that the coded information could be sent by diplomatic courier to Berlin and then on to Washington. The list of agents that would be entering the US as college professors should be in Admiral Lowe's hands before our data gathering part of the operation was complete. If the German Government decided to eliminate Hans and I, the information would be lost.

"How can we contact the US Consul in Munich without arousing any suspicion, Hans?"

"While you were helping the 'Danish Muffin', I sent telegrams to all the US Consul's offices on our route. I asked them to meet us at the trains stations. Munich is the first plant location that has such an office. We will use the, change of brief cases in a public toilet, procedure at the station and continue on to the hotel chosen for us by the Kaiser. Hopefully our followers are assigned to us for the whole trip. If they change at each location, then the exchange of brief cases will be more difficult."

"While we are in this train compartment, I will remove anything that we need to keep with us then. Hand me the notebook from

Stuttgart, that should go into the brief case. Here, put this in your suit coat pocket. Do we have enough pockets in our new suits to hold everything we need?"

"I think so. How do I look? Are my pockets bulging?"

" You look fine. I will translate the code off the underwear bands and put it on paper to send to Berlin. Right, Hans?"

"Right, Louis. If you buy an armored vehicle at this plant, Louis, it should be given to the consul's office for break down and shipment to the Washington Naval Yard." I spent the next hour or so putting things on paper to leave in the brief case.

> Message to Admiral Lowe
> Lancaster, Virginia
>
> We have managed to purchase an entire Valkyrie model number WS11WBD-0000 162-EZQ it is presently being flown to Caldwell Shipping Airfield, Copenhagen. I need to know it you would like us to use the assembly instructions in the notebooks given to us at the assembly plant to disassembly it into its major components. These components can be crated and shipped to Washington Naval Yard. We have two complete spec notebooks, I am enclosing one with this message.
>
> If you have contacts at the War Department in London, another option might be to hire a pilot to fly the Valkyrie to England from Denmark. Our next US Consul's office will be Strassburg, please advise.
>
> We have one complete notebook of specs and ordering instructions for the Panzer plant. I will enclose that copy for you. Any of these can be ordered by Ambassador Wilson and drop shipped to Copenhagen for transatlantic shipment to the Washington Naval Yard.
>
> LJ Caldwell

"Will there be two or one agent at the train station to meet us?"

"Usually two, why?"

"One can make the brief case exchange and the other can take us to the assembly plant, we can stop at the hotel after the plant visit for an overnight."

At the train station two American agents were waiting for us and I nodded and headed for the public toilets. One followed me into the public wash room area. We exchanged passwords and he took my brief case and gave me his, then he left. I waited a few minutes and took his brief case and met Hans and our driver to the Panzer Assembly plant in Munich. We arrived a few minutes early and told the driver to wait to see if a purchase of a vehicle was possible. There was no plant manager waiting for us and we could not get past the front gate, there was no gate minder. The three of us stood and talked until the time of the plant tour was at hand and still no one came to let us into the plant.

"There has been some sort of mixup about times, driver, take us to the hotel and we will telephone the plant."

"What do you think happened, Hans?"

"Do you have the plant telephone number from your first brief case?"

"Yes, driver, stop at the first public telephone booth and I will call the plant, we do not need to travel all the way back to the hotel." He stopped and I got out of the automobile and dialed the plant number.

"Hello, this is Commander Caldwell from America calling."

"Oh, hello, Commander, you got to your hotel and found the plant manager waiting for you and you talked to him about the accident at the plant this morning. Is there anything I can do for you?"

"I am not at my hotel, Miss, Professor Becker and I came directly from the train station to the plant. I am calling from just outside the plant at a pubic telephone booth."

"Our sincere apologizes Commander, the manager is waiting to see you, he has the notebook and photographs that you requested. You need to continue on to your hotel."

"Thank you, we will." I hung up and walked back to Hans and the driver..

"What did you find out, Louis?"

"The plant is closed because of some industrial accident, the plant manager is waiting to talk to us at our hotel. Have we been followed?"

"No sign of anyone."

"Good, take us to a location where we can get a cab and you can return to the consul's office, driver." He nodded his head and drove off. We switched transportation and arrived at our hotel as outlined on the Kaiser's schedule.

"The followers assumed that we would go directly to the hotel. I wonder what this is really about?"

"Did anyone ever tell you, you were paranoid, Hans?"

"Yes, the director of the Farm, that is why I am still alive." In the hotel lobby, three men sat waiting to talk to us. Two were our followers so the other was the plant manager. All three of them were engaged in a conversation. We stopped at the front desk and we were told to meet with the three men. We walked over and introduced ourselves to the plant manager and our two followers. We were told that the followers were from the Munich plant.

"Here is our letter of introduction from the Kaiser, Gentlemen." They took it and read it, "Can We keep this, Commander?"

"Of course, do you have anything for us?"

"Yes, the tour notebook similar to the one you received at Stuttgart." He handed me a leather bound book of photographs and descriptions of the assembly process.

"Thank you, I will make sure that my Uncle Teddy gets this. We are sorry about the plant accident. Was it serious?"

"Yes, it involved two worker's deaths."

"If you visit with anyone from Kaiserslautern will you tell them we did not check in here at our hotel and we went directly on to our second stop in Bavaria?"

"Of course. We regret that you did not see our processes, Professor Becker and Commander Caldwell. I have asked these two helpers to drive you to the railway station." The plant manager rose from his chair, clicked his heels, bowed and was gone. Hans and I stood and looked at our followers, then at each other. Finally, Hans said, "Where the hell are our suitcases, we forgot to pick them up at the train station." The look of surprise was evident on the faces of the two followers.

"Too many things going on at the last minute, let's walk over to the desk and cancel our rooms here and tell the desk manager you two gentlemen are taking us back to the station. First class luggage is always held until claimed by showing your first class ticket." I was not sure what Hans was thinking but I wished we were armed. The followers may have been told that this was our last stop and to bury us in the countryside.

Our fears were for nothing. The two men drove us to the train station and said goodbye.

"Look around, Louis, two more will be taking their places before we board for Rosenheim."

"You keep a look out, Hans. I am going to change our tickets and get our luggage checked."

"Louis, there will be no one waiting for us in Rosenheim, it is too small to have a US Consul's office."

"I will cable the Schneider Cutter Plant and someone will meet us at the train station, Hans. The train ride down to Rosenheim is less than an hour." We waited an hour for the next train south, boarded and found our compartment. Hans then began to ask his usual questions.

"What do you know about Rosenheim, Louis?"

"Rosenheim is a town in Bavaria at the confluence of the rivers Inn and Mangfall. It is the seat of administration of the district of Rosenheim, but is not a part of it. My grandfather has told me some things like the geography. The population of the town proper is approximately 10,000 inhabitants with up to 25,000 in the surrounding area. Rosenheim is situated in the Upper-Bavarian Alpine Foothills and, 1470 ft above sea level and covers an area of 22.5 square miles. The capital of Bavaria, Munich, is 32 miles away in the North-West direction from Rosenheim. It has a railway station at the junction of the Munich–Salzburg and the Munich–Innsbruck lines."

"Do you know any of the history of Rosenheim?"

"Yes, Rosenheim is famous for its churches of St Nikolaus and the Holy Spirit. In 1234, Rosenheim was mentioned for the first time as a market. The town's landmark is the gothic spire of the parish church St. Nikolaus (1450) with its baroque onion dome (1641). Rosenheim has very good facilities for studies in the midst of excellent weather conditions. There is a Fachhochschule Rosenheim offering various courses to the students."

"Many famous, some infamous, people have lived in Rosenheim.

Just the last names that begin with the letter F, would amaze you, Louis. Johannes Fischart was a protestant reformer. Friedrich Fishbach is a pattern-designer and author of many books. Emil Fischer is a chemist and full professor at the University of Berlin. Gustav Fischer was an African explorer. Jean Fischer was an officer in the French Foreign Legion. Johann Fischer was a poet. Kuno Fischer is a noted philosopher. Ludwig Fischer is an artist. Theobald Fischer is a noted German geographer. Von Erlach Fischer is an architect. Need I go on?"

"No, Hans, you have made your point, I am ignorant about my grandfather's heritage.

Hans took this as a sign that I needed further education. He explained the difference between a town and a Kreis, when he said, "Rosenheim is also a Kreis, which is a governmental district in the south of Bavaria. Think of it this way, Germany is the country, Bavaria is the state and Rosenheim is the county in which the town of Rosenheim is located."

"Got it, Hans."

"The neighboring counties are, clockwise from the west, Miesbach, Munich, also a city, Ebersberg, Muhldorf and Traunstein. The Austrian county of Triol is across the southern border. The county of Rosenheim completely surrounds the town of Rosenheim, Louis."

"There you go, then."

"Not only that, Louis, the town of Rosenheim is independently administered but hosts the county's administration: both town and county share the 'RO' designation for their automobiles."

"I am impressed with your research, Hans." He ignored my barb.

"The county was created in 1902 when the former districts of Bad Aibling and parts of Wasserburg am Inn were merged. The Rosenheim county is located in the foothills of the Alps, called the Chiemgau. The landscape is dominated by moraines created by the 'Inn" glacier in the last glacial period, including many lakes."

"Ja, ja. I got it, Hans. The giant ice field caused bumps and holes and when the ice melted it filled the holes." He still was not phased.

"The eastern half of the country is the largest of these lakes, also called Lake Chiemsee. The main rivers in the county are the Inn and the Mangfall, which meet in the town of Rosenheim. Mountain ranges in the south of the district include the Chiemgauer Alpen and the Mangfallge-birge which also contains the Wendelstien, at 1,383 meters or 6,030 feet for you American tourists." He was smiling.

43

Schneider Cutter Plant

Rosenheim, Bavaria

A day ahead of schedule can be a nice thing when you are about to see where your grandfather's people lived before they came to the United States. Rosenheim is a small border village, about 15,000, compared to Munich. It is located just 32 miles from the Austrian border. We could see the Alp ranges in the south of the district, the Chiemgauer Alpen and the Mangfallgebirge. We could see the Wendelstien, at 1,838 meters or 6,030 feet for us American tourists. I was smiling now, Hans was right. The train station was indeed located at the junction of the two Rivers, Inn and Mangfall, A huge double stone bridge crossed them both not far from the station.

Hans gave the porter our luggage checks and got our luggage. We were standing waiting for our guide from the Schneider Cutter Plant. A man walked up from the river Inn and asked, "Are you the Americans I am supposed to meet? My name is Ludwig Schneider and I am your cousin." He was looking at Hans.

Hans pointed to me and said, "That is your cousin. I am Professor Hans Becker from the American Embassy in Berlin." The mention of Berlin made my cousin, Ludwig, bristle. Obviously not every one in the German Empire was happy with having their capitol in Berlin.

"Bavarians are a very independent people according to my Grandfather Schneider." I was smiling and held out my hand to shake his. He did not offer to shake with Hans, he was a Berliner, obviously not someone to be trusted. I looked at Hans and winked.

"I have been sent from your great, great grandfather's plant to greet you and welcome you to Rosenheim. Come, I will take you in one of our cutters." He turned and walked down a set of stone steps to the level of the river. There sat a river boat cutter about the size of a small US Coast Guard cutter, which we boarded.

"You build boats this big for fresh water river patrols?"

"This boat is typical of what we sell to countries that have a system of lakes, locks and rivers. This part of Bavaria is not unlike the city of Stockholm, Sweden. We patrol all the rivers that are borders and those that connect into large lakes like our Lake Chiemsee. The plant that you will visit today is on Lake Chiemsee, we build and launch directly into the lake. We will have our captain run up the Inn river and enter a series of locks. Once we have reached the level of the lake we will be only a few minutes from the plant. If we made that same trip by automobile it would involve a long distance and a much longer commute time."

"Is the plant still privately owned or has the Empire claimed that also?"

"It is still in our family, Louis. For how much longer, I have no idea. The Kaiser and his plans for the Empire to occupy all of Europe are crazy." I smiled at him and shook my head, yes.

"You have a diagram of the family tree and where you are located in America, Louis. What do you think of the family?"

"I have never seen a Schneider family tree.

"There is one on this vessel, let's go below and look at it if you like." We had just started to pull away from the train station. We went down three steps and found a common area and there it was framed and hanging on the bulk head.

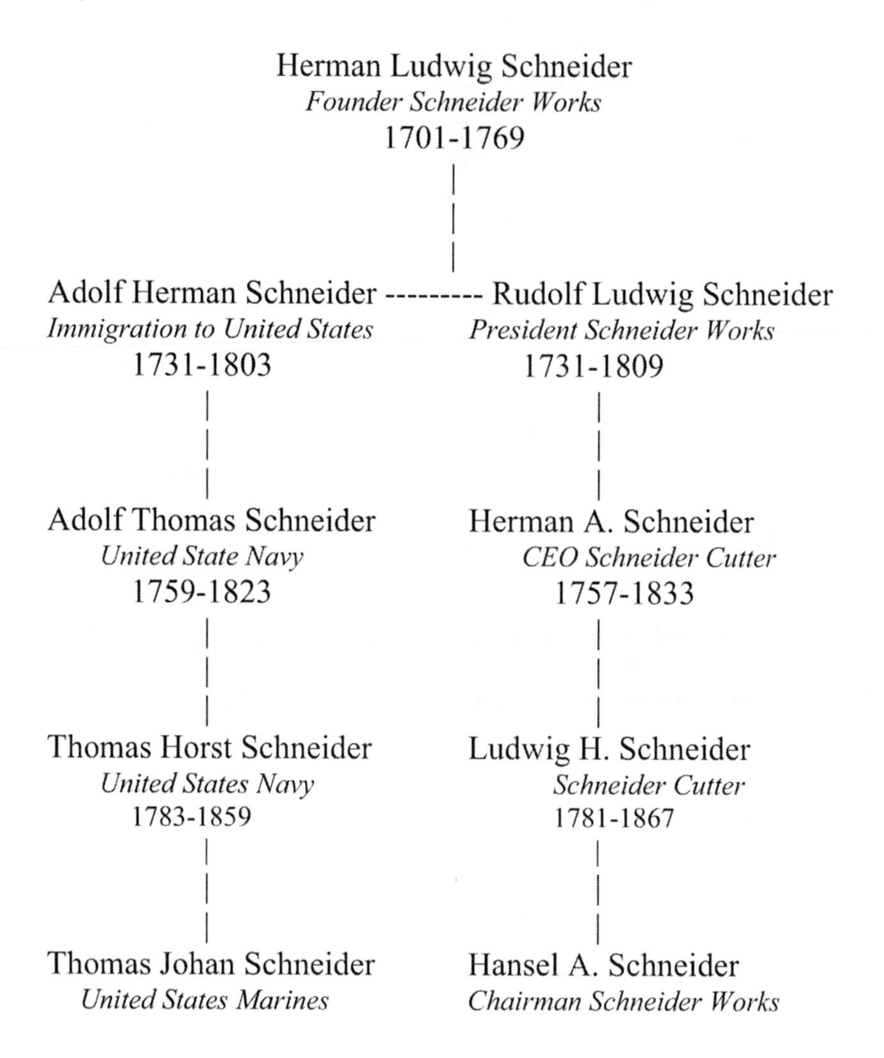

"You see, Louis, your grandfather is on the left and mine is on the right."

"That explains why my mother, Emily Schneider, is so devoted to her father. Her brother, Thomas Johan Schneider II, broke the line of succession in the US Navy. My mother picked it up by marrying a naval officer, that is how I got here."

We went back on deck and I saw Hans chatting away in German with the captain as they slowed to enter through the steel gates of a lock. The gates closed behind us and the water level slowly began to rise.

"You see, Louis, the lake is at a different elevation than the river Inn."

"I know, Ludwig, my Uncle Teddy is finishing the abandoned French project of connecting the Atlantic and Pacific through Panama. The French started from the Atlantic and stopped when they realized that the elevations were very different. My uncle solved the problem by creating a huge fresh water lake midway between the two oceans. The whole system will have two sets of locks, one coming east from the Pacific and one coming west from the Atlantic. Ships can use the huge fresh water lake to await passage in either direction."

"Your uncle must be German also, Louis, only a German would come up with such a simple solution to a complex problem." He was smiling. I decided I liked my cousin Ludwig. "Look Louis, as soon as the lock gates open you will see one of the most beautiful lakes in the world." The gates swung open and he was right. Lake Chiemsee was surrounded by foothills near the water's edge and behind the foothills stood the Austrian Alps in one direction and the Swiss Alps in the other.

"My God, Ludwig, this is breath taking!"

"Ja, the Schneider boat building facilities are just to our left on the far bank. We will be there in a few minutes. Would you care for a cold bier?"

"What is a bier?"

"You call it beer."

"Nein danka bitta." He looked at me funny." I thought bitta, was, thank you?"

"Ja, you are welcome, Louis." He began to laugh.

The Schneider Cutter Plant was an old fashioned assembly facility that was not concerned with speed of assembly or producing a certain number of boats in a week or a month. There did not seem to be a method of assembly. When an order came into the plant, one of the bays that led to the lake was selected and the entire boat was assembled until it was complete. It was launched directly into the lake and from there it entered one of the many rivers of southern Bavaria. It stayed in a river until it could travel no longer. Then it was hoisted onto a heavy trailer and pulled to its final destination during the night time only. Some of the cutters would have stopped traffic if they traveled during the daytime. I was glad that we had two days in Rosenheim. After the plant tour, where we received no notebooks, no photographs or written procedures, we were taken to a nearby beer hall and ate a huge meal. In two days, I met more cousins, uncles and aunts, it was like a family reunion, Ludwig never left my side. I slept in his house and Hans used the hotel that we had reserved. At the end of the second day, Ludwig took us back to the train station by boat. He had trouble saying goodbye and with tears in his eyes, he said, "Louis do not be a stranger to your family. You are welcome in Rosenheim whenever you can come to see us. My father likes you very much, Louis. I, of course, can not stand your ugly face." He gave me a huge bear hug and said, "Write when you can. I will too. See you next fall for sure, I have holiday and I am coming to America to see what all the fuss is about the 'New World'". He laughed again, turned and walked down the set of stone steps to the river Inn and his waiting cutter.

I turned to face Hans and said, "I am sorry that Ludwig kept me so busy, Hans. I have not had a chance to talk to you for two days. Have you spotted any followers at the hotel in last two days?"

"None, they are gone, I think. After all, this was a family reunion for you, Louis. What do you think of the German side of your family, Louis?"

"I think I am welcome to visit anytime I would like, but my home is in the United States."

"I feel the same way, Greta does not want to leave Germany and her family. When I am reassigned and leave Germany, I will ask her to move with me."

"I hope she wants you more than she wants to live in Germany, Hans. Can you afford to bring her parents to America? That might change her mind."

"That is a good idea, Louis, I will try that as a last resort." He was laughing.

44

Munitions Plant

Strassburg, Baden-Lorraine Border

Our train arrived in Strassburg from Rosenheim and we were met by representatives from the US Consul's office. They informed us that they would be with us all the way into Berlin. The US maintained a consul here because Strassburg was the capitol of Alsace-Lorraine. Two rivers are joined in Strassburg, just like in Rosenheim. These are the Breusch and the river Ill. This junction is only two miles east of the Rhine, 28 miles from France and 88 miles from Switzerland. The Ill divides into five branches inside the city. Strassburg had become a fortress since its capture from France. There is a German garrison of 15,000 men. A circle of fourteen forts and an inner rampart surround the city. The center of the city forms an oval, and it is surrounded by two arms of the river Ill. Here the streets are narrow and crooked, and the picturesque ancient houses and frequent specimens of pure mediaeval architecture, reflect a period when the city was both art-loving and wealthy. In this section, on the southeast, rises the structure for which the city is best known, the cathedral, or Minster. It is said to have been founded about 600. We were looking at the present edifice which was completed in 1176. Our guides stopped and let us walk around the cathedral. The fore part appeared to be Romanesque, and the rest Gothic. The remarkable facade, the work of Erwin Steinbach, with its galleries and rose windows caught my eye. I also noted the late Romanesque south portal, which is embellished with carved images. The tower looked to be about 500 feet high.

A scarcely less celebrated feature of the Minster is its astronomical clock, the mechanism of which was constructed in 1839-42 to replace that of the famous clock of the sixteenth century. We got back in our automobile and continued southwest past the cathedral to the protestant Saint Thomas Church, a composite edifice embracing the Gothic and Romanesque, begun about 1200. It contains a marble monument to Marshal Saxe, executed by Pigalle. Across the street is the ancient episcopal palace, identified with the Rohans, and now contains the municipal art museum. In the next block we drove past the Grosse Metzig. Its market hall dates from 1588 and is the museum of Industrial Arts. We turned to go north from the Grosse Metzig.

North of the Ill extends the handsome new quarters of the city, where in the Kaiserplatz, we saw the splendid Imperial Palace of Uncle Willy. We drove past the "citadel" built by Vauban and destroyed during the siege of 1870. Between it and the new city is the extensive arsenal of Strassburg. It was here that we would visit a modern munitions plant. Our two guides stopped giving us a tour and said, "We have received a message from Ambassador Wilson that mentions that you two are in hot water with the Chancellor. It seems that someone stole a part out of the guidance system off the Count Zeppelin on your trip to Kaiserslautern. You two are suspected of aiding a young woman in its theft. You have had two German agents following you since you left the conference. They closed the Panzer factory to your inspection and all further plants are probably also closed."

"How did we get entrance to the Valkyrie assembly plant?"

"The word had not reached them, the theft was not discovered until the zeppelin was airborne and on its way to Hamburg."

"They let us tour the Cutter Factory." I said.

"Yes, the Schneiders were notified by the Chancellor not to allow you any photographs, descriptions or plant tours. That is why they turned it into a family reunion for you, Commander."

"Why are we driving to the munitions plant then?" Hans asked.

"To make sure the intelligence is correct, if we are turned away at the plant, we are instructed to travel with you directly to Berlin so that you can travel with the Ambassador to London."

"The Ambassador is returning to Washington?"

"Princeton, actually, he has finished his work in Berlin and is returning to his post as President of Princeton University."

We had arrived at a factory within the arsenal for our tour and we were told that the factory was not in operation for the next week due to a malfunction of an important 'crimping' machine. Our suitcases were still in the boot of the automobile so we headed for the US Consul's office in Strassburg. We wanted to hand over the notebook given to us by the plant manager in Munich, we were still carrying that around with us. Hans thought it would be safer in the diplomatic pouch to Berlin than in our suitcases. We went through our entire suitcases and removed anything that looked suspicious and boxed the items for shipment to the American Embassy in Berlin. Hopefully it would catch up to us in Berlin or London.

The US Consul handed me a cable from the White House and said, "Congratulations Lieutenant Commander on your promotion to Commander. I read the cable, it was sent in the clear.

THE WHITE HOUSE
WASHINGTON D.C.

COMMANDER LJ CALDWELL
US CONSUL OFFICE
2312 RUPRECHTSAUCER
STRASSBURG, GERMANY

LOUIS, LET ME BE THE FIRST TO CONGRATULATE YOU ON YOUR PROMOTION WITHIN THE US JAG CORPS, USN. YOUR MISSION IN GERMANY IS NOW AT AN END, IT IS MY PLEASURE TO INFORM YOU THAT YOU WILL BE RETURNING TO EUROPE AFTER THE FIRST OF NEXT YEAR TO ASSUME A POSITION IN THE NLSO OFFICE, LONDON. SINCE YOU WILL BE RETURNING THROUGH LONDON WITH WOODROW, I THOUGHT YOU MIGHT LIKE TO LOOK

FOR A NICE, COMFORTABLE PLACE TO LIVE FOR THE NEXT FOUR YEARS IN LONDON'S WEST END.

UNCLE TEDDY

I handed it back to the US Consul and he placed it in a file.

"Well, professor and commander, it is time to change your identities again. You are now back in the Navy, Hans Becker, you are a Lieutenant Commander and assigned to the American Embassy in Berlin. Here are your papers Commander Becker. Commander Caldwell, you are assigned to the American Embassy, London, with travel documents so you may travel with your friend, Commander Becker on holiday to Strassburg. You will leave immediately with Lieutenants Carson and Howell, they already have their papers. Here are four coach tickets to Berlin, you leave within the hour. You best get to the train station."

"Thank you Sir, I have seen enough of the German Empire's war machine to write my report to the President of the United States. I purchased an aeroplane and it is being flown to my father's airfield in Copenhagen. Any report on that delivery?"

"No, not yet. I do have information on the whereabouts of the English agent posing as Elska Van Mauker, Commander. She was found dead at this address in Berlin." He handed me a piece of paper with the address. I pulled the only thing that Elska left with me. I compared them, the addresses were the same.

Elska Van Mauker	Elska Van Mauker
768 Zellin StraBe	768 Zellin StraBe
Berlin, Deutschland	Berlin, Deutschland

"Is the body held somewhere in Berlin?"

"Yes, it is a murder investigation, the body will not be released to anyone until the case has been cleared."

"Where will I find the morgue?"

"I know where it is." Hans looked grim.

"I need to identify the body and then visit the War Department while I am in London. I imagine she had parents living in England. I would like to pay my respects and tell them a little something of what their daughter was doing a few days before her death. It might comfort them until her body is released."

"I have no idea if the War Department has told the parents anything other than she is missing while on assignment delivering papers. There will be no request from England for the body, Commander. The British will never admit that they tried to steal something off a German zeppelin. I know you were fond of her and you can tell the Germans you knew her, but I would not request her remains for burial in Germany. That would prove that you and Hans were in cooperation with her and your life would be in mortal danger. You do not work for me and I can not order you to stay away from the morgue, but I can suggest something that you could try. You need to see the remains for closure, but you could say you do not recognize the remains as those of Elska Van Mauker." I looked at the US Consul as though he had slapped me across the face. I must have been ready to explode because Hans said, "I will go to the morgue for you, Louis."

45

Berlin

November 30, 1905

THE FOUR TRAVELERS BOARDED THE train in Strassburg and sat in the coach section near the back of a railcar so that Lieutenants Carson and Howell could protect us from anyone who would wish us harm. Hans and I began a quiet conversation.

"Louis, I know you want to find out about Elska. It is hard to accept her death. Did she live alone or did she have a roommate?"

"She had a roommate, she never told me the name, however. Why would she return to Berlin? Why didn't she stay on the train and continue all the way to Copenhagen?"

"Because you only bought her a ticket to Berlin."

"She traded that ticket for a non-stop, express all the way into Copenhagen. The train would not have stopped at the Berlin station. In fact the route would have been from Kaiserslautern to Frankfort, through Hanover and into Copenhagen. Berlin is over 150 miles to the west. I doubt the body in the morgue is Elska, it is probably the roommate. You are right to go to the morgue instead of me, Hans. The look of relief on my face would be reported immediately to the authorities."

"How did the agents know to look for her at that address, Louis."

"The aerodrome station master knew her as Elska Flensburg from Berlin. He would have her address. I think Elska used the alias more than once to board the zeppelin and make the Kaiserslautern trip. She gave him money on every trip that she made. I am not sure why the British would use a woman on such a dangerous mission."

"She was obviously good at her job. She fooled you, Louis."

"When it comes to women, Hans, your little sister could fool me. I have been scorned so many times, I have lost track."

"If she arrived in Copenhagen, someone was waiting to take her suitcase and get it into England. She probably returned to Berlin thinking she was in the clear. It will only be a few more hours and we will be there and we can find out."

"Where are we now?"

"Strassburg is straight south of Mannheim, we have passed through there and are headed to Frankfort."

"How many hours on into Berlin?"

"Probably five or six. Why?"

"These seats fold down. I am going to get some sleep."

Six hours later, Hans was shaking me, trying to get me fully awake. "Louis, wake up, we are here."

"Hans, I had a dream. It was wonderful, Elska is alive and sitting at the feet of her great uncle, Christian V."

"Let's hope not Louis, her great uncle died this week." I was now fully awake.

"Hans, why don't we all go to the morgue and only you can view the remains. If two of us show up it will look more suspicious than if the legal representation of four lawyers from Copenhagen want to examine the remains. Our luggage and the fact that we have been on a train for hours will add credibility to our story."

"No, Louis, I am going alone into the morgue. If I do not return in fifteen minutes you and the lieutenants can come to my rescue."

"We hailed a cab and went to the city morgue. Three of us waited in the cab. Hans returned with a smile on his face. "It is not Elska, Louis, it must be her roommate."

"Do they think they have Elska Van Mauker?"

"Yes, I broke down at the sight of the strange looking body and babbled in Dutch and the few words I know in Danish and told them it was Elska and that I would inform the royal house of Denmark that the grand niece and 18th heir to the throne has been killed in Berlin." I hugged Hans.

"Now what, Louis?"

"Now we can take our time, cover our tracks and I can travel with Woodrow Wilson to London." The cab continued on to the American Embassy, Berlin.

AMBASSADOR WILSON WAS HAPPY that we survived the mixup with the British operation. He had a number of pieces of information for me. The first was a telegram from Caldwell Shipping that they had received a model WS11WBD-0000 162- EZQ aeroplane from Stuttgart and a crate of spare parts. The second was a message from Lancaster informing me that the Valkyrie was to be flown by an English pilot to Barrows, England. The pilot would meet me in Copenhagen the day after tomorrow. The code word was Dodo Bird. That seemed a bit ominous, since this was the only flightless bird that I knew. He then handed me a sealed envelope that was addressed as:

ELSKA VAN MAUKER
768 ZELLIN STRABE
BERLIN, DEUTSCHLAND

COMMANDER LOUIS CALDWELL
AMERICAN EMBASSY
BERLIN, DEUTSCHLAND

I opened it.

November 6, 1905

Louis,

I am writing this in the train station at Kaiserslautern. I changed my ticket to Berlin to an express to the second location that we talked about. I had planned to take the Count, but my suitcase was over weight for some reason. If you would go to my apartment and tell my roommate that you have offered me a position with your firm, I would greatly appreciate it. She will pack my things and send them to me. I always leave her a small amount of postage money to cover things that I have forgotten when I travel. She will know what I need from the apartment.

When you arrive at my destination come to the train station and ask for a letter being held for you at the postal service window. I hope your fact finding mission here has been as successful as mine.

All my love,

Elska

"Ambassador, I will need the assistance of Lieutenants Carson and Howell. I will leave today by train from Berlin to Copenhagen. Caldwell shipping has a guest house in Copenhagen and I think the three of us will be comfortable there. We will meet the English pilot and make sure he is qualified to fly this German areoplane before we return to Berlin. I know you wanted to leave for London as soon as I arrived but this needs to be done before we make that journey."

"Commander Caldwell?"

"Yes, Mr. Ambassador."

"You and I can leave from the port of Copenhagen just as easily as from the port of South Hampton. Do you want me to book us on a Danish transatlantic vessel?"

"Yes, I think that would be appropriate, Mr. Ambassador."

"I will need reimbursement for the purchase of the Valkyrie, Sir. Otherwise, I will be a vagrant." I was smiling, I was sure that Woodrow Wilson understood the financial picture of the Caldwell family."

"Of course, Commander, German gold marks alright?" I handed him the bill of sale and he went to his desk and wrote me a bank draft in the amount of 2100 marks. He handed it to me and said, "You might need a little traveling money, Louis."

"Thank you, Woodrow, when can we leave?"

"In two hours, I am packed, I have already boxed and sent everything to my wife in New Jersey, last week. I am as ready as I will ever be."

"Hans, can you take the four of us to the train station? I need to send a telegram to Caldwell Shipping to meet us at the train station in Copenhagen."

46

Copenhagen, Denmark

December 2, 1905

Woodrow Wilson, the returning President of Princeton University and the exiting Ambassador to the German Empire, and I arrived in Copenhagen on the second of December, 1905. I found the Caldwell Shipping driver and had him load the luggage while I went to the station post office. I asked for a letter addressed to me and paid the postage due. I ripped it open.

> Dearest Louis,
> Where do I begin? Please forget that last letter, I was sure it would be read by the postal inspectors, as might this one. By now you know that my German name is not Van Mauker, it is Flensburg and I lived alone at my apartment. I do not plan on returning to my apartment any time soon. Everything is fine there until the end of the year. I think you know that I have a fine position already that I am very proud of and I will not be needing the position that you offered me in Copenhagen.
> My feelings for you are confusing to say the least, I have never felt like this towards any man that I have known. One moment I want you to come for me and tell me to forget about my present position and move to your

castle in America. Then I think, "Silly girl, this is an American agent who was on a covert mission of his own and cares nothing for you."
When you decide if we have a future and it is what you want, please make contact with me and I will come running to you.

All my love,
Elska

I folded the letter, kissed it and placed it in my breast pocket.

"At least this one let me down easy." I said to myself.

I would be home before Christmas I would deal with this after the first of the year. I left the Ambassador and Lieutenant Howell at the Caldwell guest house, with all our luggage, while Lieutenant Carson and I drove out to the Caldwell Shipping Company's airfield. We stopped at the shack that served as a control tower and terminal. Two pilots were visiting and one had a real heavy British accent.

"Excuse me, are you two employees of Caldwell Shipping?"

"Who wants ta know?"

"I am Louis Caldwell, owner of Caldwell Shipping. I do not recognize either of you, what are you doing here?"

"Waiting for you, Sir. Flight Lieutenant, Jake McDonald, at your service, Sir. This here is flight Lieutenant 'arry 'iggons. Do any of these Dodo Birds parked on the grass outside actually fly?"

"We have one under wraps, that we just purchased. Care to take me for a spin in it?"

"Right you are, Governor. Let's have a look at this, then." The four of us walked outside into the raw wind of December and towards the two seat model Valkyrie parked under a tarp. I helped him remove the tarp and I climbed into the back seat. "Wait a minute, Commander Caldwell, I have to do a pre-flight check of this machine. Where is the notebook that Barrows is all excited to see?" I reached under my seat and handed it to him. He sat down on the grass and began to read it. "He looked up and said, "This is how you build the stupid thing. Don't you have a flight manual?"

"What you see is what you get, McDonald. I am getting out of this beast if you don't know how to fly." I started to get out.

"Hold your horses, I know how to fly as well as the next chap. Let's check the petrol level."

"Auto level."

"What?"

"Every gauge is marked in German. Petrol is Auto in German." He handed the notebook back up to me and said, "I will need you to translate every gauge in this machine. 'arry, go get me some adhesive tape from the shack and a grease pencil." The other pilot ran back towards the shack. He returned with a roll of tape and a pencil. In a few minutes Jake had labeled all the switches and gauges.

"All right then, here we go, CONTACT! Harry pulled the propeller through and the engine caught. McDonald released the brakes and Harry grabbed the wheel chucks and the Valkyrie began to creep forward along the grass strip. McDonald looked at the wind sock outside the shack and positioned the Valkyrie for takeoff. I was scared to death. The engine began to really scream and the plane jumped forward and raced down the strip and gently lifted into the air. Neither one of us had a helmet or a warm jacket, the rush of the wind past our faces was freezing. I was screaming from the back seat and McDonald was smiling as he did a gentle bank and then a full turn and approached the strip for landing. It settled softly and rolled up to the front of the shack. The engine stopped its roar and the propeller stopped its turning. I had had my first aeroplane ride. It lasted only a minute or two, but it fulfilled one of the requirements for my mission to Europe. "*Ride in a Valkyrie if you get a chance.*" I looked down to see that I was sitting in a puddle of my own urine.

I climbed out of the back seat and said, "McDonald, I want a proper ride the next time I am at Barrows."

"You can count on that, Commander. Our engineers are going to love examining this machine." He turned to his co-pilot and said, " Hey 'arry get our gear and take a pee. The commander already has. We have no idea where or when we can land and purchase our fuel." He turned to me and said, "We have a rough idea of where we can land in Denmark, Holland and France, after that we are across the channel.

Wish us luck, Commander. Oh, and change your pants before you get back in your fine motorcar."

LIEUTENANT CARSON AND I STOOD and watched the Valkyrie until it was a dot in the sky headed west for Holland.

"We have a few more days here in Copenhagen before the Ambassador and I board our ship for Washington. Would you like to take a short side trip with me to Fredericia, Denmark?"

"Commander, Fredericia, is not a short side trip. We can not drive there. Denmark is a series of islands. Copenhagen is on the eastern shore of the island of Zealand. The islands of Falster, Laaland and Funin are between Copenhagen and Fredericia. Fredericia is on the eastern shore of the island of Jutland."

"I know, that is why I booked us on a day ferry from Copenhagen north, through the Straight of Oresund and directly into Fredericia a couple of hours at the most."

"What do you need in Fredericia?"

"I need to check with the hall of records for a Elska Flensburg. If we find a record, I think we will visit her parents and ask if they have heard from their daughter who went to Berlin to find work."

"Do you think she is the one in the morgue, Commander?"

"I do. I think she may have been killed by the British, trying to cover their tracks."

THREE HOURS LATER we were walking off the Copenhagen to Fredericia ferry and asking directions to the hall of records. We found it in what we would have called the county court house at home. We showed our embassy cards and told the woman working in the department of records about the slain girl in Berlin identified as Elska Flensburg. Her Danish passport indicated that she was born in Fredericia. We would like to give our condolence to her parents, but we did not have an address. She looked in her book of registration and asked,"How is the last name spelled?" We told her and she shook her head no and said, "That is not a common Danish name, there is a small village in what used to be southern Denmark, by that name. Most likely you will find the parents there. Let me get you a map and show you." She left to get the map.

"Well, Lieutenant, it looks like I have dragged you on a wild goose chase. We are not venturing back into Germany."

The clerk returned with her map and pointed to the tiny village just south of Fredericia, but now inside Germany, about 40 miles. "I have drawn the new border in black ink, here, the original border was 250 miles further south. The Kaiser has pushed the German Empire that far north into Denmark."

"I understand your feelings, I would feel the same way if I lived in the Frisian Islands which used to be Dutch. Thank you for your time. We have a ferry to catch for Copenhagen."

47

Return to United States

December 4, 1905

A Danish ocean liner is not like the transatlantic steam ships that Caldwell Shipping uses to transport goods. The *Pride of Copenhagen* was like a floating hotel and the two passengers from the American Embassy, Berlin, were going to enjoy their passage to America. If the Germans had decided to follow us, they did a good job, we never noticed anyone. Dr. Woodrow Wilson was eager to get back to his family and the first day he spent a good deal of time in his stateroom. We ate our meals together and I wrote letters to my family. I wrote a letter to Elska, or whatever her name was, but I had no address and no place to mail it in the middle of the Baltic Sea. I spent some time touring the ship and talking to the seamen that provided our passage in such comfort.

I was preoccupied with the death of the young woman in the apartment at 768 Zellin StraBe, Berlin. I guess it was the NCI investigator in me asking the questions. 1) Who was the woman they found in 768 Zellin StraBe? 2) Was she the roommate of the woman I knew as Elska? 3) Was she a British agent or was she a German agent waiting for Elska to return home? 4) Who killed her and why? Was it an accident? 5) What happened to the two agents that followed Hans and I around after we left Kaiserslautern? Were they called off after the death of the woman in Berlin? I needed more information from Hans, he had seen the body.

I decided to ask the ship's Purser if radio messages could be sent to Berlin.

"You are the second person to ask me that, Mr. Caldwell. Most of our passengers are from Denmark and we send radio messages from the ship to any point in Sweden, Germany, Holland or England until we are out of the English Channel and into the Atlantic. It is winter sailing and we can not take our usual summer route past Iceland. We will be docking for a short time in Brest, France. That will be tomorrow. After tomorrow, we will be at sea for seven days, until we enter United States waters."

"So, I have until to tomorrow to write my messages."

"You may take them directly to the radio room for transmission, but you must have a paid receipt from our office."

"My messages are for the German Chancellor's office, can I reverse the charges?"

"No, as I told the other gentleman who wanted his messages to the Chancellor's office reversed, we have no means of collecting fees from Germany."

The purser watched me as I smiled and thought to myself, "*Thank you, you just confirmed that Ambassador Wilson and I have followers on this passage.*" What I said out loud was, "Thank you, you have been very helpful."

I left the Purser's office and headed for the stateroom of Ambassador Wilson. I knocked and he came to the door. "Oh, Commander, I am glad that you came by. Did you know that you could send messages to anywhere in Europe from this ship?"

"Have you been to the Purser's office, Mr. Ambassador?"

"No, I read it in this handbook of facts that each of us have in our staterooms, why?"

"I have just come from the Purser's office. I was inquiring about radio messages to Hans in Berlin. The Purser told me I was the second one today requesting information on how to contact the Chancellor's office in Berlin. It would appear that we are being watched on this trip. I would suggest that we do not walk alone around the ship. We will be safer with each other. A single target is easy to throw over the side."

"I agree, Commander. Why did you want to contact Hans?"

"I need a physical description of the woman killed in the apartment on Zellin Street, Berlin."

"Hans is very efficient, Commander, I have that in my messages and communications to Admiral Lowe. Let me find that for you." He took out his brief case and rummaged around in it until he found what he was looking for. Here it is." I read it.

> MESSAGE FOR ADMIRAL LOWE
> BERLIN NCI STATION CHIEF
>
> ADMIRAL, I HAVE MADE THE IDENTIFICATION OF THE BRITISH AGENT'S BODY FOUND IN THE APARTMENT ON ZELLIN STREET, BERLIN. I DID NOT WANT LOUIS TO SEE THE BODY AFTER WE LEARNED THAT THE BODY WAS BEATEN TO DEATH. IT WAS A FEMALE, HAIR COLOR AND LENGTH IDENTICAL TO THE WOMAN LOUIS AND I SAW ON THE ZEPPELIN AND AT THE KAISER'S HOME IN KAISERSLAUTERN. THE FACE WAS SO BADLY BEATEN THAT IT WAS SWOLLEN TO ABOUT TWICE ITS NORMAL SIZE. IF TWO WOMEN SHARED THE APARTMENT, THAN THIS COULD HAVE BEEN EITHER ONE OF THEM. IF THE APARTMENT WAS OCCUPIED BY JUST ONE WOMAN, THAN THE WOMAN WE MET IN OUR FLIGHT TO KAISERSLAUTERN IS NOW DECEASED.
>
> THIS MUCH WE DO KNOW. A BRITISH AGENT ENTERED DENMARK AT THE TOWN OF FREDERICIA WITH THE PASSPORT OF ELSKA FLENSBURG. SHE COULD HAVE HAD ANOTHER ONE IN THE NAME OF ELSKA VAN MAUKER, WE DO NOT KNOW. SHE ENTERED GERMANY THROUGH THE BORDER VILLAGE OF FLENSBURG MONTHS BEFORE WE MADE CONTACT WITH HER. SHE MADE APPLICATION FOR EMPLOYMENT WITH THE ZEPPELIN COMPANY AND DID SIGN A CONTRACT FOR SIX MONTHS SERVICE.

The stateroom telephone rang, as I handed the message back to the ambassador. He reached out and answered it. "Hello....... yes, he is with me now......... thank you, no, there are only two us traveling with diplomatic passports....... yes, that does sound strange. Where is ship's security? Can they arrest them or detain them? .... thank you, I will tell Commander Caldwell." He hung up the telephone.

"Was that the Purser?"

"Yes, two Germans were just at his desk, inquiring about our cabin locations. Since we are preferred suite guests, he told them we could be paged and you and I would meet them in the Sail Along Bar."

"Did he mention if either one of them was the man asking for radio messages to Berlin?"

"Yes, do you want to observe them from a safe distance to see if you know either of them from your recent tour of southern Germany?"

"They know what we look like, Ambassador, we have no idea what they look like. Let me go by myself and see if they were the followers from last week. I doubt that they are. When the ship docks in Brest, I am going ashore and buying us two hand guns. Unless you happened to have two in your brief case, Ambassador." He smiled and nodded his head, no.

"Louis, did you cash that bank draft that I gave you in Berlin?"

"Yes, I have German marks."

"You had better exchange them for French francs at the Purser's office before you go ashore. I am going with you. I want some simple instruction in how to load cartridges and fire the gun before we get back on board this ship."

"Good idea, Woodrow, are you sure you are a college president?"

"I was a lawyer long before I was a college professor, Louis, and I know the law. It is always self defense when your life is threatened."

I LEFT THE AMBASSADOR'S SUITE and headed for the ship's bar when I heard the announcement, "Heir Wagner and Heir Hezein please meet our parties in the Sail Along Bar."

The two German agents froze in their tracks, "What has the idiot Purser done?"

"We will split up, you go first and I will catch up to you." The agents separated and headed for the ship's bar. The three of us entered the bar at the same time, all from different directions. I recognized both of them. They were the ones on the train from Munich to Rosenheim. They were back to finish their job unless I acted quickly. I took the one closest to me and bumped into him on purpose. He was so surprised that he did not react at first. I drove my fist up under his chin as I screamed, "Get your hand off my wallet." I was putting my wallet in his left side suit coat pocket as he was collapsing to the floor. His partner came rushing to his aide as I thought he might. I used the forward motion of his body and threw him over my hip. He came crashing down on top of his partner and had the wind knocked out of him. I started to help him up as I slipped my wrist watch into his suit coat pocket. It was over in seconds. People in the bar just sat and looked at the three of us.

"Call ship's security, bar tender, these two just tried to rob me." I punched the second agent in the face as he started to protest his innocence.

"Tell it to the captain, you thief!" Within minutes, two members of the ship's security were on the scene.

"What is the meaning of this?"

"That man took my wallet, I want it back." I was pointing at the one still on the floor trying to speak. "That one took my watch." I pointed at the one standing holding his mouth. "Search them, I want my money back." Within a minute the wallet and wrist watch were found along with black jacks, folding knives and snub nose hand guns. They opened the wallet and found my navy identification card.

"If this is your wallet, what does the identification indicate?"

"That my name is Louis Jason Caldwell and that I am a Lieutenant Commander assigned to the American Embassy, Berlin. These two tried to rob me. I want them locked up until we dock at Brest. As soon as possible I would like them taken off this ship. What has this world come to that you can not enjoy a holiday without being robbed or worse?" The members of the ship's security handed me my watch and wallet and assured me that these two would be taken off the ship in handcuffs when we docked in Brest. They would be sent back to Denmark to stand trial, since it was a crime in Denmark to board an ocean liner with a hand gun. The attempted robbery was witnessed by nearly twenty guests in the Sail Along Bar of a Danish vessel.

"Thank you. Where will these two be kept until the ship docks?"

"We have holding cells on the first deck, you will be called to testify at a Captain's inquiry, Commander."

"I would be happy to do so. Anything to get these two off of this ship, I want to relax and enjoy my vacation."

THE NEXT DAY the ship docked at Brest, France, and the captain called his inquiry into the matter. During the night, the two arrested were allowed to send radio messages to the German Consul's office in Brest. A member of that office sent a radio message to *The Pride of Copenhagen* requesting permission to represent the two arrested and his request was denied. He was allowed to meet with the two when the ship's captain inquiry was completed and the two were taken off the ship.

The inquiry began with the captain telling each of us present, the following:

"Good morning. This is an informal hearing into the charges pending against Heir Wagon and Heir Hezein of the German Chancellor's staff in Berlin. I am speaking in German because the two accused do not speak Danish. Commander Caldwell, do you speak German?"

"Yes, Captain."

"Heir Wagner, are you aware that it is a crime to bring firearms aboard a Danish vessel?"

"Danish law does not apply to members of the German diplomatic corps. Only German law applies to us and we have permits to carry fire arms anywhere in the world."

"I see, did you declare that you were on a diplomatic mission and show your diplomatic passports when you purchased your tickets to travel on this vessel?"

"Nein, we did not have to."

"Oh, yes, you did, Heir Wagner. Once you stepped on this vessel you are subject to my law and my law only. You signed a travel contract which stated that you must declare all personal weapons and surrender those weapons for safe keeping in the ship's safe. Therefore, you violated the terms of passage and you will forfeit any amount that you have paid for this voyage and you will taken from this ship. An agent of your government will meet you at the end of the gangway in thirty minutes."

"But, I protest this treatment of a foreign diplomat." He was still in handcuffs and asked for them to be removed. The captain ignored him and turned to the second agent.

"Heir Hezein, are you aware that it is a crime to bring firearms aboard a Danish vessel?"

"It is not a crime, it is our right to carry fire arms."

"Is it also your right to attack another passenger and try to steal his wallet and watch?"

"We did no such thing. We are German diplomats and we demand our release."

"How did you end up with the Commander's wallet and watch on your person?"

"He put them there."

"I see. Call the first witness from the Sail Along Bar." A man came forward and gave his name and cabin number. "Tell me what you witnessed yesterday, Sir."

"My wife and I were having a drink and two men ran into each other."

"Point to the two men, please." He pointed to Wagner and me.

"What happened after they collided?" He pointed to me.

"That man cried out, 'take your hand off my wallet.'"

"Are you sure those were his exact words?"

"Yes, the thief was not a very good pick pocket."

"What happened next?"

"The man who was yelling pushed the pick pocket to the floor. Then a second man attacked the victim and ripped off his wrist watch."

"You saw the second man, Heir Hezein, forcibly take the man's watch?"

"Yes, he was angry that his friend had been caught red handed stealing a wallet."

"Thank you. Second witness please." A woman stepped forward and answered the captain's questions. After three more witnesses, the captain was convinced that a crime had taken place.

"Heir Wagner and Heir Hezein, you are a disgrace to the German foreign service. Because you are German does not give you the right to treat other people as you please. I find you guilty of attempted robbery. We are docked at a French port of call. A member of the German consul's office has demanded your release. And you will be released as soon as the consul pays your fines. I will send a porter to the foot of the gangway with a transcript of this inquiry and my finding. As soon as he pays your fine in French francs you will be released. Your weapons were thrown overboard last night and can not be returned to you. Because you failed to act in a civil manner on this vessel, I am instructing my security members to keep you in handcuffs until you are off the ship."

WITHIN FIFTEEN MINUTES the waiting German consul was reading the transcript of the inquiry. He thanked the porter and asked permission to pay the fines at the Purser's office. He was allowed aboard ship and he paid with French francs from his brief case. The captain was standing behind a one-way mirror inside the Purser's office.

"The Commander is an unusual man, Captain, he took care of our problem on his own, without instructions from us."

"Yes, he appears to be a fine member of Ambassador Wilson's staff. Obviously, the two Germans were sent to kill the Americans traveling on my ship. No one has broken any laws of the sea, except Commander Caldwell, and he can not be arrested. But that does not stop us from enforcing the terms of our travel contracts. The Commander gave us the opportunity to get rid of the German agents. Alert ship's security that additional German agents may be aboard. We need to keep a close watch on the Ambassador until we dock in America."

> THE INCOMING MESSAGE FROM GERMAN CONSUL'S OFFICE, BREST, FRANCE, TO BERLIN READ AS FOLLOWS:
>
> OCEAN LINER, PRIDE OF COPENHAGEN, JUST DEPARTED FROM BREST. AGENTS WAGNER AND HEZEIN RELEASED UNHARMED AND ARE IN ROUTE TO BERLIN. PLEASE ADVISE NEXT ACTION TO BE TAKEN.
>
> RESPONSE FROM BERLIN:
>
> THANK YOU FOR THIS INFORMATION, MISSION PRESENTLY UNDERWAY ABOARD THE *PRIDE OF COPENHAGEN.*

Please forward all messages from last two agents on board.

Incoming message from American Embassy to:

The Pride of Copenhagen
Off the coast of France

Dear Commander Caldwell:

The two physical descriptions match those of our old friends Heinrick Hemmler and Karl Witenshon of the SS. You were wise not to confront these agents, they are known killers. Your actions were prefect to defuse the situation.

Hans Becker
Military Attache American Embassy, Berlin

The first day ended in frustration for every one.

First: Heinrick Hemmler and Karl Witenshon had been ordered to protect the American Ambassador and his traveling companion at all costs. The college professor exchange program would be destroyed if any harm should come to either passenger. In order to observe and protect them, they needed to know the cabin numbers of the two individuals. The dumbkopf Purser, had given them away just prior to their meeting with the Americans in the ship's bar. The crazy American Caldwell had attacked them and placed his wallet and watch on their persons.

Second: they were arrested before finding the second pair of agents assigned personally by the Kaiser, to assist in the protection of the American Ambassador.

Third: The Captain was certain that a murder was attempted on his ship and he had removed the threat by taking the agents off his ship.

Fourth: The security detail of the *Pride of Copenhagen* was jumpy, they had been ordered to protect the American Ambassador and his traveling companion.

Day two began with the two remaining German agents deciding what they would do. They decided to do nothing that would bring attention to themselves. They would observe the Americans in public areas of the ship and write a daily log of the observations. This log would then presented to their superiors when they arrived home.

Day three began as the ship's security detail settled into watching and protecting the Americans. The day before, they had observed two men watching the Americans and writing in a diary. They did not look dangerous and the observation was reported to the captain.

Day four began with the Americans feeling more at ease. The Ambassador and the Commander joined a bridge tournament in the lounge and won first place.

Day five began with the German agents deciding that there was no danger to the Americans from anyone on board and they discontinued the log book entries. They would report to their superiors that they had protected the Americans as ordered.

Day six began with the captain ordering his security detail to ease off the constant monitoring of the Americans. They would report only unusual happenings during the observation period.

Day seven began with the early arrival at the Port of Philadelphia and the captain's joy of releasing his passengers. His responsibility for the safety of the Americans was at an end.

48

Christmas at Seneca Hill

December 22, 1905

My Grandmother Caldwell's plans were finally coming together it had been exactly one year since I had been home to her house. When my Uncle Teddy ran for re-election in 1904, she had released his trust fund so that he could run a first class campaign. After his election, she released the Seneca Oil Trust Fund and the construction of Cranson College began. The construction had gone on for a year. The architect from Pittsburgh had done a wonderful job. The college site was spread around with the house as the center point. My grandmother must have walked the site every day. It would take another year or so for all the buildings to be completed.

My grandmother was now age eighty seven and she realized that she would probably not see the young women who would graduate from Cranson College. In fact this might be her last Christmas with her family. She wrote, again this year, to everyone in the family and invited them to attend a Christmas celebration at Seneca Hill. She still had a sense of humor, she wrote, "Most students leave college to travel to their homes for Christmas. I am asking each of you to leave your home to come to the future Cranson College, now in its second year of construction at the family estate. Carol Caldwell Cranson will host the event and I promise to come back and haunt any Caldwell who does not see fit to come home for Christmas."

We were all there. My sister was already there and I rented a automobile and drove from Washington a few days earlier. Our parents and Aunt Ruth had come by train from Washington to Oil City. My sister and I took the same team of four horses from the carriage house as last year and hitched them to the largest carriage and met them at the train station. The secret service was not amused.

"Really, Mister President, you can not be seen riding in a horse and buggy." Uncle Teddy said, "Snow is predicted for tomorrow and if my mother-in-law has a sleigh, these four fine animals will be pulling us all around the estate. You weren't here last year, were you? Get used to it. We are in the country. One of you stay with all the baggage, you other two jump on the back where the footmen usually ride. Louis, take us home."

The carriage was full, the Roosevelt family numbered eight. They sat on each other's laps. Just like last year, my parents loved it. Twelve people crammed into a carriage from the nineteenth century.

"Who has arrived, Louis?" My mother asked.

"Brother James and his family, Busy is here with her family, of course, Aunt Carol and the Cransons live here now. That will make a dining table of twenty-four, Grandma will love it."

"Has anyone come from South Carolina this year?" My father asked.

"No, they all sent their regrets, again. They have families of their own, with their own Grandma's ghost in South Carolina." We all laughed.

When the carriage pulled up in front of the house and disgorged its passengers, Louise and I went back to the station for the baggage and the secret service man left as a guard. When we returned, Grandma was holding court again like a year ago. The President of the United States was still the second most important person in the room and he was fine with that.

"I have decided that I like the term 'freshmen' for first year students at a woman's college, what do you think, Teddy?"

"I still like 'first ladies.'" He was holding my Aunt Ruth's hand.

"That is because you are the only one in this room with a 'first lady'." She still had her sense of humor.

"Mother, Bill and I have nearly two hundred early applications to attend Cranson next year, would you like to see them?" My Aunt Carol handed a stack of papers toward Grandma.

"Carol, I am sure that you and Bill are pleased." My Aunt Carol, said that most of the applications were for the two year teaching option. She did not want to encourage two year students and see them graduate from *her* college. She said she wrote to each two year applicant and reminded them that a four year teaching certificate and a bachelor's degree was the desired goal. My Grandmother Caldwell did not balk at the term *bachelor* like I thought she would..

My Uncle Bill Cranson, was the college provost and his job had been the placement of advertisements in the state newspapers for college faculty. He had hired all of the department heads and one of them had hired my sister, Louise.

"Louise, how does it feel to be a college teacher?" I asked.

"Like being a JAG lawyer, only, safer." Everyone who knew my job tried not to laugh at her remark.

Last year when I came home to Seneca Hill to visit my grandmother, I was amazed at her renewed strength and determination to see her life's goals completed. We always had a nice visit. This year she seemed tired.

"Louis, what has happened with those Jigsaw murders? Did you solve them?"

"Yes, Grandma. We found out how they were all murdered, Grandma, they were injected with a poison from the tip of an umbrella."

"What kind of poison?"

"Curari, Grandma."

"Ah, yes, you told me about that last year, I forgot. It is the poison of choice for tribes of Indians from South America. They make it from the curare plant and dip their spears and arrows in it. Terrible stuff. There is no antidote, is there?"

"Yes, we use the antidote for curarine, the chemist's version of the same poison, it works."

"Well, you would know that, Louis, you are the smartest of my grandchildren. Why didn't you bring your telephone operator friend with you for Christmas?"

"She is spending it with her parents in Washington. We are just voices on a telephone, Grandma, I don't even know what she looks like."

"You know, your sister is jealous of her!"

"She is?"

"Of course, she hates anyone who might take you away from her.

You write to her too often, Louis, she lets me read every one of your letters. She feels sorry for me, she has no idea how many times you write to me or your parents."

I like to write to my family, Grandma, it keeps me connected. Remember our conversation from last year?"

"Not really, tell me about it."

"My father and I still write to each other all the time. Mother is busy and she likes to read my letters home, but she rarely writes, why do you ask?"

"Your father and his father wrote back and forth all the time, it must be something special between the Caldwell men in this family."

"I think it was because Grandpa was a warrior first and a grandfather, father, husband, and company man second. Some men are like that, I found out from Grandpa Schneider that my Grandfather Caldwell hated injustice of any kind and he fought hard to make things right."

"In that respect, you are identical to your grandfather, Louis. Sometimes it skips a generation. Your father is not like that at all. Your father tried very hard to please his father so that your grandfather would try to be a father to him first. He knew that, that is why you have a very large collection of letters from your father over the years. Do you know that you have more letters than your sisters and me combined?"

"I had no idea."

"I know you saved them. When you get back to Washington, get them out and reread them. He is trying to make a connection with you, Louis. The connection he never had with your grandfather. Your father will continue to teach you life's lessons as long as he lives. He had your mother read each one and make corrections in his first draft so that his meanings were clear. If you reread them once a year you will always have your father and mother close to you. Maybe that is why your mother felt she didn't need to write, she already did inside your father's letters."

I could see that she was exhausted and I hugged her and went looking for Louise. It was beginning to snow and it was time to hitch up the sleigh. We spent the afternoon taking the family for rides in the horse drawn sleigh. Louise and I were wiping down the horses when our father came looking for us. He had been crying. Grandma had taken her normal afternoon nap and died in her sleep two days before Christmas, 1905. She was buried inside a crypt that had already been constructed with her and Grandpa's names neatly chiseled into the marble as the founders of Cranson College for women.

49

Washington, D.C.

January 2, 1906

When something is totally out of control and at the same time slightly off balance, most people would stop and readjust their lives. I was off balance ever since my Grandmother Caldwell died. I spent more and more time with my Grandfather Schneider talking in German, telling him of my adventures in Bavaria, asking him questions and driving everyone in JAG to stresses beyond their control. I always went into an investigation head first and before a month was completed, I was out of control. My immediate supervisor would shake his head and wonder how much longer I would live with some of the things I put my body through. My supervisor decided to see my father in the White House.

"Admiral, I am concerned about Louis. He is a JAG lawyer not a navy commando. In his last case, which he called the jigsaw murders, he was attacked by two agents of a foreign service. The agents were trained killers and they both wound up in the hospital with broken bones and closed head injuries."

"Were these agents German?"

"Yes, has Louis talked to you about this?"

"No, he does not discuss his work, he has signed a top secret White House clearance. He has spoken a lot of German around the house in the last few months. His grandfather is fluent in German."

"Oh, I was not aware that he had secret service clearance. When I try to moderate his actions during arrests, like closed head injuries to suspects, he just shrugs at me and says, 'They can not testify against me if they do not have memories of what happened to them during the arrests.'"

"Commander Morton, I do not know what to tell you. If he is not performing up to your expectations then he should be given a chance to meet your expectations or he should be transferred to NCI full time."

"Oh, I can not do that!"

"Why not? I would not tolerate such actions in this office."

"His present case was given to him because he has proved many times that the more difficult the case is, the more energy he puts into solving it and bringing the 'bad guys,' as he calls them, to justice."

"And you think this is bad thing?" I was beginning to wonder about Commander Morton and why he came to see me.

"He has his own sense of justice. He has an excellent record of convictions and an unusually high death rate. Not the death he is investigating, but people around him have a very short life span."

"I do not understand."

"A closed case is often the result of the suspect winding up in the morgue or, in more than one case, his partner is dead when the case is closed."

"Are you saying he is reckless or incompetent?"

"No."

"Are you saying that he is a genuine headache for you to manage when he is in the field?"

"Yes, that is it exactly!"

"Would you like him mustered out of the Navy, Commander?"

"God, no, if he leaves JAG, the number of solved cases assigned to the division would drop like a stone."

"I see. Would you like a little fatherly advice from this old three star Admiral, Commander?"

"Yes, Admiral, anything that will help me understand your son."

"My son idolizes his two grandfathers and their service during war time. I will give you an example, which contains both grandfathers. Louis is trying to emulate both of them, an impossible task. I lived in the shadow of my father until his death."

"Go ahead, Admiral, I will listen."

February 1865

Tom Schneider and his marines had moved inland from their landing points at Carboneras, La Pesca and Ciudad Madero. They were led by their guides sent from President Juarez's encampment in the Nuevo Leon Mountains. President Juarez had also sent 100 Mexican soldiers to help with the unloading of the armaments and supplies sent by President Lincoln. The soldiers were unarmed except for rather long knives, or short swords, that they carried in their belts. During the unloading process, 875 English speaking US Marines began to learn simple Spanish commands. The tons of supplies were stacked in a storehouse in the fishing village of Carboneras and Tom sent one of the guides and ten soldiers back to President Juarez to request horses, wagons and pack mules. Until they returned, all Tom could think of to do was train the 90 remaining Mexican soldiers. Tom had three Spanish speaking privates within his 875 marines and he found a dozen Mexican soldiers who indicated that they spoke English.

"Jose, I need to talk to you, come into my tent."

They walked off the dusty patch of ground and across a grassy area on the outside of the village where the marines had their encampment. "Jose, I will show you a map. Show me where the French have established outposts." Tom unrolled a map of northeastern Mexico.

"Here is my capitol, Mexico City. It is 400 miles from here. The French puppet, Maximilian, stays there. He has sent the French troops north to occupy our forts at Pachucal, Tampico and Tamaulipas. From Tamaulipas they sent out small groups to locate suitable places for the French to steal what they needed from the villages."

"Have they come to Carboneras, Jose?"

"No, Mia Major. They keep further to the south, in villages like Hidalgo and Santa Jimenez."

"Santa Jimenez is only 48 miles from here! They will be here next, Jose. We must act before they find the storehouse with the supplies. We must make them think that we did not land at Carboneras. We must attack and draw them away from here. Go see if Admiral Caldwell's ships have returned to the harbor." *A breathless Jose, returned and he reported sails on the horizon. My father was returning from Havana with another shipment of*

equipment and supplies. Tom and his aide were waiting on the docks as the first long boat tied up.

"Take us out to the flag ship, we must talk to Admiral Caldwell." Tom ordered.

"Can we unload first, Major?"

"Just set everything on the docks as fast as you can, my men will take it to the storehouses."

On board the recommissioned USS Providence, Tom explained what the French were attempting to do in northeast Mexico. "I would like you to take my marines from here back down the coast to La Pesca and up the river to Soto La Marina. This is south of the French at Tamaulipas. We only need one vessel, the shallowest draft. We will attack French patrols and seize the horses and wagons for transport of the supplies in Carboneras to President Juarez. I do not feel comfortable with 30,000 muskets sitting in a storehouse, we need to get them to the Mexican Army."

"I agree, Tom", my father said, "I would like to mention something that might be helpful. I would not bury any dead French in this part of Mexico. I would load them on wagons and return the bodies to the New Haven, it has the shallowest draft. The New Haven can dispose of the living, and the dead, in the Gulf of Mexico."

"The idea is to make them disappear! I like that, Admiral. Put some fear into the French."

"And one other thing, take Jerome with you and he can report back to me after the operation is over."

"Done, when can we get started?"

" Have your marines here before sundown so we can land you at night."

Before sunset a thousand men showed up for transport. "Where did all these come from? I thought you were taking 800 marines." my father asked.

"I am, I have 800 marines on this operation and 75 left to guard the storehouses in Carboneras. The extra 200 are Mexicans, eager to kill as many French as they can find."

"Do they realize, that they will be on foot until we capture horses?"

"I will try to buy horses as we move inland from Soto La Marina. I have gold in my money belt."

"I better signal for the other ketch, USS Trumbull to accompany you, Tom."

I was told a thousand men on two small ketches was a sight to be seen as they left the fishing village of Carboneras for a short run down the coast of Mexico. They stood shoulder to shoulder, some in United States Marine Uniforms and some dressed like Mexican farmers, because that was what they were until they had some training in how to fire a musket. The USS Trumbull and New Haven entered the river and stopped at Soto La Marina. It was a dark winter night and the village was asleep as the 1000 made their way towards Ciudad Victoria, the first French outpost past the Fort of Tamulipas. About ten miles into the march, they came upon a French encampment consisting of tents full of sleeping French cavalry, their horses and wagons. A single sentry was posted but was fast asleep. Two marines crept up on him, covered his mouth and placed a knife between his ribs and into his heart. The first French death was recorded by Jerome Lewis for report back to Washington. The sleeping camp was awakened by a 1000 screaming marines, some American, some Mexican. The draft horses were hitched to the wagons. The single dead French soldier was placed in the wagon and the prisoners were marched back towards the waiting ketches at Soto La Marina. Tom gave orders to take the rest of the wagons and horses directly to Carboneras and begin the loading of supplies. He ordered the supplies to be taken to President Juarez immediately.

The company was now down to 900, 800 marines and 100 Mexican nationals. As the sun rose they came upon a small village and Tom used some of his gold to buy every wagon and horse that he could find. At around noon, a dust cloud was visible on the horizon. This meant that a large number of horsemen were probably on the road towards the Fort. Tom drew his sergeants around him and told them what he wanted them to do with the horses and wagons.

The French Cavalry officer signaled for his column to halt. Six Mexican bodies lay in the roadway, near an overturned wagon, apparently dead or dying. One of the farmers raised his hand and motioned for the French to help him. The troops dismounted to rest the horses and that is when the marines raised from their cover along side the road. They rushed the column with fixed bayonets screaming, "Ferma La Fenettra." A Mexican who said he spoke French had told them it was "Surrender the fight." It turned out that it meant, "Close the window." But the result was the same, the entire column surrendered without a fight. This was more than Tom had hoped for. There was only one dead, the sentry, and many live prisoners. The horses were tied together in groups of three and a single rider was assigned to each group. The groups were told to ride for Caboneras and use the horses as pack animals to move the remainder of the supplies. Tom ordered the remainder of the company and one wagon, to begin the march back to the waiting ketches at Soto La Marina. French cavalry were used to riding, not walking and they began to complain. Some sat by the side of the road and refused to move. Tom drew his revolver, walked to the first French man and shot him in the head. The body was thrown in the wagon beside the other and he walked to a second French man and started to shoot him, but he jumped to his feet and said in perfect English, "We need to rest." Tom shot him in the foot.

"You can rest on your trip across the Gulf of Mexico. I will shoot any man who refuses to march." The wounded French man turned to his officer and translated. French orders were shouted down the line of prisoners and they began to march again towards the waiting ships. They reached them before sundown and loaded the prisoners on one ketch and the remaining marines on the other. By sunrise, the following day, my father was prepared to sail back to Havana and on his way, dispose of the living and the dead."

"That is an interesting story, Admiral. Is it true?"

"That is not important. Louis thinks it is true."

A light went on in the Commander's head and his facial expression changed. "Are you saying that your son has no concern for the enemy that he is fighting and that death is favorable to capture?"

"That is, unfortunately, exactly what I am saying, Captain. The United States is not at war at the present time. Let me tell you another story of a man who had a similar set of values, during the same war."

"Personal to Secretary Stanton:

Item One. Jefferson Davis and his cabinet are now fugitives upon the evacuation of Richmond. It is my fear that he will try to reach Kirby Smith in the southwest, and with his help, he will attempt to prolong the life of the Confederacy. I, therefore, order General J. H. Wilson to use every effort with his cavalry to capture the fleeing President. I do not wish to discuss this order with you or have you issue it through General Grant. This is a direct order from me to General Wilson. I want you to make it clear to the General that I expect Davis to be in custody before May 1st, or his letter of resignation on my desk by May 2nd.

Item Two. Issue an order for General Grant to move south until he engages General Johnston of the remaining Confederate Army trying to protect Davis' escape. You are to direct General Grant that I want Johnston's unconditional surrender, identical in terms that were granted General Lee. I am tired of General Sherman's pussyfooting around Johnston. Tell Grant that either Johnston surrenders or he has orders from me to attack and take no prisoners. I desire no input from you or General Grant on this matter. I want the war ended by May 1, 1865.

Item Three. Issue an order for General Sherman to pull out of the fight against Johnston and march towards McAllen, Texas. If he meets any Confederate resistance, he is to take no prisoners. If the Confederate mentality is to die on the battlefield, tell Sherman to do his best to kill every damn one of them from as far away as possible with artillery fire. Barring that, use the new long range rifles to drop the enemy where he stands. General Sherman is not to stop and bury the enemy dead, he is to let them lay where they fall. The message must be introduced that the war is over, only death remains for those foolish enough to resist.

Item Four. General Sherman is to remain within the US borders, but he is to send scouts into the mountains to locate Major, (make that Colonel), Schneider's marine force. President Juarez will be offered Sherman and his troops to hunt down and kill every God Damn French troop they can find. The French have been told by President Lincoln to withdraw. I will not ask them again. I will find and kill as many as I can until they get the same message as delivered to the Confederacy. The longer we wait, the more Union deaths we will encounter."

"Admiral, I had no idea your father was so blood thirsty!"

"The man in that story was not my father, it was the President of the United States. When you leave here today, Captain, I want you to consider how best you can use someone like my son. Do you want to continue to have him practice Navy Law within JAG? Or do you want to turn him loose on the enemies of this country who have sent their agents inside our borders to murder our citizens in order to steal state secrets."

"He won't live a month if I transfer him to NCI full time, Admiral, is that what you want?"

"Of course not, Commander, he has been through Lancaster and he will be assigned full time to a foreign post soon. We have an opening in NLSO, London and he may be assigned there. It sounds cold, but he needs to train many others to have his attitude and to perform overseas in our efforts to neutralize the enemy agents pouring into this country."

50

Presidential Aviation Report

January, 1906

The United States Navy reported at the end of 1905, that it had an aeronautics division. A few dirigibles and a few hot air balloons should not constitute an aeronautics division, but it did. I think the only reason that it was reported was because England's war office had undertaken the aeroplane branch of aeronautics. Four English Valkyrie bi-wing planes and one German Valkyrie were added to the dirigibles housed at Barrow, England. Since the German Valkyrie was courtesy of the US Navy, flown from Copenhagen, US Navy personnel were now training in England. We were playing catchup again because our aviation began shortly after the Wright brothers flight with a motor driven aeroplane, December 19, 1903. It was now two years later. NCI was given the task of establishing an aviation school at Annapolis, with winter quarters in San Diego. The Curtiss and Burgess-Wright hydroplanes using the Langley patents were flight tested on both sites. Dr. Langley and I were very excited to see the top secret testing. Dr. Langley continued to teach and conduct his experiments under a Navy contract. Since his secret flight on November 28, 1896, in his dirigible, he continued to experiment on a much larger version.

This dirigible used a steam engine fueled with naphtha. His first flight in 1896 was less than a mile, but today he could stay aloft until he ran out of fuel. The congressional appropriation to construct a larger aerodrome to carry 12 marines was completed in 1903.

The testing by NCI continued day and night. Mr. Glen Curtiss flew from North Island to the *USS Pennsylvania,* lying at anchor. He landed in the water, along side. His plane was hoisted out of the water and onto the deck of the Pennsylvania. The Pennsylvania put to sea and some time later she attempted to place the hydroplane back in the water. Mr. Curtiss was supervising the operation from the deck of the Pennsylvania and survived the experiment because he was not inside the plane when it sank to the bottom.

The most common joke inside the NCI was, "How do you sink a US Navy Hydroplane? Answer, put it in the water!" In Glen Curtiss' defense, he had merely applied the required floating apparatus to a wheeled plane. His engineers had not designed the attachments necessary to convert his machines into an effective hydroplane. Within a few months, the Curtiss hydroplane was capable of alighting on and starting from either land or water. Additional modifications came within a year for a second pilot, or navigator, seat with dual controls which allowed the shifting of the steering tiller to either seat while in the air. Tests were immediately begun with Burgess-Wright machines. The purpose of the tests were to see if a pilot could rise above the water from a stationary position, make a flight to and along side a ship, hoist the machine aboard, put to sea and launch again to continue a flight. Lt. John Rodgers was the first Navy flyer to accomplish this simple task. He stated that his experiments convinced him that it is impractical to launch a plane from a ship with a crane. The flight must be made directly from the deck of a vessel, either by the use of a monorail catapult or some other contrivance. When I read this report, to summarize for Admiral Lowe, I thought, my father predicted this from his Naval War College lecture before the last war. How he will love to see Lt. Rodgers and his hydroplane. This may replace the steam automobiles that he brought home when I was a child.

I continued to read. On October 11th, Lts. Ellyson and Tower started at the aviation station, Annapolis and landed on the beach at Smith's point, Virginia, 65 miles south of Annapolis an hour and a half later. The time to their destination, Buckroe Beach, Virginia, a distance of 145 miles, was 147 minutes. When near Buckroe Beach, the engine was stopped and the hydro-plane was allowed to settle in the water. The wheels were lowered and the plane was driven ashore. The last thing I read before falling asleep for the night was; Mr. Curtiss is now building a flying lifeboat, to carry 12 men. Lt. Rodgers devised a life preserver for pilot use. It is similar to a baseball catcher's breast protector and attached in the same way.

I awoke the next morning and it was time for me to begin to write my report on what I saw in Germany during the first week of November, 1905.

Mr. President:

I have just finished reading the 1905 report of **Naval Progress/ Aviation.** It is probably an accurate accounting of progress within the United States, but it is not the progress made world wide. France, Germany and Japan are far ahead of the efforts made in the United States. The trap we fall into is believing that anything worthwhile must have been invented in the United States. In the case of aviation this is certainly true. The record of accomplishment in aviation did not begin with the flight of the Wright brothers, December 19, 1903. That is the date of the first flight in the United States. It took us nearly two years, September 26, 1905, before a flight of an hour's duration was made by these American inventors. Compare this progress with the accounts that I have already sent to you of the German Empire's progress. A flight of four Valkyries left an airfield and met the zeppelin I was riding in and escorted us for over an hour. This flight was replaced by a different flight of different manufacture and then escorted us for an hour. A third flight of still another model of aeroplane escorted us the final hours of the flight. These were called long range aeroplanes. You may want to review the report sent to you of my tour of the Valkyrie assembly plant in Germany.

Henry Farman in England has made longer, cross-country flights, while Louis Bleriot, of France, has flown from France to England across open ocean. Japan destroyed the Russian fleet with bombs dropped from their aeroplanes. Some countries have developed separate air forces, which operate independently from their armies and navies. The number of pilots within the United States is estimated at less than a hundred.

The number of pilots being trained in Germany, for example, is 220 per month to keep pace with the number of airframes being produced.

The effort within the United States is research. The effort throughout Europe is development, from my observations. I shudder to read from US reports, statements like, "From such beginnings and early flights, the use of the aeroplane, as well as the mechanical efficiency and construction of the machine itself, will be researched until the beginning of 1906. Further research and theoretical knowledge of aviation must be completed to a point where the problems of the air and its navigation are well recognized." This is what I read about bi-winged aeroplanes!

Meanwhile, in Germany, the mono-wing airplane is being researched and tested. An airplane is not like an aeroplane with two wings. The airplane has a single supporting surface, whose possibilities far surpass anything presently built in America, England or France. If an aeroplane and an airplane meet in combat, it will be suicide for the pilot of the aeroplane. It is the purpose of the airplane to fly anywhere from 10 to 20 times faster than the bi-wing. A bi-wing frame is made of wood in the United States and wood and aluminum in Europe. Both versions fall apart upon emergency landings and the pilot dies upon impact with the earth. There is no wood construction in an airplane. An airplane has hollow, high tensile steel tubes for its framework. By the end of 1905, a gradual development in all fields of aviation were apparent throughout Europe, not just Germany.

This, as will be shown in this report, was in general, the tendency throughout the world, except the United States. There was not an undue imitation of successful machines by the many world manufacturers, but more or less development along original lines. This was evidenced by the fact that during the year it was estimated that some 100 different types of aeroplanes were in use. Naturally, there was also an increased number of aviators. In all branches of aviation there was considerable development, and the machines produced were of greater efficiency than in previous years. A large number of exhibitions were held in all the leading countries of the world and various competitions took place. The United States did not win a single competition. The reason for this is obvious. Vast amount of investments were made by manufacturers of machines in Europe, which already had begun to number long-established engineering firms, yet it was considered that the commercial possibilities would rest rather in the military use than in more general fields. Numerous sales were made to foreign governments, including our own purchase of a German Valkyrie. It is presently undergoing military tests in England, under US supervision. I would recommend the purchase of any and all foreign made aircraft for comparison testing.

Owing to competitions and military applications, the main aim in the design and construction of machines during the year was to increase speed, and this naturally required engines of greater horsepower, so that motors from 140 to 200 horsepower were being fitted to the more recent aeroplanes. With the increase in speed, the dangers of flight were diminished, especially under unfavorable conditions of weather and changes of wind directions. The most apparent shortcoming in the aeroplane of 1905, was the inability of the aviator to control his speed as desired, and especially to start his motor again in case of stoppage or sudden failure.

An interesting feature of the year was the construction of aeroplanes and airplanes with bodies more closely resembling that of a bird, which became most marked in the Austrian Etrich airplane. These completely covered bodies with enclosed cockpits, were first developed in the case of the German airplane design mentioned earlier. The enclosed fuselage was found much more useful to support the propeller and side planes than a construction of spars and at the same time it diminished wind resistance. Furthermore, such covering naturally involved the enclosing of the motor, and at the Paris Aviation Salon, held in December, it was noted that most of the more advanced types of machines were built with enclosed motors.

Another tendency of the year was the replacement of all cloth covered wings and fuselages with thin sheets of aluminum. At the Paris Salon, 42 airplanes were exhibited, six were built entirely of hollow steel, the rest were a mixture of steel, aluminum and wood frames. In the general design of the planes, various conditions had to be taken into consideration. The ability to warp the wings being controlled by the Wright patents, some other means was required by other manufacturers. Yet the flexibility of the planes themselves was no longer desired if smaller controlling planes or ailerons could be used. These have been found very satisfactory, and they figure in most of the aeroplanes of the day. Some device for reducing the size of the surface plane, or reefing them, was also suggested, as by telescoping, but nothing practical along these lines was forthcoming.

Taken all in all, the great tendency of aeroplane design was the reduction of wind resistance and supporting surfaces, and using the power of the motor to compensate for it. With the increased power and means of control at their disposal, aviators during the year were able to fly under conditions of wind which previously would have been considered impossible. Flights in winds up to thirty miles an hour were not uncommon, and in the long-distance trips the amount of time lost by bad weather was being greatly diminished.

Respectfully submitted
Commander Louis Caldwell, USN
January 31, 1906

51

NCI Review Board

Washington, D.C.

While I was in the process of transferring most my work load from JAG to NCI, my father was still sending me information from the White House. The improvement and changes brought about by the United States NCI Board of Review for 1905, were listed in a report and sent to the president. Teddy gave my father the report to read and summarize for him. He asked me what I had managed to obtain on foreign naval activities. He then included that information in his summary to the president. The report was divided into sections.

Naval Aeronautics

Great Britain. In England the war office has undertaken the aeroplane branch of aeronautics and the admiralty is experimenting with dirigibles. Four Valkyrie aeroplanes have been presented to the government. None of the naval officers being instructed in aeroplanes has had any practice in map-drawing from balloons, but two of the officers employed with airships have had this experience. The naval airship was launched at Barrow on May 22. It was 512 feet long, beam was 48 feet and its lifting power was 21 tons. It is propelled by two eight cylinder motor engines.

France. Experiments with wireless telegraphy from aeroplanes has been carried out at Buc, France, by Maurice Farman, using an apparatus of the Ancel type, with a four-inch spark coil supplied by four storage battery cells. The total weight of the wireless outfit is 45 pounds. Signals were sent a distance of eight miles. New experiments are being made to increase the range, using an eight-inch spark coil and a 300-foot aerial. In order to make reconnoitering flights at night, Farman has experimented with an aeroplane fitted with two electric searchlights, one on each side of the pilot's seat. The current is provided by a dynamo using the power of the motor. A battery of accumulators is carried on the biplane, so that light will not fail if the dynamo does not work. The searchlight throws rays downward 400 meters, so that, when flying at a height of 150 meters, everything below the aviator can be seen. A muffler for the motor, reduces the noise of the engine to a minimum. It is so efficient that the biplane can not be heard when flying above 100 meters. With the muffler in use, the pilot and an observer can converse freely without the use of a speaking tube. France will soon lead the world in the efficiency and number of both airships and aeroplanes. It is claimed that next year, 120 aeroplanes and 16 dirigibles will be in service within the French Navy.

As a result of experiments at Cherbourg, it is believed that an aeroplane can discover a submarine from a height of over 3000 feet, whereas the periscope of the submarine does not detect the aeroplane after 1500 feet. But it will never be easy for the most practiced air pilot to pick up a submarine at sea. For scouting, a slow air machine, making about 45 miles per hour, is deemed best. An extensive program of experiments are presently being held to include the search for submarines at various depths, in different conditions of weather and the search for surface mines.

United States. The naval aeronautics school in San Diego has the following courses of instruction; hot air balloon techniques for battleship observation, dirigible flight and observation techniques and the Burgess-Wright hydroplane flight course. Professor S.P. Langley continues to teach and conduct his experiments under a Navy contract. Since his secret flight on November 28, 1896, in his Aerodrome, he continues to experiment on a much larger version.

This dirigible uses a steam engine fueled with naphtha. His first flight in 1896 was less than a mile, but today he can stay aloft until he runs out of fuel. The congressional appropriation to construct a larger aerodrome to carry 12 marines was completed in 1903. As you know, the plans were stolen by German agents and now Germany is building a whole series of dirigibles. See the photograph from NCI, taken in Germany. *Office of Naval Counter Intelligence Photograph "Z-4"*

Professor Langley has now perfected his aeroplane wing design, called the aerocurve and it also is now being copied in Germany by Herr Otto Lilienthal. The manufacture of his aerocurve design in America has been given to Mr. Octave Chanute, an engineer at the Wright Company in Dayton, Ohio.

Battleship Armor

United States. No marked improvement is noted in thick armor. Increase in the severity of tests has not been warranted. There has been a steady improvement in the quality of thin plates made of special treatment steel. In order to obtain armor plate of greater resistance, plate both hard and tough is demanded by the increasing power of rifled guns. Compound armor has been introduced, in which a face of hard steel is welded onto a backing of softer metal of great toughness. It has been found that the welds do not hold when tested. Research is presently underway at the Naval Proving Grounds to solve this problem.

Germany. Krupp improved upon our process by using gas in place of solid carbonaceous material. But the face hardening could only be made to reach a certain depth. Continued improvements both in the energy of the projectile and its ability to remain intact while penetrating the hard face are needed.

Great Britain. In England recently, a new system of face-hardening, named after its inventor, Simpson, has been developed, but makes a plate with a perfect weld. It is claimed that this result is obtained by interposing a thin plate of copper between the two plates before welding them together. Ships launched after this date will carry 12 inches of Simpson armor plate.

Japan. Armor plate for Japanese battleships is supplied from the Kure Navy Yard, where a plant was started in 1902. The plates are made by a special secret process invented by Japanese Engineers and stolen by NCI. The latest battleship *Tsukuba* carries this type of armor.

Ship's Gun and Gunnery

Great Britain. England has abandoned the 12-inch guns for the 13.5 inch, 45 caliber gun in the main batteries of battleships and battle cruisers. The battleship *Orion* and the battle cruiser *Lion*, armed with the 13.5-inch gun have been completed. The 13.5-inch gun is nine tons heavier than the 12-inch. The weights of the shells fired have increased from 850 to 1250 pounds and the muzzle velocities have increased from 48,000 foot tons to 70,000.

United States. All future US battleships will carry the new 14-inch gun, with the 5-inch rapid fire for torpedo defense. It is recommended that all USS vessels with 12-inch guns be retrofitted with 14-inch. It is recommended that all USS vessels be equipped with 3-inch air defense guns for dirigible attacks. Dirigibles are now capable of carrying heavy bombs capable of sinking light cruisers and smaller vessels.

Italy. Le Yacht gives the following characteristics of the latest Italian 12- inch guns; length is 46 caliber, weight of projectile 895 pounds, muzzle velocity 2895, elevation for 10,000 meters range is 6 degrees, angle of fall is 8 degrees and penetration of Krupp armor is 11.1 inches.

Aerial Guns

Germany. The Ehrhardt Ordnance Works has offered for sale, aeroplane guns firing high explosive ammunition, using time fuses. NCI has purchased several of these and are testing them. When the target aeroplanes come within range, the guns fire time-fuse shell exploding several seconds apart, releasing gases of extremely high temperatures which set the target aircraft on fire.

United States. A new 3-inch aeroplane gun, based on the German model, is being developed for the navy at the Washington Naval Yard. A 6-inch gun has been designed, but not tested, to fire about 20 times per minute. It also will use an explosive shell, with a time fuse.

Projectiles

United States. The shells used throughout the fleet are slowly being improved. The new high explosive bursting charges are now a necessity in modern armor-piercing. The soft cap is still used to enable the point of the shell to "bite" on impact. Experiments with the monitor, Puritan, did not demonstrate the value of shells exploding on soft impact surfaces.

Torpedoes

United States. The torpedo of today is effective at up to 6000 yards fired from a torpedo boat. The torpedo boat is in the process of being replaced by the new submarines, ie. *USS Starfish.* The Starfish has a new torpedo that is effective up to 10,000 yards and can be fired while the submarine is in motion for up to 27 knots.

Germany. The largest torpedo now used in the German Navy has a diameter of 19.5 inches and a maximum range of 4200 yards. It is rated the same as the British 21 inch torpedo. NCI has discovered that the new 22 inch German torpedo has a range of 5000 yards at 21 knots. The Krupps have taken out patents for a self-propelling torpedo to be dropped from aeroplanes. NCI has stolen the internal specifications for a new and powerful torpedo.

Powder

United States. The Navy has introduced a stabilizer to increase the life of smokeless powder from one to ten years. The stabilizer is also an efficient and automatic detector of irregularities in manufacture. The experimental firings of powder mixed with ozokorite and graphite have given no definite results in determining the reduction in erosion of guns.

France. On September 25th, the French experienced a spontaneous explosion of powder aboard a 14,000 ton displacement vessel located in the harbor of Toulon. When NCI assisted in the determination of the cause of the explosion, they found that spontaneous ignition of a charge in the forward starboard upper 7.5-inch magazine was the cause for the death of 204 men and the wounding of 136 others. The NCI was called to assist in the investigation because the powder on board the *Liberte* was fairly new. The official investigation proved that a powder stabilizer would have prevented the disaster.

Propulsion of Naval Vessels

United States. The engineer-in-chief of the US Navy recommends that we abandon the use of turbines for reciprocating engines as are now found on the *USS Delaware* and *USS North Dakota*. The decision to abandon turbines for reciprocating engines in the new battleships *Texas* and *New York* has caused great surprise in the naval world. All other naval powers have adopted the turbine. In his annual report to the Secretary of the Navy, the engineer-in-chief says: "This decision was arrived at after an extensive investigation, including the comparative trials of the two types of machinery in the scout cruisers *Birmingham, Chester and Salem* and in the battleships *Delaware* and *North Dakota*. These tests render exact data on the subject than are available to any other government. It is found that the reciprocating engine is about 30 per cent more economical at cruising speed than the turbine and has about the same economy at high speeds."

In the Scientific American of December he also writes, "The turbine is especially suited to high speeds. The reciprocating engine shows greater reliability than the turbine. The present problem is to provide a method of propulsion in which a high-speed turbine can be made to drive a slowly revolving propeller, thus conserving both turbine and propeller efficiencies. One method is to employ reduction gear machinery, as in the collier *Neptune* (19 thousand tons). Reduction gearing as installed in the cargo steamer *Vespasian* (5 thousand tons) by the Parsons Company, has successfully completed a year's trial. In the naval collier *Juptier*, electric propulsion will be tried. One turbo-generator, maximum speed about 2000 revolutions a minute, delivers current with a potential of 2300 volts to an induction motor which drives the propeller shaft.

It has been noted that the remarkable development of heavy oil engines of the diesel type in Europe will probably prevent previous methods of propulsion from enduring. Superior economy of the oil engine, with elimination of the steam boiler and condenser, will cause us to be patient with the defects while it is being perfected. Oil supply is a great factor in which the United States is especially fortunate, producing two-thirds of the world's supply."

He also writes, "All our new destroyers are oil burners. The advantages are many. The reduction of personnel and of weight and space required for boilers is the first. The elimination of coal and ash-handling gear is the second. Easier stowage and handling of oil is another. Steam for full power can be as readily maintained as for low power. A vessel burning oil is capable of prolonged runs at full speed limited in length only by the supply of fuel. No reduction of speed is due to dirty fires or to difficulty in trimming coal from remote bunkers, with no cinders, smoke can be controlled. With oil, an evaporation per pound of fuel greater than with coal can be maintained as well. The two new battleships *Nevada* and *Oklahoma* will be oil burners and will carry no coal. Tests made on the North Dakota, equipped with both oil and coal, are largely responsible for this decision."

Submarines

France. The French submarine *Mariotte,* the largest in the world, with a displacement of 1100 tons, length 214 feet, was launched in Cherburg on February 2. The displacement of the "D" class, British Navy is 604 tons for example. It is recommended that we continue to build these as fast as possible and form a submarine fleet for both oceans. New designs should not be less than 1100 tons, length 214 feet, 6 torpedo tubes and storage for 10 additional torpedoes. A submarine salvage lighter must be built in the next few months to rescue submarines from the sea floor.

Sea Strength of Naval Powers

Great Britain. England leads all others with 56 Battleships, 41 Battle cruisers, 73 light cruisers, 140 destroyers, 49 torpedo boars, 70 submarines and no new coastal defense ships. Germany is second, the United States is third, followed by France, Japan, Russia, Italy and Austria.

Ships Currently Under Construction

Great Britain. England leads again with 9 battleships, 4 battle cruisers, 17 light cruisers, 44 destroyers, no torpedo boats, 16 submarines and no coastal defense vessels. The US is ranked third with, 7 battleships, 3 battle cruisers, 5 light cruisers, 12 destroyers, no torpedo boats and 16 submarines.

Naval Aircraft Currently In Production

Germany. The Kaiser will soon lead the world in the efficiency and number of both airships and aeroplanes. The current inventory and those in production are as follows:

120 aeroplanes (bi-winged) on a monthly basis,

80 aeroplanes (tri-winged) on a monthly basis,

16 large dirigibles (9000 cubic feet) on a yearly basis, and 6 small dirigibles (7000 cubic feet) on a semi-yearly basis.

52

NCI Investigates Langley Death

WASHINGTON, D.C.

SAMUEL PIERPOINT LANGLEY WAS BORN in Roxbury, Massachusetts, on August 22, 1835. He died in February, 1906, and by March his death was declared a possible homicide. This declaration was automatic because this was the fifth government employee to die under unexplained circumstances in the past 12 months; Dr. Ernest Abbel was an MD and a physicist, Dr. Louis Barrias was a chemist, John Farnham was a retired Navy Captain, John Hayes was a diplomat. The Department of the Navy was assigned the case from local police because Dr. Langley was a government employee working for the Navy. The case was kicked down to me from my supervisor, Commander Morton, because Dr. Langley had been on the Presidential visit to Mexico with me.

I always begin a case by finding as much about the deceased as I can. I knew Samuel Langley, he had traveled with me to Mexico the year before to investigate the deaths of Farnham, Hayes, Hanson, Phillips and Ingraham. In this first step of the puzzle is usually a clue to why the person's life ended by the hand or hands of others. Dr. Langley was a high profile individual, worked on secret projects for the US government, and was probably the only true genius of our time. When he died he was Secretary of the Smithsonian Institution, President of the American Association for the Advancement of Science, holder of the Rumford Medal from the Royal Society of London and holder of several patents, including the invention of the bolometer and the aerocurve wing design used in all aeroplanes. Step one was still to gather background, forget about the genius of the man, for now.

He was educated at the Boston Latin School here in the United States and then went to Europe for graduate education. The word *Europe* jumped off the page at me. What, when and where are not only the key factors for a newspaper reporter – they apply to a murder investigation. I found the *when* first. Samuel Langley left Boston in 1855 and returned to America in 1865 to accept an assistant professor position at the Harvard University Observatory, less than a year later he was teaching at the US Naval Academy. Why did it take him ten years to complete one or two advanced degrees?

Patience, I told myself. What country accepted him in 1855? I sent a transatlantic cable to my counterpart in the war office in London asking for information on a student visa issued to S.P. Langley during the 1855-56 academic school year. I indicated that we were investigating his possible homicide, and we had no record of his study in Europe. The following reply came in a few days.

Commander LJ Caldwell
Judge Advocates General's Office
Army Navy Building, Washington, D.C.

I have located information requested – Samuel Pierpoint Langley entered the port of South Hampton from the United States on July 30, 1855. He was traveling on a student visa issued from the British Consul's Office, Boston, dated July 1, 1855. Suggest contacting said office for details made at time of request. Contacts at the following UK colleges and universities negative for enrollment in 1855: London, Oxford, Cambridge, Edinburgh.

Cathleen Whither, Ensign Royal Navy

"*Well, Cathleen, an Ensign in the Royal Navy, indeed. When did the Brits start making women officers and gentlewomen?*" My thoughts were not on my job! I picked up the telephone and had the operator place a long distance call to Boston. I hung up, waiting for her to make the connection and call me back. I shuffled through my index cards of what, when and where. The telephone rang and I talked to the British Consul's Office in Boston.

"Thank you for returning my call. I am Commander Caldwell from the JAG Office, Department of the Navy, Washington........ Yes, Ensign Whither of the War Office suggested that I talk to you.............. A homicide, S.P. Langley, he applied for a student visa through your office. That would have been July 1855........ I was afraid of that........ Thank you anyway."

I hung up and wrote at the bottom of the index card, records not kept that far back. This was not a dead end, but it did make the search a little more interesting. I knew he left the US and entered South Hampton – wait a minute, how do I know he left from the US? I cabled Cathleen.

ENSIGN CATHLEEN WHITHER
WAR OFFICE
LONDON, ENGLAND

IT IS ME AGAIN. NO STUDENT VISA RECORDS AVAILABLE FOR 1855, ALL RECORDS NOW DATE FROM 1880'S. WHAT WAS NAME OF VESSEL AND COUNTRY OF REGISTRY CARRYING S. P. LANGLEY?

LJ CALDWELL
JAG OFFICE, ARMY NAVY BUILDING
WASHINGTON D.C.

That afternoon, she replied.

LJ – Vessel's name Lusitania, Portugese registry, route of sailing New York, Halifax to South Hampton. Any progress?

Cathleen

"I need to meet this Cathleen, she is either married or 100 years old and ugly as sin." My thoughts were always on the job, what the hell was the matter with me? Alright! Back to work we go. If Langley went to London he boarded at New York or Halifax, he did not meet the ship in the middle of the Atlantic. What, where and when; *what* did he do after arriving at South Hampton? Some variables here; one, he stayed in England, two, he left for the continent of Europe, three he left England for Australia, Africa or God knows where. I needed to check with the Langley family and get a copy of his degrees and where they were earned in Europe.

The next day, I was at the home of his widow asking some very delicate questions.

"Mrs. Langley, I am Commander Caldwell. I have been put in charge of your husband's case. I am so sorry about your loss, your husband was one of the Navy's most valuable scientists. We think this may have something to do with his unexplained death."

"What do you mean, Commander? Samuel was a loving grandfather, why would anyone want him dead at his age? He was getting ready to retire, his work was over, there was no need ....." Her voice trailed off and I switched to a new line of inquiry.

"Where did you meet Samuel, Mrs. Langley?"

She brightened and said, "England. I was a late teenager and already working on my graduate degree. I thought Samuel was very bright. That is what attracted me to him."

"Were you both US citizens studying abroad?"

"Oh, my, no. I am English, through and through, but my accent is gone since living here forty-some years." She was smiling.

"Where were you two studying?"

"Paris, my family was not happy with me leaving England to study in Paris at my age."

"I thought you met in England?"

"We did, we met on the ferry from Dover to Calais and enjoyed a conversation. We both took the train to Paris and the Sorbonne."

"I enjoyed my time there, Mrs. Langley, I studied for a short time at the Ecole des Hautes Etudes." As soon as this was out of my mouth, I knew I had made a mistake. Mrs. Langley switched to French for the remainder of our conversation. My notes were a mess. This is what I think I gained from my interview. Samuel completed his master's degree in record time and left to study for a doctor's degree at the University of Zurich. She showed me both of the framed degrees and I wrote down the dates on each for my notes. I wondered if I would get lucky and have Mrs. Langley tell me that she married Samuel and could account for the missing ten years. She accounted for her time with him in Paris. She did not go with him to Switzerland. I thanked her and returned to the Army Navy Building to send a transatlantic cable.

> CATHLEEN – PROGRESS SLOW. SAW DIPLOMAS ISSUED FROM SORBONNE IN PARIS AND UNIVERSITY OF ZURICH – CABLING EACH LOCATION TO VERIFY AFTER SENDING THIS. STILL SOME LOOSE ENDS TO TIE UP, CAN YOU CHECK ON BIRTH DATE AND LOCATION OF ANN WHITEHURST WHO CLAIMS TO HAVE MARRIED SAMUEL LANGLEY IN THE LITTLE VILLAGE OF WENDINHALL, THE LAKE DISTRICT, 1859. I OWE YOU SOMETHING FOR ALL THE WORK YOU HAVE DONE ON THIS CASE. I WILL TAKE YOU TO DINNER THE NEXT TIME I AM IN LONDON. — LJ

Within an hour a cable returned from London,

> LJ – SUGGEST YOU CHECK YOUR DEPARTMENT OF RECORDS – THERE YOU WILL FIND MY PHOTO AND BIO – I HAVE DONE SAME AT MY SIDE OF THE ATLANTIC. LOOKING FORWARD TO YOUR NEXT VISIT TO LONDON!

> INFORMATION REQUESTED HAS BEEN FOUND. ANN WHITEHURST MARRIED SAMUEL LANGLEY ON MAY 15, 1859. THEY BOTH WORKED HERE IN ENGLAND UNTIL

THEIR RETURN IN 1865. HE HAD A JOB OFFER FROM HARVARD UNIVERSITY.

SEE YOU SOON – CATHLEEN.

I needed to close the case and file a report that stated that there was no evidence of foul play in the death of 69 year old Samuel Langley. I would do that as soon as I checked with the NCI records division, I had a friend who worked there.

"Frank, how are you?"

"Fine, Louis, what case are you working on now?"

"Langley, I have been cabling an Ensign Whither in London. Do we have a set of records for this individual?"

"If he works in the War Office, I can pull the folder for you, wait here and I will get it. You will have to sign it out if you want to take it with you."

"No, I just need to check his date of appointment to the War Office, I need to know if I am working with a rookie."

A few minutes later I had the folder in my hands, I sat at a table and opened the cover. A photograph of a beautiful girl in a Royal Navy uniform appeared clipped to the stack of personnel records. I smiled as I slid it off and into my pocket. I knew this was against department policy, but I would have it copied and then I would return the original to the folder claiming that it must have dropped out and would Frank please return it the proper folder. I began reading. The file was one year old, unless she got married in the last year, she was still single. She was a college graduate, London University, and then she went on to law school. She joined the Royal Navy a year before I joined JAG, she was born in 1881 a year before me. "*Ah, an older woman.*" I thought. "*Why was this twenty-five year old beauty still unattached*?" I closed the folder, gave it back to Frank and said, "I need to make a transatlantic telephone call to London. Will you see if you can get a connection for me, Frank?"

"Sure, Louis, what are you going to ask this guy when you get connected?"

"You can listen if you would like, Frank." We waited ten minutes and the telephone rang back with our connection. Frank handed me the telephone. "I am trying to reach an Ensign Whither in the war office, can you ring through for me? Thank you." Frank raised both of his hands and turned his palms outward in the sign of 'what gives'.

"Hello, Ensign Whither, this is Louis Caldwell. How often do you use the alias, Elska Van Mauker?".

EPILOGUE

"Hello, Ensign Whither, this is Louis Caldwell. How often do you use the alias, Elska Van Mauker?"

"Oh, Louis, it is so good to hear your voice. It took you long enough to figure out who you were sending messages to across the pond."

"I figured out you were British as I soon I realized you could not speak Danish. I still have not figured out who the woman was that we found dead in your flat."

"That was my partner, Finoa McBride, we looked a lot alike. I do not have very good luck keeping partners alive."

"I have that same problem. Your German was excellent, you must have German grandparents."

"I do and you do, too. How was your trip to Rosenheim?"

"How do you know about that?"

"I keep track of the men in my life, Louis."

"Am I a man in your life?"

"You certainly are! Now when are you coming to London, I have to clean my flat."

"Do you have a double bed?"

"Yes, why?"

"Change the sheets, I am on the next ship out of New York. I have a ton of leave time coming. I will cable you from New York and let you know the ship's registry and the docking time in South Hampton. Can you meet me?"

"Louis, it has been four months since you have seen me, I am a little larger around the middle than I was at Kaiserslautern."

"Is this your English way of saying I will be a father in five months?"

"It is."

"Cathleen, I love you."

"Thank you, Louis. You are the only one for me, too."

"Cathleen, I am Episcopalian, what religion are you?"

"The same, why? That does not matter."

"Oh, yes it does, you do not know my sister. She will be traveling with me, so will my whole family, probably. Cathleen, I hate to do this to you, but could you talk to your priest in London and tell him how me met and fell in love and that we were separated by covert missions run by two separate nations. He will understand. Book us a church or a chapel or wherever you would like to get married, invite your family and friends. Tell them your groom is mentally challenged for waiting this long, oh, Cathleen, I do love you."

"I trapped you, Louis, are you sure this is what you want?"

"Cathleen, I have been assigned to the NLSO, JAG office, London, as NCI station chief. The first thing I was going to do was tear the war office apart looking for an A.K.A. Elska Van Mauker. Your face is burned into my memory, I would recognize you anywhere. I would have spent the rest of my life looking for you."

"Oh, Louis, I adore you. I have from the first minute I laid eyes on you in that zeppelin. Get your family over here so we can begin ours. I love you, Louis, with all my heart."

PREVIEW OF DAN RYAN'S NEW NOVEL ADMIRAL'S SON GENERAL'S DAUGHTER

It was June 29th and after dinner each evening, My father had talked about his life experiences from a Plebe at West Point to Admiral in the United States Navy. He was celebrating his 60th birthday, and the party had lasted three days. The first to arrive was Monty Blair with the news that Bell's air cooled telephone lines had been successfully strung and tested in Boston, he left the first night to get back to Boston. Sam and Rachael Mason had come up from Annapolis and had moved into their old living quarters for the week, they were called away by one of their children. They returned to the Naval Academy. My Uncle Robert, and Aunt Mariann, had come for my graduation and they came north with us to Pennsylvania. Uncle Robert's twin daughters, Karen and Sharon, were both married, one lived in Virginia and the other in Maryland with their families. Uncle Robert left after the second day to stop in Maryland and Virginia on the way back to South Carolina.

My sister, Ruth, had come home from Harvard with the "nice young man" she had met, a Mr. Theodore Roosevelt. She told mother that it was not serious, but they left to return to New York City and the Roosevelt's Park Avenue apartment. Carol had finished her last year of preparatory school before entering Columbia University. She left with the Peters when they continued their trip to Pittsburgh.

The hotel rooms in Franklin, Oil City and as far away as Titusville were left by our guests over the three days since their arrival. There was a definite pecking order to who left first. You could not ask the President of the United States, his Secretary of the Navy or the Commandant of the Marine Corps to stay an entire week. They stayed in the house one night and were called back to Washington.

Mark twain listened to every word of my father's nightly monologs, then announced that he would be leaving with the others back to Bermuda on the Cold Harbor. Jerome Lewis and his family were called back to Louisville because of a large murder case. Jerome was retired from the navy and was now the Chief of Police for Louisville.

Brigadier General Tom Schneider and his wife, Beth, checked out of the Oil City Hotel and moved into the spaces left by Sam Mason and settled in for the week. Won Sing still followed the President of Seneca Oil around, making fun of him at every turn.

The train for Nevada left the fourth day before I had a chance to tell my father that I would be leaving soon to take the train into Washington to see Emily

Today, June 29, 1877, the house was nearly empty. Every bedroom was no longer taken. My mother had hired more household staff for the week. The evening meals were not unlike those she organized in the White House. The main table held all the Admirals and Generals in the house, now only Tom and Beth remained. Empty chairs were now where President Hayes, a former brigadier general, and now the commander-in-chief, and Mrs. Hayes had sat. Admiral Ben Hagood and his side kick, General Chris Merryweather, had been next to the Chief of Police and his wife from Louisville Kentucky. Next to them, Colonel Sam Mason, Superintendent of the Naval Institute, and his wife from Annapolis, Maryland had been sitting. They had been seated next to General John Butler and his wife, Sally from Bermuda. The tables forming the dining hall were nearly empty. The tables had had a theme to them, the rapid response marines and their families were grouped together and some of them stayed because Tom Schneider had asked them to. The Nevada group of tables was now empty. The original Caldwell Shipping group was headed by Captain Jacobs and his family and they stayed. The original Caldwell Trading and Banking group was headed by Robert Whitehall and his family and they left on the Cold Harbor. The ATT table was half full. And so the dining room that fourth evening looked a little lonesome. After dinner, my mother said, "Welcome everyone to our home for the final installment of Jason's story. I have asked Jason to write a book about his adventures. It involves everyone who was invited to this house. As I warned you three nights ago, Jason, is a talker and he may not be finished after this party. He has decided to tell his story in three parts entitled; Calm Before the Storm, Death Before Dishonor and Lull After the Storm. The Woolfall Book Company of St. Paul, Minnesota, has agreed to publish it. You are all invited back next year, for one day, June 26th to have Jason sign a copy for you. Jason, you have the floor." She sat back down on her dining room chair and my father stood.

"Thank you everyone for coming to this special celebration. My voice is about gone, so this will be a very short chat. Did I ever tell you about how I met Louise in Ostend, Belgium and later visited her in London?"

I had heard this story many times before and I excused myself and went to my room to pack my sea bag. I was scheduled to begin my two year tour of sea duty, shortly. I told my parents that I was off to report to the Philadelphia shipyards. I decided not tell them that I would be going by way of General Schneider's house in Washington. I figured that if Emily and I did not seem glad to see each other, the disappointment to her father and mine would be less.

I found myself gazing out of the coach window as the train pulled into Union Station. I pulled my sea bag onto my shoulder and stepped from the train. I found a cab and asked to be taken to the address that General Schneider had given me. We pulled up about a half hour later in front of a three story brownstone in Georgetown. I paid the driver and took my bag up the front steps. "*What am I doing here? What if Tom Jr. and Emily are not home?* I reached for the door knocker and let it fall a few times. "*No one is home, not even a servant. I need to get to Philadelphia.*" I turned to go and the door opened.

"James Caldwell, is that you?"

Emily Schneider was standing in the doorway. "Your father wanted me to check on you and see if you and Tom needed anything. I am on my way to the Philadelphia Shipyards and it was right on the way."

"You are the same poor liar, JJ. Washington is not on the way from Seneca Hill to Philadelphia. Why did you come here?"

"To see you, Emily."

"That is better, come inside, Tom is home and will want to talk to you about the Naval Academy. I want to know what your future plans are JJ."

I felt a large lump forming in my throat, so I did not respond. I grabbed my bag and walked into the Schneider home. I sat the bag down in the foyer in front of a center stairway and waited for Emily to tell me where her brother was. I turned and she had her arms around me hugging the breath out of me. My knees turned to jelly but my mouth met hers and I did not run away to the stables this time.

"You two going to come up for air any time soon?" Her brother was smiling and extending his hand. I shook it as I kept Emily's hand in my other hand. The electricity ran up and down my arm. This was definitely not the reaction that I got with my friend in Olso. I glanced sideways at Emily and said, "Emily said you were home and wanted to talk to me about Annapolis. I graduated with my degree but I will not get a commission until I finish my sea trials. So you will finish at Georgetown with your degree about the same time, right."

"Yes, my major is business administration. I want to stay as far away from the military life as possible. Emily and I never saw our dad much, we were raised by our mother. I want a family where I see my children every night."

We all walked into the parlor, Emily and I were still holding hands. We sat on a sofa and JR sat in a chair. JR continued, "I suppose dad told you to come and talk to me about my plans to get married at such a young age?"

"JR, you will know when it is time to get married. My parents were almost 40 when they were married, that is why I am adopted. My youngest sister is not even in college and my parents are now 60. I do not want that for my family. I am planning on a military career as a hydrographic surveyor and starting my family before I am 25 years old. I just have to find the right woman who understands what military life is like, especially for someone who is mapping the ocean floor."

"How about the one sitting beside you, JJ? She talks about you all the time."

"We all three grew up together, JR. That is why she knows me so well. Your father says Emily has plenty of boy friends."

"Hello, I am in the same room! And boy friends do not count, what about that Helga person in Norway?" She took her hand away and crossed her arms in front of her.

"Do want to spend the rest of your life with me, Emily?"

"Do want to spend your life with me, James Caldwell?"

"Take a hold of my hand again. What do you feel?"

"A tingling in my fingers that runs the whole way up my arm, why?"

"I thought it was just me. What do you feel when we hug?"

"Like my knees are going to collapse."

"And when we kiss?"

"Like my insides are going to melt."

I looked at her and said, "The next time you talk to your father, ask him what I said about how I feel about you. I think he will tell you the same thing."

"Hello, I am also in the same room!" JR was grinning.

I turned to face JR and said, "How about a double wedding after I get back from my sea trails? What is your girl friends name anyway?"

"Naomi Blackford, and I can not wait two years for you to get back from the Mediterranean. We are going to get married before I graduate from Georgetown."

"Okay, no double wedding then. Emily, I am on my way to the Port of Philadelphia to join the USS Quinnebaug, it sails for Europe in four days. Tomorrow lets go shopping for your engagement ring."

"I think you better ask my father and mother for their blessing, James."

"I already have."

"What did they say?"

"I think you should hear that for yourself. There is a public telephone at the Union Station, but there must be one closer than that."

"There is one at Georgetown School of Business!" JR sounded excited.

"What are we waiting for, we need to get to a telephone so Emily can talk to your parents."

"Are you asking me to marry you, James?"

"Yes, when I get my commission in the United States Navy."

"I accept, two years is going to seem like a life time."

"I have a suggestion." JR had a devilish grin on his face. "Why wait? You two were made for each other. Tomorrow, after you get a ring, why not have the Georgetown Chaplin marry you. I will be your witness. In two years you can have the big formal wedding that all the relatives can come to and think they are seeing the real thing. Mother will spend the next two years planning Emily's wedding while you are away. I promise to keep your secret. What do you say?"

I looked at Emily and said, "It is up to you Emily. If we can not keep away from each other in the next four days, we might as well be married secretly."

She looked at me and said, "James I am giving myself to you tonight in my father's house. If you want to make something official so you can look my father in the face, then we need to do it today. Either way, I am promised to you, always have been. The date of marriage is not important to me. JR and Naomi are already sleeping together."

JR blushed from head to foot. "She is right, James. It is 1877 and young people do not get married as virgins anymore."

We locked up the brownstone and caught a street car to the Georgetown campus to find the telephone. JR knew where it was and I told the operator that I wanted to place a call to Oil City, Pennsylvania.

When I got the operator, I asked for the Seneca Hill connection. It took a minute or two and my mother answered the telephone.

"Mom, this is James.........Yes, everything is fine. I am at the Schneider's in Georgetown.......Yes, yes. Yes, I did....... She said yes, Mom." I handed the speaker to Emily.

"Hello, Mrs. Caldwell, can I talk to my father? .... Hello, dad..... I have a series of questions to ask you .... What did James tell you about how he felt about me?........ He did?....... He did not!...... He did! ...... Can I talk to Mom? .... Mom, James asked me to marry him!..... Yes, I know the boy is really dense, but I love him with all my heart......... He has to report in four days........ We are going to be married in the chapel here in Georgetown...... Of course, both families can be here by train in a day.....Yes, we will wait until you get here, I have waited all my life, I can wait one or two more days....... Yes, Mother, really..... I know that!..... Of course....... Of course........ Can I talk to James parents?"

Tears were rolling down Emily's cheeks as she turned to me and said, "I just lied to my mother, James. I told her I would wait to jump in bed with you until we were married."

"You are sending that over the telephone to Seneca Hill, Emily."

"Oh, My God. I am sorry Mrs. Caldwell I .... Of course...... With all my heart....... You did? .....Oh my, and that was in 1855?.......Do you want to talk to James?

"James, it is your father."

"Yes, dad...... I know ...... I know....... I will ask her....... I have no idea.... her brother will be my best man......can you and General Schneider wear your dress uniforms? .... I will get one from a shop here ..... I have known her all my life, ...do you trust Tom Schneider and his judgement?..... I do too ....we are going shopping for the wedding ring this afternoon...... hang on I will ask her." I placed my hand over the speaker and said to Emily, "My father asked if you would like my grandmother's wedding ring."

"Oh, James, that would mean so much to me. Is he sure he wants to do this?"

"Dad, Emily says that it would be an honor for the newest Mrs. Caldwell to wear a family heirloom from your mother. Are you sure you want to do this?"

I handed the speaker back to Emily and said, "It is your mother."

"Mom.......yes, I would......where is it .... do you think it will fit? .....I can .... yes I know where her shop is ...... twenty- four hours ..... I will try."

After an hour we disconnected and the three of us looked at each other and began to laugh and cry as we hugged each other. "My father is bringing the entire party down by train, Emily. We are going to have a huge wedding. We better get over to the Chapel and see when it is available so we can give everyone a date and time."

We found the chapel and the College Chaplin, Ambrose Flynn. He took your information and gave us list of items to bring to him in three days.

"Emily you were a student here until you graduated last year, alumni are usually not eligible to use the chapel, but your brother is still a student here and the General is well known on campus since he completed his degree as an adult."

"Thank you, Father Flynn. James and I will be very grateful if we can get married before he has to ship out of Philadelphia on the *USS Quinnebaug* next week."

"James, I doubt the Quinnebaug will leave in four days. I read in the paper that the ship is in quarantine, something about yellow fever it picked up in Savannah. No one is allowed on or off the ship for thirty days. You better check with the Department of the Navy here in town before you go all the way to Philadelphia."

"Thank you, Father, Emily and I will stop at the Army Navy Building on our way home."

We left the chapel and caught another street car for downtown Washington City. We got off in front of the White House and walked to the Army Navy Building. I handed my written orders to the department clerk and he said, "We have been trying to get in touch with you, midshipman Caldwell. You have been given a wavier from sea trails because of your undergraduate major. We are short of hydrographic surveyors and you have been reassigned from the surface warfare division to the United States Coast and Geodetic Survey here in Washington. The effective date of commission for Lieutenant JG is two years from now, or you may have the option of the rank of Ensign immediately."

"OF-1 pay grade is the same. I will accept the immediate commission as an Ensign, Sir."

"There is a note attached to your file to see the Secretary of the Navy, you must be in some kind of trouble, Mr. Caldwell."

"The Secretary is my Uncle Ben, he probably wants to congratulate me on my upcoming marriage. How do we get to his office? Oh, this beautiful young lady is my bride to be, Emily Schneider."

"We know each other. Hello, Harry, how have you been?"

"Great, Em, how is your family? Your father still running all the eligible bachelors off until James here graduated?"

"You know my dad, no man or boy could ever measure up to James in his eyes. How are Mary and the children?"

"Wild as ever. You want to go up to the Secretary's office with Ensign Caldwell, here?"

"That would be very nice, Harry. See you and the family at the Georgetown Chapel in three days if you can get off work here."

"No can do, Em. This strain of yellow fever on board the Quinnebaug is a nightmare. I have to reassign everyone who is cleared in thirty days and stop those that have been assigned from coming on board."

We left the check-in desk and started walking to the office of the Secretary of the Navy.

"Have you ever been inside this building, James?"

"Never. My father would not allow us to visit him here."

"Why not?"

"He never liked Washington, said it was the most dangerous city in the country."

"I agree, where will we raise our family, James?"

"In your father's many assignments, where did you like the best?"

"Where ever you and your family were stationed. I loved Bermuda, not because it was a subtropical isle, but because I could see you everyday."

"Oh, lady you have the love bug, bad. I hope I can measure up to what you think I am like."

"I know what you are like, James. There will be no surprises for either of us." She was smiling like her brother and blushing.

We walked around a corner on the third floor and there stood Ben Hagood. "Hey, look at you two! Are you happy, Emily?"

"Admiral Hagood, you have no idea. I figured I would have to wait at least two years to get my hands on this gentleman."

"Well, things happen for a reason. The Quinnebaug is shut down for the foreseeable future. We may have to burn the infection out of that boat. Did the clerk tell you about my letter to Annapolis, suggesting that you be given your commission immediately and be reassigned to the USCG Survey?"

"No, he did not tell me it was you. Thank you very much for this opportunity, Uncle Ben. I know you bent a few rules for me, I appreciate it."

"Nonsense, James, you graduated fourth in your class. Your father and I barely made it out of the Point. Take advantage of your opportunities, both of you. I have got to get back to work, see you at the Georgetown Chapel. I got orders from your father to show up in dress uniform so that I can be a witness for you and Emily. I would not miss this."

He turned and left us standing in the hallway on the third floor of the Army Navy building. "Want to find somewhere we can eat a meal?"

I asked.

We started back down the stairways and Emily stopped and said, "Kiss me, James."

"Right here on the stairwell?"

"No, on the lips, silly."

To say that the wedding was memorable would be an understatement. Our families and all the party goers from Seneca Hill were on a train bound for Washington within twenty-four hours of our telephone call. My father loosened his purse strings and rented an entire coach car into Union Station. Emily and I knew that her mother's main thrust would be to keep us occupied and apart until the ceremony on Independence Day. But she failed, I had never seen Emily so happy, she glowed from happiness. We were together day and night from my arrival on June 30, until Father Flynn said, "I now pronounce you man and wife."

The day of the ceremony came and the chapel was filled to overflowing. I waited with Father Flynn behind the altar along with my witnesses, Admirals Hagood and Caldwell, JR Schneider and Midshipman Kiro Kunitomo. Kiro had not started his sea trials and was awaiting deployment on the *USS Ranger*. We waited and waited.

"Why are we waiting, what has happened?" My father was nervous. He left us and came back with a box full of boutonniere. "It appears, James, that everyone is ready except us." He walked around and placed a rose bud into each of our buttonholes.

"Now, Father Flynn, we are ready as soon as I wave to the organist." My father disappeared again and the wedding march began to

sound throughout the chapel. That was our cue to leave our hiding place and walk onto the altar of the chapel. The bridesmaids, all Georgetown friends of Emily, took their places. General Thomas Schneider walked with his daughter down the aisle and stopped just before the altar. Father Flynn asked, "Who gives this woman to be married to this man." General Schneider said, "I do, I mean, her mother and I do." He was embarrassed that he flubbed his only line in the ceremony.

"Who gives this man to be married to this woman?" Father Flynn asked again.

"I do, I mean, his mother and I do." My father was grinning and laughter rang out in the chapel.

"This is where I usually say, a marriage is a solemn occasion – but I think that has just flown out the stained glass window." Father Flynn was smiling and the laughter continued. "Let me continue by saying that I am Irish and we celebrate funerals and cry at weddings. I have never seen two people so much in tune with each other as James and Emily. In fact, this comes from the two families that have shared so much together over the years. I have watched James and Emily grow up together from the time that their fathers served in Washington together. This is not a marriage made in heaven, it was put together right here on earth over a period of many years. I wish Emily and James every happiness in the years to come and to their parents, good health and long life so that they may see their grandchildren and their grandchildren's children."

He turned and began the wedding mass. I took Emily's hand in mine and knelt before the altar and repeated the responses in Latin as I did as an altar boy. Our vows were exchanged, the music filled the chapel again and we marched back down the aisle and out into the bright sunlight. A long receiving line was formed just outside the chapel and those in attendance wished us well as they took cabs to the

Hay-Adams Hotel. Our parents had an all night celebration in the ballroom of the hotel, but we left around ten o'clock and retired to our room upstairs.

We fell into bed again, this time as a married couple. We awoke the next morning to find her wedding dress across a chair and my dress uniform in pieces spread across the floor along with our underwear.

"Are you happy, James?"

"I had no idea what happiness was until June 30, 1877."

"I will take that as a, yes!"

"You may do that, Mrs. Caldwell. I promise to be with you as a husband and as a father for our children, Emily. The USCG Survey is not like the US Surface Warfare Navy. It is a separate division within the Department of the Navy. I will never be at sea for long periods of time. I will be assigned to the schooner *Palinurus* for sea duty and to the mapping section at the Hydrographic Office in Washington. We must come back into the Potomac Dockyards so that charts and maps can be made for the Navy. You and I have a financial base that most young people do not have. You need to find a brownstone in Georgetown that we can rent for a couple of years."

"Can we do that on an Ensign's pay grade?"

"I am not talking about that. I, and therefore we, own one third of a hotel resort in Nevada, a house in Beaufort, South Carolina, and a healthy trust fund. We do not have to worry about money, ever."

"James, kiss me again."

"Right here on the bed?"

"No, on the lips, silly."

LaVergne, TN USA
20 September 2010

197682LV00001B/18/P